For all the many women – the dead and those still living – who have suffered at the hands of violent men.

THE SADDEST SOUND

DEBORAH DELANO

First publication
LEPUS BOOKS
2015
ISBN: 978-0-9572535-8-2

LEPUS BOOKS

lepusbooks.co.uk

Prologue
Monday, 15th September, 1980

Graham rounded the corner of The Avenue in his lime green Ford Capri and pulled up outside his nicely proportioned three-bed semi. His wife, Irina, was in the front garden torching the cracks between the paving stones with her newly purchased Weed Wand. His heart sank. He'd been supposed to do that job yesterday and he knew she'd be quarrelsome about it. He'd meant to do it, but with all the excitement of last night it had slipped his mind. Sometimes things did slip his mind. That was dangerous for a man in his position.

Irina would not tolerate weeds of any kind and she was frantic with irritation as she ruthlessly scourged them with the jet of fire. Weed Wands were the latest thing in eliminating untidiness. Graham leaned over to the glove compartment, took out a small crucifix on a broken chain and slipped it into his overall pocket. 'Sorry, petal. Let me take over,' he said climbing out of the car.

'Leave it,' Irina snapped at him. The very sight of him increased her irascibility. He attempted a peck on the cheek but Irina turned her face away.

'Shall I pop the kettle on, love? Fancy a brew?'

'As you please, but don't splash water everywhere when you fill it.'

Graham removed his work boots and went inside. His slippers were neatly paired on the shoe rack in the hall and he put them on. He inspected the soles of his boots cautiously and, satisfied that they were clean, he placed them on the rack where his slippers had been.

He went through to the kitchen and carefully filled the kettle. As he lit the stove, Irina came into the kitchen pulling off her gardening gloves.

'How were't Mum and Dad, love?' he asked in his most placatory manner.

Irina had stayed at her parents' house the night before.

'It was lovely to see them,' Irina said, thankfully deflected from her weed-killing. And then, more hesitantly: 'Selene was there with her young man.'

Graham hated Irina's sister Selene. When he thought of her, he imagined what her head would look like spiked on a pole. He chuckled inwardly when this image came to his mind because she was a Pole. Not like Irina though, Irina was Polish just the same but she was ladylike and refined. She'd been to university in Leeds and had a degree in English literature. That's what had attracted him to her in the first place. She was educated and cultured. She knew about ballet and classical music and books. All Selene had done with a university education was turn into a fleabag hippy cunt. Graham would have dearly loved to do something about her.

'She's asked me to go along to one of her feminist meetings next week.'

'Feminist.' Graham sneered. 'Well I hope she's not put any funny ideas into your head. They're all lesbians.'

Irina flushed. She feared and dreaded any kind of discussion that might be connected to sexuality. Whenever anything came on the television involving intimacy she either turned it off or found some excuse to leave the room.

'Don't be stupid,' she said vexed and flustered. 'Anyway, what happened to the work you were going to do in the garden yesterday?'

'Something came up at yard.' Graham's thoughts raced.

Irina scowled. 'More like something came up at the pub.'

'No, one of the lads spilt his load,' he lied effortlessly. 'Derek and me went to help him clean it up and I were buggered when I got home.'

The shrill whistling of the boiling kettle punctuated their exchange. Irina went back into the front garden while Graham spooned tea into the pot. He could feel his heart racing and a tingling excitement knotted his guts. He couldn't wait to get into his den to put his newest souvenir with

2

his collection and he fingered the head of the tiny Jesus in his overall pocket as he waited for the tea to brew.

Graham poured the tea and took a cup to Irina in the garden. She was bending down with her back to him probing between the cracks with a knife. Graham felt a stirring in his groin. 'It's on the sill,' he shouted. Then he went back inside and upstairs to his special place.

The room was small, probably intended as a child's bedroom but in their case never occupied. It was his space, a kind of dressing room. He and Irina agreed that as long as he kept it spotlessly clean she would not invade his privacy. She had never enquired what he did in there. There was just enough room for a single bed, a chair and a small table.

Graham locked the door behind him and opened the door to the built-in wardrobe. It wasn't actually a proper wardrobe but a door he'd fixed across a recess. At the back of the recess was the original closet. It was where he kept his collection. He unlocked the concealed, padlocked inner door and reached into the darkness. His hand grasped the handle of a bag and he pulled it out of the closet. It was an old handbag, black wool with a gold metal clasp. It smelled of face powder and rancid old perfume. He inhaled the sublime scent of his mother.

He loved going through his things. It brought him to his true identity and he felt the power course through his veins. He opened the bag, took out each of the items and lined them up on the table. Then he put his hand in his pocket to retrieve the crucifix. He was rock hard. He put it down next to the other things. Strands of hair were caught around the head of the dying Christ. Dyed hair.

Died hair.

Words slipped and twisted in his brain. He closed his eyes and let his mind drift into blackness and back to clarity.

Then he went through his treasures. There was a ring box with 'Ratners' inscribed inside the lid and, poked into the space where the ring had been, a child's tooth. That piece of shit had been his first. He took the tooth out. It was minuscule in his big workman's hands. He inspected it in the light and put it back into its crease. He picked up the lipstick next and opened it, twisting the bottom until it was fully extended. 'Revlon Red Hot Red,' the tiny sticker on the end said. He sniffed it. It smelled of cheap perfume and animal fat. Just like the bitch who'd used it. He could see where her disgusting lips had shaped the end. His excitement mounted.

The powder compact lay next to it. The catch was broken. It had 'MC' engraved into the heart-shape on the lid. He opened it and looked at his eyes in the mirror, and then at his lips, pursing them. A few grains of powder fell onto the leg of his overall. He rubbed them away and put the

3

compact down. Then he removed his overalls and stripped himself naked, laying each item of clothing neatly on the bed.

Graham went back to his mementoes. As he touched each one a charge went through him. He was in control, the master of life and death. His decision was final. His hand passed over the silver belt-buckle and moved to the letter, never posted but neatly addressed and stamped. He'd read it hundreds of times since he got it. It was his prize. 'Dear Mum,' it began. What a bit of luck that he'd intercepted it. He'd saved a lot of heartache for some chap called Ian. He'd been sorting that little slut out good and proper. Good thing he'd finished the job for him. Graham fantasised about meeting Ian and telling him about it. That thought did it for him. His ecstasy was satisfying and prolonged.

'Graham.' Irina's penetrating voice trilled from the hall.

He quickly attended to his mess with his discarded underpants, hurriedly put his keepsakes back in the handbag and returned it to the closet.

'Just about to have a quick bath, love,' he called.

'Why have a bath when you've got the ceiling to do in the dining room?' Irina had started upstairs.

He opened the door to his room. At the sight of his naked body Irina turned in revulsion.

'Aye, sorry love, slipped me mind,' he said. 'I'll do it t'morrow wi'out fail.'

♀

One
Friday, 23ʳᵈ November, 1979

Ginny cleared a circle of mist from the bus window with her gloved hand. Outside the dank northern day seeped down from the moors, visible in the murky distance, and cast its gloom across the cityscape.

The bus had stopped outside City College. Ginny watched as students came out carrying their books and files, all long hair and black Levis. Some were hand in hand, young lovers. She felt a stab of envy for their freedom and their learning. These days even girls were staying on in education. Last time she took Michael to the doctor's with his asthma, they'd been seen by a woman GP. She was probably only a few years older than Ginny herself. Ginny hadn't known how to act. She had flushed with humiliation when the doctor asked if there was damp in the home. She felt more judged by a woman than she would have by a male doctor.

The students jostled onto the bus. A young woman sat next to Ginny. She had jet-black dyed hair, thick black eyeliner and a leather jacket thrown over a Ramones T-shirt. Ginny vaguely recognised her. Her boyfriend stood next to her in the aisle hanging onto the rail. His leather jacket had

'Sex Pistols' spelled out in studs across the back. Ginny read the spine on the folder that the girl held on her lap. It said: Art History. She didn't know what that was. Just being near them gave Ginny a terrible sense of inferiority.

The bus was packed now and even more steamed up. The circle Ginny had made misted over again and the buildings blurred wetly into the fading light. A musty smell of old wet coats hung in the air.

'Don't I know you?' said the Ramones fan. 'Didn't you go to Riverside Primary, Mr Gilkes' class?'

'Yeah, I did,' said Ginny.

'I'm Sophie James,' the girl went on.

Ginny placed her then. She used to sit on the top table—the Tigers they were called. Ginny herself had been on the Donkeys table.

'Oh yeah, you used to go round with Judy Hawkins. You at college now then?' Ginny recalled the painful moment when Judy Hawkins had called for her to go to school. Her mum had answered the door in curlers and invited Judy in. Judy perched awkwardly on the end of the sofa and looked as though she could smell something nasty. Ginny knew that their friendship was over when, on the way to school, Judy asked why her parents didn't buy a nicer house. Where would she have started on that one? She'd shrugged and resolved to avoid Judy in the future.

'Yeah, I'm doing Art and Art History.'

'That's nice,' said Ginny hoping she wouldn't be called on to comment further.

'What're you up to these days?' the girl enquired.

'Oh, um, looking fer a job at the moment. Just bin fer an interview actually at a Solicitors' office,' Ginny lied. She'd been for an interview at the meat packing factory. The man had said they didn't take young mothers on because they had too much time off work with the kids. Ginny was sure she could remember her English teacher at school telling them about a new law that meant women couldn't be discriminated against but she didn't know if this counted so she didn't bother to argue. Anyway the place reeked of blood and corpses.

'Here's my stop then,' said Ginny. It was two stops before hers really but she wanted to cut the conversation short. 'Nice to see you again.'

'Yeah, you too,' the girl replied, standing to let Ginny past.

Ginny raised her eyebrows in a smile at the silent boyfriend and pushed her way down the crowded bus.

It was nearly dark when Ginny arrived at her mum's house to pick Michael up. It was the house she'd been brought up in. A red-brick council house on a sprawling estate. She would have liked to get one herself but the council had put her and Michael into one of the high-rise blocks nearer the city centre. So it was a bus ride every time her mum looked after him.

'Has he bin good?' she asked as she hung her jacket on the peg in the hall.

'Good as gold,' her mum replied.

'Mummy,' Michael called from the living room. 'Mummy, see what I've got.'

He raced eagerly into the hall. Ginny knelt down and hugged him. She'd never regretted for a single moment her decision to keep him. When she fell pregnant at just sixteen there'd been a lot of pressure to have an abortion. It wasn't like in her mum's day. Sheila got pregnant at sixteen too but had the baby aborted by some woman in Lumb Lane. She'd nearly died of the septicaemia that had set in later. These days you could get a legal abortion on the National Health, but somehow Ginny wanted this child more than anything she'd ever wanted before. She had stuck out against her family and most of her friends. She had stuck out too against Pete, the baby's father.

Pete was in the same year at school as Ginny. They'd argued and then split up over it. He'd refused to have anything to do with her or the child, and as her pregnancy noticeably progressed he began to spread rumours that Ginny had slept around and that he couldn't be sure he was the Dad. That year had been the toughest of Ginny's short life. She'd done her 'O' levels in the boiling-hot June. She could hardly get her bump into the exam desks, but she was glad she'd suffered the humiliation though, because she passed her Maths and English.

'What've you got there darlin'?' Ginny turned to her mother. 'Mum, you haven't bin givin' 'im loadsa sweets now, 'ave yuh?'

'No, 'e's 'ad a 'nana and evap,' said Sheila defensive, though she thought her daughter's fussiness about the boy unwarranted.

Michael held out his closed fist. Ginny put her outstretched hand under it. He opened his hand and a tiny tooth fell into her palm. A bottom incisor.

'Wow,' said Ginny. 'You're getting a proper big boy now. We'll put that under your pillow and see if the tooth fairy comes.' She knew Michael had been wiggling steadfastly at the tooth since he'd become aware of the rewards on offer for such bounty.

Ginny picked her son up and carried him through to the living room smothering him in kisses as she went. Crackerjack was on the television set in the corner. It was curiously wrong to Ginny because it was in colour and she remembered it in black and white with Leslie Crowther and Peter

7

Glaze. Memory was going to be in colour from now on. Ginny didn't know if that was a good thing or not.

'How'd the interview go? Any good?' asked Sheila hopefully.

'Nah,' Ginny replied. 'The manager thought I'd be off too much with Michael.'

'How d'they bloody well expect women to live?' grumbled Sheila as she went upstairs to get ready for work.

Ginny's dad, as usual, was in the armchair sleeping off a bender. He got his dole money through on Fridays and he went straight to the pub and spent half of it. Sheila had to manage on her cleaning money. She'd done other stuff to get by as well when Ginny and her brothers and sister were younger. Ginny knew she'd been on the game. A lot of women on the estate did it occasionally to make ends meet. Like mother like daughter, Ginny thought ruefully. She wasn't going to be like her mum though. She'd got plans. She was waiting until Michael started school next year, then she was going back to college. She'd got her 'O' levels and that was enough to get her onto the Social Work course at the Polytechnic.

'Pappy snores,' said Michael

'Yeah, I know,' Ginny replied and they both giggled.

As if to comment, Ginny's dad let out such a loud snore that he woke himself up. 'Whaddya want?' he grunted bleary eyed.

'Just picking Michael up,' Ginny responded in a tone that said: and it's got nothing to do with you.

'Start picking your puzzle up, Mikey.' She wanted to leave as soon as possible now.

Ginny despised her father. Stan Hames had never held down a job. He was a useless drunk and nasty with it. She couldn't count the number of times her mum had 'walked into a door' after he'd come home rat-arsed.

'There's a couple of ham sandwiches and a bit of pork pie in the kitchen, Stan,' said Sheila coming into the living room dabbing her nose with a powder puff. She was in her cleaning smock, ready to go to work.

'Get us a few bottles of Newkie on t'way 'ome, pet,' Stan wheedled.

'Gi'us the money then,' Sheila replied abruptly. Stan fished in his pockets and found a crumpled pound note.

'You can get yourself a Babycham wi' t'change.' He handed the money over. Sheila took it from him and raised her eyebrows at Ginny.

'C'mon love,' she said. 'We'll get the bus to town together.'

Ginny finished loading Michael into his coat and shoes. She carefully wrapped the tooth in some toilet paper and put it into the back pocket of her jeans. Then the three generations set off together into the cold damp night.

Michael kissed his Gran goodbye outside the council offices where she worked five nights a week from six until eight. After stoppages she came home with fifteen pounds and thirty-eight pence. It paid the rent and meant she wasn't completely dependent on how much Stan had left after Friday in the Queen's Head.

'Be a good boy for yer mum,' said Sheila picking Michael up and squeezing him to her. His chilly, pink face pressed close to hers. She put him down and, turning to Ginny, took the pound Stan had given her out of her pocket and pushed it into Ginny's hand.

'No Mum,' said Ginny. 'We're alright honest. Anyway, what about his beer?'

'I get paid meself t'night. You get something nice fer y'supper.'

'Thanks, Mum,' Ginny was glad of the money. She'd been trying to think if there were any spuds at the flat to do mash with. Now they'd be able to get pie and chips from the chippie.

'Be careful, Gin,' Sheila added cryptically and headed into the offices.

Ginny watched her go, but her parting comment had left her with a sense of unease that her mum knew how she was paying her rent and keeping Michael in fitted shoes.

Ginny headed home, away from the lights of the town and into the dimness beyond. This area on the margins of the city was the red light district. The girls paced up and down smoking impatiently, their bare legs blue from the cold. Ginny and Michael lived in one of three high-rise blocks, emerging from a much older industrial wasteland. Derelict factories and forlorn, boarded-up terraced housing - remnants of the city's Victorian manufacturing past - surrounded these new monoliths. They had been thrown up in the late 'sixties and, just ten years on, were already riddled with damp.

When Ginny and Michael reached the chippie opposite the flats a scuffle had just broken out between one of the street girls and her pimp. A bag of chips had gone flying and the girl was being dragged by her hair, her head bent into her attacker's grip as she staggered past. Ginny pushed Michael behind her legs and flattened herself to the wall. From what she could make out, the girl owed a tenner but still had the nerve to buy a bag of chips before the debt was paid.

'Take it outside,' Danny shouted from behind the high chip-shop counter. 'Fuckin' whores,' he added to Ginny. 'Oops, s'cuse language. Didn't see you there, Mikey.'

Ginny picked Michael up so that he could see above the counter. 'Look,' he said exposing the small space on his bottom gum. 'My baby tooth come out.'

'Well so it has,' said Danny. 'You'll be getting a visit from the tooth fairy then.' Michael nodded, grinning.

'Two pies, a portion of chips, and some batter bits, please Dan,' said Ginny.

'Anything fer you sweetheart,' Danny replied, chancing his arm as he always did around Ginny.

She knew it was only a matter of time before everyone around the flats knew she was on the game herself. Then Danny's flirty banter would dry up and a cold appraising expression would replace his warm smile. She'd only done it a few times, just enough to scrape the money together to get Michael's warm winter things and pay the electricity bill before they cut her off. It was easier than leaving Michael to go out to some dead-end job, even if she could have got one. If you had a few stiff vodkas before, you could kind of remove yourself from reality. Ginny had actually once seen herself sucking some bloke's knob from above, as if she'd been out of her body.

After the chippie they went next door to the newsagents. Ginny bought a bottle of Coke and a Wall's ice-cream bar. She and Michael were going to have Coke floats after their pie and chips. It was Michael's favourite thing. Mrs Gupta leaned out across the counter and traded a ruffle of Michael's blonde fringe for a Black Jack chew.

'What d'you say, Mikey?' prompted Ginny.

'Thank you,' said Michael busy unwrapping his sweet. This transaction left Ginny with seventeen pence. She made sure she'd got a ten-pence piece, which she figured, with inflation, would meet the tooth-fairy bill.

They headed across the main road. By this time the fog had turned to drizzle. A couple of girls were patrolling the kerb. Ginny knew them both. They lived together in one of the other blocks. Sandra was tall and really beautiful with a Farah Fawcett hair do. Tracy, her mate, had joked about how the three of them should team up as Charlie's Angels on account of Ginny bearing a passing resemblance to Kate Jackson. Somehow though, Sandra's looks didn't translate into big money. Sandra struggled to get johns in this neighbourhood. Ginny thought she'd have been better off in a posh London hotel. It was Tracy who earned the most and she was dead ordinary looking and never even bothered to dress up. As Ginny and Michael approached, Sandra was busy applying lipstick.

'Hey, Gin. Awright?' said Tracy. Ginny smelled a wave of alcohol on her breath.

Sandra bent down, smothering Michael's face in the newly applied 'Red Hot Red'. It looked like she'd been crying.

'Yeah, good. Just gunna have a quiet night.' She showed them her wrapper of chips.

'Have a good one mate,' said Sandra, straightening as she released Michael from her grip.

'You too. Take care,' Ginny replied as she and Michael headed home.

♀

Two
The same day

Tracy had woken that morning with a terrible sense of doom. She knew that Sandra would be devastated if they didn't get Vincent back. It seemed to her that months and months of being careful and watching every glance had eaten its way into her very soul and undermined her sense of herself, not to mention her relationship with Sandra which she'd worked so hard to keep.

Today they'd know. The custody hearing was at half past two. She switched on the lamp in the darkened room and turned to see the alarm clock. It was a quarter to eleven. Sandra slept peacefully beside her. Tracy didn't want to wake her. She'd been up half the night chain-smoking and pacing the floor. She wanted to let her rest as long as possible. Sitting up, she looked down at her lover beside her, the soft blonde hint of downy hair on Sandra's upper lip, and her smudged mascara, adding pathos to the drama going on behind her closed eyes. Tracy knew that Sandra was dreaming because her eyes darted visibly beneath her lids, and she prayed that she was dreaming something beautiful because so much of her life had been shit.

She carefully pulled back the blankets and crept out of the bedroom. She'd wake Sandra up with a coffee and a kiss. The living room was still strewn with glasses, cans and overflowing ashtrays. Tracy picked up as much as she could carry and took it with her through to the kitchen. A few mates had come back with them to lend moral support to their cause. No one wanted to face the fact that the law wasn't known for its sympathy with prostitutes, let alone one who shared a bed with another woman. Tracy had kept an eye on how much Sandra was drinking. The last thing she needed was to turn up at the hearing stinking of booze. They'd still managed to sink a few though. Clinton alone had brought a bottle of scotch and a dozen cans of Red Stripe, and they'd smoked a fair few fatties on top. It still hadn't been enough to knock Sandra out until it was almost daylight.

Tracy put the kettle on and picked up the papers for the hearing while she waited for it to boil. They set out the unembellished details of Sandra's life. Mrs Sandra Jacques, 27, of 17 Bronte Mansions versus Mr Stephen Jacques, 36, of 42 Milton Street in the case of the custody of their child, Vincent J. Jacques, 8, also of 42 Milton Street. Stephen didn't want the kid; he just wanted to fuck Sandra up. It was all he'd ever wanted to do. He saw something lovely and he had to take it apart and smash up all the pieces. He was with some other poor cow these days and knocking ten bells out of her in months, just like he was with Sandra. Tracy was gripped by the customary rage she felt whenever his name came up. She knew she could kill the bastard, if she ever thought she had a chance of getting away with it.

She went back through to their bedroom, put the coffee cups down on the bedside table and opened the curtains. A damp grey light seeped into the room, insufficient to warrant turning off the lamp. Sandra stirred and Tracy kneeled down beside her and stroked her hair back from her face.

'Mornin', beautiful.'

Sandra started as Tracy kissed her forehead where the lock of hair had been, and then sat up, pressing her hands to her face. 'Is it time?'

'We've got a couple of hours to get sorted. Don't fret darlin'. What were you dreaming about?'

Tracy placed great store by dreams and had read loads of books on interpreting them. When she didn't smoke too much weed, she had incredibly vivid dreams herself. Often she knew she was dreaming and could even control what happened. It had been happening since she'd been a kid in the Home. It was the one part of her life over which she did have control. She'd long for it to be bedtime so she could escape the constant fear of her waking life.

Tracy had been in care since her mum died from cirrhosis of the liver when she was two. She didn't know who her dad was. No other relatives had come forward with a warm hearth and a cuddly toy to claim the child, and so Tracy had spent fourteen years at the mercy of the care system.

'I can't remember much of it but it was really weird. Really creepy feeling.' Sandra searched for her dream. 'I was down at the bins and there was this big black bird, like a vulture, just sitting there on one of the bin bags. It was hammering at the bag with its beak and making this awful noise, as if the bin bag was full of pebbles crunching. Ugh!' Sandra shuddered. 'It was horrible.'

'Umm.' Tracy pondered. 'Maybe it means we're gunna open up all the rubbish that Steve's bin doin'. An' p'raps the pebbles means we'll be taking Vince to the beach tomorrow.' Tracy strained to find an optimistic reading.

Sandra looked unconvinced. 'Anyhow.' She shook the dream off. 'Run us a bath will ya, babe?'

Tracy went into the bathroom and turned on the hot tap. She held her hand under the running water until it began to get warm. She'd never say so to Sandra but the dream didn't seem to bode well for the day ahead. It had given Tracy an indefinable sense of unease. The water ran suddenly scalding hot, as it generally did.

'Ow! Fuck it.' Tracy withdrew her hand. 'Nothing works proper in these poxy flats.' She left the bath running and went back into the bedroom. Sandra was sitting on the edge of the bed in her knickers and Tracy's old 'Stones' T-shirt lighting a cigarette.

'D'ya think he knows?' asked Sandra.

'What's to know? This is a two-bed place. He don't know I live here. Nobody can prove anything. An' we ain't 'ad no trouble from the filth lately.'

'Oh c'mon. You know what people are like round here. An' he did see us in the Swan that time together.'

'Jesus Christ. You're allowed to have a drink with a mate without bein' a fuckin' lesbian.' Tracy was sick of this conversation. They'd been over it a thousand times. It hurt her so much that the only time she had ever loved someone it had to be a dirty secret.

'Don't use that word. You know I hate it,' Sandra snapped. She loved Tracy, but she wasn't 'one of them'. To her, the word 'lesbian' had a vile ring to it, conjuring images of twisted, fucked-up women in men's clothes.

'Well, that's what it's called when you let another woman fuck you and like it.'

As soon as the words were out Tracy wanted, needed, to bite them back. 'Look, I'm sorry darlin'. Please let's not argue.' She held up both palms.

15

'Not today. Let's just see how it goes at the court. I honestly don't think he knows anything. If he did he'd already be shouting it all over the friggin' city.'

'I'm just scared. It don't do you any fuckin' good to love someone, 'cause then some bastard's got summat on yer'. Sandra held her head in her hands letting her hair form a curtain to block out the world.

Tracy sat down on the bed and put her arm around Sandra. 'We'll get him back darlin',' she whispered. 'C'mon. Go and have yer bath.'

'Do I look like a nice mum?' asked Sandra, after two hours changing and re-changing her outfit. She'd finally decided on a knee-length black crepe skirt and a fitted blue-silk shirt with little puff sleeves and four buttons at the cuff. The bedroom looked as if they'd been burgled.

'You look like a beautiful mum,' Tracy said. She was constantly overwhelmed by Sandra's loveliness. It amazed her that johns didn't go wild for her. When they worked together it was more often than not she, with her crooked teeth and broken nose, who got the first punter. Cars would slow down, and then, when they saw Sandra, sometimes speed off. It was as though they were intimidated by her. These weak, inadequate men needed a prossie who was rough, somebody they could feel superior to. Sandra's beauty made their dicks limp.

'Come as far as the swimmin' baths with me?' Sandra said.

'Whatever you want.' She'd have gone to Hell and back if Sandra had asked her.

They set out from the flats. For once the lifts were working but they smelled of piss. They tried to hold their breaths for the entire downward journey. Sandra was the first to fail and she dug Tracy in the ribs.

'Ah, you bitch,' Tracy said laughing.

Sandra hugged Tracy tight to her, releasing her grip just as the doors opened on Mrs Higson, the neighbourhood gossip and curmudgeon. Sandra and Tracy stepped out of the lift. Mrs Higson scowled at them both and turned her nose up in an ugly grimace.

'Your ladyship.' Tracy bowed, allowing Mrs Higson's entrance. Sandra laughed, and the moment gave them a tiny reprieve from the dread that they were both feeling.

By the time they reached the swimming baths the drizzle had turned to rain. Tracy was glad because it gave her an excuse to huddle next to Sandra as they shared the umbrella.

'I'll be in the George,' Tracy said, naming a pub where she knew she'd be able to find a bit of privacy in the snug.

'What if it goes against me?' said Sandra with tears welling.

'I don't know darlin'. We'll 'ave to sort somethin' out.' Tracy had no comfort left to give but she took Sandra's hand and squeezed it. 'See you after,' she said. They daren't allow themselves a kiss in public, not even a peck on the cheek. Sandra nodded and walked away. Tracy stood in the rain and watched her go.

When Sandra arrived at the family courts, Stephen was already there with his new partner, Doreen, talking to their solicitor. He saw Sandra and a big, shit-eating grin spread across his face. He was in a tweed jacket and smart trousers, and Doreen looked just about as mumsy as a person could without actually proffering a plate of home-baked biscuits. They looked like a mum and dad off the adverts. It was only Sandra who could discern the thick concealer makeup under Doreen's right eye.

Sandra's legal aid solicitor, Jane, was nice but really young. She came across to Sandra sucking a theatrical breath in through her teeth.

'Think we've got our work cut out,' she said. 'They got married last Saturday.' She nodded her head towards Stephen and Doreen.

'Yeah? Well good luck to her, she's welcome. They're just not gettin' my kid.' Sandra drew on every ounce of bravado she could muster.

'Shall we get a coffee? We've got about fifteen minutes.'

There was a vending machine; they got two cups of brown liquid and took them to a plastic table and chairs just off the foyer, out of sight of Stephen and Doreen.

'He beats her up y'know? Just like he used to beat me. An' he raped me after I split up with him,' Sandra said when they were seated.

'Um. You said before that he was violent. The trouble is, without any charges being brought against him it's only your word against his. And with the soliciting conviction against you in 'seventy-seven it'd be really difficult to make the case.'

'Oh right, so prossies can't get raped or beat up.'

'No. Of course I didn't mean that.' Jane tried to placate her client. 'It's just that judges tend to be men and, well, it's bound to colour their view.'

'I did call the police on him before I left. Isn't there any record of that?' asked Sandra although she already knew the answer. She hadn't pressed charges against him because he'd cried and begged her to forgive him. She'd been an idiot and believed the lying scumbag. More important to her then, she didn't want Vince to see his dad for what he really was.

'There were no records of the events you described to me Sandra. I'm afraid the police don't always record domestic incidents where they're unlikely to get a conviction. It looks bad on their clear-up rates. Also, the alleged rape—'

Before she could finish her sentence Sandra leapt to her feet. 'What the fuck d'you mean alleged? I know when I've been fucking raped.'

'Please, Sandra. Sit down. Of course I didn't mean to imply that you hadn't been raped. It's just legal jargon when there's been no conviction.' Jane looked nervously around the foyer worried Sandra's outburst had attracted unwanted attention.

Sandra sat back down. 'Sorry,' she said, disconsolately picking at the skin around her thumb nail. She didn't want to smoke because it might look bad in front of the court officials, so she bit nervously at the skin she had loosened instead.

A clerk appeared and beckoned the adversaries into the court. The judge slowly explained the purpose of the hearing, as if they'd all just arrived from Mars. Then he asked for information regarding the current arrangements concerning Vincent's care. Stephen's slimy lawyer explained that the boy had lived with his mother until she had been convicted of soliciting two years before. Following this, his 'caring' and 'responsible' father had taken over the custody of the boy and was unwilling to allow access to his former partner who, he felt, was a deleterious influence. The lawyer droned on about the good home that Mr Jacques provided and his recent marriage to a woman of exemplary character.

'A doormat,' Sandra thought as she listened to this rosy depiction of domestic bliss.

Then Jane stood up. She began by countering the soliciting conviction. Her client, she said, had been of good character since that time. And Mr Jacques had been in full knowledge of the way in which Mrs Jacques earned money prior to her arrest and later conviction. Indeed, he had encouraged his former wife to prostitution and lived off the proceeds of her immoral earnings during their relationship. Furthermore, her client had found two-bedroom accommodation and had furnished and prepared a room in anticipation of her son's return. And, while she still relied on welfare benefits, Jane pointed out; this gave Sandra the opportunity to be a full-time mother to her son. She asked the judge to consider the cruelty of Mr Jacques' actions in denying Vincent access to his mother's care. A mother's love, she concluded, was essential for a contented childhood.

'The girl dun good,' Sandra thought, in spite of her youth and her posh middle-class ways. She could taste victory and her temples throbbed with anxiety. Jane smiled and showed Sandra her crossed fingers as she sat down again next to her.

'There is another matter of which Mr Jacques thinks your honour should be aware.' The lawyer was on his feet again. 'Mrs Jacques has for many months been involved in a lesbian relationship and is currently sharing her home with a woman. Mr Jacques understandably feels that, at this time, it would be wholly inappropriate to expose his young son to such a relationship.'

'You fuckin' bastard,' cried Sandra leaping to her feet. Jane wrestled her back to her chair as Stephen's lips peeled back in a smile.

It took just ten minutes for the judge to return his decision that the boy should stay with his father and step-mother, and that his mother be allowed supervised fortnightly visiting rights.

Stephen and Doreen hugged each other and shook hands with the lawyer. Then that grin spread across Stephen's face and Sandra knew beyond a shadow of a doubt that this had nothing to do with Vince's welfare. The sense of powerlessness she felt overwhelmed her in a great unstoppable wave.

'Keep quiet,' Jane ordered as they left the court. 'We'll fight it.' Sandra simply stared ahead biting hard to stop her tears. She could not let that scumbag see her weak. 'I wish you'd told me,' Jane said when they got outside. 'At least we could have been prepared.'

'I'm not one o' them,' Sandra insisted. 'I do live with Tracy but I'm not that thing they said.' She wanted to explain her feelings but words failed her.

'Look, here's a number. They might be able to advise you. They're called the Lesbian Custody Group and they're based in Leeds. It couldn't hurt to give them a ring. In the meantime, I think we have to wait and try again next year.'

Sandra took the piece of paper. 'You did your best,' she said. 'Thanks.' It was still raining and she'd left her umbrella in the courtroom.

As she walked across the city Sandra replayed the events in her mind. The only way to get Vince back was to finish things with Tracy. Yet as soon as she'd made that decision she remembered how Tracy made her feel loved and respected for the first time in her life. She thought of how Tracy made everything funny, and how they'd pissed themselves about the johns they'd done, just like normal people at work, except they laughed at bent knobs and bizarre requests. Like the bloke who'd paid thirty quid to sniff Tracy's arse, and they'd cried with laughter and gone to Blackpool on the proceeds. She couldn't understand why they couldn't just be who they were and have her son living with them. Women had been screwing men for the money to raise their kids forever. Why was it immoral? Her thoughts ran round in circles.

Tracy knew the minute she saw Sandra across the bar in the George that she'd lost the case. Sandra bought a lager and lime and came through to the snug. She relayed the details of what had gone down in the court. Tracy raged and ranted, mostly at feeling impotent to change the situation.

'I think we should pack it in,' Sandra said at last. 'I'm never gunna get him back while we live like we do. I don't wanna be 'one of them'.'

'You're not one of *them*. We're not what anyone calls us. We're just people trying to live our lives. I love you. Please don't say that.' Tracy felt the terrible fear of loss. 'He'd find something else to get you with even if we weren't together.'

'But we are, and that's what he's using to keep Vince. I just can't carry on.'

'Right,' Tracy said setting her jaw against her lover, against the world, against the fuckin' unfair bastard world. 'I'm getting a drink.' So far she'd been on soda water. Now she went to the bar and ordered a large Scotch on the rocks. She downed it in one and ordered another.

By the time they left the George, Tracy had spent all the money they had. Sandra had fifty pence left in her purse and a cold resolve in her heart not to just obliterate the pain she felt with booze. She needed to know what this pain felt like so she'd be able to root out that vulnerable part of herself and kill it. She'd lost her child and she'd pushed away her lover, her only source of comfort.

It was dark and still raining as they walked towards the flats. A car passed them near the kerb and sent a great wave of dirty water onto the pavement soaking Sandra's legs.

'I'll kill the bastard,' Tracy screamed and chased the car ineffectually as it rolled inexorably on, its driver careless of their torment.

Then Sandra wept until her breath caught in painful sobs and mascara streaked her cheeks.

♀

Three
Later the same day

The lifts were out again when Ginny and Michael got to the flats. They had to climb the four flights to their floor. Michael was tired and Ginny practically had to haul him up the last flight. One strip light blinked intermittently on the landing as Ginny rooted for her key. It was right at the bottom of her shoulder bag amongst the debris of old tissues and Michael's used inhalers. The smell of cold and damp hit Ginny's nostrils as they went in. She put the electric fire on to try and warm things up a bit. The central heating didn't work and the council still hadn't sent anyone out to mend it.

Ginny put the ice cream in the freezer compartment of the otherwise empty fridge, and then put the kettle on for a hot water bottle for Michael's bed. She saw the red impression of Sandra's lips on Michael's cheek and performed a cursory spit-wash with the tissue she had wrapped his tooth in. She laid out the pie and chips in their wrapper on the floor in front of the fire, and then she and Michael sat cross legged and tucked in to their banquet.

Michael kept up a stream-of-consciousness interrogation. He insisted on knowing how pies were made, the location of the tooth fairy's residence, even the size of the moon. Was it very small, or very far away? Ginny did her best to satisfy his enquiries. The pie and chips was heavenly. Ginny hadn't eaten all day and she was ravenous. When they'd finished she cleared away the greasy newspaper and went to the kitchen to fill the hot water bottle. Michael followed her, keeping up his commentary; and now his key concerns were the coloured laces in his new Clarks shoes. He wanted to demonstrate his newly acquired skill in tying them up himself. His Gran had taught him how to do it that very day.

'Go on then, let's see,' Ginny said. As she watched his small hands awkwardly fumbling, she was completely overwhelmed by the strength of her love for him. 'You are so clever,' she said with pride in her son's achievement when the laces were knotted. 'Now let's get you in yer 'jamas, then we'll have our Coke float.' She'd decided that the extra-curricular treat would make a good bargaining tool for bedtime.

They went to Michael's bedroom. Ginny put the hot water bottle in his bed, tucking it down so his feet wouldn't get cold. Michael held up his arms, Ginny pulled off his jumper and t-shirt and replaced them with his pyjama top. Then she sat him on the bed and took off his shoes and trousers. As she knelt before him with his pyjama bottoms at the ready Michael reached out and, stroking her hair, said: 'You're pretty, Mummy. I love you.'

'I love you too,' said Ginny and hugged him so tight she thought she might hurt him.

They went back into the kitchen and made two Coke floats. Ginny even found a straw at the back of the cupboard and put it in Michael's glass. They drank them in the living room while they coloured in a circus scene in one of Michael's books.

Ginny made up a story about a boy who was so good at taming lions and tigers that they let him ride on their backs. She noticed with satisfaction how Michael rarely went over the lines. He took such care with things. By the time they'd finished the colouring and the boy in the story was exhausted from too much lion taming, it was half-past nine, well past Michael's bedtime. He was so tired that he let Ginny carry him to bed.

'Don't forget about my tooth,' Michael said as Ginny laid him down and pulled up the covers.

Ginny reached into her pocket, took out the piece of lipstick-smeared tissue, carefully unwrapped the tooth and put it under Michael's pillow. She smoothed back his fringe and tenderly kissed his forehead. 'Good-night, sleep tight, my darlin',' she said switching off his light and gingerly pulling the door to.

Ginny cleared away the colouring pencils and rinsed their glasses in the kitchen sink. She took a small bottle of vodka from the top of the cupboard, poured a hefty slug into one of the tumblers and filled it up with Coke. She took a deep swig and carried it with her into her bedroom where she sat down on her bed to do her face in the dressing-table mirror. She didn't usually wear much makeup but, on the few nights when she'd been out, she'd slapped it on and found it made her feel like someone else, and that had helped.

Ginny examined herself in the mirror. She liked her eyes. They were dark brown and set wide in her face. She'd always been complimented on them. Her chestnut hair was layered, like Chrissie Hynde's, and it suited the almond shape of her face. Ginny had always attracted attention from men and she knew it would be easy to get a regular boyfriend, even with Michael in tow. She also knew that it wouldn't take long before he was telling her what to do, how to raise her son, and just generally cramping her style. She'd seen enough of her mum's life to know that she wanted more for herself. She applied a dark brown eye-shadow to her lids, and a then a kohl eyeliner to add mystery to her open face. Copious mascara and a reddish-brown lipstick outlined in black completed the desired effect: Joan Jett's evil sister. She changed into tight white jeans and a red satin shirt.

A light knock at the front door drew her into the hall. She could make out the bulky shape of Carolyn through the glass panel. She opened it quietly and hushed Carolyn into the living room. 'He's just gone off, I think,' she said quietly, hoping Carolyn, well known for her foghorn voice, would follow suit.

'Oh okay, good,' Carolyn replied in a comically loud whisper. 'Got any fags?' she added.

'No, sorry,' said Ginny, 'but I'll get you twenty Bensons tomorrow.'

Carolyn was the eighteen-year-old daughter of her neighbour on the landing. She was a big, good-natured girl ready to help anyone out. Her mum had died recently and Carolyn hated being alone in the flat with her dad. She'd confided to Ginny that he'd been trying it on with her since her mum had been ill and she didn't know where to turn. Ginny had listened and told her to go to the police, but she could understand that, vile as her father was, he was all Carolyn had in the world. Ginny wondered if his sexual advances to his own daughter hadn't hastened his wife's demise. Carolyn and Ginny had a kind of unspoken agreement. Ginny kept Carolyn's counsel and Carolyn didn't mention to anyone that Ginny went out at night and didn't come back until four or five in the morning.

'Want a glass of Coke?' said Ginny. She hadn't much else to offer.

'Yeah, ta.' Carolyn plonked herself heavily into the sagging armchair. The few bits of furniture Ginny owned came from the Methodist church Helping Hand Society, and most of it had seen better days. But beggars can't be choosers and Ginny was grateful for their kindness, though not so grateful that she'd succumbed to the subtle pressure that the Reverend Sweet had put on her to start attending Sunday service. 'The Lord 'elps them that 'elps 'emselves,' her mum always said, and Ginny figured that this nugget of wisdom was probably good advice.

Ginny went to the kitchen, picked up her own glass and poured the rest of the vodka into it. Then she poured a glass of Coke for Carolyn. She didn't have enough vodka to share and she decided her need was greater.

'Guess what? I've got tickets for The Boomtown Rats at the Empire next Sat'd'y,' Carolyn was saying as Ginny came back into the living room. 'D'you wanna go wi' us? It's a true story, y'know. Some girl in America got pissed off 'cause she didn't like Mondays and shot a loada people.'

'Yeah, I know,' said Ginny. 'I'd love to, but it depends if I can get me mum to have Michael. Anyway, dunno if I'll have the money.'

'I got 'em off Jonesy fer havin' his kids last week, so it'll be my treat.' Carolyn looked up to Ginny and took every chance she got to spend extra time with her.

'That's lovely of you, Car. Ta very much. I'll ask me mum about Michael,' said Ginny before slinging back the last of her drink.

'You gunna be alright t'night? It could be a late one again.'

'Yeah, no probs. I'll get me 'ead down here anyway,' Carolyn cheerfully replied.

'You're a godsend,' Ginny said, putting on her bomber jacket and picking up her bag. 'See ya later.' She went into the hall and opened the front door. Then she remembered the tooth. She rummaged through her bag for the ten pence she'd saved and silently opened Michael's bedroom door. Gently and without a sound, she lifted the corner of his pillow and replaced the tooth with the money. He didn't stir. Ginny leaned over and smelled the back of his head, brushing her lips against his hair. Then she closed his door again and went back to her bedroom. On the dressing table was the ring box for the signet ring her mum had given her for her twentieth birthday last May. She put the tooth into the ring box and put the box in her bag.

'See ya later,' Carolyn called as Ginny closed the front door behind her.

There was only one woman out when Ginny arrived at the bit of kerb she'd been using near the old woollens factory. It was still drizzling. Tracy had given her stark warnings about taking someone else's patch and Ginny didn't want to make any enemies. The shops had shut and a single streetlamp cast a damp yellow circle of light, which only seemed to emphasise the darkness. Ginny recognised the woman across the street but didn't know her name. She nodded to her and said: 'Quiet t'night?'

'Too bleedin' cold,' the woman replied. 'I'm givin' it twenty minutes then I'm going up the Caribbean Club.'

'Freezin', ennit,' Ginny agreed.

A car pulled round the corner—a green Morris Minor. 'Thank Christ,' the woman across the street said. 'It's one of me regulars.'

The car stopped and the woman got in. It pulled away leaving Ginny alone on the pavement. The Caribbean Club did sound like a good idea, but Ginny hadn't got the price of her first drink so she stayed put. If she could just get herself one punter, maybe cop ten quid, that would get her through till Giro day on Tuesday.

Ten minutes went by. A few cars had gone past but they were just people on their way somewhere. It was easy to tell a punter, they slowed to eye the merchandise. Sometimes tourists did this too, just for the thrill. That was really annoying.

Ginny felt the November cold seeping into her bones, thought about giving it up and asking her brother Gary for a loan. If she could get him in private his grasping wife needn't know about it, and she'd be able to pay him back before the miserable cow found out.

Another ten minutes, and then an old Hillman Hunter began to slow as it approached the kerb where Ginny stood. As it got closer she could see that there were four people in the car. That was a bad sign. Gangs of lads didn't usually pick up working girls. A young man on the passenger side wound down the window and shouted, 'How much to suck my dick, you fuckin' slag?' Ginny heard the other passengers whoop with laughter at this dazzling wit and she gave them the finger. Then something hit her shoulder. An opened tomato ketchup portion. It splattered Ginny's jacket and caught in a sticky mass in her hair.

Fuck this, Ginny thought as she snagged the gloop from her hair with her fingers.

She decided to chance the Caribbean Club. There'd be bound to be someone she knew and could borrow the money off for a couple of drinks. She was nowhere near pissed enough for this caper anyway.

Ginny could hear the music well before she got to the club. 'Police and Thieves' came throbbing at her from fifty yards away. It was one of Ginny's favourite tunes and it lifted her spirits. A couple of black guys at the door were passing a spliff between them. They parted to let Ginny through and she caught the pungent odour of the weed. By way of greeting, one of the men said, 'Hey, where you bin hidin', pretty lady?' Ginny smiled but kept on walking.

The main room was packed and thick with smoke as Ginny entered. 'Exodus' was playing now, so loud Ginny could feel her chest vibrating. She spotted Tracy on the dance floor, pushed sideways through the crowd. Tracy looked completely hammered.

'Couldn't lend us a couple of quid till Tuesday, could ya, Trace?' Ginny bellowed. 'I'm absolutely skint.'

'Yeah, no worries,' Tracy slurred lurching in Ginny's direction. Ginny managed to steady her and they made their way to the bar. Sandra was perched on one of the tall bar-stools talking to Clinton, their pimp. Clinton was a flash bastard but he was well-liked by the girls and did actually treat them fairly. To him it was just a business like any other. He looked after the girls, provided good contacts with regular customers and always had a ready supply of weed. Ginny wanted to avoid getting to the point where she needed the services of someone like Clinton, but he'd be the one she'd have gone to if things ever went that far. Most of the pimps, black or white, were violent bastards.

'What'll you have, honey?' Clinton asked Ginny.

'Vodka and Coke please,' she replied, 'but I can't get you one back'.

'You'll find some way to re-pay me, honey,' Clinton said in his thick Jamaican accent.

'Leave her alone,' said Sandra. 'She don't need a bloody pimp. Do ya darlin'?'

Clinton chuckled and shouted the order up to the barman.

'Get us one an' all,' said Tracy.

'Haven't you 'ad enough,' Sandra cut in.

'Mind yer own fuckin' business,' Tracy replied.

Ginny hadn't seen Tracy like this before. It was obviously the drink talking, but there was an underlying antagonism between the two girls.

'Don't mind her,' Sandra said to Ginny. 'We've 'ad a bit of bad news t'day. Who's got your Michael anyway?' she added, changing the subject.

'Carolyn along my landing,' Ginny replied. 'She's ever so good an' Mikey loves her.'

Clinton handed Ginny what looked like a large vodka. She downed half of it in one gulp. Then a dub track came on that the DJ played every week and it filled the floor. The little party of four raised their eyebrows at each other in mutual agreement and joined the throng.

'Tell me something good.' Tracy mouthed the words to Sandra as they danced and Ginny felt a little needle of envy that at least they had each other. Clinton, meanwhile, had gone into his Rastaman zone. They danced the next three numbers too, and Ginny had begun to feel the effects of the vodka and the weed that Clinton had been surreptitiously passing her as he danced closer to her. Her head was buzzing nicely and she was loosening up.

'Fuck it all,' she thought. At least she had Michael and a place to live, and some good mates and a lovely mum. As she counted her blessings a commotion broke out at the door. Six burly policemen pushed their way into the club and started herding people to the back of the room. Everyone appeared to know the drill. Joints were mashed out on the floor and some people were already holding up their arms ready to be searched. A couple of guys had been cuffed. Ginny thought they were the cheeky ones she'd encountered at the door. The women were told to go home. Clinton passed Sandra something as she pressed past him on their way out. A young policeman grabbed Ginny's arm as she put her jacket back on in the entrance.

'Nigger-loving cunt,' he spat through gritted teeth.

'Fuck off you racist arsehole,' said Tracy defending her mates.

'Like to spend the night in a cell, slag?' The policeman rounded on Tracy, put his hand in the middle of her chest and pushed her roughly against the wall.

'Sorry officer, she's had a bit too much to drink.' Sandra tried to calm the situation.

'Go on and fuck off the lot of you. Fucking load of filthy whores.' The young man had asserted his power and now he wanted a piece of the action inside the club, where several more black men had been handcuffed.

The three women left the club. The rain that had been on and off all day had finally stopped, but a bitter wind cut into their faces as they walked home towards the flats. Tracy was still swaying a little but the bust and the cold night air had sobered her up no end.

'Those fuckin' wankers,' Tracy said. 'If it's not the Caribbean Club it's The Swan every other bastard week. Haven't they got any fuckin' crimes to solve?'

'Is that the gay bar up Cable Street?' Ginny asked.

'Yeah,' Tracy replied. 'It's a good night up there on Sat'd'ys. They have a drag act on. It was Diana Ross last week.'

'It is funny,' Sandra agreed. 'You'll have to come up there with us sometime.'

'Ta, I will, thanks,' said Ginny, adding, 'Is everything alright? Only I couldn't help notice you looked upset when I seen you earlier.'

'I lost the custody case to get my Vincent back t'day,' Sandra explained with a 'life sucks' expression.

'What a bastard,' Ginny said with real feeling. If anyone ever tried to take Michael off her she'd kill them.

'D'you wanna come up for a smoke?' Sandra asked, tapping the pocket where she'd slipped the little package Clinton had passed to her in the club. They'd reached the flats and the three towering monstrosities loomed above them. It was half-past one and the lights that were still on made a patchwork reaching up into the night sky.

'Thanks, but I need to get some money,' Ginny said. There were still plenty of cars about and a couple of women in sight, working a patch a bit further down the road.

'We're gunna call it a night,' Tracy said. 'But watch yerself. Poor old Maisie got fuckin' near strangled by some bastard just last week. She's still not well an' the filth ain't bin anywhere near.' The recollection revived her disgruntlement with the police.

'I will,' Ginny said as they went their separate ways.

Ginny dug her hands deep into her pocket and kept her head down as she walked towards the old woollens factory. The two women she'd seen from up at the flats had disappeared by the time she got there. She wished she'd asked Tracy for a fag before they'd parted. The factory behind her had stood empty since she was a kid. Its blackened walls were interrupted only by a row of long narrow windows toothed with jagged shards of glass. Ginny thought they probably made them like that so they let in enough light to work, but nobody could see out. She imagined what life would have been like for the people who worked there all that time ago. Not much different to now, she decided. Though Ginny didn't know it, women had been selling themselves from the very spot where she now stood since before the factory was built. The damp and cold cut through her as she tried to fasten the broken zip of her bomber jacket. She was just about to give it up and ask her brother for the loan when a car came round the corner and slowed at the kerb where she stood. It was a Ford Capri. The driver wound down the window and Ginny leaned in.

'Get in then,' the man said. He looked in his thirties and wore blue workmen's overalls. It gave him a kind of homely air.

'Don't you want to know how much?' asked Ginny.

'I'll gi' you what you ask for,' the man replied in a hoarse local accent. Ginny thought he seemed nervous. She hesitated. The car smelled of sweat and something else that Ginny couldn't place, a sickly cloying smell. 'Ten for a blow-job, fifteen for sex with a rubber.' Ginny added a fiver to the going rate half-hoping he'd turn her down.

He reached into the breast pocket of his overalls and took out two ten pound notes.

'We'll get change from the garage,' he said.

Ginny thought she'd get the fags for Carolyn while they were in there. 'Okay,' she said and got into the car. She'd probably be able to get a few bits in for Christmas as well, now.

♀

Four
The same day

Irina adjusted Graham's tie. His Adam's apple bobbed just above the perfect knot as he swallowed back emotion. He brushed a few flecks of dandruff from the shoulders of his black funeral suit and turned to stare at himself in the hall mirror. He touched the bruise on his cheek, still tender from the week before. His brother had punched him on the day their mother, Catherine, had died.

The deathbed scene at the hospital was surreal. His father, Jack, had been casually reading 'The Sun' while his brothers were discussing Leeds United's performance against Coventry the previous week. Graham had no interest in football. He had sat silent by Catherine's bed as her breathing faltered and long, aching moments passed between each respiration. When at last there were no more, Graham stood and closed his eyes tight. His brothers, unaware of Catherine's demise, had been invited by Jack to look at the page three girl, and Billy was at that moment saying: 'Look at the tits on that.' Graham began to bang his head against the wall. The congregation of male relatives looked up at him from the paper.

'Ah well. She's gone,' said Jack, adding, 'The King David, or the Saracen's?'

His brother, Dave, took hold of Graham's shoulders. Graham looked at him uncomprehending. 'Get a fuckin' grip, mate,' Dave said and led him away.

A young nurse came in and closed the dead woman's eyes. 'There's nothing to be done now,' she said kindly. And then, turning to Jack: 'Are you the lady's husband? Perhaps you could sign the necessary papers tomorrow?'

'Will you be here to help me?' the bereaved man replied, winking at his eldest son, Billy.

The four men left the hospital and made their way to the Saracen's Head. Graham had recovered his composure and walked steadily in front of the rest, although not so far that he couldn't hear their banter. They'd fallen back to their analysis of Leeds United's chances this season.

They'd started drinking whisky at three in the afternoon. Graham rarely touched the stuff, so he'd said more than he'd meant to. He'd gone on about how much he'd loved his mother, and how she'd loved him much more than her other sons. Jack Hindle had menace in his eyes as he warned him to 'Shut it!' but Graham had kept on.

'She was a slag,' Jack said at last. 'Now just shut the fuck up.' It was as if he needed to keep his hatred alive, because it relieved him of any sense of guilt or responsibility for his own philandering, which had been continuous throughout their thirty-six-year marriage.

Graham felt tears hot on his face and the scarlet blouse incident played itself out in his alcohol muddied brain. He remembered how, when he was eighteen, Catherine had bought a new blouse. She'd rarely spent money on herself so the scarlet blouse with a big ruff-collar had impressed itself on his memory. Wearing it, she looked different, her usual clothes drab by comparison. Jack had come in as he lay on the floor with his chin resting in his hands watching Top of the Pops. Billy and Dave, being older than Graham, had the sofa, and no one was allowed in their father's chair. Jimmy Savile was introducing that week's number one, The Rolling Stones' 'Satisfaction'. Mick Jagger strutted and pouted his discontent as the scene played out in their living room.

'Is that for yer fancy man, you fuckin' old whore?' Jack had raged, and then grabbed Catherine by the ruff on the front of the blouse. He ripped it from her and left her standing in her bra as her three sons looked on. Someone Jack worked with had told him they'd seen her with a man in a pub in Elland. Jack didn't need to ask questions. The blouse was evidence enough. 'Look at the piece of shit, boys,' he invited, as his wife tried in vain to gather the shredded material across her breasts. 'Never trust a woman. They're all lying fuckin' tarts.'

After that, Jack had replaced the contempt with which he'd habitually treated Catherine with something akin to revulsion. She'd become no more to him than a menial employed to keep house and provide sex on demand. Graham had often heard her screams when Jack came home drunk from the pub on Saturday nights. He'd been paralysed with fear, as if he'd been the one getting the beating, or worse. His brothers had soon benefitted from this new, utterly subservient role that his mother now played in their lives. They enjoyed complete freedom from washing, or even picking up, their clothes; from ever having to explain when they'd be in or where they were going; from asking before they finished the last of the biscuits. Only Graham still treated his mother with any respect at all, and then only when his father and brothers were out.

As he recalled the scene, Graham felt his head swimming with a mixture of drunkenness, grief and an anger that seemed to reach into his soul. He swayed slightly on his feet.

'Look at the fuckin' state of him, will ya?' Jack sneered, and then continued his withering assault with: 'Great big useless pansy.' Graham leapt forward swinging his clenched fist at his father. His brother Dave intervened and, with one hard punch, knocked Graham sideways. He crashed into a table full of drinks and onto the floor in a heap, where he lay sobbing among the spilt ale and broken glass. Billy and Dave picked him up, ashamed of their fraternal connection to a man who'd behave in such a way.

The landlord had thrown them all out after that. When he hit the fresh air, Graham threw up. The acrid taste of vomit burned his throat. When he looked up, his father and brothers were walking away. Graham gathered his jumbled thoughts and followed, like a wounded dog. He wanted so much to be part of their brotherhood but something stood in his way, something vile that he felt a need to eviscerate. Thoughts crowded his brain in random snatches as he walked.

Graham was always the brunt of their jokes, always the 'mummy's boy'. They despised him for it. Just as they despised Irina, his wife, and the way he allowed her to dictate his life. They'd nearly made him lose her once. Billy had pinched her bum, and she'd turned and slapped his face. Billy responded in kind, but twice as hard. Graham had managed to smooth things over with Irina but she never visited his parents' house again. She'd always looked down on them anyway and this gave her the excuse she'd needed to sever the connection. In some ways, he knew, she looked down on him too.

Irina was from better stock. Her Polish parents had been professional people in Krakow. They had fled the country in the early fifties, fearing Stalin's persecution of 'subversive elements', seeking a standard of living Irina's father had thought commensurate with his standing as a doctor. He railed against 'socialism' and tried to instil in his two girls a belief in their 'superior social status'. In Irina's case it had worked, and she prided herself on her family's erstwhile grandness.

Her father never recovered from the shock of the treatment he'd received in Britain or his failure to find employment in his specialist field of orthopaedics. He'd spent more than twenty-five years as a ward orderly at the city infirmary. He opposed Irina's marriage to a mere warehouseman but he'd been impressed by Graham's loyalty to his daughter when she'd had her 'illness'. He had finally relented and agreed to their union when Graham paid the deposit on the semi-detached house.

Irina, with her refined ways and her fragility, made Graham feel strong. Women like that needed protection and he'd been there to provide it. He would always protect her from the shame of being a woman. She was more than that to him. Irina was his shadow, just as his mother had been when he was young.

Now, passing beneath a streetlamp, Graham watched as his own shadow foreshortened and disappeared. Now, he would find the strength to be a man.

Alone in his thoughts, Graham had lost sight of his family. And he'd sobered up enough to know he didn't want any more to drink. He walked back to the hospital car-park filled with disgust as he relived his humiliation in the pub. His trousers were still damp with beer and his face throbbed. When he got back to his car he decided to drive around for a while to clear his head. He found a cassette in the glove-box and put it into the player. It was his mother's favourite song: 'Bridge Over Troubled Water'. Graham turned up the volume and drove. Tears streamed down his face and Art Garfunkel's high, feminine voice made his skin tingle. He clenched the steering wheel as his grief gave way to anger and self-pity. He drove to the old industrial centre of the town, to the red-light district. Graham had driven there often before with his friend Derek. They'd had a right laugh talking about the slags parading up and down. Derek had confided in him how he'd roughed one up once just for the crack. Graham felt himself getting an erection now at the memory.

The woman was walking slowly, her miniskirt stretched skin-tight across her buttocks. Graham passed her. There was no one else around. He pulled off the road onto the derelict ground behind one of the old factories. The woman reached his car. His heart was banging in his chest.

When she got into the passenger seat he saw she was plastered in crude makeup and much older than she'd looked on the street; probably not yet forty, but wearing the script of her life on her face.

'Fiver for a blow job. Ten for sex with a rubber, fifteen without,' she said matter-of-fact.

Graham made as if to look for his wallet in the glove compartment. Then he turned and punched the woman hard, right between the eyes. She retaliated, catching him a painful blow to his already injured cheek. He grabbed her by the throat and squeezed as she struggled and lashed out beneath him. He was much too strong for her and, as he pressed harder against her throat, he felt the woman go limp. Then Graham was kneeling above her. He was the one who'd decide how much and for what. He let go of her neck, snatched up her handbag from the seat beside her and rifled through its contents. Her social security payment card gave him her name, Maisie Nicholls, and her purse held ninety-two pence. He emptied the money into his hand and put it in his pocket. Then he opened his car door and pushed the woman out onto the waste ground. She rolled away onto her side and Graham threw the handbag and its contents after her.

That had been a week ago. He'd looked in the paper but he hadn't seen anything about the attack. Prostitutes were always getting beaten up; why waste column inches that could be more lucratively filled with adverts?

Graham had not seen his family since then. He and Irina had done most of the funeral arrangements. Catherine had been a Catholic and a service was to be held at the cathedral before they went on to the crematorium. First, they were to meet the funeral directors at the family home. When they arrived at the house, Jack and Graham's brothers and their wives were already there. Dave held out his hand and said: 'No hard feelings mate.' Graham shook the hand, grateful, and flushed, knowing that the wound on his face was a reminder of his thrashing the previous week.

The hearse pulled up outside. Catherine's coffin was decked in a wreath of white and pink carnations spelling MUM. They'd all chipped in for it. Irina thought it horribly undignified and working class. She thanked God that they were all travelling in their own vehicles. That way, she reassured herself, people might easily imagine it possible that the car she was riding in was just caught up behind a random funeral procession.

'Take something of your mother's. Would Irina like a piece of jewellery?' Jack spoke as if Irina wasn't there. It was as if he couldn't bring himself to address her directly.

As the rest of the mourners filed out and got into their cars, Graham went upstairs to Catherine's bedroom. Irina tugged at Graham's sleeve, indicated with a shake of her head that she didn't want his mother's old tat, and had gone to wait in the car. He knew what he wanted: the black woollen handbag with the gold clasp. He found it at once at the bottom of the dresser drawer. Graham remembered the bag from his earliest childhood. It contained everything his mother seemed to need in life, yet was forbidden to him. He had longed to know what was inside but it was always out of reach. It was her special place containing all her mystery. Now he opened the clasp. It was empty, unused for years. He slid the bag into the back of his trousers and covered it with his jacket. Then he took his mother's blood-donors badge - she'd given twenty-five pints - hurried down to the car and, pretending he needed a rag, slipped the bag under the boot-rug. Then he got into the driver's seat and set off.

'Mum's blood-donor's badge.' Graham handed the little silver heart-shaped trinket to Irina. They caught up with the funeral cars before the end of the street. The procession crawled slowly through the town towards the cathedral.

'I didn't know your mother gave blood,' said Irina, dabbing at a tiny spot of dirt on the car-seat.

The service at the cathedral was a miserable affair and very poorly attended. Catherine had a few acquaintances but no real friends. After the scarlet blouse incident, she'd only gone out to shop for food, and occasionally to mass. It seemed the priest didn't actually know his mother well, though, and appeared to have her mixed up with a woman from the choir, since he waxed lyrical on the beauty of Catherine's singing voice. No one in the family had ever heard her sing. The uncomfortable sacrament went on for over an hour. Graham thought he would faint but managed to hold himself together for long enough to escape into the cold damp day. After this they moved on in solemn convoy to the crematorium.

Graham had chosen 'Bridge Over Troubled Water' as the funeral music. He'd given his own tape to the funeral directors as they filed into the chapel. A mercifully brief rite was followed by the curtains closing slowly and inexorably around the coffin. A clunk could be heard as the tape was switched on and the song began. But it wasn't the one he had chosen. He'd forgotten to rewind the tape and the next track came on instead. The impossibly taut strings at the start of 'El Condor Pasa' filled the little chapel and Graham felt his brain tighten in response. He closed his eyes, almost losing consciousness. No one else even noticed. No other member of her family would know Catherine's favourite song from a hole in the ground.

Graham could not remember, when he thought of it afterwards, if he had actually been conscious. He fell into a trance-like state. Those looking at him would have seen a man, eyes wide open, staring at the ground. He saw a bird pecking at the shell on a snail's back in vicious blows. Then a hammer smashing into that shell, obliterating it. The great forest would overwhelm the street. A boundless force of nature. Destructive and cleansing, he would glide like The Swan—here, and gone.

After the funeral Graham felt a kind of weightlessness. He needed to be away and alone. He and Irina said their goodbyes and left.

'Drop me in the centre,' Irina said in her usual, slightly irritated tone.

Graham was glad. He needed time to think. They drove in silence to the city centre. He pulled up outside Richard Shops and leaned over to give his wife a kiss. She turned and offered him her cheek.

'I'll make my own way home,' she said.

As had been his habit since boyhood, Graham headed onto the moors. He used to bike it. He could still remember the near-sick exhaustion he felt as he reached the highest point. Now he was comfortably behind the wheel of his car and, as he gained altitude, the fog closed around him like a curtain. His headlights lit only the mist in front of him. He pulled over to the side of the road and switched off his engine. Silence. He watched as headlights appeared dimly through the shroud of mist and moved slowly towards him. The car passed him and disappeared. The longer he sat the clearer his mind became. The confusions he'd felt seemed to evaporate into the haze and a wonderful sense of clarity wiped out his fears. He knew what he had to do; the message had been crystal clear. He had a purpose, a way to make a contribution to the world. He would be that force of nature, the street cleaner of his vision.

When Graham started his engine again it was nearly eight o'clock. He'd been sitting for two hours. He drove back towards the city, and as he descended the fog cleared slightly and the moors gave way to streetlights and clusters of houses. He decided to call for Derek and take him up on his offer made yesterday as they left the yard. 'If you fancy a bevy or two after the funeral, gi' us a knock,' Derek had called after him as they'd gone their separate ways.

Derek's mum answered the door when Graham arrived, and ushered him into the parlour muttering her condolences as they went.

'How did it go, mate?' asked Derek.

'Yeah. All went off alright. Just thought I could do with that pint.'

'I'll get me coat.' Derek returned his copy of Front Page Detective to the magazine rack. 'Equal Rights Got Cath Killed!' read the lurid headline above a picture of a woman screaming in a dark, male shadow.

'Don't wait up, Ma,' Derek called as they left.

They went to Derek's local and sank half a dozen pints of IPA. Graham told Derek about the funeral, and they talked about work and cars, and Derek's true-crime magazine stories.

'Remember that slag you roughed up?' said Graham, prompting Derek to relate the story.

'Oh that old bag. She kept tryin' to get me t'go wi' her, so I give her a fuckin' good slap. Horrible diseased old bitch, it was.'

Both men had laughed then. 'Fuckin' whores,' Graham said. 'Don't hardly deserve to live.' They'd finished their pints, and it was long after closing time now.

When they got back to the car, Derek fished a packet of Juicy Fruit chewing gum from his pocket and offered a stick to Graham. 'Cover up the smell of the ale a bit,' he said.

It was close to one o'clock when Graham dropped Derek back home and headed into the city. He knew where he was going. He stopped at a bus stop pull-in and got out, loosening his tie as he walked round to the boot of his car. He took off his suit jacket, folded it neatly and placed it with his tie in the boot. Then he took out his blue work overalls and slipped them on over his trousers and shirt. He rummaged in his tool box and found his claw hammer and a large screwdriver. He put these in the right leg-pocket of his overalls. Then he drove directly to the red light district. As he passed the new flats he saw two women standing close together. He circled the block. He was looking for a woman alone. She was there on his next circuit. And, as if God himself ordained it, she was wearing the scarlet blouse. He could see it beneath her jacket.

Graham wound down the window as he pulled over to the kerb. 'Get in, then,' he said.

♀

Five
The same day

Selene left the Leeds University campus in the certain knowledge that she had failed to land the part-time fellowship she'd applied for. It had always been a long shot. Now she was back in her hometown she was struggling to find a space where she belonged, either economically or emotionally.

She had finished her degree in History at The London School of Economics three years before and, with no clear idea of what to do next, drifted into an MA course and a squat with her boyfriend of the time. She'd written a thesis on Victorian Prostitution for her masters' degree, and had spent two years steeped in the lives of the denizens of Whitechapel. On the day she'd been awarded the second degree she'd gone home to find her boyfriend in bed with one of the other women at the house. He'd behaved as if she was a reactionary threat to the revolution as she packed her things and told him he was a cheating fuckwit.

After that she had little choice but to go back to her parent's house up north. They'd been overjoyed at first to have their baby back with them, but their pleasure in Selene's return was soon replaced with disapproval and nagging. She'd chosen to study in London to get away from them in the first place. They harped on constantly about getting married, getting a job, getting on in life. They compared her unfavourably with her sister, Irina, who had been educated too but had made the sensible decision to marry and settle down nearby.

'Yes, but look at what she married,' Selene had countered, knowing her father's barely concealed dislike for Graham.

'Well she's got a lovely home,' Selene's mum, Beata, said in a tone that was final and conclusive.

But Selene couldn't let that one lie. 'She's got a severe obsessive compulsive disorder, actually.'

'Some people care about having a clean home.'

'It's not about having a clean home, Mum. Irina's terrified of something. She's not well.'

Discussions like this invariably ended in a bitter screaming match. Selene suspected they were fuelled by guilt, on the part of her parents, that they were somehow responsible for Irina's illness. Irina had suffered from mental health problems since she'd been a teenager but her father had been unable to countenance the idea that any child of his should be so afflicted. She'd fallen in love with a boy at university called Simon, and when he'd dumped her it had triggered a breakdown. Irina had been hospitalised, and it was during this time that Graham had insinuated himself into Irina's life. He'd been hanging around Irina for a while and her illness had given him the chance to be the knight in shining armour. After that he'd just behaved as if their engagement and marriage was a *fait accompli*, and Irina was too delicate to resist him. She'd just gone along with it. Her lack of ability to stop it seemed to characterise their union. Selene loathed Graham. She'd hated him on sight and nothing he'd said or done in the intervening years had altered her opinion. He gave her the creeps. It was one of the few things on which she and her father were of one mind, though they seldom ever openly shared their views.

After three months at her parents' home, Selene could stand no more and moved out. She'd started going to a feminist consciousness raising group in Leeds and had met a new friend, an artist called Izzy. It was through her that she'd been invited to take up a spare room in a recently acquired squat. It was separatist, and men were not allowed across the threshold, but she wasn't that bothered about another relationship in the near future so she'd jumped at the chance. Anyway, if she did meet a bloke she fancied they could go to his place. At least it was cheap and she'd be away from her parents.

When she first got back up north Selene did some temping in random offices. Her mother, Beata, was furious at the waste of her five years in higher education. The agency found her a short stint at the dole office, but that had ended after a couple of months when she'd called her manager a sexist. He routinely expressed the view that married women should leave their jobs and become full-time housewives. The argument they'd had was fierce, and after it the whole office seemed to turn against her, even the women she'd thought she was defending. Her qualifications seemed more of a hindrance than an aid to finding work, so eventually she'd decided to try to return to academic life.

The fellowship Selene had applied for had been in the History faculty but they'd seemed disinterested in her ideas on the history of sex work in the Leeds/Bradford area. She'd banged on for ages about her work on prostitution in Victorian London and the need to also reveal the neglected lives of women outside the capital. One of the men on the interview panel had yawned visibly, and another wondered if something on the impact of the 1842 Mines Act on the lives of women might not be more pertinent. Anyway, she'd left knowing that the bespectacled young man with his thesis on Lenin tucked under his arm would get the post.

Now, as she walked away, Selene felt relief that she wouldn't actually have to do something she wasn't all that keen on anyway. She was sick of study; it had begun to feel as though she was living her life vicariously through her books and articles and interminable analyses. She wanted to experience life at first hand. Academia kept her at a distance from everything real.

Selene walked towards the city centre wondering what to do next. She didn't want to go back to the unheated squat and the chance of running into Jenny. Jenny was the founder of the Lesbian Separatist Movement in Leeds and she brooked no arguments about men or heterosexuality. Sleeping with men was sleeping with the enemy and all men were rapists. Jenny was one of five other women who lived in the squat and, when Selene had been put forward by Izzy as a possible candidate for the spare room, Jenny and her partner Nicola had voted against it, on the grounds that Selene was heterosexual. The vote had gone three to two in Selene's favour and she'd been invited to move in, but she always afterwards tried to give Jenny a wide berth.

It was just before four o'clock now, the end of the day, too late to do any daytime activity but not yet evening. A dead time. She drifted into a Wimpy Bar and ordered a coffee. It was wet, warm and frothy, but there any resemblance to coffee ended. She cupped her hands around the mug and stared out onto the damp city street. The waitresses were starting to wipe down tables and straighten salt and pepper pots as they talked about their Friday evening plans. Selene felt her own emptiness sharpen. She had no plans for the evening, or for the weekend that would follow. She was enjoying her novel, although it was deeply depressing, and she thought she would finish that.

Selene was reading F. Tennyson Jesse's 'A Pin to see the Peepshow'. It was a novelisation of the Edith Thompson case, a cruel miscarriage of justice in which a young woman was hanged for adultery. The final chapters, describing Thompson drugged and terrified in her prison cell awaiting her fate, were a gruelling read; a kind of semi-conscious haze in the approach of death. The plight of Edith Thompson seemed to resonate with the timbre of Selene's life as she saw it at that moment.

The streetlights were starting to come on and the pavements glistened with rain. As she sat contemplating her life, Selene saw Irina approaching hunched beneath her umbrella. Irina looked so much older that at first Selene had not been sure it was her sister. She knocked on the window and Irina looked up startled. She had always been troubled by unexpected events. Selene beckoned her into the café. It had been over a month since they had seen each other, though they had spoken on the phone, and Selene knew that Graham's mum had died. Irina carefully arranged her three bags of shopping on the seat beside her before ordering a strawberry milkshake.

'Ugh.' Selene pulled a disgusted face at the thought of the gloopy sweet drink.

'I'm trying not to drink too much coffee. I think it might be causing my heart flutters,' Irina explained, engrossed in aligning her bags.

'How's Graham taken his mum dying?' Selene was solicitous more on her sister's behalf than any feeling of concern for Graham.

'Oh, he doesn't say much but I think he's been quite cut up about it really. He thought a lot of her. I've just come from the funeral, actually.'

'Did it go okay?'

'There was only the immediate family there, poor woman didn't seem to have any friends, and the way they treated her was horrible. You should have seen the wreath. It was pink carnations spelling MUM.' Irina rolled her eyes scornfully.

'Oh don't be such a snob. It sounds fine to me,' Selene snapped. When Irina was like this she seemed to embody everything that Selene hated about their parents. Since she had been married to Graham this part of Irina's personality had appeared to intensify. She never asked Selene anything about her life and she, in turn, tended not to volunteer information. Her sister would only look vaguely disappointed and uncomprehending. They talked instead about the clothes that Irina had bought, though she would in all likelihood never wear them. Irina had a wardrobe full of brand new clothes that once worn, she felt, would be forever sullied. This was another of Irina's strange obsessions.

When the milkshake arrived, pale pink in a tall sundae-glass, Irina pushed it away in distaste.

'Didn't fancy it after all?' enquired Selene.

'There's a chip,' Irina replied indicating a tiny imperfection in the pedestal of the glass. Selene knew better than to argue or try to persuade. Her sister's eccentricities had started to emerge after her breakdown and had gotten progressively worse since.

They left the Wimpy and walked together to the bus station.

'I like your new haircut, by the way,' Irina said.

Selene touched the nape of her neck. She'd had her long, straight brown hair cut and feathered at the back, and a fringe instead of a centre parting. 'Do you? I can't make my mind up,' she said grateful of the compliment.

'Yes, it really suits your face.'

Irina's bus came first. As it pulled away, she gave a little wave at Selene waiting behind the barrier. This gesture sent a swell of sadness through Selene. She recalled their childhood, and how patient her sister had once been.

Irina was four years older than Selene but she never once pulled rank or refused to play with her baby sister. For a few years they'd been close, but as they grew they drifted apart. Selene had become the prodigal daughter. While Irina had been shaped by her father's bitterness and her mother's fear and distrust, Selene had escaped. She'd found a way to be her own person and, at least in part, that was because Irina bore the brunt of their anxieties. Now Irina was stuck with a man who, in some way that Selene couldn't name, was dismantling her. As she thought of the word 'dismantling' it seemed exactly right. It was as though Graham had taken out all the screws that held Irina together and looked on, satisfied as she fell apart. Whenever Selene had any dealings with him she'd got the sense that he enjoyed his wife's troubles because it made him feel more powerful.

Selene arrived back at the squat at a quarter to six. She saw, as she approached, that the windows were lit. That meant some of the women were already there. She was glad at the thought of companionship. The house stood in a row of fine old Victorian mock-villas. They'd been built at the height of the city's industrial prosperity and, more than a century later, had fallen into disrepair. This area of town had ceased to attract the wealthy middle classes even before the nineteenth century was out. Successive influxes of immigrant communities during the twentieth century had been housed here as unscrupulous landlords turned these old family homes into warrens of shabbily converted flats. The district had become synonymous with deprivation, though it still bore the remnants of a more illustrious past, fine architecture and open parkland. Their house had once been a rich man's home with servant's quarters. The old bell-system was still on the wall in the kitchen. By the early seventies the windows and doors were boarded up. There was a hole in the roof and the staircase had completely decayed. The women squatters themselves had made the place habitable. Though it was cold in winter, the big, communal living room was cosy, with an open fire and walls hung with tapestries and art, a lot of it made by Izzy.

Selene let herself in the front door. A waft of cooking smells led her into the kitchen. There she found Izzy with Rachel and Jo, the other lesbian couple who lived in the house. Rachel was a lawyer and Jo a social worker, and between them they ran about a dozen different committees and groups. They were like two perfectly fitting halves that formed a seamless whole, both chubby and full of kindness for the world. Rachel was dark haired and Jo was blonde, like positive and negative ions. They epitomised the old joke: What do lesbians take with them on the second date? The furniture.

Selene was glad to see that Jenny and Nicola hadn't come home yet. She still felt awkward around them, knowing their opposition to her living there. There was another guest at the table who she didn't recognise.

'Hi,' Selene said. 'Smells lovely.'

'Howdy,' Izzy said. 'I'm just knocking up a frittata out of some leftovers. How'd the interview go?'

'Um. Not so good, I think. They didn't seem to go a bundle on sex workers. I'm not that fussed to be honest.'

'Oh well, their loss. I don't think you've met Kim.' Rachel indicated their guest.

Selene held out her hand. Kim stood to her full six-foot-two and took Selene's hand in hers. Selene stared down at the huge hand that held hers and then back to the face, a warm round face with deep brown eyes and wide sensual lips. 'She's our donor,' Rachel explained.

'Oh. I see. Well congratulations,' Selene stumbled on as her brain clunked into gear and she processed the information. Izzy wore a smile as broad as any Cheshire cat's.

'Hello. Lovely to meet you,' Kim said still holding Selene's hand. 'I'm saving up for a trip to Denmark but Jo and Rae persuaded me to make use of the old equipment before it finally goes.'

'She's always wanted to be a mum, haven't you?' said Jo indulgent.

'It's true,' Kim smiled and finally let go of Selene's hand.

'Well, three mums. Imagine that.' Selene sat down.

'Jesus. Sounds like a nightmare. One's bad enough,' said Izzy, and Rachel responded with a good-natured cuff around the ear.

'Actually, it's not congratulations just yet. We've been trying for ages to get pregnant and it doesn't seem to be working. I think it might be because I've been too tense at Kim's place, so we're giving it a go in our own bed,' Jo said. Selene's mind boggled slightly. She was grateful that she'd recently borrowed 'Tales of the City' from Izzy. A fictional experience of trans-sexuality was better than none at all, especially now that she was sitting opposite a trans person.

'They're not actually shagging,' Izzy helpfully explained. 'Kim's gonna do the deed with a magazine in the vestibule, then Rachel's gonna dash upstairs with the turkey baster.'

'Good plan.' Selene nodded, making a mental note never to use the turkey baster again. 'Well, I'll leave you to it then. I've got to sort my room out. It's a midden.'

'I'll come with you,' Izzy said turning off the veg she'd been frying. 'Dinner about seven, seven thirty?'

'Excellent. Wish us luck,' said Rachel.

Selene and Izzy went up to Selene's room, closed the door and then both heaved with silent laughter, holding each other until tears ran down their faces.

'It's lovely for them,' Selene said. 'It's just—'

'Fuckin' hilarious.' Izzy finished Selene's sentence. 'Also, Jenny is gonna go mental if she finds out a transsexual's been in the house.'

'Well I'm not about to tell her,' Selene said. 'Anyway, Kim's a woman all bar the shouting. Everything about her seems female except the physical stuff.'

'No. I know. I agree. But Jenny reckons you've got to be born a woman to really understand sexist oppression. Anyhow, her and Nicola are picking up a polisher for the living room floor over in Hebden Bridge, so what the eye doesn't see and all that.'

'I'll bet Kim's been through some pretty oppressive shit,' Selene said.

They heard Rachel and Jo coming upstairs and going into their room. And then Joan Armatrading on the stereo. This precipitated another bout of the giggles.

'Rae's trying to get her in the mood,' Izzy said, stifling her laughter with a fist.

The vestibule was a small room off the hall where the coats were kept and a few bits of furniture stored. They heard Kim close the door.

'At least it's nice and warm in there,' said Selene, wondering what kind of magazine did it for Kim. She thought she'd better change the subject. 'By the way, d'you think that poster's too gruesome for a bedroom wall.' She indicated her print of Beardsley's 'Salome' on the wall opposite her bed.

'Not at all,' Izzy replied. 'I love Beardsley. A good old beheading never hurt anyone.' She slumped down on Selene's bed with her head propped on one hand.

'Umm. I love it too but it's kind of sombre.' Selene was still uncertain. She too sat on the bed with her back against the headboard, staring at the image, and saying: 'I bumped into my sister Irina today in town. You know she gives me a feeling of such sadness. I can't quite put my finger on it.'

'Is she the one that's married to that bloke you don't like?'

'She's the only one, and yeah she's married to him. It's the way he looks at you that gets me.' Selene shuddered. 'He's got these horrible little beady eyes, and this way of just staring.'

'Like he's mentally undressing you?' Izzy offered.

'No. Not really. In a way, I wish it was that.' Selene shook her head. 'Anyway, it's her life, I suppose?'

They heard the front door open and Jenny's voice shouting: 'Nicola, hold your end up.'

Selene and Izzy sat up rigid.

'Oh, fuck me, it's Jenny,' Izzy said, her eyes widening in panic. Selene's mouth opened into a perfect 'O'.

Downstairs, Jenny called out again. 'It's only us. Got the polisher.' Then she opened the door to the vestibule and found herself staring confused at the back of a long, crocheted cardigan. 'Sorry, I didn't—' she started to say and broke off strangled.

Kim turned, her erect penis bobbing vibrant in her hand, a look of shock on her face. Jenny screamed and rushed at this monster using the polisher as a battering ram. It banged painfully into Kim's shins and she shrieked as she pushed the rapidly deflating object of offence back into her knickers. Jenny flung herself back against the wall. Her hand flew to her throat and a grimace of murderous horror locked her jaw.

Selene and Izzy dashed downstairs, arriving to find Kim, stricken with embarrassment, smoothing down her dress and saying, 'I'm so sorry. But there wasn't a lock on the door.'

Rachel and Jo arrived moments later looking flushed. 'Oh uh--hi Jenny,' Jo said in a strangled voice. 'This is our friend, Kim. She's kindly agreed to be our donor.'

'She,' Jenny practically howled. Her horror had evolved into furious rage. 'That's not a she.'

'I'm leaving now,' Kim said. Her face was a practised impassive mask and Selene realised how right she'd been about the abuse Kim must have suffered.

'How could you bring a man into this house?' Jenny turned her wrath on Rachel and Jo.

'Kim is a pre-op transsexual for your information, and she identifies as a woman,' Rachel defended.

'I don't care how *she* identifies. That's a man, with all the benefits and privileges of that status. He can't just decide to *identify* as a woman. He's not one and he never will be.' Jenny added an ugly emphasis to her words that made Selene fill up with repugnance for her.

Kim had gone to get her handbag and coat but she'd heard the entire exchange. 'We'll talk later,' she said to Rachel and Jo; and then, turning to Selene and Izzy, 'Nice to meet you.' Then she put her head in the air and left, sailing down the hall on a great wave of dignity. Nicola flattened herself against the wall as she passed.

'You too. Bye,' Izzy and Selene shouted after her.

'It was agreed that this house is separatist by everyone.' Jenny's tirade was set to continue.

But Rachel had heard enough. 'Oh do shut up,' she said. 'You're a rude and bigoted woman, Jenny Dean, and you've just wounded a very good friend of mine. Kim is a woman in possession of a penis, and bloody good luck to her, I say. Now go and fuck yourself.' Rachel's posh southern accent rounded beautifully on the words leaving Jenny wide eyed and speechless. She shouldered past Selene and marched imperiously upstairs with Nicola in hot pursuit.

'Anyone fancy frittata?' Izzy said, as first she and Selene, and then Rachel and Jo, subsided into uncontrollable laughter.

Jenny and Nicola didn't show up at the dinner table, much to Selene's relief. Rachel had been to the off-licence hoping they could sort things out over a few bottles of wine, but when she'd knocked on Jenny and Nicola's door, Nicola had answered saying: 'Jenny and I are considering our position.'

'She'll come round,' Jo said. 'Remember that time at the Lesbian Custody Group, when that woman said she was bisexual and Jenny threw a fit. She had her little tantrum and then she got over it.'

'I just feel rotten about calling her a bigot. She's done such a lot for the women's movement and I hate falling out.' Rachel looked concerned.

'Honestly Rae. Don't worry. She'll be right as rain in the morning. I'll give her some stick about voting for Thatcher. That should give her something else to get her teeth into.' Izzy tried to cheer things up a bit but Rachel still seemed out of sorts.

'Anyhow, it's us who should be doing the tantrum bit. That could have been the moment we've been waiting for and she was vile to poor Kim. I'm ashamed of her behaviour,' Jo said righteously.

'Yes, I suppose, if you put it like that. She was definitely in the wrong.'

'Totally,' Selene agreed.

After dinner, Rachel and Jo cleared the plates and washed up. Selene and Izzy went through into the living room. 'You build a fire and I'll skin up a joint?' Izzy suggested, producing a packet of Rizla from the back pocket of her jeans.

'You're on,' said Selene, thinking it had turned into quite a Friday night after all.

♀

Six
Saturday, 24th November, 1979

Carolyn dropped off to sleep in the armchair sometime after midnight. She was awakened by Michael calling out in the early hours of the morning. She got up and went to his room. He was still fast asleep but thrashing wildly in his bed. 'Shush sweetie,' she murmured and gently stroked his hair. It was sticky and wet in his distress. She sat on the floor by his bed for several minutes until his anguish dissipated and he lay quiet again.

Next morning at just after seven, Michael woke to find that the tooth fairy had been and had left him a ten pence piece. He climbed out of bed and went immediately to share his good fortune with his mum. She wasn't in her bed, so he went through to the living room where Carolyn lay asleep still slumped in the armchair. 'Where's mummy?' he quizzed her into wakefulness.

'Uh. What time is it?' she replied.

'Where's mummy?' Michael persisted.

'Oh, sorry Mikey. I dunno.' Carolyn hauled herself out of the chair. 'I'm sure she'll be home soon. Let's get you some breakfast.'

'I want my mummy.' Michael's face began to crumple and his mouth turned down like a sad clown. Carolyn picked him up and carried him through to Ginny's bedroom to check for herself that Ginny wasn't home. A slight unease began to take root in Carolyn's mind. It wasn't like Ginny to stay out all night. It'd been late before but she'd always been home before Michael woke up.

They went through to the kitchen and, still holding Michael in one arm, Carolyn began to search for something to give him for breakfast. Food was always Carolyn's first impulse in times of stress. Michael was sobbing by this time, his tiny chest was heaving and his breath caught, heartbroken, between sobs. He still clutched his ten pence piece.

'Hushy, Mike.' Carolyn was trying to think. She put him down and found an open box of Rice Krispies in the cupboard. There was no milk but she poured two bowls out anyway and offered one to Michael. He lashed out at it. 'That's naughty Michael. Mummy'll be home soon and I'll tell her.' Her warning sent him running into his bedroom to throw himself, still sobbing, onto his bed. Carolyn stood in the kitchen frowning and ate both bowls of Rice Krispies with her hands. She felt upset and angry with Ginny because she didn't know what to do next.

Michael's sobbing kept up for another ten minutes. When finally, it began to subside Carolyn went to him and said, 'C'mon, let's have a story.' She picked up a copy of "Fungus the Bogeyman" and began to read. Michael calmed a little and snuggled into Carolyn's side noisily sucking his thumb, occasional sobs still juddering in his chest.

They stayed like this until it was light. Ginny had still not returned and Carolyn's anxiety was growing.

At ten past nine Carolyn dressed Michael, found the spare key to Ginny's flat, put her duffle coat on and said: 'Let's go for a walk Mike. Maybe we'll see Mummy coming home.' At this prospect Michael brightened and the two of them went down to the street.

Even though it was a Saturday there was plenty of traffic heading into the city and this was a comfort to Carolyn. It made things seem normal. She wasn't sure how long to give it before she rang Ginny's mum. They crossed the main road and made for the swing park. At least Michael was now distracted by the hustle and bustle of the morning. Also the sun was shining and that put a cheerful light on things.

There was no one else about and they had their run of the swings and slide. After these pursuits had been exhausted, Michael sat on the roundabout while Carolyn pushed. When she'd reached a fair velocity she jumped on herself and they sat together as it span, ever more slowly, to a stop. Carolyn's sense that she should do something grew in the exact opposite proportion to the roundabout's inertia. 'Let's go back up to the flats Michael,' she said.

'I'm hungry and I wanna see Mummy,' he replied, beginning to look agitated again.

'Well she'll probably be home when we get back and we can tell her what fun we had at the swings.'

Carolyn was breathless when they got to the fourth floor and Michael was starting to grizzle. Two uniformed police, a man and a woman, were outside the door to Ginny's flat.

'What's up?' Carolyn almost shouted as she hastened towards them, her heart pounding. Police were never good news.

'Do you live here, Miss?' the policeman asked.

'No. I live next door. I'm babysitting her son.' Carolyn looked down at Michael.

'Hello gorgeous, what's your name?' the female officer said, bending down to Michael's level, before taking his hand from Carolyn and walking him down the hall. 'Shall we take you to see Grandma?' Michael stared at her, confused and speechless.

'Are you a relative?' the policeman continued to Carolyn.

'No, I'm her friend,' Carolyn said, her panic rising.

'Would you mind accompanying us to the station, Miss? You may be able to help us with our enquiries.' His words slammed like rocks against the wall of Carolyn's incomprehension.

'Please, just tell me what's wrong,' Carolyn pleaded, her heart by this time pounded loose in her chest.

'Not in front of the boy, Miss,' the policeman whispered.

Carolyn's legs wobbled. The colour drained from her face.

When they arrived at the police station, Sheila Hames and Ginny's eldest brother, Gary, were already there. They both looked as though they'd been hit by a train. Michael ran to Sheila the minute he saw her. His sobbing had started up again in the police car. She picked him up and hugged him. The tears in her own red-rimmed eyes welled and spilled again down her face.

'Ullo, love,' she said to Carolyn.

Ginny's body had been found at ten-past seven that morning by the dustbin men. It had been dumped behind the huge industrial skips that served the flats. Her head was shattered and her red satin shirt had been pulled up exposing her breasts. She'd been brutally sexually assaulted with an, as yet, unknown implement. Her jeans were missing, they would be found later in one of the alleys between the boarded up houses. Ginny's bag lay near her body, its contents spilled amongst the rubbish.

Seven
Saturday, 24th November

The unmistakable knock of the police woke Sandra the next morning. Tracy was still out for the count. She threw on a T-shirt and jeans and shook Tracy hard.

'It's the filth,' she said.

'Uhh.' Tracy groaned groggy.

Sandra hid the big lump of hash that Clinton had given her in the ripped lining of her old leather jacket and picked up all the torn Rizla packets she could find on her way to the door. The loud hammering had intensified in the meantime.

'Hang on, I'm just getting dressed,' Sandra yelled.

When she opened the door, she was surprised to see two plain-clothed policemen. Only uniforms usually bothered hassling prostitutes.

'Mrs Sandra Jacques? Can we come in please?' the older man said as they both held up their identity cards for inspection. Sandra checked them and let them in.

Tracy was just coming into the living room as they entered and the policemen exchanged a knowing glance.

'I'm Detective Inspector Randall, and this is Sergeant Hill.' The older man indicated his partner who was staring, slightly slack jawed, at Sandra's cold-erected nipples beneath her t-shirt.

'How well did you know Virginia Hames?' Detective Inspector Randall addressed his question to both of them.

'Who?' said Tracy.

'D'you mean Ginny?' Sandra asked.

'That's what her mum called her, Sir,' said Sergeant Hill.

'She lives in Eliot House, got a little lad called Michael,' Tracy said confirming Ginny's identity.

'Why? What's up?' Sandra said with alarm now in her voice and looked at Tracy.

'I'm afraid Miss Hames is dead,' DI Randall informed them. "We have reason to believe that you may have information vital to our investigation.'

'Oh my God. What happened?' Sandra said.

'What do you mean, "reason to believe"?' demanded Tracy, already trying to piece together the chain of events.

'First of all, Miss, would you please confirm the nature of your relationship with Miss Hames and describe to us the events of last evening.'

Tracy set out the details of the previous evening, from the time that they'd seen Ginny and Michael outside the flats, to the time that they'd said goodbye on the street after the police busted the Caribbean club. She left out the two Johns she'd done in between, stating instead that she and Sandra had gone back to their flat and watched TV together before going to the club. Sandra confirmed Tracy's account. Someone had to get money for the week and Sandra had been too upset about Vincent to fuck anyone.

'Was Miss Hames a prostitute?' Sergeant Hill asked with barely concealed disdain.

'What the fuck difference does that make?' Tracy snapped.

'If she was, Miss, it is more than likely the reason she was killed,' Hill said. It seemed to Tracy that he thought being murdered was little more than an occupational hazard for prostitutes.

'Well she wasn't a prostitute, actually,' Sandra cut in. She was getting sick of the labels everyone wanted to throw around as if they explained everything

Hill stared at them both, his distaste almost palpable. 'Get your coats, please. We'll take statements at the station.'

Tracy surreptitiously held Sandra's hand as they rode to the police station in the back of the unmarked squad car. She was no stranger to the back of police cars, but this time she'd lost her normal back-chatting persona. It had given way to a profound sorrow at Ginny's death and she frowned deeply.

'How did you know we were with her last night?' she asked Randall leaning forward.

'Miss Hames baby-sitter suggested that she sometimes used the Caribbean club and we learned from other sources that she left the club with you.'

Tracy put two and two together and realised that Clinton must have been this 'source'. Good job all the blacks were locked up last night, she thought to herself, otherwise they'd have been first in line for this crock of shit.

'Is Clint still in the nick?' Tracy asked.

'That's not relevant, Miss McCall.' Randall ended the exchange.

At the station they were shown separately into interrogation rooms where they were kept waiting for two hours. The small, adjacent rooms were both empty save for tables with chairs on either side. They had plenty of time to contemplate what had happened to Ginny. Sandra smoked the four cigarettes she had left in her packet in the first hour. Tracy stared defiantly ahead, aware that this treatment was part of the game. They weren't suspects really, but they were prostitutes, and this meant they could be treated with contempt.

Finally their statements were taken. Randall sent Hill into Tracy's room and he himself interviewed Sandra. He was less than comfortable with letting Hill into a room alone with Sandra, and there was only one WPC on duty. She drifted between both rooms with a look of measured distaste as she listened to the story of their evening in the Caribbean Club. Tracy and Sandra read and signed their accounts. Both women tried to pry details of Ginny's death from their interviewers. None was forthcoming, but when Sergeant Hill left Tracy alone for a minute to go and ask his boss how many copies he needed to take, she looked in the file he had left on the table and saw the crime scene photograph: poor Ginny's savaged body laid out like an exhibit. And worse, she recognised the bins where someone had scrawled CUNT on the fence a few weeks before. Sandra's dream came back to her. Tracy thought she had known fear; but now it gripped her, unyielding and icy cold. She shuddered. Gooseflesh erupted across her body.

It was already dark when they were released from the station.

'If you'll take my advice you'll stay off the streets, ladies,' Randall said through gritted teeth.

They headed for The Beehive, a pub where a lot of the girls drank before they went to work. It being a Saturday night, business would be brisk and Tracy and Sandra wanted to let people know what had happened. The women needed to look out for each other more. Tracy and Sandra talked over how they might be able to make their precarious lives slightly safer.

'We could take down number plates,' Sandra suggested.

'Yeah, and work in pairs more.' Tracy had looked out for Sandra in this way since they'd met. Being ready for trouble was second nature to her.

When they got to the pub it was still only five o clock. The bar was nearly empty. 'What d'you reckon happened to her?' Sandra asked.

Tracy had been debating what to tell Sandra about the photo. She finally decided it was safest to tell her exactly what she'd seen. She guessed that the bin area would be cordoned off as a crime scene and Sandra would know soon anyway. 'I dunno exactly what the bastard did to her,' she said, 'but she was proper messed up and they found her down by our bins.'

'Oh no,' Sandra gasped when Tracy told her about the photo. 'That was my dream with the bird and the horrible noise.'

'Why don't we just do one? Get out of this shit-hole city?' Tracy had no answers to give but she knew when it was time to leave a party.

'I can't till I get Vince back. You know that. You go if you want to.'

'I'm not gunna leave you, baby. Not ever.' Tracy touched Sandra's cheek.

'What a fuckin' day. I thought it was bad enough at the court. Now this! Poor cow. And with that lovely little Michael. Who's gunna have him?' Sandra was filling up with tears and Tracy rubbed the back of her hand roughly, struggling to stem her own tears.

'You two look a cheerful pair o' bastards,' said Donna, one of the street girls, coming to join them. She was a bit older than them, in her early thirties, but she'd been on the game since she was fourteen, that even beat Tracy by two years. She looked closer to fifty. She was an alcoholic and always got to the pub early for half-price doubles. Before Tracy and Sandra had started their story, three more of the regular women had come into the bar, so they waited while the newcomers joined them. Then they told about Ginny. The women listened, interjecting frequently with 'Poor cow' and 'Fuckin' hell'.

'I wondered what all the coppers were doin' round your flats. Had she got a fella?' Donna asked. They were all hoping that this was a domestic attack. That would make it normal.

'Don't think so,' Tracy said. 'She talked about going to college. She said she liked being on her own with the kid. Anyway, she went to work last night, and then she was dead. This is some random fuckin' nutcase and we all better take care.'

'Well, I've gotta go out t'night. My bloody old man'll kill me if I don't go home with at least forty quid,' said Carol, already sporting a black eye fading to yellow.

'Just make sure you take down number plates.' Sandra restated her idea like some kind of mantra.

'That's all well an' good, but how's that gunna stop us getting bleedin' slashed up?'

'We work as a pair,' Tracy said.

'Yeah' we know,' said Carol with a knowing smirk.

'What's that supposed to mean? We're in 'ere tryin to fuckin' help you lot an' that's all you can fuckin' come out with,' Sandra said and looked at Tracy. 'C'mon let's fuck off. This is a waste of time.'

'She didn't mean anything by it. Did ya Carol?' said Donna trying to smooth things out. But Sandra and Tracy were already on their feet.

'We're leaving anyway. Forget it,' Tracy said as they gathered their coats. They left the other women to their drink and the night ahead, now spiced with a twist of fear.

'You stood up to that bitch,' Tracy said when they got home.

'I'm just fed up with all the shit you get just for bein' with another woman.'

'So we're still together then? I just wasn't sure after what happened yesterday with Vince, and what you said about calling it a day.'

'You daft bastard. Come 'ere,' Sandra said and pulled Tracy close to her. They kissed, a deep urgent kiss, and made love on the threadbare sofa. Afterwards, Tracy laid her head on Sandra's stomach, listening to her inside.

Sandra stroked her hair. 'Jane gave me a card for some group that can help with gettin' your kids back,' she said after a minute.

'Jane the solicitor?'

'Yeah. They're called the Lesbian Custody Group,' Sandra said and Tracy laid still and quiet, taking in the enormity of the fact that Sandra had just used the 'L' word.

♀

Eight
Thursday, 29ᵗʰ November, 1979

Tracy looked out of the window. Snow was falling. A white patina had settled on the moors. Outside, cars swished by on the dual-carriageway and brown slush was collecting in the gutters of the street below. Sandra was with a regular — she did him every Thursday afternoon — and Tracy was watching for her return. He was a retired bank manager and they went to The Grand Hotel. He liked Sandra to call him 'Daddy'. It amazed Tracy that he paid for the room for a whole day though they only spent two hours in it. The arrangement was comparatively safe, regular customers were a known quantity, but a worm of fear still niggled with Tracy. The bloke who'd done Ginny was probably somebody's regular too.

The phone rang.

'Hello,' Tracy said cautiously, always careful in case it was Steve, or someone trying to get at them in some way.

'Hi. I'm Rachel, chair of the Lesbian Custody Group. I believe you rang the Women's Centre.' The voice was well-spoken and sounded southern.

'Oh yes,' Tracy said, trying to sound a bit posher herself and not having a clue what she meant by 'chair'. 'We were given your number by our brief, Jane Rayment. She said you might be able to advise us. My girlfriend's lost custody of her little boy.'

'Oh dear, I'm so sorry. Would you like to come to a meeting? We can't promise to get anything done, but we do offer a sense of solidarity and we have a network of sympathetic lawyers and solicitors who may be able to work with Jane.'

'When is the meeting?' Tracy asked.

'Well, there's one tonight at our house if it's not too short notice. We're in Chapeltown in Leeds.'

'Yeah, okay, we'll try to make it, but my girlfriend's at work at the moment so I'll have to see when she gets home. What's the address?' Tracy found a pen and wrote the address on the corner of the local paper. 'Prostitute Slaying: No Leads,' read the headline. 'Thanks for calling back,' She said and hung up the phone.

When Tracy went back to the window, Sandra was just disappearing from view into the flats' doorway below. She walked in the door five minutes later and out of breath.

'The bastard lifts are out again. D'you know there's thirty-nine steps between each floor.' She coughed, took her last cigarette out of the pocket of her sheepskin coat and lit it.

'All alright with Daddy Banker?' Tracy lit her own cigarette.

'Yeah. He's easy money. Just takes the poor old sod ages to get it up. He's started calling me 'Vivian' as well. No idea why.' Sandra put her hand inside her embroidered shoulder bag and pulled out a fistful of fivers and a lipstick.

'A woman phoned from the Custody Group thing. They've got a meeting tonight.' Tracy avoided the 'L' word, still nervous that Sandra would react badly or be put off. 'It's in Chapeltown.'

'Good. Let's go. We can get the train then grab a cab at the station. I feel like something good's gunna happen today. In fact, why don't we set off now and get a curry on the way? I'm buying,' Sandra said, picking up the fivers and throwing them up in the air.

They arrived at the house just before seven-thirty, nicely mellow from the wine they'd had with their meal. The things Tracy loved most about Sandra were her spontaneity and generosity. They'd never be rich because as soon as Sandra had any money she spent it on the people she cared about.

Tracy pushed the old door bell and pulled a face at Sandra that said 'Here goes!' They were nervous. Neither of them had ever been to a meeting in their lives

Selene answered the door. 'Hi. Are you here for the meeting?' she said standing to one side.

'Yes,' said Sandra and Tracy together.

Selene showed them into the kitchen where six woman were gathered around the big table. Rachel stood when they came in and said: 'You must be Sandra Jacques and Tracy McCall. Welcome.' She indicated a couple of free stools. 'I spoke to you this afternoon. We'll do proper introductions in a minute. Would you like coffee or tea?'

'Coffee, please,' Sandra said already wishing she hadn't come. She knocked Tracy's leg under the table.

'Oh yeah, me too,' Tracy said, lost in wondering what the 'introductions' would involve.

'Mind if I sit in? Izzy's gone to London and I'm just sitting twiddling my thumbs,' Selene said to Rachel.

'I don't, if no one else does,' Rachel said.

'I don't see how these issues can be relevant to a heterosexual woman.' Jenny peered disdainfully over her half-moon reading glasses. She'd got over the transsexual trauma of last Friday and was ready for another battle. Tracy and Sandra looked at each other baffled.

'I see sexuality as fluid rather than set in stone. How do you know what would be relevant to me,' Selene countered swiftly, barely managing to keep the anger out of her voice. 'Anyway forget it.' She stood up and made to leave.

'No, please, sit down,' Rachel said. This meeting is open to any woman who expresses an interest. She looked at Jenny askance.

'You're the chair,' Jenny replied, busily shuffling papers.

Tracy and Sandra looked in bewilderment around the faces of the gathered women, but at least Tracy now knew that 'chair' meant boss of the meeting.

Rachel suggested that they start by going round the table and giving a brief synopsis of their respective situations. Each of the women in turn said their name and why they were there. Jenny said that she and her partner Nicola had lost custody of Nicola's twelve year old son when they'd got together five years before. Selene privately wondered if this son, now seventeen, would be allowed in the house anyway. Rachel and Jo hadn't lost custody of anyone, but as prospective lesbian mums they needed to be aware of the pitfalls and Rachel was a lawyer, so in a position to be of practical help. Another woman called Monica said she'd lost her child after her husband had found out she'd had an affair with a woman at work. He'd left and taken the child with him to his long-term mistress' house. The poor woman was sitting next to Sandra and she looked at her plaintively, waiting for Sandra's own version of this blighted story.

'I got my kid took off me two year ago,' Sandra began. 'I got done and my ex used it to get Vince. I appealed and it took ages to all get sorted, and then me and Tracy started. He found out, and last week at the hearing his lawyer said I was—' she trailed off.

Tracy looked like a cornered animal. 'Yeah, that's right,' she added.

'Well, we've all got a lot in common and a lot of work to do,' Rachel said matter-of-factly. Selene smiled encouragingly at Sandra and Tracy, sensing their isolation in the group.

'Was there a prosecution?' Jenny interjected. 'Because it could complicate or even overshadow any efforts to work on your behalf as lesbians.' She was expert at finding a tender spot to poke, and she'd taken an instant dislike to Sandra on account of her stiletto heels and bright red lipstick.

'Yes, there was a prosecution. I got a fifty-pound fine and three months suspended sentence for soliciting,' Sandra coldly replied. Tracy's eyes widened and she tensed ready for a fight.

'Umm.' Jenny rested her case.

'All the more reason for us to be involved, I'd have thought. These women are being persecuted, not only as lesbians but as sex workers,' Selene waded in. This was territory where she felt qualified to comment and she was more than ready to have it out with Jenny in any case.

Sandra and Tracy had never heard their line of work referred to so straightforwardly before. Sex work, Tracy thought, sounded just like piecework or needlework.

'I'm afraid I agree with Selene,' Rachel said and Jo nodded emphatically in support. She went on to offer her help in challenging these decisions and cited a case where a judge had actually given custody to a woman precisely because he'd been her regular customer. This bought a touch of much needed levity to the proceedings. Rachel took down details of their case and seemed to already know Jane Rayment, which Sandra thought encouraging.

When the meeting broke up, Sandra and Tracy shook hands with everyone apart from Jenny, who'd conveniently gone to the loo, and Selene showed them out. 'Don't suppose you'd fancy a drink or anything,' she asked hesitantly at the door. 'There's a decent pub on the corner.'

Tracy looked at Sandra to check and then said: 'Yeah alright.'

Selene picked up her coat from the hall and the three of them set off to the pub. The place was packed with students. They managed to colonise a bit of table and Selene went to the bar. They all had pints and Tracy came and helped her carry them back to the table.

'Nice one,' Tracy said and took a swig. 'So why'd you wanna have a drink?' She had great difficulty taking anyone at face value. There was always an ulterior motive and, thus far in life, her suspicious nature had served her well.

'I was just interested in your story,' Selene said, thinking there was no point in being anything but completely honest. 'And I've done a bit of writing about prostitution,' she added, conscious that this must sound prying, condescending and presumptuous.

'So d'you wanna write about us?' Sandra looked mystified.

'No, not like that.' Selene was already out of her depth. 'I just thought I might be able to help in some way because I've got some ideas about the relationship between gender, sexuality and prostitution that might—' She hesitated, sensing she was losing ground. 'Er, help.' Now, she realised, they both looked mystified. 'Actually, I was feeling a bit lonely as well and just thought you seemed nice people,' she finished, spitting out something closer to the truth.

'Well why didn't you just say so?' Sandra said. 'Anyway, cheers.' She held up her pint and a relieved Selene clinked glasses with both of them.

'So who lives in that big house then?' Tracy enquired.

Selene told the two girls something of the politics of the house and the women in it. They'd heard of feminism but neither of them could really see how separatism would work.

'So what about little boys?' Sandra asked. 'What if that couple have a little boy?'

'I honestly don't know the answer to that one,' Selene said. 'I suppose they'd have a kind of cut-off age, when either they'd be asked to leave or give the child up.'

'No, I don't get that. I can understand not wanting to be around blokes. But your own flesh and blood, that's bloody ridiculous that is,' said Sandra, feeling her pain again at the loss of her son.

Then Selene told them the story of the transsexual donor.

'No, get away,' Sandra said amazed. Sleeping with Tracy was one thing but this lot were a right bunch of nutters.

'So this bloke's actually gunna be a woman, with a fanny an' all?' Tracy looked astonished. 'And can a woman be turned into a bloke then?'

'Yeah. I think so. They do it in Denmark... and here too these days. I think women can have a kind of pump-up penis.'

Tracy sprayed lager across the table in a great guffaw and Sandra held back her head and rocked with laughter. Selene was pleased to be the source of such entertainment.

They finished their pints and Tracy went up for the next one.

'Did you read about that poor woman who got killed last Friday?' Selene asked Sandra.

'Yeah. We knew her really well. She'd got a little boy. It was terrible what they said in the papers. She wasn't a prossie. She'd done a couple of blokes to get her lad kitted out for the winter. It must have been awful for her family to read about her like that.'

Tracy came back with three pints balanced in her hands. 'Fuckin' load o' bastards, them coppers and reporters. They're all in it together. She was a lovely kid.' Tracy shook her head and swallowed hard at the still-too-recent memory.

'Oh my God. I'm so sorry. I didn't realise she was a friend.'

'No, that's alright. I'll tell you what though. That was some fuckin' nutcase that done that. It was down the bins at our flats that they found her body. The police won't have it though. They're looking for a jealous boyfriend or a pimp. She hadn't got either.'

As Selene listened to the girls telling what they knew of the murder, her mind kept flipping back to Whitechapel and her thesis. Nearly a hundred years later — the motor car, the aeroplane and the bomb later — women were still getting butchered in back alleyways. Selene felt her life pivot. Maybe there was a connection between her academic work and real life after all. There was a thread between women. They couldn't change the past but they could learn from it and take its lessons into a future that could be changed. Alongside the rage she felt, Selene had a sense of something close to elation.

When eventually the barman called time, they'd lost all track of it. Selene walked with Sandra and Tracy to the main road to hail a cab to the station. 'Look, thanks it's been really nice talking to you,' Selene said. 'I meant it, if there's anything I can do don't hesitate to ask. I'm really good at writing letters and stuff like that. We haven't got a phone at the house but well, you know.' Selene felt almost bereft that the evening was over.

'We're in The Swan most Saturdays. Come if you fancy it,' Sandra said. She'd taken a liking to Selene and she thought she might prove useful in her bid to get her son back.

♀

Nine
Good Friday, 4ᵗʰ April, 1980

When Rosie was born in 1948 her parents had doted on her for about three weeks. Then they got bored. They had met at the end of the war. Her father, Ron, was American, an air-force officer, square jawed and handsome. Her mother, Stella, was a spoiled little rich girl from a family who owned a chain of grocery stores. Ron hadn't wanted to go back to the US after the war because he knew that any job he'd find would never match the glamour of his life in the air force. He loved the thrill of amphetamine-fuelled raids over Europe and the casual sex on offer in the quaint little pubs of England's green and pleasant land. Stella's money, or at least her father's money, offered a life of idle luxury. Their marriage was tempestuous because that was the way they both liked it. They fought bitterly and their quarrels usually ended in ferocious sex. After a couple of years they'd exhausted each other and they both drifted into casual relationships with other people. When Stella fell pregnant they thought that a child would put something back into the marriage. It didn't. They farmed Rosie out to anyone who'd have her. Then, when Rosie was eighteen months, Stella took off with a lover and Ron, realising that he wouldn't get anything else out of his father-in-law, went back to the States.

Rosie's grandparents paid for her to be cared for by a series of foreign housemaids. Some of them beat her. Then they paid for her to go to one of the less expensive boarding schools. As she grew, she grew wild and fearful, and crazy with loneliness. She was hopeless at her lessons but she excelled at art. Her teacher, Miss Marjorie Clewes, was amazed at Rosie's precocious talent. She encouraged her and showed her books of paintings. Miss Clewes effused over Picasso and raved about Rembrandt. It was the only time Rosie had known kindness and interest from an adult. Her painting and drawing was as dark as it was compulsive. She drew anywhere and with anything she could lay her hands on. Her art was a way for her to exorcise the sense of abandonment and rejection in her damaged heart. When Miss Clewes announced that she was leaving the school to work abroad, Rosie stole a powder compact from her handbag so that she'd have a way of remembering that people could be kind.

At seventeen, Rosie started taking amphetamines. They gave her a cold, hard, uncaring edge against a bitter world. They also gave her the ability to stay awake all night and draw. When she was eighteen, her grandfather paid for her to get a flat in London and gave her a small allowance. This she spent on paint and speed. Then, in the Summer of Love, she met James. When Rosie first saw him he was playing an acoustic guitar and singing 'Like a Rolling Stone' outside Leicester Square tube station. She'd stopped and listened, and then put a crumpled pound note into his hat. He'd looked up through his curtain of long hair and smiled, and the warmth of that smile surrounded Rosie like a summer breeze.

They went for coffee and then back to Rosie's flat where she showed James her paintings. He thought them astounding and wonderful. They made love on the floor. James moved in. He bought a paper bag with another shirt in and a toothbrush. Sometimes James injected himself with heroin. When he did that and they made love Rosie felt his tenderness for her so intense and beautiful that it made her cry. Sometimes they took LSD, tasting and smelling each other and making art together. Their love was deep and precious and the desert that was Rosie's heart bloomed sumptuous in greens and gold.

They lived like this for two years. James wrote songs and Rosie painted pictures. She loved huge canvases and filled them with scenes from her head and from her life, and from the street outside their window. James wrote a song for her called 'Deep Red Rosie' on account of the colour he always saw around her when they tripped.

Trouble lay ahead. Supermarkets had started to emerge on the high streets and her grandfather's grocery stores were losing money. They couldn't compete. Rosie's allowance was near the top of the list of 'things that could be dispensed with'. By 1970 Rosie and James were broke. They couldn't pay the rent and they got evicted from their flat. It was summer, so at first they slept in parks and under bridges. Rosie painted a living room on the bricks and they lived there until autumn turned to winter. Then they stayed on peoples' floors and sofas. Rosie couldn't paint. James earned some money from busking and occasional gigs in pubs. Rosie would stand and watch him, and when he looked at her, right through the crowd, she knew that she was loved.

In a pub in Camden Town they met Roger, an old school friend of James. He had a house in Hebden Bridge, an old mill town in Yorkshire. Hippies had drifted up there and squatted in the dwellings, deserted after the mills and factories of the industrial age had closed down. Roger asked James and Rosie to go to his house, an under-dwelling he called it, and take care of it while he went to renovate a barn in Provence. They took down the address and caught the train the following day.

Rosie loved the house in its higgledy-piggedly street hanging onto the edge of a deep gorge. She painted again. She painted the walls in great murals and her neighbours came and asked her to paint their houses too. And when she'd finished the insides she painted the outsides in camouflage against the valley side, as if the very houses had fused with nature.

One night when James was out, Rosie found a bag of heroin and a syringe. Knowing her fragility, he'd always kept his stash hidden from her. This night he'd been careless. Rosie's curiosity and her artist's need to fathom all human experience finally overcame her fear. She needed to know how James felt when he took it and to show him the intensity in their love making that he showed her. She sat on the edge of the bath, tied a rag around her arm and injected it into her vein. She vomited. And then she knew. When James came home he lifted her from the bathroom floor and carried her to bed.

After that night, they both took heroin every day. When they couldn't get it they argued and fought. When Roger came home from France the house was such a mess that he threw them out and called them 'fuckin' junkies'. They went to sleep rough in the city, where they could get heroin more easily, and put their names on the council list. Rosie got pregnant and the council gave them a flat in one of the new high-rise blocks. The baby was born an addict, and a woman from social services lifted her from Rosie's track-marked arms.

Eventually James' veins collapsed in his arms and he started to inject into his groin and legs. His right leg became infected and gangrene set in. He nearly died, but Rosie called an ambulance in the nick of time; and, although they managed to save him, the doctors had to amputate a leg. After that James rarely went out. Rosie paid for their addiction by selling her poor, emaciated body on the street outside the flats.

Though it was only April, the day had been hot, like summer. Usually it rained on bank holidays, especially up north. Rosie didn't paint much anymore. There seemed to be no need. Yet this day something felt different. Her old compulsion seemed to thrum in every cell of her body and she just had to paint. Rosie searched in the electricity-meter cupboard, found a can of black acrylic spray paint and put it in her bag. Rosie helped James to dress and brush his tangled hair, and then she kissed him before she went out. It was twilight and still warm. On the wall opposite the refuse area, she began to paint. The picture was so big that she had to stand on one of the bins to reach the top.

When she'd finished, Rosie threw the empty can into an open bin and went out to the street by the old factories. She waited on the kerb feeling sick and shaky, in need of her medicine.

The man in blue overalls seemed to come from nowhere. He offered her ten pounds to go with him into the derelict factory. She thought that she'd seen him before.

He pushed the old, broken door open and let Rosie lead the way in. Something metallic clunked in his overall pocket as he walked. And then she heard a sound like pebbles crunching on a beach. It was her skull cracking and caving inward.

◊◊◊◊◊

Graham savaged her and tore at her body until it was bloody. She was already dead by the time he pushed her jumper up and exposed her tiny breasts. Then he pulled her jeans and knickers down her thighs, raped her with a screwdriver and used his Stanley knife to slice open up her belly. Quenched then and breathing hard, he stood and looked down at his work. Next to her on the old concrete floor, her bag gaped, similarly open. Graham stooped to rifle through it and dumped out its jumbled contents. A powder compact caught his eye. He picked it up and kept it.

Graham rolled the slight, broken body under an old workbench with a casual heave of his foot, stripped off his bloody overalls, wrapped his tools up inside them and jogged back to his car.

Then he drove home to surprise his wife. He'd bought her a huge Easter egg earlier, the biggest in the shop, and he was looking forward to seeing her expression when he presented it to her.

♀

Ten
Sunday, 6th April, 1980

Mrs Doris Gilbert walked Alfie, her golden retriever, twice a day, every day come rain or shine. Since her husband, Ernest, had died three years before, Alfie had been her only companion. Her two sons had grown and gone to the ends of the Earth. Her eldest, Andrew, still single, lived a life unfathomable to Doris, in Dubai. Her baby, Martin, had married a Danish girl and gone to live in Copenhagen. She'd never even met her grandchild, a little girl near a year old now, called Elektra. What kind of name was that? She couldn't make a bit of sense of any of it. Doris wondered sometimes why she'd bothered bringing children into the world. This Easter Sunday was warm and dry and she'd walked a little further afield than was her custom. They'd found a small swing-park, and Doris enjoyed a quarter-hour sitting in the empty space imagining she could hear the wraithlike voices of children at play – as though they'd been recorded in the ether – while Alfie sniffed at trees and rummaged in the litter bin.

She decided on a whim to take the long way home and crossed the main road past the old factories. Her dad had been a weaver in the mill. She'd brought him his lunch of bread and jam there as a girl. As she walked, dreaming of long gone days, Alfie stopped suddenly at a factory door, one near off its hinges; and, tug as Doris might, he wouldn't budge.

'What is it Alf?' Doris said. She habitually chatted to Alfie as if at any moment he might reply. The dog nosed further into the broken door and strained on his leash. Doris thought that he'd probably got the scent of a dead rat and tried to pull him away. He wouldn't oblige. Out of a mixture of curiosity and nostalgia, Doris nudged the door further open with her foot. Alfie sped away from her and into the factory with his lead trailing between his legs. Doris followed into darkness made blacker by the brightness of the day, calling Alfie's name. The stench hit her within a few feet of the door and she clamped her hand to her face. She saw the dog's backside sticking out behind an old workbench, and near him a dark, congealed pool of blood next to a pair of feet in bloodied plimsolls. She turned, her screaming silent, and ran from the building.

Doris's heart pounded hard against her ribs as she regained the empty street. The warm holiday had taken most people to the nearby sea and countryside, left the city streets ghostly. She hurried as fast as she could back to the main road where she found a phone booth and dialled 999.

When Detective Inspector Randall's phone rang he was sitting in his back garden sipping a cold beer while his wife, Maggie, planted out her gladioli. He went into the hall and picked it up.

'Bill Randall.'

It was the desk sergeant at the station. 'Got a body, Sir. Bit of a mess they say. Down at the old factories near Lumb Lane. Your presence required.'

'Thanks, Sergeant. On my way.' Randall put the phone down and went back into the garden. He wasn't sorry if truth be known. He was bored witless at home, and now he had the excuse he needed to go out without inferring any problem in his marriage, or hurting Maggie's feelings. 'Sorry, love.' He grimaced rueful. 'Nasty murder by the sounds. I'll have to go in.'

'Oh no!' Maggie straightened, rubbing her lower back. 'I was going to suggest a run out to that bird sanctuary you were reading about.'

'Next week, Mags. I promise. That'd be smashing.' He didn't make eye contact as he kissed her cheek.

When he arrived at the scene, Sergeant Hill and a couple of squad cars were already there.

'We've got another one, Sir,' Hill greeted him. 'Same as the other tart last November.'

'Mind your language, Sergeant. Let's get the facts straight before we jump to any conclusions about who or what she was. How long's she been here?'

'Sorry, Sir. Dunno yet, Sir. Old lady walking her dog found it. She's with a uniform.'

'Anybody from forensics here?'

'Yep, Donovan's already in the factory, Sir.'

'Let's have a gander then,' Randall said, peering into the semi darkness.

'Definitely the same MO as the woman I examined last November, Randall. Fifty or so screwdriver stab wounds across the abdomen, and the same implement inserted with enormous force into the vagina. Smashed skull. This one's got black paint all over her hands and a couple of smudges on her face, though. Don't know if that's got any relevance. Oh and by the way, she's an intravenous drug-user.' Donovan was matter-of-fact and capable. Randall nodded wordlessly in response.

'Any missing persons?' Randall enquired of the desk sergeant when they arrived back at the police station.

'Bag-head over there.' The sergeant indicated what looked like a bundle of rags and hair on the bench with a pair of crutches propped next to it against the wall. James had been at the police station since early that morning. He had taken the last of the methadone on Friday night but when he woke on Saturday afternoon to find that Rosie had not returned he'd panicked. He hobbled on his crutches through the streets of the city, bedraggled, sweating and fearful. Finally he had gone to the accident and emergency unit at the local infirmary. They had not treated Rosie they said, but they gave him a prescription for more methadone. He went back to the flat and took half of the medicine, in case Rosie came home in need of the other half, and nodded out in the chair. When he came round the next day and she was still not home he swallowed the remaining linctus and headed to the police station. He'd refused to move until someone said they'd help him find Rosie.

Randall shook James awake and handed him his crutches.

'Has Rosie come home?' he asked almost childlike. Randall ignored the question.

'Let's get you some coffee,' he said, then waited as James dragged himself onto his crutches and ushered him into an interview room. Randall sat opposite their suspect and Hill stood behind him, their usual method of interrogation.

James told them everything he knew about Rosie's last movements: what time she'd gone out and everything he had done since. Randall prompted James to tell them more about Rosie and to describe her. He told them she was a great painter, and that she had golden hair and deep blue eyes, like an ocean, that she was small and fragile. In fact he could do better than that; and from his back pocket he drew out a wallet with a picture of Rosie inside it. She was leaning against a wall, smiling and looking directly at the camera. Randall looked at the picture and, exchanging glances with Hill, said: 'May we keep this?'

They decided to lock James up that night. He hadn't, as far as Randall was concerned, been eliminated from their enquiries. It seemed unlikely that – even if this wretched, sick young man had brutally murdered his girlfriend and main source of heroin – he would also have murdered Ginny Hames five months earlier. Nonetheless it was a precaution. It wouldn't do any harm either to have 'a suspect in custody' when it hit the press. James had collapsed when they had told him that Rosie was dead and had been carried into the cell.

'Piece of shit,' Hill mumbled to himself as he threw James' crutches in after.

In The Beehive that night, all the women were already aware of what had happened. Donna had seen the police cordon, and one of the Bobbies on duty – who she'd done a freebie for more times than she could count – had tipped her off.

'It's the same as that poor kid back-end of last year.' She was just repeating the story for the umpteenth time to Joan the barmaid when Sandra and Tracy came in.

'What is?' Tracy said. They'd been out for the entire day. Sandra had access rights with Vincent and they'd been to the open-air baths and then to the fair. Tracy got on really well with the boy and knew he could be relied upon to exclude her from the story of his day. Steve and Doreen had stopped bothering about supervision. In fact they were only too happy to get rid of the boy as many weekends as they could. Sandra was starting to get hopeful that she'd get him back, especially since she'd got a load of right clever buggers from Leeds on the case. They'd seen a fair bit of Selene in the last few months and she'd been talking to her lawyer mates about their case. Her solicitor, Jane, thought that they'd be in a position to appeal again by autumn. Sandra was in buoyant spirits.

'Another murder, same as the last. Ripped up, Tommy said.'

'Who the fuck's Tommy?' Tracy was impatient to get the story straight.

'That copper. I've done 'im hundreds o' times. He was stationed at the police barrier and he told me. Said we'd better watch ourselves. It's one o' them nut cases they reckon.'

The entire pub seemed shrouded in tension and the fug of smoke was so dense that even Sandra's eyes smarted and she smoked forty a day herself.

'At least it'll be safe t'night with all the coppers everywhere, and Tommy says they're not making any soliciting arrests for a bit.'

'Who is it?' Sandra asked. 'Do we know her?'

'She didn't get in 'ere, but I'd seen her loads o' times. Skinny little thing. Into the smack. Rosie, they called her.'

'I know who you mean. Got a fella that's lost his leg,' Tracy said.

'Yeah. That's her.'

As Sandra and Tracy walked to their patch near the underpass lay-by, Tracy had a feeling that they needed to get out of the 'life'. They'd been rubbing shoulders with women who lived openly as lesbians, women who seemed to be independent of men and their money. She turned over the possibility that she and Sandra could somehow have a different kind of life; though she couldn't begin to imagine either of them being able to get a job and get up in the mornings, and come home at night, and scrimp to pay their bills like normal people did.

They stood on opposite sides of the road, and when a blue Cortina estate pulled up in front of Tracy she leaned in the window and indicated with a nod to the elderly driver that his number plate was being recorded by her pal across the road.

'Sorry, love, but we've 'ad a couple of nasty murders here lately. We'll destroy your plate number as soon as you drop me back. It's five for a blow job and ten for sex with a rubber.'

She hadn't seen the man before so she felt wary, but given that this nutter had done somebody last night it'd be unlikely he'd be on the prowl so soon. Anyway, this old codger looked incapable of murdering his own breakfast. She got in and they drove to a nearby patch of waste ground where a tall hedge provided cover from the road. It was a favourite haunt of prostitutes and courting couples.

The man had given Tracy a crisp new ten-pound note. It would take her three days to earn that in a regular job. Tracy was wearing jeans and she began to undo them.

'No, wait.' the man said. 'I'm havin' a bit o' trouble wi' the equipment. You'll have t' get me going first'.

'Oh fuck,' Tracy thought. 'This is gunna take ages.' And it did. She stroked and wanked, and then sucked the pitiful member. And finally, after about twenty minutes, he'd managed to maintain an erection long enough to have sex, thankfully ejaculating the moment he entered her.

When he dropped her back at the lay-by, Sandra was nowhere in sight. Tracy paced up and down and smoked three cigarettes in quick succession. Then she hurried back to The Beehive. 'Anybody seen Sandra?' she virtually shouted from the door.

'Not since she left wi' you,' Joan the barmaid answered.

Tracy returned to their patch and smoked another cigarette. It'd been two hours now since she'd left Sandra alone on the kerb and she was starting to get agitated. Tracy didn't handle fear very well. Her first response was violence. She was going to kill Sandra herself when she showed up for putting her through this. Then she fantasised about what she'd do to anyone who hurt Sandra. It wasn't pretty. She was about to go back to the flat to see if she'd returned there, when a Datsun pulled up and Sandra got out.

'Where the fuck 'ave you bin?' Tracy bellowed before Sandra had even crossed the road.

'Sorry darlin'. I knew you'd worry, but he offered me twenty and we went to his room at the Fox Inn. It was bloody miles away.' Sandra held Tracy's face in her hands, and relief swept through her body as her anger melted away.

'Right. Well we're carrying knives from now on. C'mon, let's go and get a drink.'

They caught Joan just about to lock the door and draw the curtains at The Beehive.

'What's everybody 'avin'?' Sandra said, flashing one of her tenners.

'Mine's a port an' brandy,' Carol shouted up to the bar; and then, under her breath to the two women she was sat with: 'Show-off fuckin' dyke.'

♀

Eleven
Monday, 7th April

The following day was Easter Monday. The bright snap of weather had started to give way to a cold easterly wind and dark cloud. There'd been a proper session in The Beehive the previous evening as the women drank up the money they made and some went out for more. The lunchtime crowd was desultory and hung-over. Everyone took notice, when a twenty-something, suited and booted young woman appeared at the bar carrying a briefcase.

'Hi, I'm Erica Pearce from The Herald.' She held out her hand to Joan behind the bar. Joan wiped her hands on her tea-towel and offered hers in return. The rest of the pub fell silent.

Tracy and Sandra were sitting with Donna and her cousin Janice who worked a patch in Manchester. Carol and her husband were at another table with two blokes and a couple of the regular girls. Carol always swanked when her husband came in, as though she was a cut above the others, like he were some sort of catch rather than just another violent pimp. Tracy couldn't stand her and had been annoyed with Sandra for plying the old bag with port and brandy half the night.

'We'd just like to run a piece on the recent events and their impact on women's lives.' Erica Pearce smiled beatifically at Joan who stood like a rabbit in headlights before her gaze. Carol's table quickly supped their drinks and left the bar. Erica turned to look directly at Sandra. 'I wonder if you'd have five minutes, ladies. I'm buying.'

'No names,' Tracy replied. Erica mimed zipping her mouth closed and put her briefcase down next to an empty chair. She ordered a round of drinks. Everyone had doubles.

Erica adopted a concerned expression as she bought their drinks back to the table.

'Awful, isn't it?' she said as she sat down and opened her case. 'Do you mind if I make a few notes, ladies?'

'Don't write nowt about me,' said Donna. Erica beamed.

'Don't worry. It's not going to be about individuals, just a flavour of everyday life.'

They told her about the murders, and how Ginny's case hadn't been properly investigated, that she wasn't a prostitute as such and the police had got it all wrong. They told her about Ginny's little boy, now orphaned and living with his grandparents. They talked about how it felt going out on the street knowing somebody out there had brutally killed two local women. Erica bought more drinks. She herself drank tonic water, and when Donna accidentally drank from her glass she didn't touch the drink again. They talked about how they'd gotten into prostitution and the fear and violence they experienced as an everyday event. They talked about the 'kerbies' and the prices they charged, and how many they did on a good night. They talked about the number of women who were addicts, like Rosie, and those who were forced by violent partners and poverty and hungry children onto the streets. Erica made notes. She left them at just after four o'clock.

'You've been so helpful, ladies.' Erica shook everyone's hand.

They'd all had too many drinks to stop now so they stayed there until it was nearly dark. Donna needed to get more money so she could carry on boozing. The scare Tracy had experienced the day before was still in her mind and she persuaded Sandra to go back to the flat with a takeaway.

They got fish and chips from Danny's chippie and cut through the ginnel by the bins on their way back. A dim yellow light illumined the space where Ginny had been found and they both unconsciously quickened their step.

Sandra tried to banish the thoughts she had of Ginny's body lying there in the cold amongst the sacks of rubbish and brought to mind an image of Ginny dancing that night in the Caribbean Club; and of her with Michael and their chip supper. She turned her face away from the bins; and then she saw it on the wall. Her skin broke out into ice-cold prickling terror. She screamed and threw herself into Tracy's arms.

Tracy thought the killer was upon them and dropped her chip bag. 'What the fuck?' she said.

'There on the wall, it's like my dream. It's the bird from my dream.' Sandra was practically incoherent and it took Tracy several moments to gather her thoughts and make sense of Sandra's outburst. Then she saw it too. A great bird with its black wings, bigger than a man, outstretched and swooping down, dwarfing them.

'Jesus Christ almighty. What is it?' I didn't see that before.' Tracy walked up to the wall and rubbed the paint with her fingertips.

'C'mon. Let's get home.' Sandra shivered as she spoke. Tracy picked up her chip bag, put her arm round Sandra's shoulders and they hurried into the light of the tower blocks.

On the Thursday of that week, a pile of Heralds lay in the lobby of Bronte Mansions when Sandra went out for her regular weekly job at The Grand. The headline read: "Love Rat Councillor in Sleazy Love Triangle".

A couple of grainy photographs showed two middle-aged women, one the wronged wife and mother in a twinset, the other a busty blonde in a fake leopard-skin coat. Sandra opened a copy and scanned the first few pages, wondering if there was going to be any mention of the local killings. Two dead tarts in five months didn't attract attention beyond the provincial free press. On page five the headline read: "Brutal Prostitute Slaying. Body Found in Derelict Factory". Sandra skimmed the piece. There was no connection made with Ginny's murder. The article made much of Rosie's addiction problem and mentioned the baby she'd had taken away from her. Police had a man, thought to be the boyfriend, in custody, it said.

'Bollocks,' Sandra thought, and then stopped dead when she saw the article at the bottom of the same page. She read it with mounting disgust.

Prostitution: The Deadly Game. By Erica Pearce.

A quick glance at the Situations Vacant column in this edition offers the prospective female job-seeker a cornucopia of opportunities. There are office jobs, a huge range of shop work and numerous factory and manufacturing opportunities, all there for the taking. And at the same rate of pay as a man would get in the same role. Our feminist sisters had this right enshrined in

79

law back in 1975, when they won the right for all women to earn an equal wage for an equal day's work and be free from discrimination in the work place.

Why then do so many women turn to the oldest profession? It is a question that has perplexed me for years. To find an answer I had to look no further than a local pub renowned for its clientele of working girls.

There in the drab interior, I found half a dozen women drowning their sorrows in alcohol in the middle of the day as they prepared for the teatime trade. These women provide their services for five to ten pounds. They have lost their children, most have lost what looks they had in the first place and all have lost their self-respect. They risk their lives in the dank back alleys of England's cities. It is a risk they have decided is worth taking if the alternative is a day of hard graft.

None of the women I spoke with has ever held a job or been able to settle down in a marriage. They lead a chaotic existence, drifting from one casual sexual encounter to another and then back to the pub or the drug dealer. It is a measure of their lack of self-awareness that they believe themselves to be capable of raising children, and some seek to wrench their children from the loving homes provided for them by the state.

I think I can speak for all working women when I say I find this life of idleness and venality utterly abhorrent. In my view, the feminists have taken a step too far in calling for prostitutes' rights. These women have given up their right to be part of any decent society. They undermine all the principles of a healthy nation. Prostitution is deadly for the women who sell themselves to men, but it is also deadly to society, spreading disease and tearing apart the sacred institution of marriage. Let's work together to rid our fine city of this deadly game.

Sandra was speechless with rage. She raced back up to the flat, taking three steps at a time.

'Look at this shit.' She showed Tracy the article.

'Whoa, what a fuckin' bitch. I thought she was tellin' our side of the story,' said Tracy reading through it.

'D'you think the junkie girl's bloke did her in?'

'Don't be stupid. Of course he didn't,' Sandra replied, by this time incandescent. 'Them coppers want an easy mark and they couldn't give a shit what's happened to that poor cow cause she's a pro. You know what, them clever bastard feminists, they go on about women's rights an' lesbian custody an' all that but it's us who's at the bottom. We're the ones that get the shit thrown at us. I'm goin' out now an fuck some old wanker who'd prob'ly rape his own fuckin' kid if I weren't there. It's men that's fuckin' diseased. They're fuckin' diseased in the 'ead.' Tears of anger streamed down Sandra's face as she paced up and down the living room. Tracy held out her hand and Sandra pushed it away. 'No, just let me be for a minute. I'm fuckin' right t'be angry.'

Tracy stood motionless and felt foolish and naïve next to her lover. She had heard what Sandra had said and, though she could not have articulated her thoughts and feelings, she knew something was changing. The rollercoaster ride that had been her life so far was about to go downhill. She was pretty good at hanging on tight.

♀

Twelve
Saturday, 19th April, 1980

The previous evening had seen an unprecedented number of kerb crawlers in the red light district. Business was booming. Even the older women and those most care-worn had been able to charge the going rate. It was as if the second murder had added a frisson of entertainment to the usual banality of transactions made. Tracy and Sandra between them had made close to a hundred and fifty pounds, so much money that they'd decided to put some by for the following weekend when they planned to take Vincent on a day-trip to Blackpool. They'd learned from a small article in the Friday evening paper, entitled: 'Prostitute Killing: Boyfriend Released', that the police had no new leads on Rosie's murder. Ginny's death seemed all but forgotten.

They were getting ready to go out. They'd been shopping for new clothes in the day and Sandra had bought a fabulous white dress, just like the one Marilyn wore in 'The Seven Year Itch'. Tracy thought she was the most beautiful woman in the world. As usual, Sandra was taking ages to get ready, applying and re-applying her makeup. Even Tracy was making an effort and had washed her hair and put on clean jeans. They were going to a party in Leeds at Selene's house and they wanted to impress. They might be a couple of prossies but they could scrub up just as well as the next woman. Selene had said there was to be some sort of meeting beforehand, and then the party would start about nine.

Feeling flush, they'd got a taxi over to Leeds and arrived early. Selene let them in and showed them into the big communal living-room where a dozen or so women were talking. Selene asked if it was okay if her friends joined them for the end of the meeting and everyone agreed and shifted up to make space. Sandra's dress did not go unnoticed by any of those assembled but it was Izzy who said: 'Wow, that's some dress. You look fabulous.'

'Thanks,' Sandra said embarrassed, finding it awkward to sit on the bit of floor that had been proffered. Most of the women were in jeans and a couple in long 'hippy' skirts.

'Here have my seat,' Izzy went on. 'I'm still in my scruffs.' She stood and let Sandra take her place. Tracy sat on the floor at Sandra's feet and made a mental note to keep an eye on Izzy. Their entrance had disrupted the flow of the discussion that was taking place.

'Shall I go on?' a small blonde woman said.

'Sorry, Heather, please do,' Rachel replied. It seemed to Tracy that she was again the 'chair'.

'That night I called the police,' Heather continued. 'They came out but he got so angry he even hit me again in front of them because I'd called them out to him.'

'Hang on,' Rachel said in disbelief. 'You called the police and your husband continued to attack you in their presence and they went away without making an arrest.'

'Yeah. They did,' Heather replied with a complete absence of outrage. 'I left him then and went to the refuge with my two kids. I realised the law was on his side.'

Tracy couldn't help herself. 'Why didn't you knife the fucker in his bed while he slept?'

Sandra kicked her.

'I would've but I'd got my kids to think about.' Heather's response was again quite matter-of-fact.

'Thanks for sharing your experience, Heather,' Jo said. 'It can't have been easy but none of us is alone. Everyone in this room shares a common problem and we need each other to find the strength to fight back.'

After Heather's revelations the room was subdued. 'Shall we leave it there and get the wine opened?' Rachel said, much to everyone's relief.

The little troop filed through to the kitchen where there were about fifteen bottles of wine, a couple of cases of beers and a table full of food. Tracy added a bottle of scotch to the collection from her inside pocket and, realising she was famished, seized a plate of sausage rolls. She was relieved to find that this lot at least knew how to throw a party. A fact that, until this moment, she'd doubted.

'Give us one,' Sandra said sidling up to Tracy. They knew Selene and had met the women who lived in the house at the Lesbian Custody meetings, but they weren't confident about socialising with 'educated' women.

'I feel so out of place. Let's go soon,' Sandra said.

Selene was standing right behind her and overheard. 'No don't go. Have a drink. It'll soon warm up. Anyway, you look gorgeous. Where did you get that dress? I want one.' Sandra blushed as Selene continued: 'Listen though, seriously, we've got to talk about something. Rachel wants to speak to you. Can we go up to my room before we drink too much?'

'Is it about my case?' said Sandra hopefully.

'No, sorry. It's not. I didn't mean to get your hopes up. I'll get Rachel. You go up to my room. It's at the end of the corridor at the top of the stairs.'

Rachel was standing with a group of women talking about the politics of shaving pubic hair. It looked like it could get heated. Selene touched her arm and indicated that Sandra and Tracy were waiting upstairs.

'What's up?' Sandra said as Rachel and Selene came in and closed the door.

'I didn't want to talk in front of everyone because I wasn't' sure how you felt about everyone knowing that you're sex workers,' Rachel began.

'Well we don't shout it from the roof tops,' Tracy said.

'That's what I thought. It's just that I've got some information about these murders,' Rachel went on as Sandra and Tracy looked baffled. 'There's been two in Manchester and another in Liverpool. All the victims are sex workers. The police know, but it's not gone beyond the local newspapers. Basically, there's a serial killer out there preying on women and we wanted to warn you.'

'I knew it,' Tracy said. 'I seen the photo of our mate Ginny. I knew then it was a psycho.'

'How do you know about the others?' Sandra said.

'I've got contacts with a feminist legal group who've been acting on behalf of women throughout the North West. They've got ties with the police.'

'Why aren't they doing anything about it?' Tracy asked. 'The girls need to know.'

'They're trying not to create a panic and a big media frenzy just yet. They think it could alert the killer and make him more difficult to catch. While he thinks he's clever and outdoing the law he'll have his guard down.'

'And it's only working girls?'

'Well precisely, Sandra.' Rachel always said Sandra's name with the long southern *ah* sound. It made Sandra feel strangely warm towards Rachel. She was too posh to know any better.

'That's why the NRFA are getting involved,' Rachel added.

'Who're they?' asked Tracy.

'The Northern Revolutionary Feminist Alliance. They're working with a collective of Manchester sex workers to try to educate women about safe practices, health issues and stuff.'

'Thanks for the tip-off,' Sandra said. 'We can at least tell the girls in The Beehive.'

'That's why I wanted you to know immediately. We'll have to look out for ourselves, I think, since it seems the law won't. Anyway we've got a party to go to,' Rachel added. 'Let's keep in close touch. Maybe through Selene?' She looked to Selene for confirmation.

'Fine by me,' Selene said. Tracy and Sandra nodded their approval at the suggestion.

'C'mon then, let's get fuckin' hammered,' said Tracy lightening the mood.

'An excellent proposal.' Rachel smiled.

Downstairs, people had drifted back into the living room. Tracy joined Izzy and the two of them started up a little joint-rolling enterprise. Sandra disappeared into the kitchen with Rachel and Selene. She'd relaxed a little more now that she felt that they were in Rachel's confidence. She liked the feeling of being accepted without judgement.

'You pass yours round an' we'll smoke mine,' Tracy said. She didn't like the look of the dodgy looking home-grown that Izzy was skinning up with.

'So are you with anybody?' Tracy asked, sucking hard on her joint to get it going.

'Nah. Young free and single. To be honest I'm not that bothered. I'm trying to get a show together so I'm really involved in my own head, if y'know what I mean.'

'Show?' Tracy enquired.

'Yeah. I'm a painter and I do a bit of sculpture too. I might be able to get a space in a gallery in Camden this summer. So I'm working on getting my best pieces and some new stuff together for that.'

'D'you earn money from it? Do people buy that shit? Sorry I didn't mean your stuff's shit, just that I—' Tracy passed the spliff to Izzy who took a long draw and started coughing.

When Izzy recovered she said: 'No that's okay. I know what you mean. Come up to my room and have a look if y'like. And yes, some people do buy that shit but I sign on as well. I couldn't live off my art. That's my dream though.'

'Okay. I'll just let Sandra know where I'm going.'

'Bring her?' Izzy shrugged.

Tracy went through to the kitchen. When she saw Sandra standing with Selene and a group of other women talking and laughing, cigarette in one hand and long drink with ice in the other, her heart fairly missed a beat. She felt at once an uncouth yob and blessed that she knew love so deep.

'Darlin',' she said tentatively. 'I'm just going up to Izzy's room to look at her paintings.'

'Oooh la la,' Selene said. We've heard that one before.' Several women laughed and Tracy blushed to the roots of her hair.

'No, I was just asking if you want t' come,' she explained to Sandra.

'Yeah okay. I'll just get a refill and follow you up.' Sandra held up her near empty glass

'You should,' Selene said. 'She's a really good artist.'

Izzy's room was crammed full of the paraphernalia of painting and art. One wall was lined with books stuffed haphazardly into a precarious looking homemade bookcase. There was an easel with a half-completed female nude, it's fuzz of pubic hair shaped into a skull and crossbones. Paints and inks, brushes and linseed oil were strewn everywhere. Many finished pieces stood around the available bits of wall.

'Blimey. You've been busy in 'ere,' Tracy said, unequal to the task of commenting on art. She and Sandra began to examine the work. There were many abstract landscapes and cityscapes, vibrant fractured suns sewn with gold thread and darting birds, white against blue-black skies.

'Is that Rombalds Moor?' Sandra asked, pointing to a canvas of jagged grey rock interspersed with flashes of greens and purples.

'Yeah, it is,' Izzy said. 'You must know it well.'

'I used to go up there as a kid with my dad,' Sandra said, and Tracy, who had been trying to work out the skull and crossbones, spun round in alarm. Her concern was unfounded because Sandra was carrying on seamlessly. She had never before heard Sandra speak about her dad in any context other than fear and hatred. At least never before she was completely rat-arsed.

'It's a really good paintin',' Sandra was saying to Izzy who looked overjoyed. 'My son's named after an artist. Well, not really—more a song about an artist. "Vincent" by Don McClean. It was number one the week I had 'im. I used to love that song.'

'Yeah, so did I,' said Izzy. 'I had the album in fact.'

'What's this s'posed to mean?' Tracy interrupted the little bonding session, pointing to the skull and crossbones painting-in-progress.

'I don't know really,' Izzy replied. 'It can mean a lot of different things—danger, poison, secrets. In Spain it sometimes marks the entrance to cemeteries.

'How d'you think of stuff,' Tracy asked

'It just happens when I start work.' Izzy tried her best to answer. 'It's a bit like magic.'

Sandra, meanwhile, had picked up a huge reference book of birds that was lying under a pile of books on the floor. 'Look, Trace! That's it,' she suddenly said.

Tracy and Izzy joined Sandra. In front of her she held up a picture of a condor, its dinosaur-head tiny against its huge black body. Izzy looked puzzled. Sandra explained about her dream of the previous year that had etched itself on her memory, and then the weird graffiti down at the bins.

'Wow. That is bizarre,' Izzy said.

The three of them went back downstairs. Loads more women had arrived. The Pretenders album had been jacked up as loud as the mackled together stereo system could go, and some women who'd already had enough to drink were dancing. Sandra and Izzy went to join them. Tracy went into the kitchen where she found her bottle of Scotch, still all-but untouched, and poured herself a very large one.

By half-past two the party had started to thin out. Sandra found Tracy asleep on a bean bag. A little unsteady on her feet herself, she tried to rouse her. 'C'mon. It's time to go,' she said shaking Tracy and pulling ineffectually at her arm. Tracy woke, sat up, picked up the bottle still beside her and took a swig. Sandra pulled her to her feet. They found Selene and Izzy going through the records looking for something mellow to put on.

'We're off,' Sandra said.

'How're you getting home? You can crash here y'know?' Selene said.

'Nah. Thanks, but I'd but sooner sleep in my own bed if you know what I mean. We'll walk up to the main road and hail a cab. It's been a really good night though. Thanks.'

Tracy swayed slightly and slurred: 'Yeah. Good one.'

They left and walked up to the main road, quiet now after the two o'clock club-chucking-out rush had dissipated. Sandra, holding Tracy under one arm, waived down a lone black cab and they climbed in.

'It's fare-and-a-half at this time o' night,' the cabbie warned them.

'Fine. Just drive,' Sandra replied.

Tracy's mood was suddenly bleak.

'D'you fancy 'er then, that Izzy?' she challenged Sandra.

'Oh shut it. What the fuck are you on about? You've 'ad too much.'

'Well you spent most of the night followin' 'er about.'

'No I didn't. We danced for a bit, but everybody was dancin'. I danced more with Selene. Every time I came to get you, you were just huggin' that fuckin' bottle of Scotch.'

'Oh, is that Rombalds Moor?' Tracy imitated Sandra's voice in a nasty ingratiating tone.

'Do not fuckin' do that!' Sandra warned her angrily.

'My son's named after an artist,' Tracy continued. Sandra landed a punch on her jaw. Tracy lunged back at her, but was too drunk to the land the blow.

The cabbie, who'd been observing in his rear-view mirror, pulled up with a screech of brakes. 'You can get out an' fuckin' walk. I'm tellin' yuh,' he said.

'Sorry, mate,' Tracy slurred.

'You're off your face you are. Now out you get.'

'Fuck you!' Tracy summoned her wits. She got out of the cab, slammed the door hard behind her and walked away in an almost comedic zigzag motion.

A lime-green Ford Capri pulled slowly past their stationary cab unnoticed.

'Please, love.' Sandra's tone was reassuring. She leaned forward towards the driver. 'I'll look after her. She's alright. She don't mean any harm. We'll pay double time.'

'It's a tenner on top if she throws up,' the driver cautioned. 'And I want the money up front.'

Sandra searched in her bag for her purse. It wasn't there. 'Look, I think my mate's got my purse in her pocket. I can't find it.'

'Yeah, I've 'eard it all before. Now fuck off.'

'I swear on my kid's life. If she hasn't got it, I'll get it for you when we get home. You can come up to the flat with us. Women are gettin' murdered on these streets.' But, just as she finished her sentence, Sandra's hand, still scrabbling inside the voluminous bag, struck against her purse. 'Here it is, anyhow. I've found it' she said relieved. She handed over two crisp tenners and the driver pulled away from the kerb. Tracy was nowhere in sight.

They crawled slowly along the road. Sandra's heart raced. A pounding set up in her temples. She was afraid to get out and look for her in case the cabbie just fucked off with her money and left them stranded. They'd gone too far down the road. Tracy couldn't have got that far in the state she was in. 'Turn round, please,' she said.

'It's your money.' The cabbie shrugged and swung the car round.

Then Sandra spotted her, staggering out of an alley doing up her jeans. They pulled alongside her and Sandra opened the door shouting: 'Where the fuck 'ave you bin? Get in!'

'Havin' a slash. Whaddya think? Silly cow.' Tracy climbed back into the cab.

On the other side of the road a young woman with a duffle coat slung on over her pyjamas hurried along, her hands jammed deep in her pockets.

Thirteen
Saturday, 19th April

In her second year at Leeds University, Elle had started to doubt the wisdom of moving out of halls and into a house-share in Chapeltown. It was well placed for the campus and her best mate Lisa lived there too, but she found she didn't get along so well with the other two girls in the house. They lived like pigs and, more often than not, Elle had to clear the kitchen before she could even start cooking her own tea. She was going to have to stand up to her housemates. Standing up to people was always something that terrified her.

Earlier that evening she'd snapped when she went into the shared living-room to find that one of them had been sick on the floor, more than likely the previous evening when they'd been pissed, and hadn't bothered to clean it up. Only Lisa was in the house, and so it was she on the receiving end of Elle's anger. Elle was sorry for that, but she had a tendency to take out her grief on those whose love for her felt unconditional. Their row had been heated but after they'd both stormed off to their rooms, Lisa had come and tapped on Elle's door and they'd patched things up and made a pact to have it out with the others in the morning.

After that, Lisa had tried to persuade Elle to come out to the Union bar, but she couldn't face getting ready and all the performance of flirting with blokes that the evening would be bound to entail. She felt more like curling up in the warm and watching rubbish Saturday-night telly. She also wanted to write to her mum to thank her for the set of saucepans she'd sent. 'Suit yourself,' Lisa had said. 'Shall I fetch you chips if we get some on the way home.'

'No, don't worry. I'll be asleep by then. Ta anyway,' Elle had replied. She'd made herself some cheese on toast and took it up to her bedroom; the living room reeked of bleach and cold sick. She changed into her winceyette pyjamas and lay on her bed to watch Bob Monkhouse presenting Family Fortunes on her little portable TV while she ate. When that ended, she couldn't find anything equally brainless to occupy her, so thought she'd set pen to paper. She knew how much her mum loved to get letters. She even took them to the hairdressers with her and read them out to the other women, a captive audience trapped in curlers and hairdryer hoods. Elle smiled at the thought of it, and how daft her mum could be.

Elle rifled through her bag, found a biro and file paper and cleared a space on her desk—which was littered with notes for her essay on Jung. Sitting down, she stared into the space ahead of her while she searched for the right words. She picked up the hair-bobble on her desk and tied back her hair, stretched her arms behind the back of her chair and flexed the stiffness from her neck and shoulders. Then she began.

Dear Mum

I've been really busy this week. I've got two big essays to hand in by the end of next week. I've got one to write on Jung - he was a student of Freud but much cooler - and another one on clinical practise. I'm dead interested in Jung: the bit I'm on is all about dreaming and the existence of a collective unconscious, the idea that the species might have a kind of psychic unity. Do you remember when I was a kid and me and Dad used to dream the same thing sometimes? It's funny, but reading about Jung makes me think of Dad a lot. My tutor thinks I can get a first if I work hard enough.

The house-share's going well. I know you disapprove but it's really clean and I get on with the other girls. Lisa and I have got the two rooms on the sunny side of the house, so it's lovely and light. Also the kitchen is a good size so I've been able to cook proper meals. Thanks so much for the saucepans. They're great. I feel like a proper grown-up now I've got my own set of pans.

Sorry to hear about Mark's leg, but I'm sure he's not complaining about having to have six weeks off school. Tell him I said to get on with his exam revision instead of watching daytime telly.

I hope Ian finds a job soon. It must be difficult for you both. Is he doing a bit more around the house? You can't work full-time at the shop and then come home and do all the housework and cooking, Mum. You'll make yourself ill again. I couldn't believe that you've been married for ten years. Is it something special, like wood or brass? A weekend in Paris sounds very romantic by the way.

I went to the Lakes with Lisa and Sara (from the Ethics course) last weekend and it bought memories of dad flooding back. I could almost see him standing waving at us from the top of Scafell. I used to hate hill-walking then, but now I can really see why Dad loved it. It's funny how you change as you grow up.

Elle stopped writing then and chewed on the end of her pen. She stared again into space. She put her pen down and re-tied her hair back from her face. She picked up the framed picture on the desk. It was a photograph of her dad taken in his army uniform during the war—smiling, handsome, hands in pockets. She kissed the image and put it back on the desk. Then she picked up her pen again.

Mum, I've got something to tell you, something that I should have told you years ago but was too much of a coward. I think in some foolish way I was trying to protect you. I don't want to disrupt your life and upset things at home but I feel that if I don't say now you'll spend the rest of your life living a lie. I can't keep this bottled up inside me anymore. Ian abused me from when I was thirteen until I was seventeen years old. It started about two years after you got married. Do you remember when Aunt Mary was ill and you had to go away for a week. That's when it happened first. He bought me that new bike I'd wanted for ages, and he said, in return I was supposed to look after him, like a wife would. I knew it was wrong but he sort of made it seem normal. He said if you knew he loved me like that it would kill you, and that you'd hate me and be jealous. He said that if I told you he'd say I'd made it up, and that I'd end up in an approved school. He told me that a lot of girls did it with their stepdads anyway and it was nothing to worry about. When you came back and you were so upset about Aunt Mary dying I couldn't say anything, and the longer it went on the more I came to blame myself. That's how it was for the next four years. I felt filthy, I still do. I'm so sorry that it has taken me this long to say anything. I think reading Psychology at uni has kind of dislodged things in my head and made me understand what really happened. Mum, please know that I love you and only want you to be happy, but I can't change the past. I will never be able to feel normal around men. I always steer clear of relationships and I think this is why. You keep asking me about boyfriends, well now you know. I will understand if you don't want to hear from me again and, though that would break my heart, I will live. I would sooner live with a broken heart than bear this dreadful weight any longer. Please, please, please forgive me. I love you more than anything in the world.

Elle xxx

Elle re-read the letter. Would she send it? She knew she must. She folded it neatly into four, found an envelope in the desk drawer and a single first-class stamp in her purse. She propped it up against her dad's photo to post the next day. Then she tried to sleep. She tossed and turned for what seemed like hours. She heard her housemates coming home and then racketing about in the kitchen before going to bed. She thought she heard a bloke's voice too on the landing, no doubt someone's Saturday conquest. Elle watched her alarm clock click to two-thirty and realised, beyond a shadow of a doubt, that if she left it till morning she'd lose her nerve.

She got up, put on her trainers, picked up the letter and put it in her shoulder bag with her keys. She found her duffle coat and put it on over the top of her pyjamas. It wasn't that cold and she was sure there was a post box on the main road.

◊◊◊◊◊

Graham watched her walking along. He'd been waiting to see a woman alone but he'd been unlucky. He had thought he'd have to give it up for the night. And then he spotted her. It was a sign, and he knew she was the one because the song had been playing when he first saw her. It didn't have to be playing, apart from in his head, but this time it was uncanny because it was actually on in his car as she rounded the corner from a side street. He had parked up and waited on the next street-corner, just out of sight near an alley that ran at the back of the shops. As she walked past, he bent over double and called out in a strangled voice: 'Miss, please help me. I'm injured. I think I need an ambulance.'

The girl turned and left the light of the main road, hurrying to his aid. 'What is it?' she said alarmed when she reached him, bending to see his face.

'It's this,' Graham said, producing a claw hammer and smashing it with all his force into the top of her skull. He caught her falling body and dragged her into the alleyway out of sight. Ripping open her duffle coat, he kneeled over her supine body and stabbed her twenty-three times with his sharpened screwdriver. Her pyjama top, still buttoned, was sopping with blood and viscera as Graham mutilated her corpse with his Stanley knife. He yanked down the elastic waistband of the pyjama bottoms and crudely carved two cross strokes into her lower abdomen. A kiss, he thought, smiling satiated. Then he picked up her bag and snatched the first thing that came to hand: a letter. He put it in his trouser pocket. He was drenched in blood.

Lucky again, he thought, that he'd taken the yard keys out with him. He could let himself in and clean up before going home.

♀

Fourteen
Sunday, 20th April

Elle's body was found early on Sunday morning by revellers returning from a party. Four young men, students in their first year at university, laughing and still high on hashish and alcohol, practically stumbled over it as they made their way to their flat above the butcher's shop.

'Oh no! No, no, no, no, no!' Winded, the first of the men to see it staggered backwards into one of his friends.

They had no telephone in their flat so the students had run together to the nearest phone-box on the main road. By eight that morning a police cordon had been placed around the body and the four young men were at the police station, drinking black coffee sober as judges, the savage designs of violence indelibly etched on their lives.

Lisa was a little perturbed when she couldn't rouse Elle for breakfast. Her unease increased when she found her housemate's bed unoccupied and unmade. It wasn't like Elle not to make her bed the minute she got out of it.

Still, Lisa reasoned, she could be getting some fresh air in the park, or have popped out for a pint of milk. Except they had milk. And bread.

At two that afternoon she phoned the police and within five minutes two plain-clothes officers were on the doorstep. She was taken to the police station where, at three-twenty pm, she identified the body as that of her best friend. The local police liaised with the Sussex force, and Elle's mother and stepfather learned of her loss late that evening.

The media frenzy started the following day.

Innocent Victim.
Tragedy: Top Student Slain.
Monster Stalks the North.
Frenzied Attack.
No Woman is Safe.
Police Believe Student May Be Victim Number Six.

The headlines were predictable, even in the broadsheets. A large picture of a smiling Elle receiving an award at the school prize-giving, and one with her brother and stepdad on holiday aged sixteen accompanied most of the articles. Beneath the same pieces, small passport-size photos of the other victims also appeared, two of them taken in police custody after arrests for soliciting. Sometimes, alongside these, a shot of the red light district: a lone woman leaning down to an open car window. No one who saw them could be left in any doubt that Elle was the first victim who hadn't been asking for it.

The Beehive was doing a roaring trade. Police had suspended arrests for soliciting in cities across the North West and women were turning up in droves from Birmingham, Newcastle, and even London to conduct their business unhindered by the law. In fact the huge police presence on the streets gave the girls a sense of security. Surely he wouldn't strike again with everyone on red alert.

Sandra was livid as she hurried to the police station the following Thursday. On the Wednesday evening a vicious row had started between the local women and the invaders from out-of-town. One of Donna's regulars had been poached by a Brummy woman, and catcalls soon degenerated into fisticuffs. In spite of Sandra's protests, Tracy had been drawn in when one of the women pulled a knife on Donna. When the police had finally arrived Tracy was kneeling on the woman's chest with the knife to her throat. She was arrested along with six other women and held overnight. They were all released without charge. Tracy called Sandra from the station to bring her a T-shirt, the one she'd been wearing had been ripped from her back.

'That's attractive,' Sandra said ironically when she saw her lover at the station. Tracy's jaw was swollen and she had several deep claw-marks on her cheek.

'I was tryin' to break it up. Donna was getting' the shit kicked out of her. The fuckin' load of bitches went for me.' Tracy was indignant not to be heralded as a returning hero.

'Why have you got to be defending that lot? They wouldn't do owt for you.' Sandra was unimpressed. 'We've got Vince this weekend an' look at the state of you.'

'I'll just tell him he should see what the others looked like when I'd finished with 'em.'

'No you fuckin' won't. I don't want him thinking fightin' an' all that shit is good. Don't you think he's had enough of that.'

'Oh, hello Tracy. Nice to see you've been let out. Let me take care of your smashed-up face.' Tracy said sarcastic.

Sandra rolled her eyes. 'For fuck's sake,' she mumbled as they headed towards the flats.

When they arrived back outside Bronte House, a longhaired man on crutches was fumbling around near the bins. Who the fuck's that? said Sandra.

As the two women approached the man, Sandra found herself holding back. She hated going anywhere near the bins with that bird thing on the wall.

'What's up, mate?' Tracy stepped close to the man.

James looked up. Sweat had beaded on his forehead. He held an Instamatic camera in his hand. 'I'm trying to take a photo of my girlfriend's artwork,' he said. 'She was murdered and I want to record it before they paint it out.'

Sandra caught up with Tracy. 'Is she Rosie, the girl that was found in the factory?'

'This is the last painting she ever did.' James indicated the condor with a crutch. 'I'm making her work into an exhibition.'

Sandra's skin blanched and the cold prickling she had experienced when she first saw the bird overwhelmed her with a shudder.

'When did she do it?' Tracy said.

'It must've been the night she died,' James replied, pointing to a mark just below one of the great wings. That's her signature and the date.' Tracy peered, made out a small 'R4/4'.

'She always did that, so she'd be able to remember stuff. Like a signpost in life,' James explained.

Tracy looked at Sandra without knowing what expression she wore. It was somewhere between puzzlement and terror.

'I'm so sorry, love.' Sandra touched James' arm. 'Can I take the picture for you?'

James handed Sandra his camera. She took three shots of the image. When she handed it back she noticed his hand was shaking. 'You couldn't lend me the price of a bottle of linctus, could you? I'm not very well,' he said.

Sandra took out her purse and handed him a five pound note saying: 'Okay, love. You go an' get your medicine.'

♀

Fifteen
Friday, 25th April

The next morning Sandra took the bus across the city to fetch Vincent for the weekend. Doreen answered the door. Her left wrist was in plaster.

'What've you done?' asked Sandra.

'Fell over in the yard.' Doreen avoided Sandra's eye.

Vincent came rushing downstairs, threw his arms around his mum and buried his face in her coat. Sandra stroked the back of his head.

'Look. What's goin' on, Doreen? He won't pack it in while you lie to protect 'im. Believe me, Doreen. I know 'im.' Sandra's tone was sympathetic and Doreen faltered slightly before she regained her façade. 'Here's his things.' She handed Sandra a small rucksack and closed the door.

Sandra shrugged and bent to kiss her son. 'Get off, Mum,' he said wiping lipstick from his cheek with his sleeve. 'Are we goin' t' Blackpool?'

'You bet yer life we are.'

'Is Tracy comin'?'

'D'you want her to?'

'Yeah. She's takin' me on the Big Dipper.'

'Well she's comin' then,' said Sandra.

When they got home, Tracy was busy making tea. She'd learned to cook a bit from one of the workers in the home and she wasn't bad at knocking up a blue-cheese flan. She'd also made cheese straws from the leftover pastry. These were Vince's favourite.

'Hope you don't mind, but I've invited Ginny's little lad Michael to come to Blackpool tomorrow.' Tracy looked nervously at Sandra. 'I bumped into him, in Sainsbury's with her mate Carolyn, the big girl who lives along her landing, and Ginny's mum. Poor woman looks done in. I just felt so sorry for them. Her mum's not well and she's struggling with the boy. He's fucked up. Whoops sorry, Vince.' Tracy checked her language.

'Poor little fella. You don't mind, Vince, do ya? He's only four. He won't be any trouble. You can help look after him,' Sandra said.

'He won't be allowed on the Big Dipper,' warned Vince.

''Course not. He's far too little. We'll let yer mum take 'im on the teacups while we go on the dipper,' Tracy replied.

'Okay,' Vince agreed, blowing fiercely on his piping-hot cheese straw.

They picked Michael up the next morning in a taxi. Sheila Hames did look ill. She'd lost three stones since last November. The only thing that kept her going was the care of Michael, a task to which she felt wholly unequal. They'd told Michael that his mum had died in an accident. He didn't fully grasp that she wasn't ever coming back. He still woke most nights screaming for Ginny. He would do this intermittently for the rest of his life.

They stood in the hall while Sheila buttoned Michael into his coat. Stan Hames was noisily splashing himself with water at the kitchen sink, like an old animal at a watering hole. He was getting ready to go out for his Saturday lunchtime drinking session.

'It's ever so good of yuh. He's 'ad it rough,' Sheila said. Tracy and Sandra nodded sympathetically but neither found any words of comfort.

'D'you wanna see my garage?' Michael asked Vince.

'You go an' see what Michael's got,' Sandra urged her son.

'C'mon then, Mike,' Vince said, adopting a fraternal tone beyond his years. He took Michael's hand and lead him through to the living room.

'She wasn't what they said in the papers, Mrs Hames,' Tracy began, trying to think how to say what she meant.

'She was a great kid and a wonderful mum,' Sandra continued. 'You need to look after yerself, y'know. Michael needs you. 'Ave you 'ad any help?'

'No nowt.' Sheila shook her head. 'Young Carolyn's bin as good as gold. She usually 'as 'im every Friday for me. He's so up an' down though. I'm worn out.'

'Course you are, love. Well we're glad to help out. You have a nice rest t'day. Put yer feet up. We'll have 'im back fer supper.' Sandra touched Sheila's arm.

'Here's his money,' Sheila tried to push a pound note into Sandra's hand.

'Don't be so daft,' Sandra pushed it back.

'This is our treat,' Tracy said.

'If you're sure,' said Sheila uncertain.

Michael and Vince re-appeared from the living room just as Stan came into the hall in his singlet. He ruffled Michael's hair and nodded at Tracy and Sandra before going upstairs to dress. Sheila bent to kiss her grandson and tucked the pound out of sight.

As soon as he was in the taxi Michael started crying.

'Can Gran come?' he asked.

'Your gran's gunna have a lovely day to look after herself and we're gunna have a brilliant time on all the rides. We'll get a bucket and spade and build sandcastles, and we'll have ice-cream,' Tracy jollied, but the boy's lip still quivered.

'Can we have Coke floats?' Michael sniffled his words through sobs and snot. Tracy had to look out of the window because tears had welled in her eyes and the lump in her throat was painful.

Sandra pulled him onto her lap and hugged him. 'We can have whatever you want, darlin'.'

'D'you wanna go with this?' Vince had fished a Star Wars action figure from his mum's bag. Michael took it and squirmed off of Sandra's lap.

'What's his name?' Michael asked.

'It's Luke Skywalker, in't it?' Vince said amazed by Michael's ignorance. 'I'm gunna see "The Empire Strikes Back" when it comes out. You can come if you like.'

Michael looked at Sandra and Tracy. Though he was too small to know about Star Wars, he was big enough to know a grown-up had to be with kids.

'As soon as it's out we'll go, all of us together. I wanna see it anyway,' Tracy said. 'It'll be brilliant if I've got two blokes to take me.'

That day at Blackpool was the first time since Ginny's death that Michael Hames was able to forget his sadness. For a few hours at least, he was just a carefree little boy. Tracy engineered a magnificent sandcastle with a gully that ran twenty feet to the sea. Vince and Michael were her loyal workers.

When the sea finally made its inevitable incursion and filled the moat, Michael jumped in the air and clapped his hands and Vince ran a circuit of their construction whooping loudly. 'Look, Mum!' he shouted.

Sandra had been reading Cosmopolitan in a deckchair, trying to keep warm in the brisk April breeze. She was duly impressed. Impressed with her son for his kindness and sensitivity towards Michael; impressed with Michael for his strength and will to survive; and impressed with Tracy, who had such capacity for joy and compassion. 'It's bloody marvellous,' she said.

'It's bloody marvellous,' Michael echoed, and Tracy, Sandra and Vince howled with laughter at his simple glee.

'Shall we go to the fair now, Mike?' Tracy said still laughing, and took his hand to brush the sand from his legs and feet.

'We can't leave the castle.' Michael looked horrified at the prospect of simply walking away from the product of their labour.

'It's okay, sweetheart, the sea will come and wash it away in any case,' Tracy said.

'No!' Michael was unmoved. 'I'm staying here.'

Sandra kneeled down in the sand in front of him. 'Some things are beautiful and perfect, then they get washed away by the force of nature. But you'll always have that beautiful memory. It'll live in your mind. No one can take that away from you, Michael.' She picked him up and started up the beach. He did not resist. Tracy and Vince collected their socks and shoes and followed, kickboxing as they went.

Michael fell asleep on the train going home. He was still clutching the monkey Tracy had won on the firing range as she carried him from the station to the taxi. When they dropped him off at Sheila's it was nearly nine o'clock. He wakened just enough to kiss everyone goodnight.

'You don't need to feed him tonight, Mrs Hames, said Tracy. He's eaten his own weight in hotdogs and ice-cream.'

'Thank-you.' Sheila's reply was heartfelt. 'You are good.'

Sandra and Tracy took the taxi home to the flats. The streets were thick with trade. The plan was for Tracy to work that night, to replenish some of the cash they'd spent at the seaside; winning the monkey alone had cost three quid.

When Vince went into the bathroom to get ready for bed, Sandra said: 'Don't go out again. I'll put Vince to bed and we'll have a drink together.'

'What about the money?'

'Fuck the money. We'll sort it out tomorrow.'

'Okay. That'll be nice. I'm knackered from all that sandcastle-building to be honest.'

Sandra went into Vince's bedroom and tucked him into bed. As she leaned in to kiss him goodnight she saw that he'd been crying.

'What's wrong, darlin',' she said concerned.

'Nothin'.'

'Haven't you had a nice day?'

'Yeah, I've had a top day.'

'Is it anything to do with yer dad, or Doreen?'

Vince stayed silent.

'C'mon, if there's something you need to tell me, let's have it.'

'Can I come and live here with you and Tracy? I don't wanna live at Dad and Doreen's anymore.'

'Of course you're gunna live here with us. I'm workin' on it right now. Has something happened?'

'I just don't like the sounds at night, Mum. I'm frightened.'

'What sounds?' Sandra felt her hackles rising.

'All the shoutin' and bangin' and other stuff.'

'What other stuff?'

'She screams, Mum. It's 'orrible.'

'Don't you worry, my darlin'. Mum'll sort it out.' She closed her eyes and the years she'd spent at Steve's mercy flashed before them. She couldn't allow him to warp her son's life. He was too good, too precious. She clenched her teeth to stop the rage she felt in her heart from engulfing her. Then she swept aside his fringe and kissed him gently on the forehead. 'Night, night darlin',' she said softly, consumed inside by a hard cold fury.

♀

Sixteen
Wednesday, 30th April

Selene held up her finished banner for Izzy to admire. In huge bold paintbrush strokes it read: CALL A CURFEW ON MEN. Reacting to the media psycho-killer frenzy that had ignited after Elle's murder ten days ago, the police had advised women across the North West to stay home after dark. Terror had spread around the country like a virus. He could travel anywhere. No woman was safe. The tone of the police instruction was clear- no *decent* woman would need to be out after dark unaccompanied by a man.

Selene's squat had been the command centre of operations by feminist groups. They'd finally managed to have a phone installed and Jenny had come into her own as head cook and bottle washer of the action. She had coordinated women from all the major cities of the North West, and after some subtle pressure from Rachel had also included the fledgling prostitutes rights group. Rachel was in correspondence with feminists in the US working to decriminalise prostitution, it had become her *bête noir* of late. She had carefully persuaded Jenny to her cause by making Jenny think that it was her own idea and once Jenny had an idea she was a bull terrier with a bone.

Selene and Izzy had been given the task of creating twenty five banners with assorted slogans and they'd requisitioned the living room as their workshop. Izzy painted the words and Selene stapled them to the posts.

'Feels like bein' a Suffragette,' Selene said.

'Good innit?' Izzy replied.

'It's like we've got something definite to fight against, a clear enemy. D'you know what I mean?'

'Yeah, I think I do. It's like this man is a cancerous boil that's finally erupted on a poisoned body. At least there's something to see and cut out,' Izzy said, thoughtful.

'That's exactly it. We won't cure it but it'll help us diagnose the disease.' Selene liked Izzy's analogy. She held up the next banner: STOP VIOLENCE AGAINST WOMEN.

'Who is he?' Izzy said. 'What the fuck is in his head?'

'Ten thousand years of patriarchy fused with psychosis. He's nobody and he's everybody. I bet when they get him he's a *normal* bloke. He's not going to be a monster but they'll try to make him one, it makes it possible to isolate him from the society that created him.' Selene had clearly given the matter some thought. 'It's like when I was doing my M. A. and I did a fair bit of research on the Jack the Ripper thing. They tried to make him a character in a Victorian melodrama. He was a surgeon, an aristocrat, a prince, an evil Jew, a demented Pole. You know what, he was an ordinary bloke. He must have been. He was invisible precisely because he was a nobody. He must have lived in the East End, he'd have had to have a place to clean up. How many aristocrats lived in Whitechapel?'

'Yeah, I reckon you're right you know.' Izzy considered Selene's thoughts then asked, 'Are your mates Sandra and Tracy coming out for the march tonight?'

'Yeah, they're coming to the house first to see Rachel and their solicitor Jane about Sandra's custody case, then we're all going together.'

'Good. They are so exposed out there. I just don't know how they live with that level of fear and violence.' Izzy had just finished a WOMEN UNITE TO RECLAIM THE NIGHT banner. It was embellished with the 'woman' symbol and a crescent moon in a purple night sky. She stood back to regard her handiwork.

'I think it's all they've ever known, so it's all about degree I'd guess,' Selene said.

The post dropped on the hall floor and Izzy went to collect it.

'Something for you from the uni and a giro for me, at long fuckin' last,' she said, handing a frowning Selene a chunky envelope with a University of Leeds stamp across the seal.

'They've got some nerve.' Selene had opened the letter and begun to read. 'They only want me to come for a second meeting about my PhD proposal.'

'What, the sex workers thing?'

'The very same. Only now it's worth something because we've got our very own ripper on the loose. Honestly Iz, they laughed me out of the room in November and what, a week after this shit hits the papers they're interested. Bastards.'

'So you're gonna tell 'em to stick it?'

'Don't be stupid. There's a research grant and an associate fellowship on offer and I'm broke.' Selene smiled, her brain now in overdrive.

Sandra and Tracy arrived at the squat at just after six that evening. Rachel showed them into the kitchen where she and Jane Rayment were already drinking coffee. It smelled divine.

'Coffee?' Rachel asked.

'Please.' They both nodded and sat down.

'How's it going with the access situation, Sandra?' Jane enquired.

'Yeah, that's fine. Steve couldn't care less about when I see Vince. He just needed to prove his point. We have 'im at least once a week, but I want him with me permanent. I don't want him in the same house as that bastard.'

'It might not be as easy as all that. We're still waiting on the date for the appeal hearing.' Jane shook her head and did her breathing in through her teeth thing.

'Well I'm gunna just take 'im out of that 'ouse. I'm not 'avin' 'im frightened.'

'Is Steve being violent towards him?' Rachel asked.

'No, not to Vince, but he's definitely beating Doreen up, and worse from what Vince says. It's just horrible, scary shit. I don't want my kid exposed to it. What's he gunna learn about how to be a man?'

'Sandra, don't do anything stupid that could prejudice the judge against you,' Jane warned.

'Wouldn't it just show that I loved him and cared about his welfare if I just took him away?'

'That's not how the law would see it, especially given that you are a sex worker in a lesbian relationship. You have to be realistic, Sandra.'

'It's right what she says, whether we like it or not,' Tracy agreed with Jane.

'Let's look at another angle,' Rachel said. 'How about getting the social services involved? If he's abusing his wife, there could be grounds for taking Vincent into the protection of the courts and in practise that could mean you'd have custody in all but name and we'll deal with the legal niceties later.'

'I like the sound of that. When I saw Doreen she had a broken wrist and from what Vince said he's raping her as well.'

'Unfortunately Sandra, they're married so the rape part of it's not illegal, but we can get him on the broken wrist if Doreen can be persuaded to admit it was Steve.'

Sandra and Tracy sat open mouthed. 'It's not against the law to rape your wife?' Tracy said incredulous.

'No Tracy, it's not. The law deems that marriage is consent to sex.'

'Fuckin' 'ell, at least we get paid for it,' she said.

'I've never been on a protest march before,' Tracy said to Selene as they stood outside Leeds Art Gallery. It was eight thirty and the march around the city centre was about to start. There were about five hundred women, which wasn't a bad turn out considering the speed with which the thing had been arranged. Fear is a powerful motivator. There were also a few men among those gathered with their candles at the ready. Jenny was making it her business to go around rooting out male interlopers, however well-intentioned they might be. Selene noticed Jenny talking at some length to one of the men and shuffled closer to make sure Jenny wasn't being her usual offensive self.

'Well, could I interview a few of the women for a puh-puh-piece in the Post? Just get a few reactions to the police stance.' A tall man with a mop of shaggy dark hair was reasoning with Jenny.

'And misrepresent them no doubt,' Jenny responded frostily.

'No, I think the police's attitude is crap. My article is going to cover the women's views.'

Selene stepped closer. The man was halfway decent looking. 'Can I help you?' she butted in. 'I'd be happy to give my views on the police or any other aspect of the issue.' She was glad she'd washed her hair and put her favourite jeans on. This fellow was actually quite attractive. Jenny moved away, disgruntled to harangue another man.

'Oh uh, yes. Thanks so much. I'm Jon.'

Selene took his extended hand. His grasp was warm and firm. 'I'm Selene.'

'That's a luh-lovely name. Not very English,' Jon stammered.

'Thanks. My folks are Polish. Look the march is about to start. Perhaps we could meet in The Duck about ten?' Selene was surprised at her boldness. The letter from the University had given her confidence a boost.

'I'll be there.' Jon held out his candle. 'Do you want a spare?'

'Don't mind if I do,' said Selene.

Selene joined the slow moving procession snaking along The Headrow in a river of lights. It took her a while to catch up with Sandra and Tracy and the others and she was flushed when she finally found them.

'Who's got herself a fella then?' Tracy teased.

'He looked like a bit of alright,' Sandra said approvingly.

'D'you think? Actually he's a journalist. He wants to do an article on the march and the women's action.'

'Watch them bastards. We made that mistake, didn't we?' Sandra turned to Tracy. 'Right fuckin' bitch, pretending to be on our side, then writing a load of absolute bollocks about us.'

'Don't worry I'll be on my guard. Come with me. He probably won't show up anyway and I need to talk to you about something. I need a big favour.'

Then the sound of five hundred women singing 'We Shall Overcome' took the moment and Selene, Sandra and Tracy joined the throng. It felt good. Tracy smiled at Sandra who was singing her heart out. Sandra gave her a sharp dig in the ribs just in case she was taking the piss. She wasn't.

It didn't take much persuasion to get Izzy to join them for a post protest drink. The Duck was heaving when they got there and the four of them had to fight their way to the bar. Jon was already on his third pint. He waved from the other side of the bar when he saw Selene and made the universal 'do you want a drink' gesture, but Sandra had already caught the eye of the barman and shouted up their order. Selene made her way round the bar and the company found a corner with a bit of a ledge to put their drinks on. Selene introduced Jon to the other three women. He shook their hands and Selene noticed what a nice smile he had.

'So you're a journalist?' Tracy said suspiciously.

'Yeah, well trying to make ends meet. I'm fuh-freelance. What line of work are you in?'

'Yeah I'm freelance as you might say.' Tracy grinned and all the women smiled down into their pints.

'Did you say you worked for the Post?' Selene queried.

'No, but I might to able to sell a puh-piece to them on the protest, maybe from the feminist perspective.'

'Don't you think a feminist would be best placed to write that?' Selene challenged. There was something about his stammer she found captivating.

'I am a fuh-feminist, but I take your point, that's why I want to get to understand what it fuh-feels like to be told you can't go out after dark. I agree that as a man that's something I don't understand on any real level. I'll tell you what though. I'll donate any money I make to the Violence Against Women campaign.'

'That's fair,' Tracy said.

Izzy and Sandra both agreed.

'Well, we seem to have settled that quarrel pretty quickly.' Selene smiled and looked directly into Jon's eyes. He didn't look away. 'I'm just nipping to the loo,' she said and, leaving the others exchanging getting-to-know-you information, started the sideways squeeze through the crowd. The bar was packed mostly with women from the march, so Selene minded less the virtually full body contact needed to move around. Then she saw Graham, standing alone, leaning against the wall. Just watching. A cold shiver went through her, the feeling that people said you get when someone walks over your grave. She ducked behind a pillar and into the toilet. He was the very last person she wanted to see or have a stilted conversation with, but she wondered why he was in Leeds in a pub full of women. Was he seeing someone behind Irina's back? She wouldn't put it past him. Yet she was certain he was alone. He just had a look about him, that sly caution. Her curiosity was not enough to tempt her to engage with him and by the time she came out of the toilets he was gone anyway.

'Fancy another?' Jon asked when Selene had fought her way back.

'Yeah, but shall we go somewhere quieter for last orders?' she replied.

'We're gunna get the last train. What was the thing you wanted to talk to us about?' Sandra said.

'It's just that I've got an offer of a second interview at the uni and I think you two can help me but I need to talk to you properly. Can I come to yours tomorrow?'

'Us help you with a uni interview? Bloody 'ell girl, you'll be lucky,' Sandra said dumbfounded.

'Trust me. You can help, but we need to talk.'

'Okay, we'll both be in after five.' Sandra and Tracy said their goodbyes and made their way out.

Izzy found her own excuse. 'Rachel and Jo have just come in. I'm gonna see what they thought to the protest. See you at home,' she said and glugged down the last of her pint.

'I know a quiet little bar not far from here. If we get there sharpish we might get a lock in,' Jon said.

'Are you working, or is this you asking me to go for another drink with you?' Selene hadn't been out with a man since she'd moved back to Leeds and she wanted to be certain of the protocol.

'It's me asking you for a drink,' Jon said.

'Well this is me saying I'd love to then,' Selene replied.

They walked together through the city streets under an opalescent full-moon.

'I don't think I've ever seen a moon so big and bright,' Jon said.

'Ah ah. You've guessed my secret identity. That's what my name means you know; The Goddess of the Moon.' Selene liked the interpretation. It was free kudos in feminist circles.

'Now you mention it, I did know that actually. So do Goddesses mingle with mere mortals?'

'Only if they're especially well-behaved.'

They'd reached the pub. Jon held the door open.

'After you. Oh divine spirit that tends mortal souls.'

◊◊◊◊◊

Graham sat in his car with the engine idling. He had a good view of the door of The Duck and he watched the women leaving, mostly in pairs or groups. He was waiting for one to leave alone. He jumped when a policeman knocked on the window, but quickly regained his composure and wound down the window.

'Waiting for someone?' the young officer enquired.

'Yes mate. My girlfriend's been on the march and I want to see her home safe. You can't be too careful these days.'

'Well you can't park here, mate. There's a car park just round the corner on the left.'

'Oh thanks.' Graham wound up his window and pulled slowly away. He'd have to bide his time.

♀

Seventeen
Thursday, 1st May

Selene woke with a muzzy head in a tangle of bedclothes. She couldn't believe the change in her fortunes. In one day she had a possible job offer and what might turn out to be a new relationship. She and Jon had enjoyed several more drinks and talked about the politics of murder. Then he'd walked her home. It was a warm moonlit evening and neither of them had been in any hurry for it to be over. He made her laugh and he was good looking. Result. She could live without the latter but had found 'being funny' in very short supply among the men she'd dated. They'd kissed at her door and she liked his mouth and the way he didn't try to ram his tongue down her throat, like her ex had always done. They had a date for Saturday night. In spite of her hangover she felt a fabulous little bubble of joy in her heart. She climbed out of bed and went to find Izzy to share her good news.

Izzy wasn't in her room so Selene went down to the kitchen where Jenny and Nicola were-making lunch. 'Morning,' she said. 'Have you seen Izzy?'

'Afternoon actually, and yes, but she's gone out to get a canvas stretched,' Jenny replied, her admonition of Selene's getting up so late clear in her tone. 'Did you do an interview with that man?'

'Oh yes, and no. I mean, kind of.' Selene didn't feel like sharing the story of her evening with Jenny and Nicola.

'Well either you did or you didn't, surely,' Jenny persisted. 'I'm just concerned that we get the right kind of press coverage. We hadn't actually elected a press spokesperson on this issue.'

'I went for a drink with him but it wasn't an interview. He's a really nice guy.'

'Oh, I see,' said Jenny. 'Well I'm sure I don't need to remind you that this is a separatist household.'

Selene held her temper. Nothing was going to ruin how good she felt today. 'Jenny, I agreed to those terms when I accepted my room here and I would never dream of breaking that contract. Neither would Jon, he fully accepts that women need space of their own.'

'Oh, Jon is it? You don't waste any time.'

Selene turned and left the kitchen; she would not be drawn out by Jenny, but she doubted that she could go on living under the same roof indefinitely. Then the memory of Graham in the pub came back to her and she decided to call Irina.

Her sister answered breathless after about twenty rings. 'I was in the loft doing a basket,' she explained. Irina always had a hobby that she obsessed over. At the moment it was basket weaving.

'I was just wondering how you're doing,' Selene said casually.

'Oh we're fine. But I'm glad you've called because I wanted to talk to you about Mum and Dad's ruby wedding anniversary. Shall we go in together on a gift—get them something special?'

'Oh God yes, I'd forgotten. That's a good idea. Is it at the Polish Club?'

'Yes, the thirty-first of May. What shall we say, twenty pounds each?'

'Yeah, fine,' Selene replied wondering where she'd get twenty pounds from. 'By the way, I thought I saw Graham last night after the Reclaim the Night march. He was in the pub but he'd gone before I had a chance to say hello.'

'I thought that was in Leeds,' Irina said.

'Yeah it was.'

'Well it couldn't have been him then. He was working late at the yard. They'd had a rush order.'

'Oh, I must have been mistaken. It was so busy in there.' Selene's need to protect her sister from any potential upset kicked in immediately. What she didn't understand was why he'd driven all the way over to Leeds for a drink. 'Anyway, I'll let you get on. When do you need the money by?'

'Why don't you pop over with it next week, we can have an afternoon together and think what to get them.'

'Okay, I'll call you when I know what I'm doing.'

They hung up. Selene didn't want to mention her interview, or Jon. It was all too soon and she didn't want her mum and dad jumping to any conclusions.

She drank two pints of water and ran herself a hot bath.

There was a lovely smell of frying onions when Sandra opened the door to Selene that evening.

'Tracy's doing a Spaghetti Bolognese. You haven't 'ad yer tea, 'ave yuh?'

'No and I'm starving. That'd be lovely. Thanks.'

'Awright?' yelled Tracy from the kitchen.

Selene sat down on the sofa and thought how cosy the flat was, then checked herself. Why shouldn't it be? Just because these women earned their living from prostitution didn't mean they had to live in squalor. Sometimes her middle-class values just snuck up on her. Class was stamped through people like Blackpool rock.

Tracy came through drying her hands on a tea towel. 'Fancy a beer before tea?'

'I'd love one. Hair of the dog actually. I had a stinking hangover this morning.'

Selene told Sandra and Tracy how her evening had gone and that she had a date for Saturday.

'He seemed like a right nice bloke. I'm really pleased for yuh,' Sandra said.

'I thought you were a lesbian at first, y'know,' Tracy admitted. 'I s'pose I just assumed—because of that house and all the feminism stuff.'

'No. I knew she weren't,' Sandra said confidently. 'I'm not really either. I mean I know that's how everybody sees it but if I weren't with Tracy, I wouldn't be with another woman.'

'I'm just so irresistible,' Tracy joked.

'Yeah, I do understand. You fell in love with a person and their gender was irrelevant,' Selene said.

'Yeah, that's exactly it.' Sandra liked the way Selene said things. 'Anyway, what's the story with this interview?'

Selene explained about her previous work on Victorian prostitution in the East End and her proposal to look at sex work in contemporary society

117

focusing on Leeds and Bradford. She said how when she'd first been interviewed they weren't interested but now—

'Now, we've got 'Jack' again and everybody's interested,' Sandra finished her sentence.

'That's about the size of it, yeah. But what I'd like to do is base it on a series of in-depth interviews with women in the sex industry. My favour is—will you two start me off? But it's not exactly a favour because I'd want to pay for your time.'

'Fuck off. No you won't. I'll gladly do it, but you en't payin'.' Sandra was adamant.

'But if I get the fellowship I'll be getting paid, so it's only fair.'

'No way,' Tracy agreed with Sandra. 'It'd be a way we could pay you back for all the help with the custody case.'

'But I've only written one letter and passed a couple of messages.'

'It's more than that. You've made us feel welcome in your house and that means a lot to us—don't it, Trace?'

'Yeah, you never talk down to people,' Tracy added.

'That's brilliant. With that definite, I can really sell them my proposal.' Selene felt a twinge of embarrassment at her privilege in the face of their trust and generosity.

'I'll dish up, and then we'll take you down The Beehive. Better get you ready fer this interview.'

They ate their tea on their laps watching the news. Terrorists had seized the Iranian embassy in London. 'Load o' fuckin' bollocks,' said Tracy. 'What's on the other side?'

'I tell yuh what I don't get,' Tracy was saying as they went into The Beehive. 'Why do Rachel and Jo live in that squat? They must be bleedin' loaded. She's a lawyer fer chrissakes.'

'They're trying to buy that house actually, but also they've put a lot of their personal money into the women's refuge. They're totally committed people, real socialists.'

'Blimey, it en't often people put their money where their mouth is.' Sandra sounded impressed.

Selene was grateful that she was with Sandra and Tracy because she would never have dared come into this pub alone. She realised that she'd have been afraid to be thought a prostitute, even by other prostitutes. If her thesis was going to have any value she had a lot of clutter in her own psyche that needed clearing out.

Tracy went to the bar while Sandra and Selene chose some music on the jukebox. Donna was slumped in the corner asleep. Tracy came over with the drinks; she'd bought a large gin for Donna and she waved it under her nose like smelling salts. Donna came to.

'Donna, Selene, Selene, Donna,' she said. Selene smiled and nodded.

'Hello love,' Donna said, sitting up and straightening her hair. 'Thanks, Trace, you're a good girl.' She held up her drink as 'Too Much, Too Young' by The Specials came on the jukebox.

'This one's for you mate,' Tracy said.

'Y'cheeky sod,' Donna chuckled. They sat down. Donna immediately began on the murders. 'I'm petrified. I've bin tryin' t' keep t' me regulars an' that, but I can't pay me rent this week. I had a bloke the other night, frightened the fuckin' life out of me, he did. Started on about: "Oh, what if I was him?" I said: "Stop the car! Y'can go an' fuck yerself." And d'you know what? The bastard wouldn't let me out. I jumped out at the lights. He was laughin' his bleedin' head off. What's that all about?'

'Arsehole,' Sandra commiserated. 'Why don't you work with us for a bit? We're taking down number plates for each other—then we rip 'em up when they drop us back.'

'Yeah, an' we make sure they know we're doin' it as well,' Tracy added.

'Don't it scare the punters off?' Donna seemed uncertain. 'Anyway, look at me I'd always be the last to get a john, then what?'

'You look fine, y'silly cow—but yeah, it's not a perfect plan,' said Tracy. "Are you carryin' a knife or summat t'defend yerself with?'

'Always 'ave done love, since I got that beatin' off that scouse fucker.'

They talked for the next two hours; about men, marriage, kids, money, violence, pimps and the murders. They kept drifting back to the murders. Selene felt she'd learned more about gender, power and prostitution that evening than in the entire year she spent studying it for her graduate research.

They'd called Selene a cab from the pub. As she got in, Sandra and Tracy walked away towards their patch under the viaduct and it hit her properly for the first time what they did to earn money. It suddenly became real to her. She felt horribly afraid for them, and she promised herself that in her work she would invest these women's lives with the dignity they deserved. The drink had made her love everyone so much that an unbidden tear blurred her vision. She turned and waved as her cab passed them. Tracy did the thumbs up. As she turned back round a lime green Ford Capri passed on the other side of the road, and Selene felt a peculiar sensation, as if a cold finger tugged at her gut.

♀

Eighteen
Later

The first punter to appear was a bloke who Tracy had done about four times before. He was elderly but that's how she liked them; sensible, no messing about and clear about the money. Sandra ostentatiously took his number plate anyway. It had become a habit.

Tracy got into the old boy's Vauxhall Viva and Sandra was left alone. Another woman was visible on a corner but too far away for company. Sandra lit a cigarette and blew two perfect smoke rings into the clear night sky. She felt in her bag for the penknife that Tracy had bought her. 'Cut through the fucker's jugular,' she'd said, demonstrating its exact location on her own neck. Now Sandra opened out the blade and put it in the pocket of her leather jacket, at the ready. She re-applied her lipstick. A green Morris Traveller slowed down but, as often happened, it sped off when Sandra moved towards it. She saw it stop and pick up the other woman. She lit another cigarette off the butt of the one that she'd just finished.

'Doin' business t'night, love?' the man in blue overalls said affably as he leaned across the passenger seat winding down the window. He was smiling and chewing gum so that his jaw moved from side to side.

'Seven fer a blow job, twelve fer sex,' Sandra said.

'Oh, the full Monty, I think. Jump in,' the man replied.

Sandra got in, allowing her split-front skirt to open slightly as she did. If you got them going early it took less time later she'd found. She noticed to her satisfaction that he shifted in his seat and rearranged the front of his overalls.

'I'll drive out a little bit, somewhere quiet. We can do it in't back seat.'

'If it's more than half an hour the price goes up,' Sandra said.

'Don't you worry about t'price, I've got plenty in me pocket,' the man said, still smiling.

They drove for about fifteen minutes. Sandra began to feel agitated. She wanted to get back so Tracy didn't have a fit when she turned up late. The man hummed to himself. 'Like a bit o' music?' he said at last and took a cassette out of the driver's-door compartment.

'Yeah, whatever,' Sandra replied. This bloke was starting to get right on her nerves. She took her lipstick out and traced the outline of her lips in the mirror on the back of the visor, her reflection blurred black and white in the semi dark. The driver stamped on the brake. The sudden lurch sent Sandra's lipstick flying. 'Bloody 'ell. What's goin' on?' she said, feeling on the floor for her lipstick. Her hand touched instead on a small metal pin and she came up with a blood donor's badge.

'Nearly missed the turning,' the man replied as he turned down a bumpy track. He pushed the cassette into the player and fiddled about rewinding it as they continued down the rutted lane. Sandra didn't like it. Something was wrong. 'Look, either stop an' get on with it or forget it,' she said.

The punter pressed play.

Sandra recognised the song. It was El Condor Pasa from the Bridge Over Troubled Water album. She remembered it from when she was going out with Steve, in the days when it was fun, before the violence started. And then it all fused together in her brain; her dream and the junkie girl's graffiti, the Condor. Sheer terror struck her in her chest like a chunk of brick. The blood drained cold from her head and panic howled through her. It was him. She was going to die. She'd never see Tracy again. She'd never see her son again.

'Stop! Stop the fucking car now an' turn around. I've changed me mind about this—I want you to take me back.' Sandra tried to be assertive, but every muscle of her body was tensed rigid and her hands were shaking.

The man stopped the car and switched off the headlights. The night was all but pitch dark—only a timid sliver of moon peeping out from behind curtains of dense cloud to mitigate the blackness. 'Get in't back,' he said in a voice that felt like cold marble.

Sandra opened the passenger door and bolted, tried to run back up the lane hopelessly crippled by her stilettos. She could hear his breath close behind, and the remorseless squelch of his boots in the mud. Any second now he'd have her. She turned and saw his looming bulk, the hammer raised—and then it was coming down, forcing past her upraised hand, grazing the side of her head. There was blood. She could feel it hot on her neck as she turned, plunging headlong, moving forward, not quite falling. His body hit her like a train and Sandra was face-down in the mud, his full weight pressing down on her.

Tiny sounds came from her throat as she struggled to breathe and the man turned her over. He ground his knee into her chest as he pulled the Stanley knife from his pocket and flicked out the blade with his thumb. She tried to look at his face as he touched the blade against her throat, but all she saw was a snarl of bared teeth. He pulled her skirt up, ripping at her tights and knickers. Sandra let it all go then, slipping into a gurgling darkness as he raped her. He was finishing as she resurfaced and, weirdly, the image that filled her mind as he came inside her, was Vincent playing on the beach with his skinny ribs and sticking up hair.

The man zipped up and reached for the hammer. Sandra knew she must kill or be killed. Her knife was in her jacket pocket. Then, as he raised his arm to bring the hammer down, it was out and gripped tight in her hand. She thrust upward hard as the hammer descended. Her skull cracked under the impact and she heard a sound like a beach pebble crunching underfoot. But her knife blade was deep in his arm then; she could feel it grinding on bone and hear him squawking. And then he was struggling to his feet above her, black against silvery clouds, holding his forearm and cursing as blood dribbled through his fingers. 'Fuckin' mad bitch cunt,' he snarled and kicked blackness into her head.

◊◊◊◊◊

A light came on at an upstairs window. The house was no more than a hundred yards away. He felt exposed. The countryside held out no cloak of invisibility. Graham aimed one last ferocious kick at the whore's head and then pushed her lifeless body into the ditch at the side of the lane with his foot. A downstairs light came on. He picked up the hammer, the Stanley Knife and vicious cunt's little penknife, and ran back to the car. He sparked the engine and reversed as fast as he dared back up to the main road. His arm throbbed and his shirt sleeve was soaked in blood.

Graham's heart raced as he sped back into the lights of the city and home. His thoughts were jumbled. He'd need to explain his injury to Irina. She thought he was working late then going for a drink with Derek. He couldn't say he'd done it at work. That lie could too easily be uncovered. He had to have her complicity. A plan formed as he drove. 'That fuckin' cunt,' he thought. He was sorry he'd not had time to slice the bitch, show the world the filth that was inside her. He'd made the mistake of doing it with her. That's what had bought this mess down upon him. He didn't usually get an erection until afterwards. 'Fuckin' bitch cunt,' he murmured to himself as he steered with his knees, trying to staunch the flow of his blood with his other hand. Then he saw the penknife on the seat beside him. For a moment, he considered keeping it. But no, it would hold nothing but bad memories. He wound down his window and lobbed it with his good arm as far as he could. It arced through the night and landed in a stream running parallel to the road.

He parked up on his drive. The car would have to wait until morning. He'd give it a deep clean. He was going to have to sell it anyway. He'd need a car not registered in his name. That problem was for another day though. He took his bloodstained shirt off and pushed it under the seat. He'd burn it in the fire bin the next day. Noiselessly he opened the front door. The house was silent. Good. Irina was asleep. He went to the kitchen and took a swig from the bottle of whisky. He swilled it round his mouth and splashed a little on his face. He crept upstairs, went into his room and took a T-shirt from his drawer. He smeared a little fresh blood from his wound on it and put it on. Then he climbed the loft ladder, the latch was open. It had a large nail sticking up from the frame, that Irina had complained about and he'd been meant to fix. He clattered down the ladder with as much noise as he could make and lay on the landing holding his arm.

Irina appeared from the bedroom pulling on her dressing gown.

'What's happening?' she said, still sleep-confused.

'I've hurt me arm bad, love. Help me up.' He held up his right arm.

'Oh my God,' she said. 'Get in the bathroom quick.' Irina followed him in and held his arm over the sink.

'What on Earth were you doing?' She blew out her cheeks as she approached him and grimaced. 'You've been drinking whisky. You know how it affects you.'

Graham pretended to swoon. Irina held him up.

'Stay there!' she said and went to the airing cupboard. He observed himself in the bathroom mirror. There was a wide stripe of blood dried on his cheek. He rubbed it clean. When Irina came back she was cutting up an old towel. She began bandaging Graham's arm with it. 'You need stitches in this. It's a nasty gash. How did you do it for God's sake?'

'I'm sorry, love,' Graham began his fiction. 'I wanted to surprise you. I was going take one o' your baskets t'make a gift for yuh mum and dad's ruby anniversary. Fill it wi' all red gifts an' flowers. Show willin' like. Then I lost footin' on't ladder an' caught me arm on't bloody nail as I fell.'

'You idiot. Why couldn't it wait till morning? I can't stop the bleeding. You'll have to go to the hospital.'

'No. It'll be fine.' He took the end of the makeshift bandage and pulled it tighter round his arm. 'If it's still like it in't mornin' I'll go then. I'll sleep in't spare room t'night, love, so I don't disturb you.'

'Well just make sure you put another towel down on the sheets. There's enough cleaning to do as it is,' she grumbled and went back to bed.

The next morning Graham set a fire in the bin and burnt his shirt, pants and trousers. Then he set about the car. He'd put an advert in Exchange and Mart to sell it tomorrow, he decided. He fancied a change anyway. The blood was hard to clean off but it didn't show up too badly on the dark material and anyway it was only his blood. His left arm pulsed with pain—bitchcuntbitchcuntbitchcunt. When he'd finished cleaning the seats he got the vacuum cleaner out and went meticulously over the passenger seat looking for hair. As he pushed the nozzle under the seat something clattered noisily up the pipe. He stopped and undid the Hoover bag. It was Sandra's lipstick: Revlon Red Hot Red. He smiled to himself. Somebody up there was definitely on his side.

♀

Nineteen

Done with her punter, Tracy arrived back under the viaduct in twenty-five minutes. She waited on the kerb and smoked a cigarette but decided not to do another till Sandra got back. After half an hour she walked across to The Beehive. It was in darkness. She walked back to the viaduct. Still no Sandra. She smoked another cigarette. She walked back up to the flats. Sandra wasn't home. It was two o'clock. She left the flat and went to the Caribbean Club. That too was in darkness. She kicked the door. No one answered. 'Where the fuck are you, girl?' she said aloud.

Tracy went back to the flat. Maybe Sandra was doing one in a hotel, an all-nighter perhaps. It had happened once before. She finally fell asleep in the armchair at around four. She woke at seven. It was raining heavily. She checked the bed. It was empty. They were due to have Vince again this weekend so Sandra would definitely be back by ten. She'd planned to try to draw Doreen out on the broken arm. She'd definitely be back soon.

Tracy paced around the flat randomly opening cupboards and drawers, as if she'd find some evidence of Sandra. When Sandra still wasn't back by ten she left the flat and walked to The Beehive. It had stopped raining. The cleaner was just opening up. 'I need to see Joan.' Tracy pushed past the cleaner into the bar.

Joan came downstairs in her nightie. 'What's up?'

'Did Sandra come back in after we left last night?'

'No love, she didn't, an' I was in the bar till closing. 'En't she come home?'

Tracy span round and walked back to the viaduct, then back to the flat. When Sandra wasn't there she started crying in fear and frustration. 'Where the fuck are you?' she moaned.

Tracy ran all the way to the cop shop. 'My friend is missing,' she said clearly enunciating each word.

The sergeant looked up from the desk. 'What seems to be the matter Miss, uh McCall isn't it?' It was the one who'd booked her after the affray.

'My friend is missing,' Tracy said again.

'And which 'friend' would that be?' the copper said raising a weary eyebrow.

'Sandra Jacques. She didn't come home last night and I know she would have because she's got to pick her son up today.'

'Well maybe she's gone to fetch him.'

'No, she'd come home first to change. I know her.'

'Right then. Let's take down some details. What's your full name and address?'

Tracy wanted to leap over the counter and smash his face in but she went through the motions as he painstakingly filled forms. Then the two they'd seen about Ginny's murder walked in through the door—Inspector Randall and Sergeant Hill.

'Sandra's missing,' Tracy said urgent.

The desk sergeant looked up from his papers: 'Sir, I'm just completing the—'

'Since when?' Randall cut him off.

'Since last night.'

'Hang on, Tracy. Let's not be jumping to any conclusions,' Randall said. But he did at least seem to be listening and taking her more seriously than the plod on the counter.

'C'mon, I know there's summat wrong fer fucks sake,' Tracy said clenching and unclenching her fists.

'Calm down, Tracy,' Randall said soothing. 'Let's have a sit-down and go through it.'

Tracy followed them through to an interview room and recounted the events of the previous evening to Randall while Hill jotted things down on a pad: the time that Tracy last saw Sandra and the names of the people they'd been in the pub with that evening.

'How much had she had to drink, Tracy?' Randall asked.

'Some, not much. She wasn't pissed. I'd bloody say if she was.'

'Have you tried the hospitals yet?'

'No I'm gunna do that next.' Tracy thought about Vincent. Someone would need to go to Steve and Doreen's and say something. She'd do that after.

'Well there's not much we can do at present but wait for her to turn up. Let us know the minute she does, please.' Randall imbued his voice with a confidence that he did not feel.

'But you need to start looking, don't you? Tracy snapped.

'We can alert our beat officers to keep an eye out, but until we have more information on what's happened here there's not a lot else we can do.'

'What are you on about, more information? I've give you all the bloody information.'

Randall meant that they needed a body, but that wasn't what the witness wanted to hear. They didn't need any hysterics. 'Let us know when she turns up,' he repeated, then stood to indicate that the interview was at an end.

Tracy left the police station and hurried back to check the flat. Sandra wasn't there. She grabbed a cab to The Royal Infirmary. Silly cow must have had an accident, knocked herself out, or something. She had to be there.

Selene woke at half-past eight. She felt fine and figured that she must be getting more used to drinking alcohol. The house was quiet. She went down to the kitchen and made herself some coffee and toast and took it into the garden. It had been raining, but now a warm spring sun was shining on their little yard. Her thoughts were on the research she was planning and she'd decided to take today to get her new proposal together. She was grateful for the help that Sandra and Tracy had offered. It gave her the primary resource she'd lacked in her previous work. Thinking of people as a resource was repellent, she knew, but she'd find a way to make it up to them. She'd grown to like and care about them a lot. Tracy's cut-to-the-bone sense of the world and her gift for "'avin' the crack" as she said; and Sandra—Sandra had a kind of deep wisdom and a warmth that emanated from her and made her easy to be with. She really hoped they made it as a couple. They seemed to be made for each other, but relationships were tough, especially if you were a lesbian prostitute. Selene smiled—what a crazy couple of mates to have joined up with. She was aware too of the distance of class and education between them, an invisible, but she hoped not impenetrable, barrier.

Selene finished her toast, then went back to her room and tidied her desk in preparation. She wound a sheet of paper into her typewriter and began: *Sex work in a patriarchal society: a feminist perspective.* By midday she had a two-thousand word proposal. She'd been utterly lost for hours in making words fit together. She blinked and stretched, and then sorted the sheaf of papers into order. The phone rang and she ran downstairs to get it. It was a long-winded message for Jenny from a woman at the local authority about the route for the next 'Reclaim the Night' march. As she listened she'd doodled on a piece of paper by the phone. 'Jon', she realised now she'd written in teenage-girlish bubble writing. She screwed it up as the front door opened. It was Rachel. Selene promised to pass on the message and hung up. 'Hi, everything ok?' she said turning, wondering why Rachel was home so early.

'Yes, fine, I've left some papers here so I thought I'd grab a sandwich too. I'm glad I've seen you though. I've just been speaking to Jane, Sandra's solicitor. She's got a date for the appeal in September. I know Sandra will think that's ages, but it isn't at all, and she'll need time to get the boy prepared for the change. Jane's writing to her today. Will you be seeing her anytime soon?'

'Yeah, next week. I'm framing some interview questions and piloting it with them.'

'Good, because I've got some other information. Jo's been digging around at work and she's spoken to a social worker in Manchester who was involved in taking Doreen's child into care three years ago.'

'Doreen's got a kid? Sandra doesn't know that.'

'No, I know. We don't know the circumstances but it'll likely play in Sandra's favour. Do let her know, but just be sure she handles it with care. She must let Jane deal with things.'

'I will. But she's not daft by any means, and she'll do whatever it takes to get her son back,' Selene said a little defensively.

'No, I know she's a long way from daft, but I'm guessing she does have a hot-blooded side,' Rachel said with a smile.

'Yeah, you've maybe got a point there. She'll be delighted. I'll give them a ring a bit later.'

Rachel went through to the kitchen then and Selene back up to her room. Re-reading her proposal, she knew this was going to be the best work she'd ever done.

Bert Jacobs woke late. He'd normally be up and about by six but he'd had a rotten night with his back. He'd taken a couple of sleeping pills in the end and now it was gone eight with the chickens still not fed, nor Bessie milked. He pulled on his Wellington boots and went out into the yard. The chickens squawked around him in a raucous gaggle. Tonto, his border collie, was a ball of nervous energy, leaping up at him snappish. 'Slow down boy,' he soothed to no avail. The dog replaced its impatient leaping with a ceaseless running from one side of the yard to the other, skidding each time to a halt before turning.

'What the dickens?' Bert muttered and went back into the house. He'd have to go and see the quack. He couldn't have many more nights like that without some seriously strong painkillers. Bert called the surgery and the receptionist said he could come in just after nine. Tonto was still inconsolable when, at ten-to, he pulled himself awkwardly into the Land Rover and set out down the lane. Every bump sent a wave of agony up his spine. 'Sod it,' he said to himself as the post van turned into the lane. Now he'd have to reverse to let him past. He winced in pain as he turned and put it into gear—then realised that the van had stopped. Terry, the postman, was getting out, and then peering into the ditch.

Bert climbed uncomfortably down from his vehicle and limped slowly up the lane. 'Alright, lad?' he asked as Terry turned towards him ashen faced.

♀

Twenty

Tracy arrived at the Accident and Emergency department feeling weak and shaky. She knew she should eat something, but her stomach was churning riotously. There was a queue of people at the desk in varying degrees of trauma. The boy in front of her had his arm bent at an obscene angle that no arm should ever be bent into, and a woman held a blood soaked towel at her chin. Tracy rushed to the toilet and vomited until all she could taste was bile.

'Please God, please God, please God,' she muttered to herself. She'd never had any reason to suspect that there was a God in heaven but she was all out of options today. When she got to the counter, the nurse was brusque and efficient.

'I haven't dealt with anyone by the name of Sandra Jacques but if you take a seat in the waiting area I'll check admissions when I've got a minute.'

Tracy waited. She had bitten her thumbnail so low it bled. After seven minutes she went back to the desk.

'Wait here,' the nurse said swivelling her chair back and looking heavenward. She went away and re-appeared two minutes later. 'Nope, no one admitted of that name.' Then becoming aware, at last, of Tracy's agitation, she added: 'I'm sorry. You could try Leeds or Halifax. If there's an accident it depends where it is and which ambulance service gets there first.'

'Can you phone them and ask?' Tracy was using all the willpower she had not to get angry. She knew she'd get further faster if she could hold her temper in check.

'Hold on. I'll try for you.' The nurse had softened a little.

'Thanks,' Tracy said. The nurse got on the phone. Tracy couldn't hear what was being said behind the heavy security glass. Obviously a lot of people did lose their temper here.

'Try Halifax, a woman has been admitted who hasn't been identified yet. It could be your friend. Other than that, nothing, I'm afraid.'

Tracy was already halfway across the casualty hall before the nurse had finished her sentence. She jumped into a cab waiting outside. It seemed to take forever in the Friday traffic to get anywhere, and every light seemed to be on red. When she finally got to Halifax Accident and Emergency department, she was told again to wait among the sick and injured. Fifteen minutes elapsed during which time Tracy had bitten all the rest of her nails to the quick. Then a young doctor appeared.

'Miss..?' he enquired.

'Tracy McCall. I'm looking for my girlfriend, Sandra Jacques.' She'd given up trying to be oblique about their relationship.

'Hi, I'm Doctor Thomas, Mr Emerson's registrar. Come with me please,' he said. 'We've had a woman admitted who we've been unable to identify. Perhaps you can help? The police have been informed.'

'What's happened to her?' Tracy didn't know whether this was good or bad news but it was better than the awful emptiness of nothing.

'Let's wait and see if it is your friend. The lady's in surgery at the moment but you may be able to identify her personal effects.'

Tracy was taken into a little anteroom to wait again. The young man disappeared. When he came back he was carrying Sandra's leather jacket and her shoulder bag. The collar of the jacket was stiff with congealed brown blood. Tracy's hand went to her mouth as she swallowed back more bile.

'It's Sandra's,' she said with terror sweeping over her. 'What happened?' Tracy's heart was hammering against her ribs.

'Are you a relative?'

'No. I told you she's my girlfriend.'

'I'm sorry. We must contact the next of kin first. Do you know who that is?'

134

'I'm her fuckin' next of kin. Now tell me what's happened to her before I punch your fuckin' teeth down yer throat.' Tracy had, at last, lost the battle with her temper. It was fortunate for the young man that at that moment Inspector Randall and Sergeant Hill were shown into the crowded space, for Tracy was about to make good her threat.

The Halifax police had finally passed the information concerning the unidentified victim to other stations at two that afternoon. Randall and Hill had gone straight to the hospital. If she pulled through she might be able to identify her attacker, and he could be their man.

'This person has made a threat against me and I want her ejected from this hospital at once,' the registrar said pompously to the two officers and the nurse who'd come in behind them.

'I just wanna know what's happened to Sandra. I am her next of kin. She en't got nobody else.' Tracy had returned to pleading mode.

'She's very distressed,' Randall said in her defence, much to Tracy's surprise. He turned to her. 'Are these Sandra's things?' Tracy nodded. 'What injuries has she sustained?' he asked the registrar, in a tone which said: I'm in charge here now.

'She's received two blows to the skull, one very serious, and a good deal of bruising to the head and body with some internal bleeding. She's been in surgery for the last two hours.'

'What are her chances?' Randall looked at Tracy as he said this.

'We don't know honestly. It depends how much injury to the brain has occurred. Mr Emerson is an excellent surgeon.'

Tracy leaned her head against the wall and sobbed into the crook of her elbow.

'I'll be needing to speak to whoever examined Mrs Jaques when she was admitted,' Randall said briskly.

The waiting game had begun again, but now it had a different quality. Tracy got herself together. She went to the toilets, splashed water on her face and head and took some deep breaths. Someone had got to speak with Vincent. He'd be waiting for Sandra with his bag packed for the weekend. The registrar had assured them that Sandra wasn't going to be available for comment or visiting that day. She'd go to see Vincent, then come back and wait for Sandra to come out of surgery. She wasn't going to think about 'if'.

'Hiya Trace. You're late. Where's mum?' Vince said as he bundled past Doreen at the front door.

'Hang about, mate,' Tracy said. 'You're not gunna be able to come this weekend.'

'Well me and Steve are going—' Doreen started saying.

Tracy cut her off. 'Yer mum's in hospital, Vince. She's havin' an operation today and, all bein' well, I'll come an' get you to visit her, prob'ly Sunday.'

'What's wrong with her?' Vincent sounded frightened.

'She's had an accident.' Tracy tried to indicate to Doreen that she wanted to speak in private.

'I wanna go now,' Vince said.

'No one can see her at the moment, mate, honest, otherwise I'd take you.' Tracy raised her eyebrows at Doreen and she finally got the message.

'You better come in,' she said unwillingly.

Tracy went into the sitting room and gratefully accepted the mug of tea that Doreen offered. It was the first thing that had passed her lips that day. Doreen's efforts to get Vincent to go upstairs to play fell on stony ground. He wanted to listen to whatever Tracy had to say and refused to leave the room. Tracy and Doreen talked about the weather and the new supermarket that had opened up down the road. Then Steve came home. 'What's she doing here?' he said brusque, indicating Tracy with his head.

'Sandra's in hospital,' Tracy said making a conscious effort to keep this conversation focussed on Sandra and Vince.

'Why, what's up with her?' Steve replied.

'Go upstairs and play, Vincent.' Doreen tried her previous request again in Steve's presence.

'Get upstairs,' Steve said to Vincent, the threat implicit in his tone.

Tracy noted it and kept her focus on reassuring the lad. 'I'll see you later, Vince.'

'No you won't, sweetheart. You shouldn't be anywhere near my son,' Steve said. Then he turned to Vincent: 'Get upstairs now.' Vince ran out of the room in tears.

'Let's keep this about Sandra, shall we?' Tracy said and thought about plunging the knife in her pocket through his heart. 'She's been attacked. They don't know how long she'll be in surgery. She's been hit over the head and she might—' Tracy couldn't finish her sentence because actually saying this out loud made her cry, and she pushed her fist into her eye to stop the tears from falling down her face. Doreen's hands flew to her mouth in horror.

'Who's attacked her?' Steve said, slightly less confrontational.

'We don't know yet. The police are waiting for her to come round. I'm going back to the hospital now. What're you gunna tell Vince?—'cause I don't think Sandra would want 'im frightened or anything.' Tracy was trying to keep her tone slightly submissive and cajoling. 'I've said she's had an accident.'

'We'll keep it to that then,' Steve agreed. 'And you can keep your trap shut,' he added pointing at Doreen.

'I'll ring you when I know any more,' Tracy said and handed Doreen her empty mug. 'Thanks for the brew. It were just what I needed.'

Tracy went back to the flat and collected some of Sandra's things—knickers, slippers, toiletries. She looked for a nightie but she'd never seen Sandra wear one. She'd have to go and buy one tomorrow. Great swollen tears poured down her face as she carried out these mundane tasks and she rubbed them away on the sleeve of her jacket. A little part of her head kept thinking that there might not be a tomorrow for Sandra, however hard she tried to push that thought away.

It was visiting time when Tracy arrived back at the hospital and droves of well-wishers clutching flowers and grapes followed the byzantine corridors in search of their loved ones. Tracy went to the front desk and asked where Sandra was. She could hear herself speaking as if in a dream. She had no idea how she would continue to live if Sandra had gone.

'I can't tell if she's out of surgery yet,' the receptionist said. 'Go down to intensive care. I'm sure they'll be able to help you there.'

Tracy set off following the directions through the hospital maze. The staff nurse at the desk in intensive care was capable and professional. She recognised Sandra's name at once.

'Ah yes and you're Miss...?'

'Tracy McCall. I'm Sandra's next of kin.'

'Sister perhaps? Is she unmarried?' Tracy caught the word 'is'. She was alive.

'No girlfriend, lover, partner. Please just tell me how she is?' Tracy would have the fight later. For now, if Sandra was okay she couldn't care less what anyone else's problem was.

'That's fine then, Tracy. Sandra's back from surgery but she's not come round from the anaesthetic yet. She should be awake in the next hour, if you'd like to wait.'

'How did the surgery go?'

'Sandra's had some bleeding on the brain, so we won't know for sure until she's awake. I'll tell you what the surgeon said though; he said: "That's one very hard-headed woman".' The nurse smiled.

'Yeah, I know,' Tracy said proudly. Then she took a seat and waited.

Thirty-five minutes later a doctor appeared.

'Miss McCall. Mrs Jacques is awake. It might be helpful if you were to speak to her, but not for too long, five minutes or so for tonight. She's sustained quite a nasty fracture to the skull and we've drained a significant bleed on the brain. There may be some memory loss, I'm afraid. Don't be too concerned if she doesn't recognise you tonight. Memory is a tricky beast. She may recover things later.'

Sandra lay surrounded by drips and monitors, her head completely bandaged. Tracy sat by her side and offered her hand. The doctor looked on. It was clear that he wanted to see how Sandra would respond.

'Sandra, it's me, Tracy. I'm here.'

Sandra blearily opened her eyes. 'Babe,' she said, and squeezed Tracy's fingers tight.

♀

Twenty-one
Saturday, 3rd May

Tracy woke knowing that from this day on things would be different in her life. When Sandra was well again they'd make decisions about everything. One thing was for certain, they'd have to get Vincent back. Tracy's hatred of Steve had hardened during her visit yesterday. She felt pleased with herself for handling the situation with him so well. She realised that caring for other people was a real responsibility. She had put her driving need to batter the fucker to one side. There were better ways of doing stuff. When she'd phoned to update him last night he'd been almost polite, and had even said a gruff 'Thanks' at the end of the conversation.

She smoked a cigarette in bed and made a mental shopping list of things Sandra would need in hospital. The nightie was going to be a problem. She knew from the vision that came to her mind when she thought of this garment that she'd get the wrong thing. All she could imagine was something pink and nylon with a ribbon woven into the neckline. Sandra wouldn't be seen dead in such an item. Selene was always elegant—even though she was mostly in jeans and tops, she wore clothes well. Sandra had remarked on it, she'd actually used the word 'elegant'. Tracy decided to phone Selene later and ask for help. She would have to call in any case to let her know what had happened. The thought of speaking to someone was a comfort. She stubbed her cigarette and climbed out of bed.

The kitchen was bare and Tracy was ravenous. She hadn't eaten anything at all yesterday. She threw on some jeans and a T-shirt, went out to the local greasy spoon and ordered the fry-up with everything, plus chips. She devoured her meal in minutes and topped it off with a chip butty. As she went to the till, Tracy felt in her pockets for the money to pay. There was a pound note and a bit of small change. She had twenty pence left when she'd counted out the coppers onto the counter and she threw it into the tips saucer. 'Fuck it,' she thought. 'I'll have to do a punter to pay for the things Sandra needs.' The prospect filled her with dread. She was sure that the same person wouldn't strike twice so quickly. But Sandra had lived—maybe he knew she was alive and still had the compulsion to kill. But there really was no choice.

Tracy went back to the flat and ran a bath. While the hot water dribbled out she went to phone Selene. It only rang once before Selene picked up. 'That was quick,' she said.

'Oh, hi Tracy, I thought it might be Jon. We're supposed to be going out tonight.'

'Yeah, of course—sorry I forgot. Look I've got some bad news. Sandra's been attacked. She's in hospital with a fractured skull and she's really bad.' Having to talk about it made a lump come into Tracy's throat and her words petered out.

'Oh my God. No. Is it him?'

'We're not sure. She only woke up from surgery last night and she couldn't say much, but she'd been hit with a hammer over the head and that's what's happened to the other women.'

'When did it happen?'

'Thursday night, after we left you.' Tracy told Selene the story of her last thirty-six hours. 'Listen, I've got a favour to ask,' she ended.

'Absolutely. Anything I can do, just ask it.'

'Sandra needs a nightie and I don't know what to get. She likes how you dress and I thought...'

'I'll go into the city now and get it,' Selene said before Tracy had even finished. 'Shall I bring it to the flat? I can easily jump on the train and come across. When can I see her?'

'That'd be brilliant, mate. Ta. She's really groggy at the moment so I'm just gunna go in today. She's in Halifax. They took her there after they found her.' Tracy realised just how much she'd appreciate a bit of company and someone to talk to. 'It'd be great if you could come over when I get back.'

'Consider it done,' Selene said, glad to have a useful task to perform. They hung up and Selene stared ahead at nothing in particular and remembered seeing Graham's car as her taxi had pulled away on Thursday night. It couldn't have been him. There were loads of Capri's around and it was dark. She could have been wrong about the colour. She found Graham totally repugnant but he couldn't have anything to do with this horror—not her own brother-in-law. It was unthinkable—yet the killer was almost certainly somebody's brother-in-law. A niggle opened up in a dark corner of her mind.

Selene went through to the kitchen where, as luck would have it, the whole house seemed to be assembled in various stages of cooking and eating. Selene relayed the information she had and tried, unsuccessfully, to field the barrage of questions that followed. Even Jenny seemed genuinely shocked and concerned and refrained from any comment about prostitution being the oldest form of slavery.

Then the phone rang again. This time it was Jon. 'Hi. It's me,' he said nervously. 'Did you remember we said about going out this evening?'

'Yes, of course I did. I don't have that many offers of dates you know.'

'Oh, I didn't mean...'

'No, I know you didn't. Anyway listen, something's come up. My friend Sandra's been badly hurt. You met her briefly the other night. I need to go shopping in the city centre, and then go over to Bradford to see her partner. So I'm not sure when I'll be done.'

'I could meet you in Bradford. I could pick you up from your friend's house, even if it's late. Especially if it's late.'

'Yeah, okay. I don't see why not.' Selene gave Jon Sandra and Tracy's address and instructions on how to get into the flats. 'It's a dodgy area, so watch yourself,' she added. 'See you around nine?'

'Yeah, that's great—and don't worry, I can look after myself. I'll see you then.'

When she'd put the phone down Selene had a moment's doubt. What if it was him? What if she'd just given the killer access to her friends? She knew this was rubbish but paranoia was an infectious disease. It worked its way into every aspect of your life and thought. How powerful it must make this bastard feel to know that because of his actions every woman in the land had to fear and suspect every man.

Tracy left the flats and walked down to the underpass. She had her army lock-knife open in the pocket of her leather coat. There was plenty of lunchtime trade. It took less than five minutes for a car to pull over. It was a man about fifty with a comb-over. He drove to a quiet road by the cemetery and ten pounds exchanged hands. Tracy began to wank him off. She felt nauseous.

'I've paid fer a blow job,' the man said and tried to push Tracy's head into his lap.

She pulled the lock knife from her pocket. 'Touch me and I'll cut your fuckin' dick off.'

The man's penis began to deflate and he held his hands up. 'I don't want any trouble,' he said feebly.

'Open your fuckin' wallet, shithead,' Tracy said. The man did as he was told and Tracy emptied it of notes. There were three tens and a five. She put them into her coat pocket and backed out of the car. The terrified man pulled away before she had a chance to close the door. Tracy fell to her knees on the soft earth and spewed her barely digested fry-up under a hawthorn edge. Tears streamed down her face.

Sandra woke up at eleven in a private room off the main ward. She had a drip in her arm and a monitor bleeped rhythmically beside her. A metal kidney bowl stood on the locker. She tried to think what had happened but a jumbled patchwork of random thoughts seemed to have replaced her ability to reason.

'Good, you're awake.' A nurse had come in to the room to adjust the drip. 'Can you manage a drop of water?'

'A cup of tea'd be lovely,' Sandra said. Her mouth was sticky and dry.

The nurse held Sandra's head up and handed her a small glass of water. Staff Nurse Susan Beale, her name badge said. Sandra gulped the water down and immediately bought it back up into the kidney bowl.

'Umm,' said Susan. 'That's what I thought. Any pain?'

'No, not exactly, but my head feels really weird.'

'Well you've had a very nasty injury, Sandra. You're a lucky girl to be alive. Do you think you'll be up to seeing two policemen this afternoon?'

'Yes I think so. Has my friend Tracy called? Is she coming this afternoon?

'Yes, she has and yes she is. We practically had to throw her out last night.'

'Can I have a ciggie?' Sandra asked.

'You're still too poorly.' Susan rolled her eyes and left the room.

Sandra looked around, but moving her head was difficult and strange. She reached up and felt her head completely encased in bandages and tried again to remember. Nothing came except the certain knowledge that she'd encountered the killer. Of that much she was certain, everything else was a haze. She drifted in and out of consciousness.

Next time she opened her eyes Tracy was holding her hand. Her face broke into a luminous smile but it was obvious she'd been crying.

'What're you grinning at, weirdo?' said Sandra keeping her head very still. The pain had started to kick in.

'The most beautiful woman in the world,' Tracy said completely unselfconscious.

'Look, I've got you some stuff. Soap, deodorant, toothbrush and toothpaste, your make-up bag, Vimto cordial.' Tracy held open her Boots carrier bag. 'Selene's getting you a nightie. I'll bring it in tomorrow.'

'Have you seen Vince?'

'Yeah, I said you'd had an accident. Shall I bring him to see you tomorrow?'

'What do I look like? Will he be scared?'

'No, you're fine.'

They were interrupted by a light tap on the door followed by the appearance of Randall and Hill.

'Hello, Sandra. Are you well enough for a few questions?' Randall pulled up a chair to the edge of Sandra's bed and Hill stood at the bottom staring gormlessly.

What the fuck's he gawping at? Tracy thought but managed with a great force of will not to actually say.

'Can you tell us what happened on Thursday night, Sandra?' Randall said.

'Not much. I can't remember any details but I know it was him.'

'Why are you so sure?'

'I don't remember how I know. I just do. Anyway they said I've bin hit over the head with a fuckin' hammer. What more d'you need to know?'

'It's just that there are aspects of the attack you suffered that don't fit with what we know of his behaviour.'

'If Sandra says it was him, then it was.' Tracy was starting to lose it.

'How many clients did you see that day, Sandra?'

'Get the fuck out of 'ere,' Tracy shouted.

'No. It's okay, leave it. They've gotta ask.' Sandra moved her hand onto Tracy's arm in an effort to calm her down. 'I had a regular at a hotel in the afternoon. That was all.'

'Were the clothes you were wearing clean when you went out that night? Sandra I'll ask you this straight out. Could there have been semen on your skirt and under-things before you met the assailant?'

'No, definitely not. I always make 'em use condoms. Anyway I had a bath when I got home and changed into clean clothes. A friend came over for tea—we had Spaghetti Bolognese.' Sandra felt a compulsion to list everything she could remember.

'Then what happened Sandra?' Randall's tone was coaxing and solicitous.

'We talked, and then we went to The Beehive. Donna was in there.' Sandra stopped. The haze was back. 'I don't remember leaving the pub,' she said and looked at Tracy.

'Selene got her cab and we walked down to the underpass. I got a punter and you took down his number. I was back in half an hour and you'd gone, babe.' Tracy recalled the night with pain carved in deep lines across her brow.

'Can you describe the attacker, his car, what he was wearing?' Randall persisted.

Sandra shook her head slowly from side to side. 'It won't come. When I try to think of him I just see a blank space.'

'Why're you interested in the semen?' Tracy asked.

'Because none of the victims so far has been sexually molested. We don't see why that would suddenly become part of his pattern.'

Sandra closed her eyes. 'I need more painkillers,' she said.

Susan, the nurse who'd seen Sandra earlier; and the doctor who'd performed the surgery came in straight after the police had gone. 'How're we doing today, Mrs Jacques?' he said reading her notes at the bottom of the bed. Sandra told him about her pain and her memory loss.

'You're a strong young woman, Mrs Jacques, and you may well recover memories of your ordeal, but we know very little of the workings of the human brain. You're suffering from something called Dissociative Amnesia. Basically, your brain has wiped the memory of your trauma. So I'm not able to tell you when, or if, that memory will resurface. You may well find other areas of your memory affected, or suffer from mood changes. The blow to the skull was severe and the period of unconsciousness unusually prolonged. We must be patient and see how things develop. For now, the only thing I can deal with is the pain. We can make you comfortable.' He turned to the nurse. 'Morphine, just until tomorrow,' he said.

'Visiting time's over now, I'm afraid,' Susan said.

'Five minutes please,' Tracy pleaded. 'We've hardly had any time to ourselves.'

'Well, just until I sort out the injection. She'll be asleep after that anyway.' Susan smiled kindly at them both and went about her business.

'So he raped me.' Sandra touched her temples, her brain pounding as she tried to process all the information. It hurt so much she could hardly see.

Tracy simply nodded as a great cavernous emptiness opened up inside her heart. Sandra had lived but they were both profoundly damaged forever.

♀

Twenty-two

'Wow. That looks like summat you'd go to a party in,' said Tracy as Selene pulled the Biba nightdress from a swanky department store bag.

'Is it wrong?' Selene frowned.

'Oh no. She'll love it. It's gorgeous. How much do I owe you?'

'Nothing. The women in the house had a whip round so I got this as well.' She pulled a silk kimono from the bag. 'Even Jenny and Nicola chucked a few quid in.'

'Blimey. Thank you.' Tracy didn't know what to say. She was unused to the kindness of virtual strangers. 'Can you stay for a coffee or a drink?'

'Of course, if I'm not intruding. Look, if it's okay I asked Jon to pick me up from here at nine so I've got a couple of hours. If you've got other plans I can ring him and—'

'No, that's great. To be honest I've bin looking forward to a bit of company, and I can't face all the questions and shit that I'll get in The Beehive.'

'Well then, that's great. I'd love a drink if you've got one.'

Tracy fixed two whisky and cokes and filled Selene in on Sandra's condition.

'Have the police got any leads yet?'

'No, I don't think so. They don't think it was this killer bloke 'cause they reckon she were raped and that's not what he usually does.'

'Oh no, that's horrible. What does Sandra say?'

'It were definitely him, she says, but she can't remember after we left the pub with you. I just wanna kill whoever this cunt is.'

Selene flinched at Tracy's use of that word, but now wasn't the time to tackle patriarchal semantics in language.

'I know. No, I don't know how you must feel,' Selene corrected herself, 'but I'm trying hard to imagine.'

They carried on talking and drinking until they heard a little tap on the door.

'Oh my God is that the time?' Selene looked at her watch, it was ten to nine. 'Can I invite him in for a drink?' She'd gotten the feeling that Tracy really didn't want to be alone.

'This is yer first date. You don't wanna be hanging round a miserable bastard like me.'

'As it happens I'd rather be here. I wouldn't have a nice time while I'm worrying about you. Honestly, I'm better off here and if he minds then he's not the sort of bloke I want to be with.'

Tracy nodded. 'Thanks,' she said quietly and opened the front door.

'It's Tracy isn't it?' Jon said holding out his hand. 'I took the luh-liberty of bringing a drink.' He held up his off-licence carrier bag.

Selene and Jon left Tracy at two-thirty that morning. She'd drunk twice as much as either of them and fallen asleep in the chair. They hauled her to bed between them. Selene managed to get her boots and jeans off and cover her with a blanket. Tracy was murmuring and mumbling throughout the process but Selene couldn't make out what she was saying. She propped a note on the mantelpiece saying she'd ring in the morning and they crept out of the flat.

'That was really thoughtful of you,' Selene said as they tried to hail a cab.

'What was?' Jon replied.

'Realising that Tracy might need cheering up.'

'Well, good job I did, really. It's much worse than you'd said on the phone.' A black cab had started to slow down. 'Would you like to come back to mine, or shall we get the cabbie to stop at your place first?' Jon tried to be casual but his heart was in his mouth.

'Your place is fine,' Selene said as they got into the cab.

He lived in a second-floor flat in a three-storey converted house. A waft of Patchouli drifted out as he opened the door. It was her favourite smell.

'Nice place you've got.' Selene noted the anti-Nazi league and Rock against Racism posters on the kitchen wall with approval.

'I tidied up a bit this morning,' Jon admitted. 'Yeah, it's alright for the money and the landlord's decent. D'you want something else to drink?' He ran his fingers through his mess of curly hair and smiled.

Selene shook her head and bit her lip. She walked over to Jon as he leaned against the sink and stood on tiptoes as she kissed his mouth. He lifted her into his arms and she wound her legs around his waist as he carried her into the bedroom.

'It's been ages,' Selene said twiddling with Jon's chest hair after they'd made love.

'Yeah, me too,' Jon said. 'But I could easily get into the habit again.'

They talked until dawn. Selene shared feelings with Jon that she'd never told her ex in the three years they were together. She told him about her family and her sister Irina's psychological problems. She talked about her time in London and the work she was planning to do if she got the offer of the PhD from Leeds University. She explained the dynamics of the relationships in the separatist house and allowed herself a bitch about Jenny.

Jon laughed. 'I'll make sure I give her a wide berth then.'

Selene even confided in him her hatred of Graham, and the niggling concern she'd felt about seeing his car in the red light district just before Sandra got attacked.

'Well, if it was his car. He'll get interviewed by the police and have to account for his whereabouts.'

'Really,' Selene said. She hadn't thought of this. She could do some digging when she saw Irina next week and find out if he'd been questioned.

'Yeah, I'm pretty sure they're monitoring all the cars that use that area.'

'Right. Anyway, I've chewed your ears off about me, me, me. What about you? That's not a Northern accent.'

'No, I'm a soft southern pansy, from Reading originally. Nice middle-class mum and dad. One brother, a graphic artist. Always wanted to write, so I did English at Luh-Leeds Uni and I've been trying to scrimp a living at scribbling ever since. Done a fair bit of work for different leftie newspapers and magazines but it don't pay the rent. Can I ask you something?'

'Anything.' Selene braced herself for the thing that was going to ruin it all. He was too good to be true. There was bound to be a catch.

'How did you meet Tracy and Sandra?'

'Why?' Selene frowned suspicious.

'Because it's pretty obvious they're prostitutes and it's pretty obvious that you're a feminist academic. It's seems an unlikely friendship, that's all. Don't get me wrong. I'm not judging at all. I think Tracy is a cool woman and Sandra seemed really nice too in the pub the other night.'

Selene explained about the lesbian custody group meeting, and how she'd felt lonely and they'd gone for a drink and she just hit it off with the pair of them. 'In a way I've always felt like a bit of an outsider, and somehow they understood that without anybody having to say anything. I'm from a foreign family so I never fitted in well at school, and I've absolutely never fitted in my family. They're both really decent people and they're a laugh. Also, I suppose I must have some subconscious interest in prostitution. It seems to be becoming my life's work.'

Selene looked up into Jon's eyes to gauge his reaction. He kissed her and she reached beneath the sheets. When finally they slept, the morning sun slanted through the blinds and striped their entwined bodies in its amber glow.

♀

Twenty-three
Wednesday, 7ᵗʰ May

Selene found herself that morning in a state she had never before experienced, and guessed it was how people felt when they talked about falling in love. She'd spent the rest of the weekend with Jon and then waited for him to call. He did on Tuesday evening and they'd spent two hours talking on the phone until Jenny came into the hall huffing and puffing about 'communal living and consideration for others'. It was Selene's interview in the morning and Jon had been helping her to prepare and rehearse possible questions.

She couldn't tell now if the churning in her guts was at the prospect of the interview, or just a symptom of being in the throes of a new relationship. She'd lost her appetite and half a stone since Saturday. Her interview suit looked positively baggy and she decided to be a rebel and go in jeans. If they didn't like it they could screw themselves. She felt sure that she could find a taker for her work somewhere else.

Selene ate a slice of toast and drank a cup of black coffee. The house was silent and empty. Izzy was staying in London, getting her art show ready and the rest were all out at work. She decided to call Irina to arrange to visit after the interview. She hated going anywhere she might bump into Graham, but she could get there for three o'clock and leave before he came in from work.

Selene caught the bus on the main road and travelled into the city with the rest of the unemployed young mums with squalling kids and grannies on their way to buy a quarter of brisket from Woolworths. Selene had a warm smile for everyone today.

When she arrived she was ushered straight into the office where the same panel she'd met before sat in front of her, except this time they beamed winning smiles her way. Selene took them through a brief synopsis of her plans and the primary research she had lined up. They lapped it up, and this time no one mentioned the 1842 Mines Act. Selene restrained herself from pointing out that this piece of legislation was itself responsible for thousands of destitute women turning to prostitution. After thirty minutes of discussion on the practical and ethical concerns around the proposal, they asked Selene to wait outside whilst they conferred.

Ten minutes later she was offered a research fellowship with a generous grant, and a small salary in exchange for six hours of lecturing and tutorials each week. This time she wanted it. They shook hands, and Selene could have fairly skipped down the stairs as she left. Then she thought about Sandra lying in the hospital with her head smashed and a moment of doubt crept in. Was she really doing something worthwhile that would help women and reveal important depths about their lives, or was she using them to show how clever she was? She'd better make damned sure she did a good job, because now it was about real people who she cared about, not long dead whores in a dim and sepia past.

Irina looked awful. She opened the door in nightclothes and slippers. The curtains were drawn against the sun and the television was on in the living room. 'I'm just watching House-party. Put the kettle on.'

Selene went into the kitchen. It was clinically spotless and stank of bleach as usual. Taking care not to spill anything or make a mess, she made two mugs of tea and went through to the living room. Irina never looked up from the television set. Selene could have wept to see her like this. 'Alright, Sis,' she said rubbing Irina's arm.

'Ssh. Mary's got a personal alarm,' Irina said.

Selene decided to just watch, since it was clear that Irina wasn't going to be able to talk until this was over. In the TV show, Mary had produced a portable alarm and was expounding the benefits of being able to scare off would-be attackers. The other women cooed and nodded sagely at each other. 'It gives out eighty decibels,' Mary said.

'Umm, incredible,' said a woman in a pink blouson. 'Now tell me, what is a decibel?'

Selene chortled with laughter but Irina's eyes never left the screen. When it was over, Selene stood up and switched the television off. Irina looked at Selene as if seeing her for the first time. 'Why aren't you dressed sweetie?' Selene asked. 'Are you feeling poorly?'

'No, I'm fine. Sorry, I just got involved in the telly and forgot the time.' Irina went upstairs to change.

Selene picked up the wedding photo on the mantelpiece. The two mismatched families: Graham's great horde of relatives to the left, all smiles and rambunctiousness in their wedding outfits; and, unsmiling and stiff, just Selene and their mum and dad to the right. Next, she picked up the shot of the couple alone. Graham's hand under Irina's arm as if steadying her and his eyes, black as jet, shining into the camera. Irina's expression was unreadable.

'I thought about a new dinner service. I've seen some lovely plates with a red and gold edge that Mum'd love.' Irina came back into the room.

'Yes, it's a good idea. You're much better at that stuff than me. Can you get it and take it over to them, though?'

'Graham's already offered to do any running about needed for the do. He's been ever-so good. He won't let me go anywhere alone these days. He even waited the other day while I was in the hairdressers. Silly so-and-so, he dotes on me.'

'That's nice,' Selene said without feeling.

Irina appeared not to notice. 'Well you can't be too careful. What with this maniac about. He's even killed a decent girl, they say in the papers— but you can't be sure.'

'Can't be sure of what?'

'Can't be sure she was a decent girl—I mean, out in the middle of the night. What woman goes out alone in the middle of the night?'

'Any woman. Me, for example—people who work late, go to parties, can't sleep, like the moonlight. Anyway, why can't prostitutes be decent women for God's sake?' Selene couldn't suppress her anger at her sister's attitude.

'Oh don't get all political on me. Graham says—'

'Graham says what?' Graham said then. They hadn't heard him come in.

'Oh, we were just talking about the murders. I was saying you thought the student girl in the papers probably was one of them, but they were sparing the family's feelings.'

'Oh aye. No nice girl would be out walking t'streets in't middle o' the night.'

'So are you saying that prostitutes are asking for murder and mutilation?' Selene was horrified.

Graham smiled. 'Those old bags know the risks they take. They're like murderers 'emselves, spreading diseases.' Since he'd done the last whore he'd had stinging whenever he peed. He was sure he'd got a dose of something.

'That's a ridiculous comparison. And nobody should have to risk being murdered trying to pay their rent or look after their kids.'

Graham ignored Selene and turned to Irina. 'Got a fella comin' to have a look at car. I can get hold o' that Volvo t'morrow if he buys it. I'm goin' to gi' it a quick onceover.'

'I'm just leaving anyway. A good friend of mine's been attacked—a prostitute as it happens, and I'm going to visit her in hospital.' Angry, Selene spoke before she'd thought it through.

'A prostitute?' Irina stared at her sister in disbelief.

'Oh aye, and when did this happen?' Graham asked trying to sound nonchalant. He'd been scouring the press for information about his latest victim. When he'd found nothing he'd hoped that the body hadn't been found. The wound in his arm throbbed, reminding him of his panic-forced mistake.

'Last Thursday night.' Selene stared directly into Graham's dead eyes.

'You should watch the company you keep. Folk could get the wrong idea about you.' Graham kept the nasty little smile on his lips. He quickly tried to calculate the risks he ran if this 'friend' of his cunt sister-in-law was the bitch who'd cut his arm.

'That's why I'm leaving, Graham,' Selene countered.

'Don't squabble you two,' Irina said, eager to reframe their intense loathing as a family tiff.

'I'm teasin'. C'mon, don't be like that. Gi' us half an hour an' I'll gi' you lift t' hospital.' Graham realised he could do with finding out exactly what had happened.

'That's right, Selene, he's always winding people up. Take no notice o' the silly beggar.' Irina looked indulgently at her husband.

This was how Graham always behaved around Selene. He insulted her and then pretended it was all a laugh. If she didn't give in, it made her the miserable bitch who couldn't take a joke. She smiled and said: 'Yeah right, I need to go now though. Thanks for the offer.' The thought of being in a car alone with him gave her the creeps.

The doorbell rang and Graham went to answer it. They heard him greet the man who'd come to look at the car. Selene rifled through her bag and found her purse. She handed twenty pounds to Irina. 'The dinner service,' she said. She pecked Irina on the cheek. 'Take care. I'll give you a call soon.' Then she stopped. 'I thought Graham loved that car. You said he'd spent a fortune tinkering with it. Why's he suddenly selling it?'

'Oh, I don't know. He said he's fed up with it and fancies a change. You know what men are like with cars.'

'It's funny you know, I could have sworn I saw his car last Thursday night in the centre of Bradford. Could it have been him? Just that the police are questioning everybody and I wondered if you'd been bothered.' Selene hadn't been able to find a more subtle way to ask. She'd almost decided to leave it but somehow she couldn't, even if it meant upsetting Irina.

Irina thought back. 'Thursday,' she frowned. 'That was the night he'd been out with Derek and came home plastered. He was that drunk he cut his arm open climbing into the loft. It could have been him I suppose. He would've given Derek a lift home. We haven't had any police here though. I'd be able to tell them he was too drunk to stand, let alone murder anybody,' she laughed.

'Oh well, that's good.' Selene smiled and nodded conspiratorial. 'Don't tell him I asked. I don't want him to think I'm checking up on him.' She knew that Irina wouldn't want to exacerbate the antipathy that already existed between them.

'He's a good man really,' Irina said. 'He just can't hold his drink.'

As Selene saw herself out, she heard Irina switch the television back on.

'It's a lovely clean car,' the man in the front seat of the Capri was saying as she passed.

' 'Bye,' she said to Graham. He nodded his head once and now the false smile he wore for Irina's benefit had disappeared.

Graham had in fact been questioned by the police at the yard where he worked. Wherever feasible, the police preferred to eliminate men without alerting their wives to the possibility that they used prostitutes. He told them he'd been for a drink with his mate Derek and then gone straight home. The red light district, where his car had been logged, was on the way. Derek had confirmed the story. They'd had a pint together after working on a late order.

'Will your wife be able to confirm this?' the constable had asked Graham.

'Definitely,' he'd replied with a wink, inferring that they'd had sex. Underneath his shirt the wound in his arm throbbed rhythmically.

155

'Ah, I see. Like that is it? I'll leave you to it then.' The constable pocketed his notebook with a knowing smirk.

♀

Twenty-four
Saturday, 31st May

'Sure you're gunna be alright on yer own?' Tracy was uncertain about leaving Sandra alone in the flat for any length of time. She'd been home a week and still hadn't been out. Tracy had popped out to the shops a few times but she'd made sure to be back within half an hour. Vince had been to stay, and in spite of the warm weather they'd stayed in and played Monopoly to the point of exhaustion. They'd tried Cluedo as well, but gave up when Sandra carefully examined all the tiny weapons in a kind of trance.

Today, Tracy waited for Jon to pick her up to start giving her driving lessons. Since Sandra had been attacked, both he and Selene had been rocks that Tracy held fast to. Jon had driven her back and forwards to the hospital and Selene had been like a big sister, looking out for her and giving sound advice but not taking any nonsense. When Tracy fell into self-recrimination, Selene threw down the road-block of personal choice. When she drifted into hopeless depression, Selene reminded her that Sandra was alive and needed her to be strong. She'd opened her heart to them both about her life and her fears, and the pressing need to find a way to earn money. She was pretty sure that the mad 'on the game' existence that she and Sandra shared had long-since passed its highpoint. That's how the driving lessons had come up. She could definitely see herself taxi or delivery driving and Jon had volunteered to get her started.

'I'll be fine. You go,' Sandra said.

'I'll only be a couple of hours. We're gunna drive out somewhere quiet in the countryside to start off with.'

'Somewhere quiet in the countryside,' Sandra repeated, deep in thought. She was sat in front of the dressing-table mirror just staring. Something was different. Her hair was gone. They'd shaved her head for the surgery and a sand-coloured film of re-growth now covered her skull. But that wasn't it. There was something different that wasn't visible. She touched the scar on the crown of her head.

Tracy came up behind her and, leaning down, gently kissed the reddened ridge of flesh and said: 'You are more beautiful than ever, d'you know that?'

'Don't be stupid. Look at me, for God's sake.'

'I am looking at you and I mean it.' Tracy held her ground. 'When you had all that hair it hid your face. You were always beautiful, now you take my breath away every time I look at you.'

Sandra took Tracy's hand and kissed her palm. A tear dripped onto her wrist. 'It'll be alright, won't it?' she said.

'Of course it will, babe. I'm gunna get a job. We're gunna have Vince back with us soon and we'll have a nice life like we said. We'll be a little family, just us.'

There was a tap at the door. 'You certain it's okay?' Tracy checked again.

'Just get some ciggies on yer travels.' Sandra tried to smile reassurance.

Tracy kissed her head again and went to answer the door.

Selene scrutinised herself before the full-length mirror. She was wearing a floor-length halter neck cotton-print dress and hippie sandals. She liked what she saw. She felt good about herself and she was happier than she could ever remember. This was the first weekend she hadn't spent with Jon since they'd met a month ago. She was going to her parents' fortieth wedding anniversary party, and she wasn't ready yet to expose Jon to her family. He'd offered to come, and part of her wanted to say yes, but she also knew that her mother would badger him about marriage and her father would look down his nose at Jon's long hair and 'freelance' status. She just couldn't bear to have her life judged by them.

Her work was going well. She'd spent a lot of time with Tracy and Sandra recording conversations and allowing her thesis ideas to develop and mature. They'd both endured predictably terrible lives, and at times she'd had to swallow back outrage and horror because they regarded it all as normal. Her middle-class indignation served no one, so she listened and occasionally interjected to clarify. 'You were how old when that happened?' 'Did you go to the police?' 'How do you think that affected you psychologically?' She'd had tears in her eyes at times from both crushing sorrow and uncontrollable laughter. They had an inimitable way of turning even the most appalling events into an absolute scream. The attack on Sandra had given her the opportunity to have unrestricted time with the pair of them. Sandra had suggested it. She wasn't going out just yet and was glad of the chance to talk things through. This was a time of change for them and Selene could see they were benefitting from speaking about their past.

They'd also spent a lot of time talking about the future: what Sandra and Tracy would do to earn a living; how they would get Vincent back. And her own thoughts about Jon. She was trying not to rush things. She was crazy about him and she was pretty sure the feeling was mutual. Tracy thought he was great and that she should just get on with it and stop worrying. Sandra was more circumspect. She could see why Selene was being careful. She liked Jon and could see he was a great match for Selene, but relationships needed a lot of thought, and anyway, why not enjoy just hanging out like teenagers? There was no need to start making commitments.

Selene hung a Celtic silver-moon pendant around her neck. It sat perfectly on her collarbones. Jon had given it to her the previous evening. He said he just wanted to buy her something and he'd remembered that Selene was Goddess of the Moon. It was the first time that she'd been given a gift by a man that she actually liked.

'Selene,' Izzy called up the stairs. 'Your taxi's here.'

Selene grabbed her patchwork shoulder bag and went downstairs.

'Are you coming back tonight?' asked Izzy.

'Yeah, definitely. I won't be late. Are you going to be in the pub?'

'Yeah, if you are. I feel like I haven't seen you for ages, what with your new job and a new bloke.'

'I'll be home by nine at the latest. We can catch up then.'

'Good one, mate. See you there.'

Selene gave the cabbie the address of the Polish club in Bradford and screwed her courage to the sticking post. This entire thing would be an ordeal but one that must be borne.

When she arrived, her mother immediately began dragging her around a lot of elderly people Selene only vaguely knew, introducing her as 'my daughter, the professor'. Selene had gone beyond the point of contradicting her mother, since her wild exaggerations held little or no meaning for anyone else. Some of the people to whom she was introduced spoke only scant English in any case. Selene smiled and nodded politely. Her father wore his usual scowl of disapproval. She made her way across the hall to greet him.

'Hi, Dad. How's it going?' Selene kissed her father on both cheeks.

'Better now that you're here my dear girl. I can't stand these events. It's only for your mother's sake. She likes to show off as you know.' Jakub Bartowski had retained a thick Polish accent in spite of living in England for more than thirty years.

'Yes, well let's all put a brave face on it.'

'You've got a post at last, I hear.'

'Yes, it's going very well. I'm starting my research, and I'll begin a little teaching and tutoring when the new academic year starts in October. I think I'll enjoy it.'

'Well done. I'm very pleased. You've worked hard and you deserve success. You'll be the one to carry the family honour.'

Selene did not reply. Whenever her father mentioned the family honour it usually preceded a lengthy diatribe on the disappointments life had dealt him. 'Shall I get you a refill?' She took his empty glass from his hand and went to the bar. As she returned she noticed that Graham was talking to her father. She did a body-swerve into her Aunt Anka in an effort to avoid him but her father had seen her approaching and beckoned her over.

'I was just telling Graham here that you have a post at the university.'

'Yes, I'll be doing some research.' Selene would have to have this conversation about thirty times this afternoon and she certainly didn't feel like having it with Graham.

'Research about what?' Graham swigged from his pint of beer.

Selene was on the point of lying but said: 'It's about the lives of prostitutes, and the relationship of prostitution to patriarchal society.'

Graham spat his beer back into his glass. 'Pastry what society?' He laughed. 'What's to research about them mucky tarts?'

'Patriarchal—it means male dominated. And them 'mucky tarts', as you say, have productive and important lives. I'll be arguing for the complete legalisation of prostitution and total autonomy for women who choose that life to manage their own business affairs.' Selene's reply was curt and her father shot her a look of disapproval.

'For the lips of an immoral woman drip honey, and her mouth is smoother than oil; but in the end she is bitter as wormwood, sharp as a two-edged sword. Her feet go down to death, her steps lay hold of Hell. That's what The Bible says,' Graham said smugly, his eyes penetrating Selene with sheer hatred.

'Wow. That's some quote. You've clearly got an interest in the subject. I didn't realise you were a Christian. How long's that been?'

'Selene,' interrupted Jakub, pointing a warning finger at his daughter. 'That's enough of religion and politics. This is your mother's day.'

'Aye well I don't go to church or owt, but I know God's will when it comes to them old bags.' Graham couldn't resist the last word. He turned to beam at Jakub. 'Have you managed to get down to the cricket, Dad?'

'I'm going to find Irina.' Selene walked away.

Her sister was in the kitchen washing glasses. 'These are already clean,' Selene said, holding a glass up to the light.

'They're disgusting. Mine had a dirty smudge of lipstick. I don't want Mum and Dad's guests drinking out of dirty glasses,' Irina admonished. 'Anyway, if you want to be helpful, dry up.'

Selene took up a tea towel and did as instructed. She spent the rest of the afternoon being polite to people with a plate of hors d'oeuvres in one hand. When she saw she'd been seated next to Irina and Graham for the sit-down meal she surreptitiously swapped her name plate. She couldn't tolerate another exchange with Graham. The rest of the day, boring though it was, passed without incident. The mostly elderly guests began to drift away shortly after the meal had finished. By eight o'clock Selene, Irina and her mother had tidied the room, and her father and Graham had stacked the chairs. Selene went gratefully to call a cab.

'No, don't be daft,' Irina called when she saw Selene pick up the phone. 'Graham's taking us all home in the new car. He's got a great big Volvo now,' she said and raised her eyebrows.

'No, it's out of his way. Honestly, I'll have a cab here in—'

Graham took the phone from Selene's hand and smiled. 'If I can't take my own sister-in-law home it's a poor show,' he said. 'Besides, I want to show off my new motor.'

'Come along, Selene. We're not leaving you here waiting for a cab and I promised I'd lock the hall.' Beata Bartowski was busy herding the group through the front door as she spoke.

Selene climbed reluctantly into the backseat with her parents. She prayed he'd drop her off first. He didn't. First he dropped Jakub and Beata at the end of their cul-de-sac, and then he headed for his own home.

'Look, you don't have to drag all the way over to Leeds. I can get a cab from here.'

'No you won't, it'll cost a fortune,' Irina said, leaning over to kiss Selene goodbye.

'No trouble at all. I fancy a spin out in't motor anyway.' Graham smiled. 'Hop in't front seat.'

Selene had no choice but to accept. Graham spent the thirty-minute journey chatting amiably enough about engines, and the laziness of his colleagues at the yard who failed to complete the appropriate forms when filling orders. Selene was only required to nod and utter agreement every so often. She stared out of the passenger window.

'It's got four speakers as well.'

'Uh. What has?' said Selene.

'New motor.' He keyed the cassette-player on. "The Boxer" by Simon and Garfunkel came on halfway through, and Selene decided she preferred listening to Graham droning along with the endless *lie-la-lie* bit than listening to him talking. He took her to her door and insisted on waiting until she'd successfully opened it before leaving.

'Can't be too careful these days. Good luck wi' new job,' Graham shouted from the car with that small, empty smile playing on his lips.

Selene watched him go. A frown wrinkled her brow as she saw him indicate to turn right. He'd need to turn left to go home. A right turn took him into the city. She frowned. Maybe he was just going for a drink.

♀

Twenty-five
31st May

Reeva groaned inwardly as another hugely obese patient was wheeled onto the ward. She'd painfully pulled her back trying to give a bed bath to a thirty-stone man last week, and it was still giving her gyp. She should have been home by now, but the night nurse who took over at eight pm had called in sick and she'd had to hang on for relief to arrive. It was half-past nine now, and still no sign of any agency staff. She'd have to phone home and let her babysitter know she was going to be late. Levi answered after two rings.

'Where's Natalie, Son?' Reeva asked.

'Upstairs putting Desi to bed,' he shouted above the din of the television at what sounded like full volume.

'Turn that thing down and get Natalie.' Reeva didn't need any more nonsense today.

'Nat-a-lie,' she heard him bellow, 'it's Mum.'

Reeva heard the sound of Natalie galumphing downstairs. 'Hi, Reeva. Something up?'

'I'm waiting on someone from the agency before I can leave tonight. Can you hang on for a while? It shouldn't be much after ten.'

'No problem. Oh, by the way, Delmar came to see the kids earlier. That's why I'm so late getting Desi to bed. He'd brought loadsa sweeties and it's been murder gettin' them settled.'

'Oh, useless bloody man. Sorry he just turn up unannounced. Thanks honey. See ya later then.' Reeva shook her head in frustration. She was well beyond loving that man. He was the father of her children and he'd passed them his gorgeous bone structure and beautiful conker-brown skin, but that was about all he was ever going to do for them. Their top grades at school; Desi's award for ballet; Levi's piano certificates; and the fifty or so other achievement accolades they'd got plastered all over the kitchen walls: those were all down to her.

On a couple of occasions in the last year Delmar had come over and weakened her resistance with his charm and fine ganja. He'd even bought her the solid-silver nurse's belt-buckle she'd coveted for her birthday— though he'd then borrowed thirty pounds from her that she'd never seen again. Reeva was under no illusion that he was ever going to be any kind of proper father to her kids.

As she replaced the receiver, she spotted Sister Donovan coming down the corridor. 'You better get off, Reeva,' the sister said. 'I'll finish off the drug trolley rounds. It's all quiet on the skin ward.'

'Thanks, Sister. I was just speaking to my sitter. She's okay for another hour or so.'

'How are your two?'

'They're fine. Levi's gettin' a proper handful, he'll be eleven next month, and my Desi was eight last week. I just don't know where the years go.'

'Ah well, I don't envy you those teenage years you've got to look forward to.' Sister Donovan laughed. 'Off you go now. We'll manage here just fine.'

Reeva went to her locker and took out her coat and bag. She took off her belt and put her hands to the small of her back, stretching upwards to ease the ache developing there. She put her belt in her bag and set off for home. She'd be glad of her bed tonight, that was one thing for sure.

The twilight was just turning to dark as she left the hospital. The wind had got up and the sky was overcast with fast moving clouds intermittently exposing a near full-moon. Reeva quickened her step to catch the ten o'clock bus. When she looked behind, she saw the number thirty-two approaching and broke into a run. She was just yards from the stop and waving to the driver but he sailed on past without slowing down. He'd seen her alright. She knew that. If she was white he would've stopped. 'Bloodclaat,' she growled through gritted teeth. The next one would be ages

164

at this time of night. Reeva decided she'd be quicker walking. If she cut across Woodhouse Moor she'd be home before ten-thirty. She pulled her coat around her and stepped out.

◊◊◊◊◊

Graham was frustrated. He'd driven around the city for over an hour without seeing a woman alone. He couldn't go home. He wouldn't be answerable for what could happen if he did that. His cunt sister-in-law was responsible. She'd been winding him up all day. She thought she was somebody, better than him—with her clever words and her sarcastic remarks. He wanted to rip her open. He wanted to let all the poison and disease spill out of her filthy hole.

Graham's heart began to race and his breath quickened. He pulled over to the side of the road and let his head slump forward onto the steering wheel. He knew he needed to calm down, otherwise he'd make mistakes. He couldn't afford any more mistakes. He pushed his tape into the player and hummed along.

Then he looked up and there she was, as if by magic, just disappearing into the park. He jumped out and ran to the boot. He smiled as he picked up his hammer and chisel, a craftsman contemplating his work. He put them in his overall pockets, crossed the road and hurried through the park gates. The woman's course would take her diagonally across the open grass. He could scarcely believe his luck. This was definitely meant to be. He ran ahead with the wind at his heels. His heart pounded out a rhythm in tune with his exhilaration. 'Excuse me,' Graham called out to her as the woman reached a group of rhododendron bushes, their flowers drooping and brown. 'You've dropped something, miss.'

The woman turned around and Graham slowed to a walk as he approached her. 'I didn't mean to scare you, miss. It's this,' he said and smiled. He had taken the sharpened chisel from his pocket. He lunged forward and pushed it into her belly with all the force he could muster. The woman screamed and stumbled back as pain exploded in her guts. He put his hand over her mouth and gyrated the tool before withdrawing it and then stabbing her again. This time she fell moaning to the ground. Graham held his chisel, now dripping blood, in both hands and knelt down by her body. And then he raised the weapon with both hands and slammed it ferociously and repeatedly into her prone body. She had already been dead for several minutes when he used the bloodied chisel to penetrate her vagina. He'd never done it with a black woman before and the novelty intensified his excitement. He stood up when he'd finished and noticed that her eyes were open. 'Don't look at me you black cunt,' he said, and then took his hammer from his pocket and used it to obliterate her face. 'No mistakes this time,' he muttered to himself as he worked. When he was done, he took her huge handbag and emptied its contents onto the grass. The big silver belt-buckle caught his eye. He snatched it up and put it in his inside pocket.

Graham left her there on the open parkland next to the bushes and walked briskly back towards the main gate. There was no one in sight and he slowed his pace a little to enjoy the feeling of omnipotence that surged through his veins. He removed his overalls before leaving the park and wrapped his tools up inside them. When he got back to his car and gunned the engine his song picked up where he had left it. He sighed content, closed his eyes and listened for a moment. He'd given the world its saddest sound

♀

Twenty-six
Monday, 2nd June

The terrible suspicions opening up in Selene's head widened just a little further when she read the headlines in the papers on the following Monday morning. She regularly bought the Guardian, but today she picked up copies of the Mirror and the Sun as well. They all carried front-page news about the murders.

Manhunt as Possible Eighth Victim Discovered in Leeds Park', appeared beneath the Guardian's main headline about the UK economy sliding into recession.

The Sun and The Mirror both carried two-inch banners: BLACK NURSE BUTCHERED and MUM OF TWO FOUND SLAIN. Both tabloids referred to 'innocent victims' and relayed police advice to women to: Stay indoors at night unless accompanied by a trusted male'. The Sun carried a strapline: HAMMER MAN—reporting that the police believed the killer could be a craftsman of some kind on account of the tools he used.

'Some proper nutters about, I hope you girls are taking care,' the newsagent said as he rang up Selene's papers.

'Yeah, you're not kidding,' Selene replied, not bothering to take issue with the implication that women should be under curfew.

Selene took the newspapers home and read all the accounts over her first coffee of the day. Graham had been in Leeds on Saturday. Why did he head into the city centre? Selene decided to phone Irina. She would have to find a way to casually find out when he got home.

Irina answered almost immediately. 'Hello,' she said sounding nervous.

'Hi, it's me. Just wondering if you'd spoken to Mum and Dad? Did they enjoy the night?'

'No, I haven't spoken to them, but they seemed to. It all went off okay anyway. Why don't you give Mum a ring?'

'Yeah, I will do later. Did Graham get back okay?'

'Yes fine.'

'What time did he get in?'

'Oh, I've no idea. I went straight to bed and out like a light after all that Polish vodka.'

'Well, thank him for the lift. There was another one of those murders on Saturday you know.'

'Yes, I've got the paper in front of me. Terrible. Those poor children— and she was a nurse, they say. You don't feel safe in your own bed.'

'No, I know. Anyway, I'd better get off—I've got an appointment later.' Selene tried to make her arrangement to go to Tracy and Sandra's place sound more official than it was as a way of finishing the call.

'See you soon then,' Irina said and hung up.

Selene's doubts had in no way been allayed. She replayed Graham's biblical quote in her head. All she could remember was something like, 'her feet go down to death'. Goose flesh stood out on her arms as she recalled his face and his lips twisting around the words. She tried hard to separate the feelings of revulsion that she'd always held about Graham from these new fears. There must be loads of examples of people whose hatred of someone led to false accusations. The phone rang and interrupted her thoughts.

'Hiya. It's Tracy. Listen, mate—can we put it off till later in the week? Only Sandra's got one o' them fuckin' terrible headaches she's bin gettin'.'

'Yeah. No problem. Oh, bummer though, I hope she feels better soon. Give her my love.'

'Yeah, well we're going to the place they found her with Randall, one of the coppers on this murder case, tomorrow.'

'Is she ready for that?'

'I dunno. But to be honest I'd try anything to get her feeling right again. Maybe it'll loosen something up in her head. D'ya know what I mean?'

'Yeah. Yeah I do, but it could be really tough on her.'

'Well she wants to do it.' Tracy sighed. 'She's just trying to get the memory back all the time. She wants to nail that fucker.'

'Good for her. She's a courageous woman. Did you read about the woman on Saturday night by the way?'

'No. What? Has he done another one?'

'Yeah. In Leeds. She was found in Woodhouse Moor Park—a nurse apparently, two kids.'

'Oh fuck me. Somebody's gotta stop this fuckin' maniac. This is gunna set Sandra back.'

'I know. I thought that. Anyway, you get back to Sandra and I'll speak to you later.'

'Yeah. Give us a buzz on Wednesday or summat.' Tracy hung up.

Selene went back to her newspapers and her thoughts. The dregs of her coffee were bitter and cold. 'Hammer Man,' she thought. That's going to catch on.

A blinding whiteness—a lightning fork of black energy cracking through Sandra's skull. She sat shivering and drained, holding her head in her hands.

'Go to bed. I've drawn the curtains and made it all cosy in there.' Tracy knelt in front of Sandra with a damp flannel in her hand. She was finding it hard to cope with the fallout from the attack. The physical headaches she could handle, with a bit of love and the super-strong painkillers that Sandra had been prescribed. It was the weird empty bits that Tracy struggled with; when Sandra was just staring into space; the fear and fragility that seemed now to dominate her. She walked Sandra to the bedroom holding her arm and plumped the pillow ready as she lay down. 'There, darling, it'll be better soon,' she murmured.

Tracy went into the kitchen and popped two of Sandra's tablets out of their foil bubbles. She threw them onto the back of her tongue and washed them down with a slug of Johnnie Walker. Then she went to the bedroom and climbed into bed, wrapped her warm body around Sandra's back.

They woke up at half-past eight that evening. Sandra's headache was gone. Tracy told her the news about the latest victim. Sandra simply listened shaking her head. Then she closed her eyes and tears streamed down her face.

Tracy made egg sandwiches and they ate them watching "Minder".

Next morning, Randall and Hill woke them at ten-to-ten, hammering, as only police can, on their front door.

'We'll come down to the car in five,' Tracy said through the small crack she'd opened up in the door.

They threw on their jeans and T-shirts and splashed their faces with cold water. Sandra put on a huge pair of shades.

'How come you still look fuckin' glamorous at this hour of the mornin'? You haven't even brushed your teeth for fucks sake,' Tracy grumbled as she locked the flat door.

'Some people just have it,' Sandra quipped back.

'Get lost, bitch,' Tracy said relieved that the mood of the day was easy. There'd be enough shit to deal with if this little jaunt did dislodge anything for Sandra.

As they made their way across to where Randall and Hill were parked, Sandra noticed a council workman preparing to paint over the huge Condor that Rosie had painted on the night she died.

'Leave that alone,' she screamed. Randall and Hill both looked up. Sandra was running towards the man with the paintbrush.

'What the bloody hell are you on about,' the man said. 'It's first on me list today.' He fished his schedule from his overall pocket. Randall and Hill walked across to the bins.

'Somebody who died did that,' Sandra said turning to Randall. 'It was that skinny girl, Rosie. She did it the night she died.'

'Really,' Randall's interest was piqued. 'How do you know?'

'We spoke to her fella a coupla days after. Look she signed it,' Tracy said pointing to the R4/4 at the corner of the work.

'That'd explain the black paint.' Randall addressed Hill. 'Leave this for the time being, please,' he said flashing his badge at the council workman.

'All the same t'me, but I'll have to get you to sign my job sheet. It's more'n my job's worth.'

Hill scribbled something on the man's piece of paper as he packed up his brushes and paint.

Tracy and Sandra climbed into the back of the unmarked Ford Granada. Tracy was glad they'd come in an unmarked car. It showed a bit of respect. Hill drove at breakneck speed while Randall turned and asked Sandra questions about her recovery. Tracy hadn't forgotten the way he'd stood up for her at the hospital. That was decent of him. She still wanted to smash her fist into the side of Hill's smug bastard face though.

'Glad to see your hair's growing back Sandra. It actually suits you short like that,' Randall said quite genuinely.

'Yeah, well I didn't have much choice, did I?' she replied, watching as the city dwindled to countryside.

After fifteen minutes or so, Hill indicated left and turned into a rutted country lane. They drew to a stop about a hundred yards along. Tracy took Sandra's hand and squeezed it tight. Sandra had lost her earlier sassy *joie de vivre*. They all climbed out of the car.

'This is just about it.' Randall indicated a ditch at one side of the road, by now overgrown with vetch and meadow grass. Sandra silently stared into it. She closed her eyes. Nothing.

'We think this is where a struggle of some sort took place,' Randall said, pointing to the dusty gravel. Forensics had found tyre tracks, boot prints and a fair bit of blood, but none of it had produced any leads. He kept this to himself, not wanting to provoke Tracy's animosity and distrust of the police and their abilities.

Sandra still felt nothing. A border collie came racing along the lane barking. Tracy flinched and moved to one side. She didn't trust dogs.

'Tonto. Pack that up,' Bert Jacobs shouted as he limped at a pace down the lane.

'Good morning, Mr Jacobs. This is the young lady whose life you may have saved,' Randall said.

'It were nowt t'do wi' me. It were postman seen her first. How are ye now, love?' Bert said, his compassion clear.

'I'm gettin' there, thanks,' Sandra replied.

'Well you certainly knew your first aid, Mr Jacobs. One of the paramedics on the scene mentioned it,' Randall persisted.

'Oh aye, you were poorly when we found you,' Bert said to Sandra.

'I don't remember owt about it,' Sandra explained.

'Happen that's best?' Bert suggested.

'Well yeah, but I want to be able to identify the man who did this to me before he does it to anybody else.'

'You're a brave girl,' Bert said. 'Fancy a brew?'

They followed Bert down to the farmhouse. Tonto trotted alongside licking Sandra's hand.

'He's fond o' you. It were 'im that found you really. He were barking in't night. Woke me up, he did. And the state of 'im that mornin'. He'd bin keeping you company alright.' Bert gave Tonto a rough ear scratching.

'Glad somebody was looking after me,' Sandra said. Tracy scratched Tonto's other ear. Maybe dogs weren't so bad after all.

'Have you noticed any other people or strange vehicles in the lane since the incident, Mr Jacobs?' queried Randall.

'It's quite usual for perpetrators to revisit crime scenes,' Hill said trying to impress his boss.

'No nowt. I'm not always here, mind you. Milk and sugar?'

They gave their orders for the strong tea Bert was brewing in the pot. He took a leather tobacco-pouch down from the mantelpiece and started rolling a cigarette. 'Any chance I can pinch one o' them from yuh?' Tracy said picking up the pouch.

'Aye love, sorry, I didn't realise lasses smoked roll-ups.'

'They do these days, Mr Jacobs.'

'Call me Bert,' he said.

'Tracy,' she held out her hand and Bert shook it. 'And this is Sandra.'

'Aye, I know your name, love. I asked after you at t'hospital later in't week.'

Sandra smiled warmly at Bert. She was trying hard to get pictures in her mind but nothing came.

'It might help if you'd go through exactly what happened that night and morning as you recall it,' Randall prompted Bert.

Bert began with when he'd gone to bed that night and finished with the ambulance pulling away with Sandra inside it the following morning. She could imagine the scene Bert described but it wasn't a memory.

'We think it likely that the attacker was frightened off when your downstairs lights came on,' Randall said.

'Well I'm awful glad summat good's come from my bad back,' Bert said. 'Can you remember nowt love?' he turned to Sandra.

'Nothing. It's just a blank.'

'Well, you come back here anytime you like, aye and bring yer pal.' Bert patted the back of Sandra's hand. 'I'm right glad you've pulled through. I shouldn't o' liked the thought on it if not.'

♀

172

Twenty-seven
Friday, 6th June

Sandra had agreed to do the first of several in-depth interviews for Selene's PhD dissertation and Selene had arrived at noon with her tape machine and notebook at the ready. The pair spent the afternoon locked in an intimate exchange about women, rape, prostitution, feminism, childhood, relationships and money. Sandra was in possession of a deep sense of philosophy born of experience that astounded Selene the more as she got to know her. She'd run away from home at fifteen with a ten-shilling note in her pocket. No one came to look for her or even reported her missing. She'd known that they wouldn't. Her father was a brutal drunk who'd driven her mother to an early grave and her step-mother loathed her. Selene suspected sexual abuse, but Sandra didn't seem ready to talk about that and Selene didn't want to push it. Her tape ran out after ninety minutes but she was so engrossed in the discussion that she didn't even notice. She'd have the salient bits in her memory anyway.

Tracy had gone out with Jon for another driving lesson. He was impressed with how quickly she picked things up, though getting her to stay within the speed limit seemed impossible. Tracy loved the feeling of control she got from being behind the wheel, and the sense of possibility and escape. She could be hundreds of miles away in a few hours.

'How's it goin' then with you two?' Tracy asked as she sped along the dual carriageway.

'Yeah, good. I'm really hoping she feels the same as me, otherwise I'm screwed.'

'Oh I think she does, man. I don't know her that well but I don't think she's had much luck with fellas, so she might just be a bit wary.'

'She can take all the time she needs. I just enjoy being near her.'

'Yeah, I know how that feels.'

'You really care for Sandra. I can see that. How's she doing after all that shit?'

'It's tough. I'm trying to be there for her—you know what I mean? But it's hard to cope with. I just want a fuckin' time-machine and make it never happen.'

'Start changing down approaching the roundabout,' Jon said.

Tracy shifted easily through the gear changes. 'Listen, are you two busy tonight?'

'No plans. Why?'

'Just that I'd like to get Sandra out of the flat and I was gunna suggest goin' for a curry. I just think it'd be easier for her if we were mob handed like.'

'Sounds like a plan. Let's run it up the flagpole when we get back.'

When they opened the flat door all they could hear was the sound of Sandra and Selene howling with laughter. 'What's the crack?' asked Tracy.

'I was just tellin' Selene about that punter that fell in the—' Sandra couldn't finish her sentence for laughing. Selene was rolling around on the sofa clutching her sides.

Tracy turned to Jon. 'Oh yeah. This really posh geezer parked his car right next to a ditch with a stream in it and he wanted to get out and do it in the back seat. He just opened his door and disappeared. Daft bastard sprained his ankle.'

'Well if you don't look where you're parking...' Jon felt slightly awkward. This was the first time that what Sandra and Tracy did for a living had been talked about openly in his presence.

Sandra and Selene wiped their eyes and started to pull themselves together. 'I'll put the kettle on,' Sandra said.

'Bollocks to that. It's Friday night. Let's have a proper drink.' Tracy looked at Jon.

'I'd love one. Ta,' he said.

'Good idea,' confirmed Selene.

Sandra went to the kitchen and came back with four bottles of Pilsner. Jon started skinning up a joint as they swapped stories of their respective afternoons.

'You'll be ready for the test before autumn,' Jon said.

'Really?' said Tracy.

'No doubt about it. You're a fast learner and you'll be a great driver.'

Tracy glowed with pride and embarrassment. Nobody had ever said she was good at anything before. Jon handed her the joint and she took a deep drag.

'Oi! Give us a go on that,' said Sandra.

'I thought you were leavin' it out for a bit,' Tracy said as she passed it over.

'Yeah, well—I just feel like it tonight.'

'Go for it,' Jon said, already sticking the papers together for another.

Selene was less certain. 'Are you sure? If you haven't since...'

'No honest, it can't do any harm and it might do me some good. I've bin like a bleedin' cat on a hot tin roof. It might help me to relax.'

'It's not too strong, just a bit of home-grown,' Jon reassured Selene.

They drank and smoked and giggled their way through the next hour.

'How about going out for a curry? We haven't done that for ages.' Tracy decided to chance her suggestion with Sandra.

'What about my hair?' Sandra suddenly looked crestfallen and reached up to her head.

'You look stunning,' said Selene. 'It just looks really modern and funky. I mean it.'

'Yeah,' Jon added. 'It looks amazing—just like Mia Farrow.'

'Now you're takin' the piss,' Sandra said.

'I'm not, honestly,' Jon pleaded.

'He's not, darlin'. I keep tellin' yer you're beautiful. C'mon, let's go out. It'd make a change,' Tracy cajoled.

'Awright—just let me put a bit o' lippy on then.'

Sandra went into the bedroom. Tracy silently held up two crossed fingers to Jon and Selene and grinned like a Cheshire cat.

Sandra came back after a minute. 'Can't find me lippy anywhere.'

'Try mine,' Selene dug through her bag and handed Sandra her L'Oreal 'Champagne'.

'Not my colour but I'll give it a go.' Sandra stood in front of the mirror and applied the lipstick. 'Not bad, actually,' she said.

'Yeah, it suits,' Selene agreed. 'Give me a bit to put on now—then you keep it. I've got another at home.'

'Thanks, you sure?'

'Absolutely.'

'C'mon then, I'm starvin',' Sandra said. She could feel the synapses in her brain connecting. The smoke had done her good and the warm summer evening felt full of possibility. 'I've got something to show you,' she announced when they were outside. She led the party across the shabby grass to the bins. Something was shifting in her head. Maybe it was the dope and the beer; maybe it was all the talk with Selene of things that she'd never really thought about before, or maybe it was the visit to 'crime scene earlier in the week. But there was an opening, like a 'tip of the tongue' sensation. She put her finger and thumb into the corners of her eyes and blinked, trying to loosen the thoughts. The feeling passed.

'One of the murder victims done that the night she died,' said Sandra. And then she and Tracy between them related the story of Sandra's dream, and how she identified the bird at the party in one of Izzy's reference books; and about their meeting with James. Tracy showed them Rosie's signature.

'She was a fantastic artist,' Jon said, stepping back to take in the gigantic graffiti. He had to stand twenty-foot away with his back to the fence of the bin area to take in its dimensions. It was swooping, claws fully extended to seize its prey.

'Wow. I'd like to show Izzy that. What a terrible loss of such a great talent,' Selene agreed. 'But it's weird—the dream and the connection with this painting. Is that why you're so sure that it was him?'

'Sort of, but it's more than that. I just know, that's all I can say.' Sandra's frustration was palpable. 'Jon. Would you do something for me before we eat?'

'Name it.'

'Will you take me back to the place where they found me again?'

'Sure, show me the way.'

'Do you really wanna do this, babe?' Tracy held Sandra's arm and looked into her face. 'Nothing happened when we went on Tuesday.'

'Really, I do. I feel different today. Please, let's just do it.'

'If you're sure, babe,' said Tracy. 'Can I drive? I know where it is.' Jon threw her the keys and climbed in the passenger seat. Selene wore her worried frown.

They drove with all the windows open in the warm breeze singing along to Echo Beach on the radio. The mood had lightened, and they might have been any bunch of hipsters 'faraway in time'. Tracy had to brake hard when she saw the lane turning coming up fast. 'Sorry,' she said. 'Didn't realise it was this soon.'

Sandra grabbed hold of Selene's hand and squeezed tight. A jolt of flashback went through her electric. Yet it still wasn't a solid memory.

'You okay?' asked Selene.

'Don't know, just a weird feeling.'

'You don't have to do this, Sandra.' Selene had a knot of empathetic fear in her stomach.

Tracy pulled to the side of the lane. They got out and wandered aimlessly around kicking at the gravel. 'Is that the farmhouse where the lights came on?' Selene asked, shielding her eyes from the low, evening sun.

'Yeah. His jeep's not there—looks like the old boy's out,' replied Tracy. 'Nice old fella.'

Sandra had walked away from the other three up the lane, and now a sickening feeling of the ground coming up to meet her made her sway and hold her head. It felt as if, if she could hold her brain still for long enough the memory would come back. Tracy was at her side in an instant.

'What's up, babe?'

'No nothing. It's okay—just a weird sensation, as if I was falling to the ground.'

Tracy put her arm around Sandra's shoulders. 'C'mon, let's get out of here,' she said.

'No. Just a bit longer. Please—I can feel something about this exact spot.' She stood at the place where Randall had said a scuffle might have taken place.

Selene joined the other two women. 'Is there something, Sandra?' She took her arm and both she and Tracy leaned in, staring deep into Sandra's eyes.

'It's like a black shape at the edge of my vision. I just can't bring it into focus.'

They stood like this for more than a minute. Jon watched them leaning against the car. 'When shall we three meet again', he thought—but thought better of actually saying for fear of making too light of such a solemn situation.

Sandra closed her eyes and took a deep breath. 'Okay, I'm not getting it. Let's go and eat something. Everybody must be ravenous,' she said.

They climbed back into the car. This time Jon drove and Tracy got in the back with Sandra and held her close.

Sandra had recovered her equilibrium by the time they'd eaten, and she'd surprised herself at how unselfconscious she felt with her new-look hair. Tracy relaxed enough to start calling it her prison haircut. It was still only ten o'clock when they called for the bill and Jon invited them back to his flat for a nightcap.

'Yeah, that'd be really nice. If you two lovebirds don't want to be alone,' Sandra said.

'Don't be daft—we've got the whole weekend anyway,' Selene said, reddening.

They piled back to Jon's flat, full of Biryani and chapattis.

'I've still got an unopened bottle of single malt from last Christmas if anybody's interested in that,' Jon ventured.

'Oh, now let me see,' Sandra teased. 'That's going to be a really tough one for Tracy.'

'I'll fix it. Jon, you put some music on,' said Selene.

Tracy picked a record sleeve at random from the huge pile stacked against the wall and settled to rolling a joint while Jon leafed through the stack of albums next to the stereo. 'Any requests?' he asked.

'No, you choose.' Sandra still had a sense of something peripheral, just out of sight, but she didn't want to take up any more of the evening with her stuff. Tracy was laid back for the first time in ages, and any more talk of the attack would just send her back to her angry place.

Jon put on 'London Calling' by the Clash.

'Brilliant, love this,' Selene said coming into the living room with four tots of whisky in her hands.

'Not sure about all this punk stuff,' Tracy said. 'Some of it just sounds like a fuckin' racket. This is alright though—I like the Clash.' She'd finished making her joint and she scraped the detritus into the ashtray and put the record sleeve to one side. Sandra picked it up. She examined the two men on the cover: one short in a scarf and cardigan, the other taller and peering above his partner's head. Sandra traced the outline of Art Garfunkel's hair with her finger, and then she turned the album sleeve over and read the track list. She felt a million miles away, as if she was completely alone and sounds in the real world were muffled and indistinct—like people were talking in another room and she was a child drifting into sleep. The other three were engaged in a discussion of the relative merits of John Lydon's new band PiL.

'He's made a good move with Jah Wobble as—' Jon was saying when Sandra interrupted him.

'Play "El Condor Pasa".' She felt like she was moving through water as she handed him the sleeve. Jon lifted the stylus from 'Brand New Cadillac' without a question.

Selene looked quizzical. 'What is it, Sandra?' she said.

The stylus clunked down into the groove and they all listened. As the trembling opening notes played, Sandra felt the hair on her neck and arms stand frozen. The watery distance she'd felt disappeared, replaced with just a memory, clear and solid and completely terrifying. 'This was on in his car.' The chilling sense she had took form and jolted her back into the room. 'He was messin' with the cassette to get it to come on and I knew it was him. I knew it as clear as I'm sitting here. I knew it was him. It's the Condor, that fuckin' horrible bird from my dream—like what was in the book, and what Rosie drew on the wall.'

They all stared at her. Selene spoke first. 'Do you remember everything Sandra?' She was afraid for her friend.

Sandra nodded slowly. Tracy knocked her drink back in one gulp.

'He's got short black hair, almost shaved at the back, and horrible little dead eyes. His breath smelt of fish-paste and chewing gum. He was wearing blue overalls. Average build and height but really fuckin' strong.' Sandra's hand went to her mouth as the flood of memory began to overwhelm her.

'What type of car was it, did you see that?' said Jon. There was a sense of urgency now; as if, if they didn't get it all out here the chance would be gone forever.'

'It was a Capri, I think. I'm not sure what colour.'

'Give me that sleeve,' Selene said, pointing to the "Bridge Over Troubled Water" album as the dawning horror of her worst suspicions solidified. She glanced down the track list on the back. 'This is my brother-in-law Graham's favourite. You know, the one I've told you about,' she said to Jon. 'I was sure I'd seen his car the night you got attacked, Sandra. D'you remember, after we'd been in The Beehive, I got a cab and I saw his car go by on the other side of the road? Only I couldn't be sure it was him. He's got this cassette in his car. I know he has because he took me home after Mum and Dad's do last weekend and "The Boxer" was playing in his car.'

'Hang on, hang on. Are you certain about this? We can't jump to conclusions. Does the description fit?' Jon tried to get all the facts straight in his own mind.

'Perfectly.' In Selene's mind there was little room left for doubt. 'Sandra, can you identify him?'

'Definitely. And something else—I stabbed him with that penknife you gave me.' She looked at Tracy. 'He raped me, and I stabbed him before I lost consciousness.'

'Oh fuck me,' Selene said, as any possible remnant of doubt was swept away. 'Graham cut his arm open that night. Irina told me he did it in a fall.' She put her fingertips to her forehead as she spoke.

They looked at each other in stunned silence.

'I'm gunna kill him,' Tracy said, her voice cold and steady; and she picked up Sandra's hand and kissed her knuckles. 'He's a fuckin' dead man.'

♀

Twenty-eight
Saturday, 7th June

They talked the night through, going over every substantive detail that Sandra had remembered and piecing together the mysterious improbabilities that had bought them to this night: the death of their friend Ginny; Sandra's weird dream of the Condor and the rubbish bags full of pebbles; their meeting through the lesbian custody group; Selene's thesis on prostitution; Rosie's painting, and Izzy's book on birds of prey.

'Why'd you pick that Album sleeve up, Tracy? I haven't played that in ten years,' Jon said. He was beginning to share the women's clear perception of forces at work that were beyond rational explanation.

'I dunno. I just picked one out of the stack. D'you think it's like some special thing to him?'

'Yeah, I do,' Sandra said. 'That's how I knew it were him as soon as I heard it. It's not gunna make any sense to anyone else but I did.'

'I think we go to the police in the morning,' Selene said.

'An' he gets put in a nice little hospital somewhere, with every fuckin' thing he's ever gunna need. No—I'm not scared to knife that fucker through the heart. Just tell me where he lives and you don't need to have anything else to do with it.' Tracy was not going to be talked down.

'Darlin' you'll get done, and then I'll be on me own again. You'll get life an' he'll never have to answer for all the misery he's caused. He'll never have to know Michael's growing up without his mum, nor that poor nurse's kids. He'll never have to face the mums and dads, an' all them people whose lives he's fuckin' ruined. He'll never have to face his own missus. You'll be lettin' him off light. You'll be doin' him a favour.'

'She's right Tracy,' Selene added. 'Let's make him suffer living out the rest of his miserable, despicable little life.'

Tracy bit the inside of her cheek and sighed. 'Okay,' she said to Sandra, 'but if you change your mind ever, I'll do him, and I'll go to prison if I have to. I'd give my life to protect you.' She was the worse for several generous single malts, and tears started to well in the corners of her eyes.

'I know you would, sweetheart. But you don't have to. Anyway, it wouldn't be protecting me, it'd just be revenge. I want us to be more than that.'

Tracy nodded.

'Shall we get some sleep?' Jon said. 'That's a sofa bed. I think we should stay together tonight.'

It was just after five and the sun was coming up over the city. Jon and Selene lay whispering intently in the semi-darkened bedroom, unable to switch off from the appalling reality they all now faced.

Only Sandra slept that morning. Tracy leaned on her elbow and smoked as she watched her lover's closed eyes darting from side to side.

At nine, all four of them set out for the cop shop. They detoured first to Selene's house. Jon waited in the car while the women went in and Selene dug out her photos. She showed Sandra a portrait taken of Graham and Irina the day they'd got engaged.

'That's him. Not a shadow of a doubt about it,' Sandra said. 'D'you think your sister knows? How could it be possible that she don't?'

'No, I really don't think she does. She's not well—she's mentally fragile and he controls her. He always has,' Selene said, though a small part of her harboured a terrifying doubt.

Inspector Randall had been at the station since six. He'd been working fifteen-hour shifts trying to get a lead on this case, but every breakthrough had slipped, like sand, through his fingers. He felt like a man shadow boxing, exhausted and empty, and no one but himself on the ropes. The investigation was a vast monolith of file cards, records of interviews and scraps of inconclusive evidence. This morning he tried to sift through a new folder full of imponderable notes, receipts, even a bus ticket to Bolton. He rubbed the creases from his forehead. He felt about as much in control as a man trying to fill out his pools coupon in a high wind.

Sergeant Hill came and plonked a steaming mug of coffee on his boss's desk. 'That prossie's at the desk Sir,' he said.

'Which fuckin' prossie, man? Be specific.'

'That one that got assaulted—Sandra.' Hill harboured thoughts about Sandra that made him assume everyone would know which prossie he meant.

'Show her in,' Randall said and sipped his coffee.

Hill went out to the front desk. 'You can go through now, Sandra,' he said.

Tracy and Selene stood up with her.

'Uh I don't think he meant all of you.' Hill tried to corral them back onto the bench seat.

'Tough, we've got stuff to say that needs all of us. So do one.' Tracy pushed past him.

'I'll wait here,' Jon said.

Hill followed them through to Randall's office. 'Sorry Sir, they just pushed past me.'

'Fine, just get another chair,' Randall said rolling his eyes. 'Now what can I do for you ladies?'

'We know who he is,' Tracy stated baldly.

'Okay, let's start from the beginning shall we. Have you remembered some of the attack you suffered, Sandra? Can you identify the man responsible?'

Between them they recounted everything that had happened in the last twenty-four hours, omitting the weed they'd smoked.

'And you say Miss—'

'Bartowski.' Selene filled in the blank.

'Miss Bartowski. Thank you. You say that this man is your brother-in-law?'

'Yes he is.'

'Could you explain to me why you came to suspect that he may be the perpetrator?'

'I saw him after we'd been out the night that Sandra was attacked, or at least I thought I did. I'll be frank, Inspector, I did have suspicions about him based on my distrust and dislike of the man. I dismissed it all as my overactive imagination. I only really felt certain last night after Sandra's memory of the night came back to her. She described him, and she also described an injury she inflicted on her attacker. It matched an injury that I knew my brother-in-law had sustained on the night of the attack. Sandra's just now confirmed my suspicions from a photograph.' Selene spoke clearly and decisively but she decided not to focus on the more circumstantial evidence of the Simon and Garfunkel cassette. Millions of people owned that record.

Randall listened. He was clearly surprised at Selene's middle-class vowels. 'And how do you know Sandra and Tracy?' Although he knew the question was inappropriate, he was struggling to see her connection with Sandra and Tracy.

'We're friends,' Selene said holding his gaze and resisting the urge to explain that she wasn't a prostitute.

'Your sister is...?' Randall paused, staring with a mixture of bafflement and curiosity.

'Irina. And I'm certain she's not in any way involved. She's extremely fragile, mentally. He controls and manipulates her. She can't see any wrong in him.'

Randall nodded as he scribbled random words on the pad in front of him: Irina; fragile; control.

Sandra cut in. 'Yeah, and I had a dream about that bird the night before he got Ginny, then that girl Rosie drew it on the wall by the bins. It's a condor, and it was that song that were on in his car and that's how I knew it were him.' She blurted out her words in a torrent.

Randall thought for a moment and then said: 'Ummm—can I suggest that, when we take the statement, you stick to the salient facts—stuff that can stand up in court? The visionary aspect could be problematic, Sandra—a decent brief might turn it against us.

'What are you gunna do about it?' Tracy demanded.

'I'm going to ask the man to come in for questioning and we'll take it from there. We'll need you to identify him, Sandra. Will you be willing to do that?'

'That's why I'm here. Get him off the fuckin' streets before he kills again.'

'We'll take some formal statements first, and then we'll make an arrest.'

The formalities took until lunchtime. They left the police station and Jon dropped Sandra and Tracy back at the flats.

'You hungry?' Jon turned to Selene after they'd said their goodbyes.

'Starving. Let's buy some sandwiches and drive up onto the moors for a picnic.'

'Done.' Jon nodded.

♀

Twenty-nine

Randall read the statements cautiously. Was this his man, as Sandra seemed convinced? Or was he just a disgruntled punter? Why hadn't he raped the other women? Why had he driven into the countryside? The other victims had been found in the alleys and dark corners of the city. He had used a hammer, but a lot of men carried tools in their cars. Randall turned it over in his mind. He was desperate for a break in the case. Other forces were involved and he knew his days were numbered unless something happened soon. At this late stage in his career he had suddenly found himself at the epicentre of an investigation that seemed to confirm the inadequacy of the police force. The media were starting to run critical editorials about the lack of progress being made. Hammer Man: the Evening Post headline read. No new leads as police fumble in dark. Randall felt he was being portrayed as a hopeless plod and this soubriquet that the bastard had now acquired didn't help either. 'Hammer Man sounds like a fucking comic book hero', Randall thought to himself. 'And we sound like a bunch of fucking incompetents.'

'Shall we send a squad car, Guv?' Hill said.

'No, let's handle this ourselves. I don't think we'll meet any resistance. Have a panda on backup in case he tries to do a runner.' Randall picked up his tired old suit-jacket with its musty sweaty odour, sniffed it and put it back on the chair. He'd go in his shirtsleeves.

Graham was cleaning an old engine in the garage when Randall and Hill pulled up outside his house. He glanced up and nodded affably at the two men who got out.

'Mister Graham Hindle?' Randall asked.

'That's right,' Graham replied wiping his greasy hands on an old tea-towel.

'Would you get yourself cleaned up, Mr Hindle, we'd like you to accompany us to the police station to answer a few questions,' Hill said.

'What about?' Graham controlled the pitch of his voice and shifted into caring family man mode. He really believed in himself.

'Just clean up here, sir—we'll explain back at the station.'

He went indoors and Randall and Hill followed. Irina glanced up from the TV.

'I've got to go out fer a bit, love,' Graham said blocking her view of the old black-and-white movie she was glued to.

'Get out of the way, I'm watching this,' said Irina

Randall and Hill exchanged glances. They'd need a warrant to search the place, but finding a judge to sign it on a sunny Saturday afternoon wouldn't be straightforward. No matter—Randall had a feeling that this fellow wouldn't be back home any time soon.

Graham followed them meekly out to the unmarked police car. Irina kept her eyes fixed on Barbara Stanwyck and Fred MacMurray. Would they get away with murder? Not if Edward G. Robinson could help it.

'What are you going to do about your sister?' Jon asked Selene. They'd eaten their sandwiches and started to stroll a moorland path.

'I don't know. That's what I've been thinking about actually.'

'I thought so. You've gone really quiet.'

'It'll destroy her. She's pretty fragile anyway. I'll have to go and explain what my role in this has been.'

'Would you like me to come with you?'

'No. Thank you, Jon, really, but I think I have to do this one alone. I'm not really here with you right now. There's too much going on in my head. I think I need to call her and check that he's gone, then go and see how she is.'

'Let's go then.' Jon was unable to keep the disappointment out of his voice. 'Will you at least let me wait for you? I'll go in a pub or café nearby and you can come and meet me afterwards.'

'I might be ages and I don't want to ruin your weekend.'

'It's a bit late for that. Look, I'd just be sitting about like a miserable bastard at home. I really want to feel near you and be there for you. Sorry, this is horribly selfish of me, I know.' He knew she needed the space to sort this one out but he couldn't help himself. 'Anyway, what if she does know? It's got to be a possibility.'

Selene stopped and stared ahead. Then she turned to him and said: 'Okay, wait for me in The Golden Hind—it's the pub on their estate.' She was aware that her heart was pounding.

They stopped at a call box. Selene heard Irina's voice and pushed her ten-pence piece into the slot. 'It's me—I need to see you now. Has Graham gone?'

'Yes, he's had to pop out for a bit. Come round if you like. Is there something up with Mum or Dad?'

'No, I'll see you in ten minutes.' Selene put the phone down. At least, if Irina did know, she was playing dumb really effectively.

Jon dropped Selene off a few doors down and watched her walk to the door and go in. He wasn't going to The Golden Hind. He was going to wait right here, afraid all the time something terrible might happen to her.

'What's the panic?' Irina said as she let Selene in.

'Irina,' Selene began when they'd sat down in the living room, 'Graham's been arrested by the police, hasn't he?' Distracted by the TV, she leaned across and turned it off.

'Well, yes, I suppose they were policemen. I expect it's some driving nonsense. I hope he's back before six—I've got a lovely piece of fresh haddock and it won't keep. He's always speeding in that car and—'

She would have wittered on an on if Selene had not interrupted. 'He's not been arrested for speeding, Irina. They're questioning him about the murders. He's been identified by one of the victims who survived.'

'Don't talk rubbish, Selene. You've never been fond of him, I know that, but it's some sort of mistake. It must be. They're questioning lots of men.'

'Not one's who have wounds that match those inflicted by the victim.' Selene knew she had to keep talking straight to get through to her sister who'd become adept at avoiding any inconvenient truths she encountered.

'What wounds?'

'That cut on his arm that you told me he'd done in a fall.'

'He did that on the bloody loft ladder. I was here in the house.'

'Did you actually see him do it?'

187

'Well no, but I heard the commotion when he fell. He woke me up with it, and he was stinking of whisky.'

'But you didn't see him do it—did you?' Selene persisted.

'He's not a mad man, Selene. I know him. He's kind and loving, and he'd do anything for me, anything at all. I know I'm not easy but he never complains. You've no idea.'

'Do you sleep together?' Selene was going for broke. She knew he had his own room and had long suspected that they slept apart.

'None of your bloody business—but, as a matter of fact, yes we do, occasionally. That goes stale in most marriages. There're much more important things. You'd not know that though.'

Selene ignored the cheap dig. 'They're very likely to question you too, you know? So you need to be ready, because asking if you sleep together will be the least of it I'm sure.'

'How do you know all this anyway?' Irina suddenly realised that her sister was somehow more involved than she'd so far admitted.

'It was my friend that was attacked and she's identified Graham from that engagement picture of the two of you. I went with her to the police. She had her skull smashed with a hammer, just like the other victims. The only reason she's still alive is because a nearby house put the lights on and scared him off.'

'How come she was looking at that picture? Anyway, it's five years old.'

'Because she described him and his car—and she described the cut she made in his arm. I realised it was him and showed her the picture. There was no doubt in her mind, Irina.'

Irina stared at her sister open-mouthed. 'You've betrayed me and you've betrayed your family. This is all a lie.' She was agitated and picking wildly at the cushion on her lap. 'What about Mum and Dad? How could you do such a thing? It's all lies. Now get out of my house. You've always hated him and you've always been jealous of what we've got.'

'Irina please, you have to be ready to face the truth. I'm trying to help you.'

'Get out,' Irina screamed and hurled the cushion at the lifeless television set.

'Can I get Mum and Dad to come over?' Selene didn't want to leave her sister alone.

'No! Don't you dare involve them in this. Just get out.'

Selene left her there and closed the front door behind her. Then she cried. She cried for her sister and for Sandra and for all the victims, and she cried for herself. Could she be wrong about this? Jon got out of his car and walked towards her. She virtually fell into his arms and he held her tight and wiped the tears from her face with his thumb. They got into his car and pulled out of the tree-lined avenue onto the main road. Selene still had her head in her hands when a panda car with a male and a female officer inside passed them on the other side of the road.

Graham was shown into the same room that Sandra had been interviewed in after Ginny died. He was cleaning grease out of his fingernails with a paperclip he'd found on the desk when Randall and Hill came in.

'Can we get this over quickly? Missus'll worry, like,' Graham said casually. He'd figured out that the bitch who had lived must have somehow identified him. He wouldn't put it past his cunt of a sister-in-law to be involved somewhere along the line either. She'd actually stood there and admitted she was friends with the tart. She'd got no shame. He could hardly credit that she and Irina were of the same stock. He'd already got a plan worked out.

'Okay, Graham.' Randall switched on the tape and took a matey tone. 'Would you take us through what you were doing on the night of May the first? It was a Thursday, if that helps jog your memory.'

Graham rubbed the stubble on his chin and looked pensive. He was right, it was that filthy pro. He allowed a few moments to pass and then said: 'Now let me see. Aye, I reckon it were't night I'd been fer a bevy wi't pal Derek.'

'What time was that exactly?'

'I dropped him off at home at about half-past eleven. Then went home meself. Aye, an' I know I shouldn't o' bin drivin' like, because I'd had a few.'

'You owned a Ford Capri at that time?'

'Aye, that's right. It'd started playin' up so I got rid o' it.'

'Mr Hindle, please remove your shirt and show me your right arm.'

Graham complied with the request. His injury was mostly healed now, but still sore looking and clearly untreated by professionals. It was going to scar badly.

'How did you sustain that injury?' Randall asked.

'I done it that night. I were in't loft at home an' I lost me balance. As I say, I'd had a few too many. I caught it on't nail sticking out o' wood.'

'And your wife will be able to confirm that?'

'Aye, she seen me do it,' he confidently replied.

'Did you go to the hospital? That looks like a nasty gash.'

'No, I didn't realise how bad it were till next day, an' it'd stopped bleedin' so I left it. Wish I had now like, because it'll be a nasty scar. Look what's all this about?' He put his shirt back on.

'Mr Hindle, you've been identified as the perpetrator of a very nasty sexual attack and in the current climate we need to establish your whereabouts on a number of occasions during the last seven months or so.'

Graham pulled his most indignant look. 'D'you mean you're questioning me about the murders o' them prostitutes?'

'Yes, Mr Hindle—and not all of the victims were prostitutes of course,' Randall said coolly.

Graham bit his tongue. He wanted to argue but that would be silly in this situation. If only he'd had a chance to speak to Irina and prepare her for this. He stuck to his story. He feigned poor memory but said he'd been home with his wife, either watching television or in bed, on all the other dates that Randall named. He added that his wife would be able to confirm his story.

Randall tried another tack. 'Do you ever use prostitutes, Graham?'

Graham already had this one worked out. 'Aye, once or twice like, a lot o' men have been wi' 'em.'

'And what do you think of them? Ever had a dose of something nasty?' Randall switched back to matey.

'Oh aye, a bit of a rash, but it were nowt. They're right mucky, en't they? But when wife's a bit low like, well, a man's got needs.' Graham knew his car must have been spotted in various red-light districts so there was no point in denying any contact.

'Did that annoy you? The rash I mean.'

'No, not really, it were just one o' them things.'

Randall switched the tape off. He could see this was going nowhere. If the wife did alibi him, there'd be little or no evidence barring the word of a convicted prostitute. It could go to trial, but equally, he might not even get it past the prosecution department. He didn't care much for his story and he'd got a weird feeling about this man, but he couldn't afford to fuck-up on this one.

'Can I go then?' Graham asked.

'Not just yet, Graham. We'd like to organise an identity parade. Would you be prepared to assist us in eliminating you from our enquiries?'

Graham considered his options and calculated the risks. 'Well, if I can help Inspector,' he said earnestly.

'Take Mr Hindle down to the cells please, Sergeant,' Randall said smiling.

Irina heard the loud knocking at the front door but she didn't answer. The blinds were drawn but she could see their shadows trying to peer in the windows. Then they went to the back door and rattled the handle. She kept still and quiet. She needed to see what Graham would say when he came home. 'Hello? Mrs Hindle? Anyone home?' a woman's voice called through the letter box.

Irina shrank down onto the sofa. Her mind was a whirl of minutiae: the haddock, the dust motes settling everywhere she looked, the dirty hand print Graham had left on the door handle. She heard them crunching away on the gravel path. A car door opened and closed, then another. Irina waited, holding her breath. She heard the engine start. They pulled away. Irina cradled her legs in her arms and rocked herself slowly backwards and forwards.

♀

Thirty

Sandra had positively identified Graham at six o' clock that evening. He'd been lined up with six other men, volunteers selected on the grounds of age and race. Two were policemen and a third was a drunk from the cells who bore an uncanny resemblance to Graham. Still Sandra did not hesitate, 'Number five,' she'd said, 'the fuckin' sick monster.'

Graham was formally arrested on suspicion of attempted murder and taken back to the cells beneath the station. It was at eight o'clock that evening, a Saturday, when most people were out partying or home watching television, that Randall finally got access to Irina. He didn't want to force entry, any procedural cock-ups on this one could jeopardise his case. He'd had enough dealings with slick bastard lawyers to know that he had to play things by the book. Finally he'd had Graham call her and tell her to open the door.

'Just tell them the truth,' Graham said, and then handed the phone back to Randall with a shrug.

Randall's palms were sweating as he drove into the avenue with WPC Sharon Maguire. This could be him. This could be the big break in the case.

He'd had his doubts, given that Sandra was so far the only victim who'd been raped in the normal way—if such an act could ever be described as 'normal'. Yet he'd seen so much of it in his thirty-five year career, and there was so much more that never passed before him, that normal was probably more accurate than he or anyone cared to admit. He trusted Sandra. She was a common prossie, but there was something decent about her and he had absolutely no doubt that she thought this was their man. If he could make it stick, if they found further evidence, if the wife didn't alibi him, this could be the one he'd be remembered for. It would be the pinnacle of a pretty average career so far.

Irina answered the door calmly enough and admitted them to the clinically spotless living room where the television was blaring at full volume. He asked her to turn it off. The whole house reeked of fish— haddock, he thought; he'd missed his own tea and had eaten a portion of chips in the wrapper on his desk. Randall sat down on the edge of the armchair and indicated the sofa to Irina. WPC Maguire remained standing, a sentry on duty, arms behind her back and feet slightly parted. 'We need you to think very carefully, Mrs Hindle, about the questions we are going to ask you, because anything you say may be used in evidence in a court of law.' Randall noted the nervous twitch that momentarily distorted Irina's eye. 'Now, can you remember at what time your husband came home on the night of May the first? I believe that was the night he injured his arm?' Randall was trying to size this woman up. She was clearly very tense but also had a kind of belligerent look about her.

Irina thought for a moment. 'Yes, it was about midnight,' she lied. She had no idea when he came home. She'd taken a sleeping pill and the first she knew of his arrival was hearing the crash when he fell out of the loft. She'd just imagined that it was about this time because that would give him time to drop Derek off and get home. 'He'd been out with his friend Derek and came home steaming.' This much was true as far as she knew.

'Are you sure about the time?' Randall pressed.

'As far as I can remember. What were you doing at that precise time? I'm not a memory man,' she said angrily.

'Please explain to us about your husband's injury. In as much detail as you can, Mrs Hindle.'

'I heard him in the loft clumping about. I got up to see what he was up to and as I came out of the bedroom he fell down the ladder with an almighty thump and caught his arm on a nail sticking out of the frame. I can show you the nail if you like. He still hasn't fixed it.' She lied again. She knew from Selene's visit that this injury was important and she had to make sure that that she gave her husband all the support she could. After all, he'd supported her through all the bad times. He'd been there for her when she didn't want to live anymore. It was what wives did, support their men. Anyway, she knew he was innocent so it was only a white lie.

Randall asked about the dates of all the other murders. Irina dutifully claimed that, as far as she could remember, on all the nights in question Graham had been tucked up in bed beside her. She embellished with additional 'facts' where possible. For example, she did actually remember the night of her parents' ruby wedding anniversary, and though she had been tipsy and went to sleep as soon as her head hit the pillow, she said she had a clear memory of Graham coming back from dropping her sister off because they had discussed the day's events together. She painted a picture of Mr and Mrs Normal-Married-People. She even said they were trying for a baby. In her own mind she wanted her version of events so badly to be true that it actually did sound real and plausible.

Randall could feel his blaze of glory slipping away. 'How would you describe your sex life, Mrs Hindle?' He knew this was going nowhere.

'Perfectly normal.' She flinched at answering the question but she was glad that Graham's impotence had been better in the last six months or so. They'd had sex six or seven times. Graham had his eyes screwed tight shut while they'd done it, which was a relief to her because she hated being looked at.

'Mrs Hindle,' Randall was running out of patience, 'what do you think of a man who'd brutally murder and mutilate young women—a nurse with two children and a student with a promising career ahead of her?'

'Well, he's a freak. Of course he is,' Irina said angrily. 'But my Graham's a kind and loving husband who wouldn't harm a fly.'

'The killer is almost certainly someone's kind and loving husband. You do understand the consequences for anyone who'd aid and abet a murderer, Mrs Hindle? An accessory to murder would go to prison.'

Irina just stared at him. Her single concern at that moment was the grease stain on Randall's lapel. She wondered if it would come out with vinegar.

They left it at that. Randall didn't mention that they'd search the house in the morning in case she tried to destroy evidence. He'd let her stew overnight and take her in for further questioning in the morning. He did tell her that Graham had been arrested and would be held in custody for the time being.

'D'you think she's lying, Sir?' Maguire asked when they got back in the car.

'I think she's protecting him, yes. There's something wrong here,' Randall added shaking his head. 'Let's see what the search throws up in the morning.'

Irina watched them leave from behind the blinds. Then she went upstairs to Graham's room and tried the door. It was locked. She bent to peer through the keyhole. All she could see was the single bed neatly made and the table top. It was empty and wiped clean. She went back downstairs and into the garage. Graham had left his keys on the work bench. She had to try four different keys before the locked room opened. There was nothing in there other than the bed and a table and chair. She opened the built-in wardrobe and looked through Graham's suits and shirts. She went through the pockets—nothing there but a used tissue and a fifty-pence piece. There were three sets of blue overalls wrapped in cellophane in a neat pile on the floor. She picked them up—all were exactly the same, medium size and from the same workman's store in town. Irina closed the door and went back downstairs. She switched the TV on. Dallas was just finishing.

Randall was back at his desk at seven the following morning. He'd taken Maggie a cup of tea up to the bedroom but she'd groaned and turned over. They'd argued when he'd arrived home at nearly midnight. She'd said she felt like a widow. He'd promised her the holiday of a lifetime after this case. She'd said she just wanted an ordinary married life, with a partner to share things with. She pointed out that he hadn't even met his two-month old granddaughter. He knew she was right and well within her rights to complain. He'd only had about three weekends this year. If he was honest with himself, he wasn't interested in babies, or weekends spent with annoying relatives. And though he loved her, he wasn't especially interested in spending weekends with his wife either. He hated shopping. He loathed picnics and walks across the moorland paths. The moors, to him, were where the bodies of children lay in hastily dug shallow graves. He knew his wife would have had a happier life if she'd divorced him decades ago, but she was from a generation who didn't divorce. They bore their burdensome husbands with fortitude and thought themselves lucky if they didn't get a beating on a Saturday night.

He was shuffling through the case notes. One of the files was labelled 'Psychological Profile'. He opened it. Usually these things were a lot of twaddle, and American twaddle at that. He'd only given it a cursory glance before. Now he read with more interest. The phrase *possible collector of souvenirs* caught his eye. The fact that handbags had been found at the scene, in most cases emptied out, had given rise to this idea. Nothing had been reported missing by relatives and purses containing cash hadn't been taken. Who knew what a woman kept in her handbag anyway? It was uncertain whether or not the contents had spilled in the struggle that might've ensued. *'The perpetrator in this event would re-live his crimes through these items. He would see them as trophies. They might have particular significance to him.'* Randall pondered the notion.

At ten past eight the phone rang. 'The search warrant for your suspect's been signed, Sir,' said the duty sergeant.

'Thanks. Give it to Hill when he comes in.' Randall replaced the receiver. Thirty minutes elapsed while he examined the crime scene photographs. He picked up the photo of Rosie's body turning it this way and that, trying to make out the items scattered around the body. He wondered why she'd done the huge bird graffiti. Who knew what went on in the mind of a junkie, beyond finding the next fix? Perhaps he'd have another word with her useless boyfriend. The phone rang again.

'DI Geoff Pulteney, Sheffield squad,' the voice on the other end said. 'We've nabbed your Hammer Man, lad. Thought it politic to let you know early. You'll no doubt want a pop at him yourself once we've handled the initial interviews—but he's coughed the bloody lot.'

'You what?' Randall was dismayed.

'Ronald Palmer. Fifty-two. He hit a prossie over the head with a hammer last night. She legged it and ran straight into a couple of bobbies. Blood all down her face, apparently. They chased the culprit and caught him red handed, as it were. He'd got a Stanley knife in his pocket as well. We've searched his flat and it's covered in news cuttings about it all. Proper fuckin' nutter.'

'It's a bit of a coincidence, Geoff, because I've got somebody in the cells as we speak. He's been identified by one of the victims. Chap called Graham Hindle. Wife's alibied him though, so we've only got the ID of a prossie, and one that's had memory loss at that. It's not a lot to go on. Listen can I come across this afternoon. A few loose ends to tie up here first.'

'Super says we'll handle the initial interviews. Maybe give us a buzz in a couple of days, lad? Once we've gone public.'

Randall put the phone down. 'Fuck it,' he said aloud.

'Fuck what, Sir?' Hill said, coming in with the signed warrant in his hand.

'Sheffield think they've got him. Fucker's confessed to the lot.'

'Will we still need this?' Hill asked waving the piece of paper.

'Who knows? Maybe we'll find a sharpened chisel with blood and hair all over it, or a fucking big sign with an arrow saying: clues this way.' He snatched the warrant from Hill's hand and picked his smelly jacket up. 'Let's go and see.' he said.

♀

Thirty-one

Graham and Irina's house gave up no secrets to the search team. His cupboard where he kept his souvenirs deceived the eye and when Hill pulled back the clothes hanging in front of it he saw only the wooden panelling that Graham had used to disguise its opening. They did find a hammer and a set of tools but they were hardly enough to charge a man, in possession of a spotless record, with murder. Nearly every man owned the same kit. They duly bagged them for forensics anyway. At the station, Irina had steadfastly repeated her story of the previous evening. It was completely true to her now. Randall had no choice but to release her at five on the Sunday afternoon. He did believe Sandra thought Graham was the killer and maybe he was the man who attacked her. He'd always been concerned though that, in Sandra's case, the M.O. was different: the rape, the countryside location. He decided to hold Graham until he'd got a medical and psychological report on Sandra. He needed to see how well her story would hold up in court before he made any decisions that could further undermine his judgement.

Sandra stood open-mouthed when Randall and Hill called at the flat and explained that they hadn't found any evidence and certain other circumstances had thrown the arrest into question.

'So are you gunna release him?' Sandra could barely believe they were letting him go. She was certain he was the killer. She should have let Tracy kill him after all.

'I've applied to hold him for ninety-six hours, but after that, if I can't charge him, I'll be forced to release him, Sandra. It's the law I'm afraid. Now, would you be willing to see the police psychologist? I need to know if your version of events would stand up in court. If it gets that far and then he's acquitted, that's the end of it, he's a free man.'

'So you wanna see if a bent slag's word's good against some upright, married man? Can't you get any other evidence on him?'

'We've searched his house, Sandra, and found nothing. Also, his wife has given him an alibi too, for the night of the attack.'

'Yeah, fine. I'll do it. When?' Sandra asked, resigned. She'd always known the police were useless—this just fuckin' proved it.

'Tomorrow morning. Ten o clock. Sandra, you do realise that even if we charge him with rape and GBH, he'll make bail in all likelihood.'

'GBH?' Tracy had come to the door. 'It's fuckin' attempted murder at the least,' she said.

'We'll have to wait and see, Tracy. There's no sense in getting agitated. We are dealing with this and we will get to the truth, I promise.' Randall spoke with a confidence he did not feel.

'Hold me coat,' Sandra said to Tracy as she was ushered into a police station interview-room next morning. Tracy took the old leather flying jacket and sat back down on the bench to wait. She could smell Sandra's perfume on the sheepskin collar. The desk sergeant's eyes followed Sandra as she walked past him and into the tiny room. Tracy glared.

The stout, balding man behind the desk didn't look up but indicated the seat opposite him as he continued perusing his notes. Witness assessment wasn't his normal role. He was a Doctor of Psychology who freelanced assisting the police in dealing with traumatised victims and talked at training sessions. Sometimes he was also called upon to suggest motives for seemingly motiveless crimes. The new-fangled science of psychological profiling was emerging in an America, where John Wayne Gacy, 'The Killer Clown', had been arrested earlier that year for the rape and murder of scores of young boys. Thrill-killing was a phenomenon growing at a furious rate. The new scientific approach pioneered by the FBI had not so far breached the traditional reserves of British policing, and most murder

200

detectives still relied on old-school commonsense techniques. The man who sat opposite Sandra felt vaguely irritated to be called upon to intervene in this case.

Sandra sat down and breathed out audibly through her nose. The stout man introduced himself as 'Dr Heaney,' and began: 'Now Sandra, please explain to me a little about what happened on the night you were attacked'.

Sandra went through everything she remembered. Now that she had regained the memory it seemed more vivid than ordinary recall. At times she had to bite back tears as she relived the ordeal. She ended at the point where she stabbed Graham. 'And then I woke up in hospital,' she finished her account.

'Umm, yes—and you suffered a form of memory disruption?'

'Dissociative memory disorder.' I'd blacked out the event.'

'Let's leave the diagnosis to the experts, shall we Sandra? Now, how certain are you that the memory you've now regained is real?'

'Completely certain.' Sandra didn't care much for the drift in this conversation. She cared even less for the next question.

'Tell me about your arrest for soliciting three years ago.'

'What's that got to do with anything?'

'That's what I'll be the judge of,' the doctor said smiling broadly.

'Look, somebody nearly killed me and he raped me. Let's talk about getting him locked up.'

'Just answer the question please, Sandra.'

'I was a prostitute and I got arrested for soliciting. What's to say about it?'

'And you violently resisted the arrest.'

'No, I didn't. I just didn't let that bitch copper push me like that and I pushed her back.'

'Ummm.' Heaney looked again at his notes.

'How long have you been involved in a lesbian relationship?'

'This is nothing to do with anything.'

'Again, Sandra, please answer the question.'

'About three years.'

'Are you both prostitutes?' Heaney's expression was one of measured disgust.

'We were prostitutes.'

'Do you think that your sexual involvement with this woman is a means of escaping from the life you've chosen?'

'Chosen? Oh yeah, during my perfect childhood and education I decided I wanted a career on the game. Good money if you don't mind the antisocial hours and constant threat of violence and rape, and the hatred of every other fucker in the world. It just happens. Don't you get that? When you've got nothing you've got no fucking choice. You sell your arse.'

'You could have sold your labour,' Heaney said smugly.

'What—at fifteen? Look, let's forget this. You're not interested in getting this murdering bastard.'

'Do you see yourself as sexually normal Sandra?'

'Yeah, I do as it happens.'

Heaney maintained his thin-lipped grimace and inclined his head slightly. 'The man you've identified. You say in your statement that you were shown a picture of him before the identity parade.'

'Yeah that's right. We wanted to make sure it was him.'

'Well don't you think it highly likely that what you've actually done is recognise him from that photograph?'

'Oh fuck you.' Sandra stood and left the room. She slammed the door behind her.

Tracy stood up and held out her lover's coat, Sonny Bono to Sandra's Cher.

'C'mon, let's get out of this fuckin' place,' Sandra said.

'So can I kill him now?' said Tracy when they got outside.

Sandra leaned her head on Tracy's shoulder and let the tears she'd bitten back pour down her face.

Sheffield murder squad charged Ronnie Palmer with murder after finding several strands of women's hair and three different types of blood in his squalid council flat. They charged him with assault first, so as to hold him while they compiled enough evidence to progress with the murder charges. In spite of his personal misgivings, Randall had no choice but to release Graham after the ninety-six hours was up. The shrink's report on Sandra had been damning. Heaney doubted the case, such as it was, would get past the prosecutions department. A lesbian streetwalker with a record of violence and a memory disorder wouldn't stand very much probing.

Sandra phoned Selene to let her know what had happened.

'You're joking,' Selene said.

'I wish I was. Apparently your sister's given him an alibi as well. I could bring a civil case, they said, but let's be honest—who's gunna believe a prossie?'

'Irina's given him an alibi?' Selene repeated appalled. 'What, for all the murders, as well as the attack on you?'

'Yeah, from what Randall said.'

202

'This is absolute bollocks. She couldn't possibly know what he does or where he goes. She's out of it on sleeping tablets most nights. I'm going to speak to her again. She threw me out on Saturday but I can't let her do this.'

'Good. I was hoping you'd say that—but think about it first. If you push her away you're gunna push her further towards him. From what you say she's pretty dependent on him.' Sandra had no intention of just leaving things as they were. She'd suffered more than her share of misogyny in her life and she was about to start fighting back. 'Also, she could be in danger herself. I wouldn't fancy living with him—would you?'

'I already thought that, but he kind of controls her. Look, leave it with me. I'll tread carefully.' Selene hung up the phone and leaned back against the wall. 'I don't fuckin' believe it,' she said to the empty hall.

Graham arrived home on Tuesday morning with a three-day beard. He phoned into the yard where he worked and said he'd gone down with a stomach bug and that he'd be in the next day. The manager warned him he'd get a bollocking for not phoning in on the first day of sickness, but since Graham was a good worker he'd leave it at that. He gave Irina a hug in the hallway.

'Mind my blouse,' she said wriggling away. 'Phew, you could do with a bath.'

'I'll run one now. Thanks, love,' he said holding her away from him. He knew that her alibi had been important for him. 'You know that you mean everything in the world to me and I'll always be here for you whatever happens.'

'How come that prostitute identified you?' Irina had been waiting to ask this question.

He let go of her arms. 'Because your sister showed her a photograph of me and told her I'd done it. It's all come from her you know. I don't want her in this house again and I don't want you having anything to do with her either. She's a hateful bitch. Just because she's jealous of you, she's trying to split us up by getting me locked up.'

'They searched the house you know.'

'How did they get into my room?' Graham said as casually as he could manage.

'I found your keys and opened it before they came. Why do you keep it locked anyway? There's nothing in there.'

'It's to do wi' when I were a boy and not havin' me own room and privacy, love. I don't know why I lock it. It just makes me feel like I've somewhere proper private like—somewhere that's just me own.' Graham's relief that neither the police search nor Irina's intrusion had uncovered his special secret gave him a renewed sense of invincibility. Lying was so easy it was almost scary.

'What if we had a child? That room'd be ideal as a nursery.' Irina didn't so much want a child as a sense that she had control over something. It was hard for her to keep everything pinned down. She felt she had no centre. A baby growing inside her would fill that void.

'Oh aye love. I'd do it up for t'nipper then,' Graham tried to reassure her with his easy manner. Then, unbidden, the thought of his Stanley knife slicing through Irina's swollen belly was in his mind's eye. He closed his eyes and shook his head, and the idea dissipated.

'What's up?' Irina had noticed his gesture.

'Nowt, love—just a bit of a headache wi' everything that I've been through at police station. I'll go up and run that bath.'

Irina watched her husband climb the stairs, listened as he turned the tap on. 'You should have got stitches in that arm,' she suddenly found herself shouting.

Graham came onto the landing and looked down at her, locking her gaze. 'Aye, love—'appen I should've at that.'

♀

Thirty-two
Thursday, 17th July

The café where Steve had asked Sandra to meet him was tucked down a side street in a row of random, dingy shops. It sat between a haberdasher and a greengrocer, opposite an estate agents. He'd said he had something important to tell her about Vincent so she had no choice but to agree to see him. Tracy had argued with her about it. 'He just wants to trap you into going back with him,' she'd said.

'He's married to that Doreen,' Sandra replied, bemused by Tracy's suspicions.

'Exactly,' said Tracy.

Steve was sat in the corner nursing a coffee when Sandra walked in. 'Wow,' he said leaping up and pulling a chair out for her. 'Love the new hairdo.' He sat down opposite and touched Sandra's hand. 'How've you been keeping, love, wi' everything?'

Sandra withdrew her hand. 'Where's Doreen?' Sandra said realising Tracy had probably been right on the money.

'That's what I wanted to see you about actually. Shall we get a bite to eat?' he said and summoned the waitress.

Sandra knew precisely what was coming. She'd seen enough of this man's 'charming' side to know when he'd got it on full-blast setting.

'No, I don't want anything to eat.' Sandra turned to the waitress. 'Thanks—I'll just have a coffee.'

'Yeah, same for me.' Steve looked disappointed. 'How about going for a drink after? We could go up to 'The Old Cock'—remember the nights we had in there?'

'Can we just talk about Vincent, please Steve? What d'you wanna tell me about him?'

'Yeah, yeah—he's doing all right, hey?'

'Yes.' Sandra held her palms upward and stared into Steve's face.

'He's got your good looks, that's for sure.' Steve moved to touch Sandra's short-cropped hair.

Sandra moved out of reach. 'Cut the crap, Steve. What's this all about?'

'Me an' Doreen have split up. She's moved out.'

'What d'you want me to do about it? Anyway, where's Vince now?'

'He's at school. I just thought that maybe we could share stuff to do with Vince more. You could even think about moving back in. We'd be like a family again. It's the best start in life for a kid, en't it—havin' his own mum and dad, like?

'Oh yeah, I remember that well. Like you beating the shit out of me when I was pregnant with him—and then trying to pimp me out a week after he's born.'

'Sandra, I've learned a lot. I know what you meant to me, now. You're the only one I've ever really loved, girl.'

'Fuck off, Steve. Look, Tracy and me'll have him anytime you like. If you don't want custody anymore that's great. We'll get in touch with the social services and—'

'Do us a fuckin' favour, Sandra. You can forget all about that dyke. I told you I'm not having my kid brought up around perverts.'

'You are the biggest fuckin' hypocrite. What about when you ask me to do that girl while you watch us? How's that different, then?'

'Of course it's different. That was just to give our relationship a bit of spice.'

'I'm not gunna argue with you, Steve—and I'm not gunna let you insult me and Tracy either. If you want me to have custody of Vincent I'm more than happy with that. It's all I want from you. We are never, ever, gunna be this happy fuckin' family thing. D'you get that?' Sandra stood up to leave.

'I'll never let you have him back, at least not till you see sense. The law agrees with me, Sandra. I reckon that knock on the head's turned you weird.'

The coffee arrived then, and Sandra relished the fantasy of throwing the whole steaming mug in Steve's ugly face. But she left the café and walked back to the high street instead. Jane Rayment's office was less than a fifteen-minute walk away and Sandra decided to pay her a visit. Steve was on the ropes—now that she was immune to his tactics she recognised his desperate, morally bankrupt scrabbling for the selfish shit that it was.

Jane Rayment was standing with her assistant in the reception area looking over some case notes when Sandra dinged in through the door of the Purvis and Dawes solicitor's office. 'That's spooky,' she said. 'I just this minute called you, Sandra. We've had a breakthrough in your case.'

'Yeah? I'm not surprised—stuffs happening a lot to me like that lately.' Sandra closed the door behind her and followed Jane into her cramped office space. 'What's happened?' she said, moving a heap of files from the chair to sit down.

'Steve's wife Doreen has gone into a women's refuge. She's recovering from a fractured jaw and bruising to the back and spine.'

'Where's Vince?' Sandra said, alarmed now the full picture was emerging.

'Vincent's fine. Social services took him into care yesterday pending a review. You can visit him if you like. They'll need to make sure you're in a position to take charge of him—but you could have him back in a couple of weeks.'

'Thank God for that. I'm sorry for that dozy cow, though. Is she pressing charges?' Sandra felt her anger rising. 'That piece of fuckin' shit. You know he's just had the front to ask me to go back with him? Not a word of any of this crap.'

'I'm not sure of all the facts. It's come from one of the women who run the refuge. She says she wants to, this time. But it happened before with her last partner, and she had her own child taken away. Seems Doreen's a serial victim of domestic violence.'

'Jesus. The bastard's not laid a finger on my boy, has he?'

'No, Sandra. There's no evidence of any kind of physical abuse. You'll need to be the judge of whether Steve's harmed him in any other way. Emotionally, I mean.' Jane reached over the desk then and took Sandra's clenched fist in hers. 'Nearly there now,' she said.

♀

Thirty-three
Friday, 8th August

Selene couldn't let things lie. No matter what the police said, she knew she was right about Graham. Ronald Palmer, the so-called suspect from Sheffield, had been released into a mental care facility after his story crumpled under deeper investigation. Selene had read in the newspaper that it had eventually become apparent he was merely an admirer of the real killer when his version of events failed to acknowledge salient facts about each case which the police had not released to the press. Palmer had been convincing enough though, and his knowledge sufficiently detailed to keep them hooked and busy for ten days trying to make the case stick.

Exasperated, Selene had returned to Inspector Randall to reiterate her suspicions. He wasn't entirely dismissive, she thought, and he'd actively encouraged her to use Irina's familial affection to break down the alibi she had given Graham.

'We could re-arrest for the attack on Sandra Jacques, Miss Bartowski, but we've not a shred of evidence for any of the other—' Randall had paused to select the word with caution before deciding on "events'. I'll

209

keep our conversation on file, Miss. Just between you and me, I'm keeping an open mind about Mr Hindle and his alibi.' Forensics had drawn a complete blank with the tools taken from the house. The tyre marks and blood found at the scene of the attack on Sandra had been common to millions.

Selene had phoned Irina several times since she'd thrown her out of the house over a month before. The first time, Irina had slammed the phone down on hearing Selene's voice. The second she'd said she didn't want anything more to do with her, ever. But at the third call she'd softened slightly and they'd had a short conversation about the results of their father's recent medical scare. Selene had blatantly used their dad's prostate trouble as an 'in' with Irina. She knew she'd be able to get a response on this, and she'd tried to extend the conversation into the 'So how're you doing?' territory. Next time, Irina seemed more willing to simply chat. Selene interpreted her sister's thaw as being down to her having no friends, or even neighbours that she spoke to, and this isolation had weakened her resolve to cut Selene off. Irina also knew that she'd lied. She knew this and she had buried it under multiple layers of self-righteousness and fear. Her disorders had been crippling over the last few weeks. As long as Irina stayed occupied with the things she could control, she could maintain some sort of precarious sense of normality.

This afternoon when Irina picked up the phone to Selene, she was almost relieved that her sister had called. Her anxieties were getting on top of her and now she'd started to fear Graham. He'd acted the perfect husband after his arrest, been kind and considerate to her despite the awful strain he was under—but something made her flinch away. Their occasional awkward episodes of sex had now dwindled to nothing, with Graham preferring to sleep more often in his own room. She'd grown to hate and to fear that empty little room. It was like a poisonous heart at the centre of her home and she felt its toxic presence leaking silently into every corner. 'Hi Irina. It's me,' she heard her sister say.

'Oh hello. I'm glad you called. I was just thinking about doing a bit of gardening, then realised I needed to get weed-killer. I might pop out to the shops.' Irina knew that she would not be able to do this but saying it to someone was like trying on a dress in a store. You knew you weren't going to buy it, but it allowed you to flirt with the idea safely for a minute or two.

'Oh good. Yes, you should pop out for a bit. It'd do you good to have breather. How've you been anyway?'

'Yes,' Irina replied vaguely. 'Do you think they'd sell it in the hardware shop?' Speaking to Selene felt like communicating with someone at the other end of a long dark tunnel, where sound distorted and her own voice echoed back so that Irina could barely distinguish who had said what and to whom.

'I'm sure they would.' Selene could sense Irina's strangeness. 'Look, shall I come up and get you? We could go together.' This was the first time she'd suggested a meeting. She didn't like how Irina sounded today. She'd been there when Irina had her breakdown years ago and she thought she knew the signs.

'Oh no, don't,' Irina practically shouted. 'Graham might come back early. He often does these days.'

'Well meet me somewhere then.' Selene knew this was a long shot.

'Oh no, I couldn't do that,' Irina said, as if it were completely obvious that a young able-bodied woman could not go out alone in the middle of the day in the city where she had lived all her life. 'Not today. It's too late. Maybe one day next week.'

Selene couldn't let it go. 'I could get my friend Jon to give me a lift. We could pick you up and go for a coffee, then get whatever gardening stuff you need. Graham needn't know.' She was completely aware that she was accepting a situation of extreme domination by pandering to Irina's fear of Graham, but going on the offensive would only alienate her sister again after she had patiently begun to rebuild trust between them. 'Which day?' She needed to pin her down.

'I'll give you a ring about it. I would like to meet your boyfriend.'

'Yeah, of course—but do me a favour and don't mention it to Mum and Dad. I don't want them getting their hopes up about marriage and all that.'

'There are worse things in life than finding a good man and settling down you know.'

Selene thought finding a bad man and settling down was probably a lot worse. 'Yes, I know but—' she was saying when the phone went dead.

Graham came in through the access door from the garage carrying an armful of bags stuffed with groceries. 'Who was that on the phone?' he challenged.

'Just Mum,' Irina said.

Graham frowned. 'I've just been up there with your Dad's prescription.'

'Oh, you know how she likes to chat. Anyway, what's all this? I wanted to go to the shops this week.'

'Thought I'd save you the bother, love. I got you something. Close your eyes and open your hands out.' Graham took a bottle of 'Charlie' perfume out of his overall pockets. He found the smell of Irina sickening just lately. And when she was having her period he found it almost impossible not to retch when she came near him. He looked at her to check her eyes were shut tight, and then dropped the box into her hands.

211

'I don't know when I'll wear perfume. I never go anywhere.' Irina turned the box over distractedly.

'Get dressed and put some on now, then. We could go for a drink this evening.'

'Okay. I'd like that,' Irina said and went upstairs. 'Make sure you put the shopping away in its proper places,' she called back to him from the landing.

Graham went through to the kitchen and started unpacking the shopping. He'd got a thrumming sound in his head. It wasn't a pain exactly, but a sensation that he'd been experiencing more and more lately. It'd been more than two months since he'd done the black bitch. Since his arrest, he'd decided to give things a while to cool down. Then he'd suggest his plan to Irina. They'd move down south, make a new start somewhere else where nobody knew them, away from Irina's family and especially his cunt sister-in-law. They could really make a go of it then. He'd wait for a message, something to let him know that he was ready to start again. He thought about Selene and imagined himself stabbing her eyes out with his screwdriver. Since those nights he'd spent in the cells he kept feeling her eyes on him, as if she was watching his every move. His heart beat slightly faster as he allowed himself the luxury of this fantasy. Usually he tried to box these thoughts off, keep them for the moments he spent in his own room reliving his accomplishments. Sometimes they crept into his ordinary life. One day, he knew, it was inevitable that his different lives would merge into one perfect entity. When that happened he'd be complete and the whole world would know his might.

♀

Thirty-four
Friday, 12ᵗʰ September

'I can do it myself, Mum.' Vince wriggled out of Sandra's grip as she buttoned his jacket. He'd been living with Sandra and Tracy since the end of July and the novelty had begun to wear off. They'd had a brilliant summer though, the best ever. Tracy had passed her driving test and they'd bought an old Mini Traveller for two-hundred quid. They'd been everywhere in it, camping in North Wales, Blackpool twice and countless picnics on the moors. Michael Hames had come with them on the camping trip and they could see he was starting to heal. He'd always be damaged, but Sheila said he was having fewer nightmares and didn't wake up screaming so much in the night. He'd certainly slept like a log in the little two-man tent he and Vince had shared.

The start of a new school term had bought with it a regularity of commitment that Sandra and Tracy were finding difficult to manage. On three mornings already this week, Tracy had rushed Vince to school in the car, arriving just as the rest of the kids were coming out of assembly. They were more organised this morning, thought Sandra, as she licked her hand

and tried to plaster down the tuft of hair sticking up at the back of Vince's head.

'Get off, Mum.' Vince ruffled his head and the tuft sprang back up.

'Have you got your dinner money?' Sandra shouted as Vince slammed out of the flat-door. She watched at the window until he appeared walking with Robbie, his mate from the flats who went to the same school.

'Bloody hell! He'll have that door off its hinges if he slams it any harder,' Tracy said coming into the living room still bleary eyed from sleep.

'What're we gunna do about money?' Sandra said, ignoring Tracy's complaint. 'We can't manage how we are and I'm not risking losing him again. There's too many people coming and going.' She'd been waiting to tackle Tracy since three teenagers had appeared at flat door at midnight with £7 in loose change asking for a quarter. Tracy had been making ends meet by dealing hash for Clinton since they'd stopped turning tricks.

'I've got an idea as it happens,' Tracy replied confidently.

'Let's hear it then.'

'I'm starting me own business.'

'Doing what exactly?' Sandra was taking no prisoners today.

Tracy lit two cigarettes and handed one to Sandra. 'Removals and light haulage,' she said.

'With a Mini Traveller? Have you completely lost the fuckin' plot?'

'Of course not. I'm gunna buy a van and put an advert in the paper. There's a lot of women'd feel safer with another woman doing jobs an' stuff for 'em.'

'And what're you planning to buy this van with—Monopoly money?'

'No, and a little bit of faith and encouragement wouldn't fuckin' kill you, would it? I'm trying my best. I'm gunna offer an investment deal to Rachel.'

'Rachel at Selene's house?' Sandra was baffled.

'Yeah, she's loaded and she might want to support a woman's business. If she put up two grand to get me started I'd either give her the money back after I was on me feet or I'd offer her ten percent of the business.'

'You've actually been planning this?'

'Yeah, I have, and I'm gunna ask her on Sunday when I drop you off.' Selene had a plot to get Irina and Sandra together and it had been arranged for that Sunday afternoon.

'D'you really think she'd go for it? Has she even got that sort of cash?'

'I dunno, but Selene said she's minted and she's right fuckin' generous like. It's worth asking, that's all I'm saying.'

'Okay, it might be worth a try, but I don't wanna feel beholden to anybody.'

'No, I know that. Neither do I, but I'm really willing to give it a go. I'll just run it past her and we can do it all proper like. I mean she's a fuckin' lawyer. If she can't make a contract I don't know who can. Anyway, if it don't work out I could always sell the van and just pay her back. If she says no I've got some other ideas anyway.'

Sandra nodded thoughtfully and pulled Tracy towards her. 'Shall we go back to bed then?'

Tracy grinned and picked Sandra up in her arms. 'Arghh! Fuckin' 'ell— me back!' She dropped Sandra on the sofa. 'That's my business plan fucked,' she said laughing as she dived, with an athleticism that surprised even her, on top of her girlfriend.

As Selene passed the closed bathroom door she could hear the faint murmurings of Rachel and Jo's voices interspersed with the sound of retching.

'Hold my hair back,' Jo said kneeling pitiably in front of the toilet.

Rachel stood behind her wearing an expression of alarm. 'Jesus, I hope this bit's over soon.'

'Not as much as I do,' Jo replied between heaves.

Down in the kitchen Izzy was making toast and had made a start on the washing up when Selene came in.

'I reckon Jo's pregnant,' Selene said to Izzy's back.

Izzy spun around wide eyed. 'Really?'

'Yeah, she's throwing up in the bog, and it's the second time I've heard it.'

'Brilliant. That'd explain why she'd only sip at that bottle of Guinness last night. D'you want some toast?'

Izzy had got back from London just the night before and they'd had quite a celebration at the house because Izzy's show had been a great success. She'd sold half-a-dozen pieces and had commissions for another five. She and Selene had sat up after everyone else had gone to bed and talked. Izzy told Selene about the crazy life she'd been living in London, and Selene told Izzy everything that had happened over the last couple of months to do with Graham—the night when Sandra remembered everything, the arrest, the police, her estrangement from Irina and subsequent, hesitant, renewal of relations.

'Love some. Thanks.' Selene poured herself a coffee from the little pot Izzy had going on the stove and picked up a thick slice of toast.

They sat at the table and Izzy picked up the conversation of the previous evening. 'What are you doing about Irina?'

'I'm seeing her on Sunday. She's agreed to come out with Jon and me but I'm planning to bring her here and get her to meet Sandra.'

'Will she be able to handle that?' Izzy sounded doubtful.

'I don't have a choice, Iz,' Selene said. 'We've got to confront her with this before someone else dies.'

'You really think it's him, don't you?'

'There's not a shadow of a doubt in my mind—and I'll tell you what, I think the police think so too but they've got no evidence. I'm sure they're watching him.'

'Um—that smells heavenly,' Rachel said as she walked into the kitchen.

Jo was behind her. She gagged, turned and ran back upstairs. Rachel watched her go before turning to Selene and Izzy smiling proudly.

'She's up the duff, I take it?' Izzy said.

Rachel nodded. 'We wanted to be sure before we said anything but we reckon she's about nine weeks.'

'Is Kim the father—mother, I mean?' Selene stumbled over the correct handle.

'Yes, she is. She's absolutely made up with it. She will actually be post-op by the time the baby's born, but we're not really sure yet how it's all going to work.'

'I don't think anybody's sure of that, however so-called 'normal' they are,' Selene said.

'Yep. True enough,' replied Rachel. They heard the bathroom door open. 'You wait—she'll appear any minute starving and eat half a loaf.'

♀

Thirty-five
Sunday, 14th September

'See you tomorrow, love,' Graham called as he left the house.

Irina waited until she heard his car pull away before she came out of the bedroom. He'd gone for his Sunday lunchtime pint with Derek promising he'd sort the garden out when he got home. Irina was going to her parents for the day and staying over. She'd omitted to tell Graham that Selene was picking her up with her new boyfriend. She didn't dare mention Selene's name for fear of the terrible expression that, since the business with the police, contorted Graham's face whenever her name came up.

As she passed Graham's room she tried the door. It was locked. She quickly bathed and dressed and put on a little mascara. She felt utterly washed out, with all the medications she was on, and she didn't want Selene's new man to think she was unattractive. The mascara didn't help much so she added a smudge of lipstick. It felt like drawing a face on a featureless mask. She quickly realigned all the cosmetics in the bathroom and went downstairs to wait.

Jon hooted as they pulled up outside, on the stroke of one o' clock, just as Selene had promised. He looked at Selene and reached out to touch her hair but she moved away as she saw Irina hurrying out to the car. The sisters kissed perfunctorily on both cheeks and Selene introduced Jon. Irina shook his hand and climbed into the back seat.

'Hope you don't mind but Jon's got a few bits to do this afternoon so he's going to drop us at my house then pick us up later for tea at Mum and Dad's.' Selene had everything riding on Irina being able to cope with a slight change of plan. Jon nodded pleasantly into the rear view mirror.

'No, that's okay. Will your housemates be there?' Irina said.

She seemed surprisingly cool about it, Selene thought and answered nonchalantly: 'Some of them, I think.' She felt desperately afraid for her sister and at the same time wanted to slap her into reality.

Irina chattered incessantly, asking Jon a million questions without even waiting for an answer. Selene's anxiety grew and she cast a sideways glance at Jon who was still nodding and smiling uneasily into his rear view mirror. As instructed, Jon dropped them at Selene's house. If he was honest with himself he felt a little aggrieved that he'd never set foot in his girlfriend's home and he'd been working his way up to asking Selene to move in with him. She gave him a peck on the cheek as she got out of the car.

'Nice to meet you at last,' he said to Irina but she was already out of the car. She gave him a curious little wave. He waved back and pulled away.

Sandra and Tracy were already drinking coffee with Rachel and Jo at the kitchen table when Selene and Irina arrived. Vincent was in the backyard kicking a ball against the back wall. Selene introduced her sister.

'I can see the resemblance,' Sandra said shaking hands with Irina who flushed and giggled nervously.

'I'm gunna cut out in a bit, the picture starts at three,' Tracy said. She was taking Vince to see The Blues Brothers at The Odeon. 'Can I have a quick word please, in private—Rachel, Jo?'

'Sure. Let's go into the living room,' Rachel replied.

Tracy followed Rachel and Jo out of the kitchen with a quick look back at Sandra who smiled at her encouragingly. Irina fiddled in her handbag whilst maintaining a monologue on the variable quality of wicker table mats. Sandra excused herself to go to the toilet.

'Sis,' Selene said sitting down next to Irina and taking her hand. 'Things aren't quite right, are they?'

Irina's face was blotchy and a little puffy and she stared into her lap. When she looked up at Selene her eyes were starting to fill up. 'I don't know what's happening to me,' she said.

'Is it like before, when you were ill?'

'Maybe, I don't know. Everything seems out of control and I'm scared all the time.'

'What are you scared of?'

'That's just it. I don't know. Graham's been so kind and helpful but—'

'Please don't take this the wrong way, Reenie,' Selene said, reverting to her sister's childhood name, 'but are you scared of Graham?'

Irina shook her head slowly from side to side, but before she could respond Sandra came back into the kitchen. 'Sorry, am I interrupting?' she said.

Irina dabbed at her eyes with the corner of her hanky.

'No, sit down Sandra,' Selene said. 'I'd like you to explain to Irina what happened to you—if that's alright with you.'

Selene had already discussed tactics with Sandra, and she judged that the time was now ripe to push things forward—especially as Irina hadn't just taken off in defence of Graham. Before Sandra had opened her mouth Tracy came back into the kitchen and called to Vince in the yard. She put her two thumbs up to Sandra and winked at Selene.

'Nice to meet you,' she said to Irina and, 'See ya later, chicks,' to Sandra and Selene.

Selene had to smile, in spite of the gravity of the afternoon, at the thought of anyone calling a woman 'chick' in this household. Vince ran in and Sandra grabbed him and planted a kiss on his cheek.

'S'later, Mum,' he said and looked at the plate of Hobnobs on the table. Selene nodded and he grabbed one.

'Whaddya say?' Sandra prompted.

'Ta, Selene,' he said. Tracy held up his jacket and the two of them left.

Rachel stuck her head round the door next and said she and Jo were going over to Kim's place. Jenny and Nicola were away for the weekend so they could talk now without any further interruptions.

'Is that your boy?' Irina asked Sandra.

'Yeah, he's a handful,' Sandra replied proudly.

'I'd have liked a son,' Irina said plaintively.

'Well it's not too late. You can't be much older than me.'

Irina just nodded tight-lipped, not quite smiling.

'Reenie, we need to talk to you about something really, really important,' Selene cut in.

'Is this your friend who—?' Irina indicated Sandra with her head.

'Yes it is.' Selene gestured to Sandra to take over.

'Look, love. I know this must be ever so tough for you, but will you please just hear me out, and then you can tell us what you make of it. Your sister's been a real friend to me and I wouldn't do anything to hurt her or anyone she cares about,' Sandra began.

Selene carried on holding Irina's hand. Sandra, to Selene's surprise, went right back to her childhood and her abusive father. She talked about leaving home at fourteen, her violent relationship with Steve, and the horrible dream she'd had the night before she'd lost Vince in the custody battle. She talked about being on the game, and as she said the words, Selene felt Irina flinch and squeezed her hand tighter. She said how she and Tracy had met Selene at the custody group, and then she began on the night she'd been attacked and nearly died. She described Graham's car, and she described him in every detail she could remember. She said he'd put 'El Condor Pasa' on in the car and Irina's eye twitched noticeably at this. Sandra continued to the point she'd blacked out just after having thrust her penknife at him. Her fingers went to the ridge of scar tissue beneath her hair as she spoke.

'I think I got his arm,' Sandra said, 'but maybe it just ripped his overalls.'

Irina flinched again. 'What is it?' said Selene.

'No, nothing.' Irina's eye was twitching more wildly now.

Sandra looked thoughtful as she relived that night again and another small detail came back to her. 'When he stopped suddenly, I dropped my lipstick and I felt on the floor for it. I couldn't find it but I picked up a blood-donor medal thing instead. I just left it on the floor.'

'You never said that before,' Selene said surprised.

'No, I've just remembered it this minute.'

Irina stood up. 'I'll have to use your loo, please.'

'D'you think she knows summat?' Sandra said when Irina was out of earshot.

'Definitely. She's always just defended the bastard before but now she's really listening, and she's terrified of him. I know her. Being here is taking every bit of strength she's got and she wouldn't be doing this if she wasn't already part-way there,' Selene replied confidently. 'We're going to get him, Sandra.'

Irina was gone for several minutes. Selene went to the door of the downstairs toilet and heard the sound of her sister retching. 'Reenie—are you okay?' she called.

Irina was rinsing her mouth at the sink. Her mind was a kaleidoscope of images fusing into chaos: the night she'd bandaged Graham's arm; the blood-donor badge; the first dance at their wedding; the dirt behind the sink; the weeds between the paving slabs on the drive; the upside-down tin of baked beans in Selene's kitchen. And, as she looked up, she saw reflected in the mirror behind her the collage of feminist cards and posters that Izzy had randomly pinned to the wall. *A woman needs a man like a fish needs a bicycle* caught her eye. And another with an image of a woman receiving corporal punishment above the slogan: *If my husband ever finds out...* Irina swayed and held on to the sink, and then called back: 'Yes fine.'

Selene heard the toilet flush and Irina opened the door ashen-faced.

'Can we go to Mum and Dad's now?' Irina's voice was businesslike.

'We can as soon as Jon gets here. Is it what Sandra's just said?'

Irina just nodded. She went back into the kitchen. 'I'm sorry,' she said calmly to Sandra. 'I think you're brave, but I can't help you.'

'Brave?' Sandra said. 'Lucky to be alive, I reckon, 'cause this man's a mental murderin' bastard.'

'I can't help you,' Irina said again. 'I'll wait outside, if you don't mind Selene. I need a breath of air.' She picked up her bag and left the room.

Selene shrugged her shoulders and held out her hands. 'I'm so sorry, Sandra. I really thought we'd got her to face the truth. But she knows more than she's saying—maybe she just needs time.' She shook her head and looked at the floor.

'Well, if we're right, that's the one thing we don't have.'

Selene just nodded silently.

The dinner that evening at the Bartowski house was painful. The two tangling threads of Beata's conversation were the virtues of Graham, who had been a model son-in-law during Jakob's illness, and Jon, his prospects and intentions. Jakob, meanwhile, was morose and clearly in a great deal of discomfort. Jon courted her mother's good opinion and empathised with Jakob with a manly stoicism that made Selene cringe. It was a mistake to introduce Jon to her parents. It had been the kiss of death for her teenage relationships. Some sense deep inside told her that, if her parents liked him, then there was no way that she could.

At the forefront of Selene's thoughts were the events of the afternoon. She had left the house feeling that she had betrayed Sandra's trust and confidence. Every time she tried to catch Irina's eye, or speak with her in private, Irina obfuscated or found some meaningless chore that must immediately be performed. When Jon and Selene were preparing to leave at nine o'clock, Irina was already in pyjamas. She shouted goodbye from the sofa but never took her eyes from the television. Selene knelt in front of her. She couldn't leave things as they were.

'Come to one of our meetings at the house next week. It'll do you good to get out.'

'Ummm. Ring me,' Irina said trying to see the television over Selene's shoulder.

'Please come again soon Jonathan.' Beata held Jon by both hands.
'Thanks for the lovely meal, Mrs Bartowski,' Jon said.
Jakob held out his hand and Jon shook it. 'Goodnight, sir,' he said.
In the car Selene burst into tears.
'What's happened?' Jon said alarmed.
She blew her nose into a screwed-up tissue and briefly set out what had gone down with Irina at the house and how she felt about leaving Sandra like that. She did not say that she'd recoiled when he'd complimented her mother and called her father 'sir'. Instead she said: 'Would you take me home? I'm just so tired.'
'Sure,' he said, knowing that somehow he'd blown it.

That night Irina tossed and turned in her childhood bed until four am. When finally she slept, she dreamed that she was nursing an impossibly tiny human baby in the back seat of a car. Graham was driving, and he turned and smiled at her as he pulled up, and Irina got out. It was raining shards of broken glass and one of the pieces struck her arm. She dropped the baby and, as she bent to pick it up, a great bird came swooping down from the dark sky and snatched it from her grasp.

♀

Thirty-six

Colleen Doherty had lived in Liverpool for the last ten years. She'd come from Dublin, originally seeking an abortion. At the tender age of sixteen she'd fallen in love with a charmer. If kissing the Blarney Stone gave you the gift of the gab then Timothy Monaghan must have had his tongue down its throat. He was handsome too. He'd a fine mop of red hair, and a way of looking at a girl that made her knees give way. She'd said no to him twice already when he'd walked her home and tried to get her to go down the alley at the back of the shops. She was still a virgin and her dadda would, quite literally, have killed her for bringing that kind of trouble to the door.

Her older sister, Mary, had been thrown out and disowned when she'd fallen pregnant unmarried at twenty-two. She'd been sent to the convent and her child had been taken from her at three months. Colleen always thought it particularly cruel that they'd waited three months, just enough time for Mary to bond with the child before they ripped him from her arms. Colleen didn't want to end up like Mary. The last time she'd heard anything from her sister she was down and out and living with a man in a derelict house in Hackney. Mary had written asking for a three-pound postal order that had been hidden in her bedroom drawer to be forwarded to her. Her dadda had screwed the letter up and cashed the postal order himself.

When Timothy had started to chat to another girl at the youth club, Colleen knew she'd lose him if she didn't let him have his way. The next day she'd gone to his house to listen to 'Moondance', Timothy's new Van Morrison album. His mum and dad were out, and by the time 'Glad Tidings' came on she'd lost her virginity. He'd been kind and gentle, and though it hurt a bit when he first did it, she'd loved the feel of his body pressing against her and his warm breath on her cheek. He'd whispered 'I love you' in her ear as he lay spent on top of her. She was so happy that day in Timothy's bed, eating soggy biscuits dipped in tea and listening to him talk about his plans for the future. He'd got a place at UCD to study History and Politics, and he knew everything there was to know about Van the Man. 'Caravan' had remained her favourite song of all time, in spite of the pain it brought her.

The next time Colleen had seen him he was cool with her though, and said he'd phone her in a few days. He didn't phone, and when she'd called at his house his mum had said he was out—but Colleen had already seen his bedroom curtain move. The following week her friend Patsy said she'd seen him in Phoenix Park with another girl on his arm.

When her period didn't arrive the next month Colleen began to fear the worst. As the days ticked by her desperation grew. She had a habit of fingering the crucifix at her neck when she was worried. It was real gold, a confirmation gift from Brigid, her beloved grandmother. She rubbed savagely at the tiny twisted body of Our Saviour when she picked up the phone in the booth to call Timothy's number. She pushed her ten-pence piece in when the pips went and Timothy's dad answered.

'Can I speak with Timothy, please?' Colleen asked. Her heart was in her mouth and her legs crossed. It was odd but she always wanted to pee when she used the telephone.

'I'll see if he's in. Who is it calling?' He was very well-spoken and Colleen felt herself flush even more.

'It's Colleen.' She heard the phone go muffled as Timothy's dad put his hand over the receiver.

'He's not in.'

'When will he be in?' Colleen asked, almost certain Timothy was standing there next to his dad with that cocky look on his face. She had a pain in her chest and a lump of fear and heartbreak in her throat as she spoke.

'Now my dear, Timothy is very busy preparing for his university place. I'd leave it for a few months if I were you.'

'I can't leave it, Mr Monaghan,' Colleen heard herself speaking but didn't know where the words were coming from. 'I'm having Timothy's baby.'

There was a silence at the end of the phone. Colleen's bladder felt swollen and she hopped from one foot to the other. Then Timothy spoke. 'Are you sure you're pregnant?' He didn't bother with any tactful enquiries as to Colleen's health or state of mind.

'I'm a month late and I've been regular as clockwork since I was fourteen.'

'How do you know it's mine?'

'Because I've never done that with anyone else, Timothy Monaghan.'

'You'd better come over,' he said and put the phone down.

Colleen felt a tear roll down her face, and a warm trickle of urine down her leg.

An hour later she'd changed her clothes and was ringing the bell of Timothy's house. Even the porch felt cosy and well-heeled. Timothy's mum answered. 'You'd better come in,' she said, looking as though she'd as soon admit Myra Hindley into her home.

Colleen was ushered into the sitting room. The meeting which followed was brief and well-organised. Mrs Monaghan was a healthcare worker and explained to Colleen, as if she were retarded, that a legal abortion could be had in Liverpool at a cost of three-hundred pounds, plus lodging in the city and travel expenses. Five-hundred would cover the entire cost and the Monaghan's were prepared to put up the money if Colleen could provide proof that she was pregnant. She should report to their house again the following day when Mrs Monaghan would administer a pregnancy test.

'But I don't want an abortion, I want my baby.'

'Now look here young woman. You have no means of supporting a child, and Timothy has been very open and generous in admitting that the child could be his, although proving that might be much more difficult. You've chosen to behave like a slut and now you must live with the consequences. We are prepared to help you and, if you don't mind my saying, this is a very generous offer. We don't want anything to get in the way of Timothy's prospects. You'd better think very carefully before making your decision.' Mrs Monaghan's lip curled in distaste as she spoke.

Colleen looked at Timothy. 'What do you think I should do?'

'You should take my mother's advice.' He didn't look at her as he said this.

Colleen remembered their afternoon together, and the Van Morrison album, and the lies he'd told her. If she'd had a gun in her hand she'd have shot him dead. 'I'll come back tomorrow,' she said picking up her bag.

Colleen went back to her own scruffy house and lay on her bed to ponder her fate. She heard her father come in from the pub and the usual fight begin with her mother. She used to try to intervene but now she didn't bother. There was no point. Something smashed downstairs and Colleen turned her face to her bedroom wall. The four faces of The Beatles stared down at her, a promotional gift from the White Album. An image which had haunted her since she'd read the newspaper reports about The Manson Family case entered her mind—an eight-months pregnant Sharon Tate having her baby cut from her womb by this demonic band of hippies. Colleen screwed her eyes against the vision and put her head beneath a pillow.

She went to the Monaghan's house the next day and peed in a tube that Mrs Monaghan gave her. Timothy was out. She was given an address of a clinic and a guest house in Liverpool, information about sailing times, and an envelope containing five-hundred pounds in cash. As Mrs Monaghan let her out she said: 'Don't ever come back to this door.'

Colleen did sail the next day for Liverpool. She told her mum she was going there to look for a job.

'I would, if I were you,' her mother had replied.

She didn't go to the guest house or to the clinic. She found a cheap lodging house in Toxteth and got a job as a waitress in an Italian restaurant. She wrote to her mum and told her how well she was doing. She knew she wasn't facing facts but everything she'd ever been taught said it was murder to have an abortion. As one month rolled into another, the question of an abortion became academic. It was already too late anyway by her reckoning. When she began to show, she was already six months pregnant, and still friendless and alone in a strange city. Her boss at the restaurant noticed her growing belly and told her to leave at the end of the week. Colleen had saved some of her five-hundred pounds, so for the next few weeks she eked out an existence on that money.

She spent her days walking around the city—from park to cathedral to dockside, and then back to her little room to watch her portable telly. She'd noticed on her travels a family-planning clinic, and she tried to muster the confidence to go in. It took three attempts, but finally she pushed open the door and went to the reception desk. The woman at the desk allowed her eyes to travel from Colleen's face down to her belly and back again. She told Colleen to sit down and wait with a frown of disapproval. Colleen sat in the corner and picked up a copy of Cosmopolitan. 'Sex Survey' the cover read, 'Tell us your likes and dislikes'. It had not occurred before to Colleen that such preferences existed, let alone that they could be the subject of a survey. Someone had completed the survey and, as Colleen read their answers, a stout woman with a girl who looked younger than Colleen came and sat down next to her.

' 'Allo, dear,' the stout lady said smiling. Her enormous gold-rimmed glasses poked through her carefully arranged beehive hairdo. The young girl sat in silence; lank, greasy hair falling around her face.

'Hiya,' Colleen replied.

'Ah, from the old country, are we?' the woman said laughing. 'In a bit o' trouble are we, dearie' Her Irish lilt was a comfort to Colleen.

Colleen smiled and nodded. 'You could say that.'

'Get a girl looked after early, I say. That's what I'd call responsible parenting.' The woman nodded towards the girl who still said nothing.

'Is this your daughter?' Colleen ventured.

'In a way, dearie, in a way. As close to me as a daughter anyway, aren't ye Katie?'

The girl looked from under her hair at Colleen and nodded unsmiling.

'I'm Mrs Faerie—Rita. And what's your name, dear?'

'Colleen.'

'Ah, now that's a lovely name, so it is. And are yer all on yer own, dear?'

'Yes. I'm staying here for a bit. My folks are in Dublin.'

'Why don't you come back wi' me an' Katie fer a bit o' supper?'

Over the next few months, as Colleen's pregnancy progressed, the Faeries insinuated themselves into her life. It was easily done. She had no one, and their big old house in Catharine Street was always a hive of activity. The Faeries had two sons, but several other young men and women seemed to live there in the warren of rooms that extended over its three floors, and many more dropped in and out at all hours of the day and night. The first time Colleen witnessed a middle-aged man going upstairs with Katie, the greasy haired silent girl, Mrs Faerie explained that he was her uncle and was going to help her with her homework.

Colleen wasn't entirely naïve and she realised that the Faeries weren't exactly above board, but they made her feel so welcome, and she'd begun to build a friendship with one of the girls who lived with Patrick and Rita. Angie, she was called; and she had a way to make you giggle that took away the constant pain and loneliness. Certainly no one in the house judged her, or even commented on her growing belly.

When her five-hundred pounds had dwindled down to fifty, Colleen knew she'd have to leave her little bedsitting room. She confided her problems to Patrick and Rita and they immediately offered her a bed. They'd a cellar room that they'd be happy to clear out for her, though once the child was born, Patrick said, she'd have to contribute to the household expenses with a little bit of work.

By the time Colleen went into labour she was already installed in the cellar at the Faerie house. Patrick Faerie had shoved the huge pile of electronic consumables and shirts still in cellophane that were stored there into one corner and set up a little electric fire to keep the place warm and dry. Nonetheless, a patch of damp crept up the wall unabated and the chill went through to Colleen's bones. But beggars can't be choosers and she was happy just to have a roof over her head.

Rita and Colleen's new friend, Angie, mopped her brow as the contraction's came. The Faerie's had insisted on having the child born at home. Rita said she'd delivered scores of babies and Colleen didn't need the looks of disgust that she'd have to endure on a maternity ward. The labour was miraculously easy. After just three hours, a little girl slithered into Rita Faerie's waiting hands and let out an ear-piercing scream.

'She'll be the daughter I never had, so she will,' Rita said as she handed the child to Colleen.

'She'll be Brigid, for my grandmother,' Colleen said.

The most peculiar thing about the whole process was the ghost. When Colleen was in the throes of agony just prior to the birth, a black man in livery had stood behind Rita Faerie. Colleen thought he was shining shoes. He had a huge gash in his forehead. When she'd mentioned it afterwards, Angie had explained how the house had been built by a slaver, and it was rumoured that one of the slaves had been beaten to death in the cellar. Colleen shivered and asked Patrick if she could move upstairs. She and Brigid were installed in a room next to the Faeries' bedroom. That way, Rita explained, she'd be on hand to help with the little one.

In the weeks that followed, Rita Faerie took over the raising of Brigid and encouraged Colleen to go out and have a bit of fun. She was reluctant at first, but Rita always seemed better than she was at quieting the baby; and every time she looked at Brigid she could see the Monaghans and feel her shame in their presence all over again.

On Colleen's seventeenth birthday, Patrick had handed her and Angie a little packet of white powder and a ten-pound note and told them to have a good night out. It was amphetamine sulphate and it made Colleen feel on top of the world, buzzing with confidence and wellbeing. When she looked at herself in the mirror in the toilets she thought she looked beautiful. She wished Timothy Monaghan could see her, then he'd realise what he'd missed.

That evening Angie confessed to Colleen that the Faeries ran a shoplifting ring and did a few other things on the side. She herself had had sex with a couple of Patrick's 'friends', but she said he'd always looked after her with money and a bit of sulphate after.

'It's only sex, nothing kinky—Susie does all that stuff,' Angie explained. 'And it's not as if the big shops can't afford to lose a few bob. It's dead easy in Marks and Spencer.'

By the time Brigid was a year old Colleen was shoplifting and working as a prostitute for the Faeries. She'd also developed a taste for speed. It certainly made it easier to do the shoplifting and the sex. She had little to do with Brigid—Rita seemed to think it best for the baby that she didn't know who her mother was.

'It'll only confuse the little mite,' Rita reasoned as she slipped Colleen another wrap of powder.

Gradually, as Brigid grew, Colleen slid into a world of drug addiction. Her drug of choice shifted to heroin and her desperation for its golden warmth drove her to an amorality that she would never have known existed in her former life.

Finally, five years later, when she argued with Rita Faerie about Brigid, Patrick threw her out of the house. 'I want my child back,' she'd screamed on the steps outside.

'You've no child here. Now get gone or you'll be sorry,' Patrick said and flicked a wrap at her. Colleen ripped her tights scrambling in the gutter to pick it up.

Colleen had a series of pimps who paraded themselves as boyfriends. By 1980 she'd already tried five times to come off heroin and sort her life out—but there was no life better for her than the oblivion the drug offered. On this day, her last, she'd fought with her latest pimp because she didn't have enough money from the previous night's work and he wanted her gold crucifix in payment. It was the one thing she had that linked her to her real life—the life she should have had. The life where Timothy Monaghan loved her and married her; and where they lived in a fine house with a porch, and he gave her presents on her birthday, and they had three children—two girls and a boy. It was the one thing that reminded her of home and her grandmother who'd been kind to her. She'd held on to it in spite of the shivers and pain in her neck and back when she couldn't get the drug. Somehow something, a punter or a loan, always came along and saved the crucifix. Colleen read it as a sign. One day, she planned, she'd give the necklace to her daughter. When the pimp had grabbed at it the clasp broke and Colleen snatched it from the pavement. As she stooped he'd kicked her savagely in the ribs and walked away. But the crucifix was still clenched in her palm.

◊◊◊◊◊

Graham whistled his tune as he sauntered down Hardman Street, hands in pockets. He'd decided to steer clear of Bradford and Leeds for a while yet, and Liverpool was an easy drive away. He was careful to check that he wasn't being followed, because on one or two occasions he'd felt sure he was being watched. With Irina away at her parents' for the night he could enjoy his day without worrying. He thought he'd have few pints and get in the mood, and a nice little pub down a side-street looked inviting. He went in and ordered a pint of mild. There was a pool table at one end of the bar and he put his twenty pence down with a nod to the two players already on the table. He was feeling confident tonight. He won three games straight— it was day when he just couldn't do a thing wrong. It was still light until nearly nine, so he drank a couple more pints before he set out. 'Better get back t'missus,' he joked to the barman as he downed the dregs of his pint.

Before he'd walked more than fifty yards Graham needed to pee and he went into a darkened alleyway behind a derelict church. 'Fancy the best blowjob in Liverpool?' an Irish voice said behind him.

Graham zipped his fly and turned round. 'Oh aye love, but not here. Let's go back to my car and have a bit of privacy.'

Colleen's body was found the following day near the ponds in Sefton Park by two twelve-year-old boys truanting from school. She was face down, half her body and one arm in the water. The back of her head had been battered with something heavy. When the forensic team turned her body over they found that her belly had been ripped open and her intestines spewed on the muddy ground. And, where her eyes had been, were two gaping holes, congealed with blood and brain matter.

♀

Thirty-seven
Monday, 15ᵗʰ September

Jakob dropped Irina off at noon. He had insisted on driving her home despite the pain he was suffering. He'd always been protective of his eldest daughter and hadn't much liked the look of her yesterday. He was certain something had happened between her and Selene, but when he'd raised the issue with Beata she'd dismissed it, saying it was probably her 'time of the month'.

The first thing Irina noticed as she waved goodbye to her father was that Graham hadn't done the weeding; the cracks between the paving on the drive were green with meadow grass and mind-your-own-business.

The house seemed chilly and had a strange smell, like an empty house, Irina thought as she let herself in. She took off her shoes and put them on the rack inside the front door. Her head was a jumble of thoughts and her heart beat erratically. She went to the kitchen first and took out her cleaning equipment and the bleach. Then she set about scouring the house from top to bottom. She started in the bathroom, and then went from room to room, bleaching skirting boards and doors and even the headboard of their bed. It was odd, she thought, that there was no sign that Graham had slept in it the night before. She tried the door to Graham's room but it was locked. She looked for the keys but couldn't find them anywhere. She peered through the keyhole but there was nothing to see other than the usual empty table and immaculately made bed. In the dining room, she noticed, there were still watermarks from when the bath had flooded months ago. She made a mental note to tackle Graham about it when he got home.

As she cleared out the kitchen cupboards, an image of the upside-down baked beans can in Selene's kitchen came to mind, and she scrubbed harder in the corners until the image faded. Her hands were sore and reddened by the time she'd finished the house, but she went straightaway next to the front garden and began attacking the paving with her Weed Wand. When she heard Graham's car turn the corner, Irina didn't look up. She listened as he turned off the engine and got out of the car.

'Sorry, petal—let me take over,' he said.

'Leave it,' Irina snapped and carried on scourging the cracks. He tried to kiss her but she turned her head away. He smelled of something that even the bleach in her nostrils couldn't camouflage. Like liver, she thought.

'Shall I pop the kettle on, love? Fancy a brew?' he said.

'As you please, but don't splash water everywhere when you fill it.'

Graham went indoors. Irina carried on with her work for a few minutes and then followed him inside.

'How were't Mum and Dad, love?' Graham asked.

Irina could tell he was wheedling round her. 'It was lovely to see them,' she said. Then, more hesitantly, she continued: 'Selene was there with her young man.' Since he was on the defensive this might be an opportunity to see how Graham reacted to mention of her sister. 'She's asked me to go along to one of her feminist meetings next week.'

'Feminist.' Graham was repulsed. 'Well I hope she's not put any funny ideas into your head. They're all lesbians, you know?'

Irina felt herself colour. She couldn't bear the thought of Graham thinking about lesbians, especially if her sister was involved. It was so rare for Graham to mention anything to do with sexual behaviour that, when he did, the incongruity was excruciating.

'Don't be stupid,' she snapped and quickly changed the subject. 'Anyway, what happened to the work you were going to do in the garden yesterday?'

'Something came up at yard,' Graham said with an expression that Irina couldn't read.

'More like something came up at the pub.' Irina desperately wanted him to admit to having had a skin-full with Derek and flaking out on the sofa.

'No, one of the lads spilt his load. Derek an' me went to help him clean it up and I were buggered when I got home.'

Irina went back out into the garden and carried on her weeding with renewed vigour. She heard him come to the door and put her cup down but she kept her back turned as she knelt, now prizing loose the remaining globs of moss with a knife.

'It's on the sill,' he shouted, his voice strangely high. Then she heard him go upstairs. After a few moments she followed him inside. She listened from the bottom of the stairs, heard him open the wardrobe and rummage about inside. Then, strangely detached, she watched her feet ascending the stair-treads one after another. She felt like a burglar. She panicked then— fled back downstairs and into the kitchen and started robotically wiping down surfaces. There was a mug-ring where Graham had made the tea and she rubbed at it frenetically, then stopped and stared at her palms. Her hands were still red and angry looking. Her thoughts were a nightmare of random images as she brought her inflamed hands to her face and rocked gently back and forth. She stood like that for several minutes until her mind had settled. Back in the living room, she noticed again the water-marks on the ceiling and started once more up the stairs. In his room she could hear Graham grunting soft and rhythmic. Irina's stomach muscles clenched. 'Graham,' she called in a voice she tried make sound calm.

'Just going to have a quick bath, love,' he called back.

Irina continued upstairs. 'Why have a bath, when you've got the dining-room ceiling to do?'

Graham opened the door naked and Irina turned away revolted. 'Aye, sorry, love. Slipped me mind,' he said. 'I'll do it t'morrow wi'out fail.' Then he walked along to the bathroom, went inside and closed the door behind him.

Irina heard the water running and, as he swished it back and forth, he was humming the song that had played at his mother's funeral: 'Lalalalalalalalalala, *yes I would*, lalalala.' Irina stayed standing on the landing for a minute, and then noticed with an eerie feeling that he had left the door to his room ajar. Irina pushed it silently open and tiptoed in.

Graham's underpants were crumpled untidily on the floor. Irina picked them up. Vomit rose sharp in her throat as she realised they were sticky. Then she noticed a hair, half blond and half brown, hanging from the table, just a single strand. She picked it up and wound it around her fingers. It was strong hair, and she tightened it until it indented her flesh. Entranced,

Irina stared at her bound fingers, then opened them, snapping the hair, and watched as it drifted down onto the carpet.

Irina ran from the room. In the bathroom, Graham was now whistling that hateful tune. She froze, remained stock still for a moment staring at the closed door, and an unfamiliar peace wrapped quietly around her. The kaleidoscope of images stopped and a single repeated phrase replaced the turmoil. 'I think I got his arm,' said Sandra over and over again in her head.

Irina went purposefully downstairs. She found the card with his direct number on it that Inspector Randall had given her in case she remembered anything important. Irina calmly picked up the phone and dialled. When the Inspector answered she heard herself say,

'It's Irina Hindle. I need to withdraw the alibi I previously gave to my husband.'

'Is your husband at home now, Mrs Hindle?' Randall asked her.

'Yes, he's in the bath,' Irina replied, still with the same sense of calm.

'We'll be there in ten minutes.'

Irina replaced the receiver, went into the front garden and continued her annihilation of the unruly weeds between the cracks in the paving stones.

Graham's fingers were still pink and wrinkly from his bath and he stared at them as he sat in the back seat of the squad car. Randall explained to Irina that she would travel with a female officer in a separate car to the station, and that she should expect a long night.

'I know that,' she said.

As the squad car pulled away, Graham looked up from the backseat and smiled at her—a funny little half-smile—and he nodded his head slowly, like a man satisfied with a job well done.

Epilogue
May, 1982

When his alarm clock hauled him awake in the spare bedroom, Bill
Randall had only been back asleep for half an hour. He'd been restless, and
had got up at three to make himself a drink, and then decided to get into the
chilly guest-bed so as not to wake his wife. She'd been longing for this day
for years and he'd been dreading it. He'd turned sixty at the beginning of
the month and, after thirty-seven years, this was his last day in the Force.
Dumped back in civvie street at the end of the war in 'forty-five, he hadn't a
clue what to do with himself next. He'd enjoyed the camaraderie of army
life, but in peacetime it seemed pointless—without the punctuation of
occasional intense action and terror the long periods of boredom would be
unbearably extended. Randall wanted a job he could get his teeth into,
something to stretch him, make his mum and dad proud. He'd done well at
school and won a scholarship to the local grammar, and it was a chance
meeting with an old teacher, Mr Greaves, that had led him to the Force.

'You've an incisive mind, young Randall,' old Greavsy had said. 'I can see you with a career in the police. An ambitious young chap like you could do a great deal worse.'

Now he lay for twenty minutes turning over in his mind what the day likely held in store. There would be the usual presentation by the Chief. It was his turn for the gold carriage-clock that he'd so often taken the mickey at when other knackered old coppers had shuffled out of the game. Then there'd be a few drinks with the lads, but that would be strange; they'd all be back at the station on their next shifts and he'd be— well, he didn't know what he'd be doing. Bill Randall hated golf and he didn't have any hobbies. He did enjoy a good book, and there was an entire library for him to catch up on, but otherwise the future was a scary blank page. He'd promised Maggie the holiday of a lifetime and they were planning a road trip in America in the autumn—but after that was over how the hell would he fill his time?

Randall took a deep breath and swung from the bed. His morning rituals took until seven-fifteen when he went down and made tea, and took a cup back upstairs.

'Mags,' he whispered, putting the cup down on his wife's bedside table.

She opened her eyes and sat up. He plumped the pillows behind her head and sat down on the side of the bed.

'Had a bad night, love? Your big day today, eh?' Mags smiled blearily and touched his newly shaved cheek.

'You could say.' Randall's smile was rueful.

'Oh, don't be like that, Bill. You've had a wonderful career and now it's your turn to have a bit of peace and family life.'

'Wonderful?' he repeated, sounding baffled.

'Yes, wonderful. All those lowlife crooks you've locked up. And you were the man who finally got that monster Hindle off the streets.'

'Not before he'd managed to murder and defile all those poor young girls.' Bill Randall shook his head and swallowed hard to stem his grief. Whenever he thought about Graham Hindle he felt, with a terrible crushing guilt, that he should never have been too afraid of being wrong to press his suspicions harder. It had been spineless not to accept the word of a known prostitute, when in his heart he knew she was right; and another woman had died at Hindle's hands – at least one – because he was a moral coward. That was something he'd have to live with.

'Bill, you did everything you could. You caught him in the end.'

'No I didn't, Mags. His sister-in-law and a couple of street girls did that. I just took the credit.'

236

'You've got to get this stupid guilt out of your head. It's pointless. No one blames you but yourself.'

'I know, love. I've just got a few mixed emotions about today, and I expect that's making everything seem a bit darker than usual.'

'Once you've been out a month you'll love it. It'll just take a bit of getting used to.' She leaned forward and hugged him. 'Think of America. We'll be like Bonnie and Clyde, without the machine guns.'

Randall laughed and kissed her cheek. 'I know I haven't been all I should be in the husband department, Mags. I've neglected you and the kids, but I'm going to make it up to you all from now on.'

'Oh pack it up, Bill. You've been a great dad and the kids think the world of you. Now get to bloody work. I'll do you a nice steak tonight when you get back. I dare say you'll be half-sozzled.'

Randall arrived at the station at just after eight. ' 'Mornin', Bill,' the desk sergeant called. 'I'll bet you've been looking forward to this one. Two more years and it'll be my turn.'

'Not half,' Randall lied. His office was still in disarray since his abortive attempt to clear his desk earlier in the week. Files were strewn everywhere and a couple of cardboard boxes stood empty on the floor. He picked up one of the Hindle files. Irina Hindle's statement was on top, and beneath it, the confession he himself had taken from Graham that night he arrested him, near two years ago now. Hindle was in Ashworth high security hospital at Her Majesty's pleasure. They said he'd settled in there—no doubt it was cushy compared to getting stabbed in Wakefield nick where he'd been remanded pre-trial. Apparently no one had seen who did it, but the knife had pierced deeply enough to enter Hindle's bladder. The medical report suggested that he'd suffer periodic incontinence for the rest of his life. Randall thought it a pity that it hadn't been fatal. It may have been just coincidence that at the time a close friend of Ginny Hames' brother was doing six years for armed robbery on the wing where they'd lodged Hindle.

Randall shovelled up an armful of buff folders and put them in one of the cardboard boxes. He went over to his filing cabinet. In the top drawer was a bottle of Scotch and a chipped mug with World's Greatest Dad printed on it. He put them both in the other cardboard box. He knew what was in the next drawer down, and he was aware that he hadn't opened it since Hindle's trial had finished. Somehow he hadn't been able to face it. He opened it now, and inside, in separate sealed plastic evidence-bags, were Graham's souvenirs. No one was really sure how many victims there'd actually been. Hindle himself changed his story several times, and prostitutes got brutally raped and murdered so often that it was difficult to tell where a vengeful pimp stopped and a deranged serial-killer started. Hindle claimed he didn't even know if he'd always stolen items from the victim's handbags. He'd said in his confession that it had 'helped it last', when he had.

The largest plastic bag contained the handbag itself. Randall recalled the day they'd found it in the hidden compartment inside the wardrobe. Another surge of angry regret welled up. He'd never know why he'd let that fool Hill lead the first search back in the July. Randall tossed the handbag to one side and picked up each of the smaller plastic bags in turn. There was Reeva Taylor's nurse's belt-buckle. Ginny Hames little ring-box with a child's tooth inside. Rosie Johns' powder compact. Colleen Doherty's crucifix. Eleanor Gifford's letter. And Sandra's lipstick. He smiled at that. She'd survived the bastard, and from what he heard, she and Tracy were making a proper go of things. Certainly they hadn't crossed his path in the last eighteen months.

Randall opened the bag with the letter in it and was reading it again when Sergeant Hill came in. ' 'Mornin' Sir,' he said. Randall didn't look up. 'Need any help?'

'Oh no, Hill, sorry. Thanks.'

'What do we do with all that crap, then? Hill asked casually. 'File it in case there's an appeal?'

Randall had never been very fond of Hill. He wasn't the sharpest tool in the box, and his attitude to women and black folk left a lot to be desired. Randall was no feminist, but he was old school when it came to how he treated and spoke about women. Now he was retiring, he allowed himself the luxury of letting his dislike show. 'It's not crap, Sergeant Hill,' he replied formally. 'It's peoples' belongings that have been taken from them in the commission of brutal crimes. Now, if you'll excuse me, I'd like to get on.'

'Only asking,' Hill said disgruntled and left the room.

Randall put the letter back into its envelope and all the plastic bags into the cardboard box with the mug and the bottle of Scotch. He knew what he had to do now, at least for the first few weeks of his retirement. There'd be no appeal in this case. He was going to return all the things to their rightful owners.

On the following Monday Randall woke up feeling unusually well-rested and he lingered over his coffee until it was gone ten. It was a lovely fine morning and Maggie was in the garden planting out her hanging baskets. Randall thought what a boon to his life she'd been, the good food and the nice things all around him she'd nurtured, and that included their children.

He dreaded to imagine what a miserable and grey existence he'd have had as a single man, though he'd many times wished it over the years.

'I'm taking Carrie and Jake swimming this morning, fancy a dip yourself?' Maggie said, coming in to wash her hands at the kitchen sink.

'I've got a few bits and pieces to clear up first, love—maybe next time.' Randall loved his grandchildren but he'd never really had time for the hands-on involvement that Maggie had, and he was uncertain of how to negotiate these new dimensions to his relationships. 'I'm starting on that little project I mentioned yesterday as it happens. No time like the present.'

'Oh good. I think that's such an important thing to do. Just don't get too involved, Bill. You've no idea what kinds of messes you might find.'

'I know, I know. And don't fret. I'm doing this as much for myself as anybody else, to be perfectly honest. The yanks call it 'closure', I think, filling in the gaps to make sense of something. I really need to do it, Mags.'

'Where will you start?' Maggie said, still scrubbing at her hands.

'I thought I'd just pop over to see Ginny Hames' mum this morning. But if it's all the same to you I'll drive down to Hove tomorrow to see Eleanor Gifford's family. That's probably the toughest call and I'd like to get it over with.'

'Like a bit of company?'

'Really love? It's a long drive.'

'I'd enjoy the ride—and anyway, we could get a B&B and a bit of sea air, make a night of it.'

'Okay, you're on. You'd be a massive soddin' improvement on Hill as a sidekick anyway, and a lot more fanciable.' Randall gave his wife a hug from behind as she stood at the sink.

'Don't start that bloody malarkey, Bill Randall. I've got children to take swimming.' She turned and kissed him. 'But if you're back here by four and still fancy your chances, you never know your luck.'

'You're on,' Randall said to her back as she disappeared upstairs.

Sheila Hames was pegging out washing when Randall pulled up. He could see her from his car and he watched her for a few moments shaking out little T-shirts and trousers, obviously Michael's. He picked up the ring box and put it in the pocket of his jeans.

'Mrs Hames,' he called.

Sheila looked up startled, and then fearful when she recognised Randall from the investigation that had stretched out for most of the last two years.

'Nothing to worry about, Mrs Hames. I know coppers can be an unwelcome sight,' Randall smiled. 'Anyway, I'm a retired copper now.'

'You'd better come in,' Sheila replied nervously. 'There's nothing up is there?'

'No, not at all. I just wanted to see how the young chap's doing.' He followed Sheila into the kitchen. He was uncertain of what her reaction to the ring box would be and he wanted to test the water first.

'He's getting there, but it's not been easy. He's sleeping through more, but he still has his nightmares every so often. We had 'eck of a job getting 'im t'school when he first started as well.' Sheila filled the kettle.

Randall frowned, concerned. 'I expect it's all left him very clingy.'

'He'd scream the house down and hang on to me for dear life. It were 'orrible, Mr Randall. He'll go to our Gary. He's been a big help. Michael goes there every other weekend. Young Carolyn 'as 'im every so often, but she's courtin' now. And say what you like about 'em, them girls, Sandra and Tracy, have been as good as gold with 'im. They take 'im everywhere and he loves Sandra's little lad, Vincent. It's a lot to take on, though, at my time o' life.'

Randall listened and it occurred to him just how much of his role these last thirty-odd years had been as a social worker. Sheila took down two china cups and saucers and it nearly broke Randall's heart because he knew he was getting the Sunday best.

'How're you coping yourself? You don't mind if I call you Sheila?'

'No, please,' Sheila said setting down the tea. 'To be honest with you I haven't even 'ad the time to grieve. I miss her terrible, Mr Randall. She was my baby girl, an' she were a good girl. Them papers make stuff out but they don't know the half of it. She was a good mum and she'd have done anything for that boy.'

'I think I know that. You find out a lot about a person in my job. It's not much comfort I know, but we're certain she didn't suffer.'

'I can't think about that. I only think about her as she was. Sometimes it's as if she'll walk in the door, come to fetch Michael—or running in from school when she were little. She was always starving an' she'd run to that cupboard an' scoff down a bowl of cereal.' Sheila's voice gave way and she wiped the tears from the corners of her eyes with her apron.

'At least Michael knows his mum loved him and that he's loved and cared for now, and that's more than a lot of poor little buggers have.' For all his years of dealing with grief and misery, Randall was at a loss to somehow find the magic soothing words. He sipped his tea. 'That's a smashing brew, Sheila.'

She tucked her hanky back into the pocket of her apron and nodded her gratitude for the compliment.

240

'There is something I need your advice on,' Randall went on. 'As I was clearing my office on Friday I found something that I didn't know quite what to do with.' Randall took the ring box from his pocket. Sheila recognised it straight away.

'I wondered what had happened to that after the trial.' She took the box from Randall's palm and opened it.

'Why do they keep 'em alive, Mr Randall? I don't want torture—I just don't want Michael to have to grow up knowing that animal's still living.'

Randall only nodded. He shared Sheila's view on this and begrudged every penny of his hard-earned tax that went into Hindle's keep.

'Can I keep this now?' Sheila asked. 'It came out the day she died, you know. I was watching 'im for her while she went to an interview.' Sheila took the tooth out of its crease.

'That's what I wanted to know, whether you wanted it back or not.'

'It's not mine, Mr Randall. It's Michael's, and I know he'll want to make that decision when he grows up. I'll just keep it by for him.' She put the tooth back into the box. 'Thank you for thinking,' she said.

'Are you sure about this?' Maggie said, putting Elle's last letter to her mother back into its envelope. She was perched on the edge of the bed in the guest house in Brighton that she'd booked on the telephone the previous evening. Randall was drying off from a shower.

'The woman's already read it. She did that when it was found eighteen months ago. It was the last letter Eleanor ever sent to her mum. If it was our Lizzie, wouldn't you want it back?'

Maggie thought for a moment then nodded. 'I suppose I would, but my God it must have been so hard for her to read, and then to be presented with it again. Tread very carefully, love.'

'Treading carefully is my stock-in-trade. If she doesn't want it, at least I'll find that out, but I've got to let the woman choose.'

Randall dropped Maggie off by the North Pier. 'I'll meet you in the Galette place at one.' They'd arranged to have lunch then a wander around the shops.

Hove was a fifteen minute drive and Randall rehearsed what he'd say to Christine Gifford on the way. He'd spoken to her on the phone to arrange a time to call. 'An Inspector calls,' he thought to himself irrelevantly as he pulled up outside the well-kept little terraced house. A boy of about fourteen opened the door before Randall had time to knock and showed him into the dining kitchen.

'You must be Mark,' Randall said. He'd been careful to research all the correct names before setting out on his task.

'Yeah, that's right,' the lad said. 'Mum's just finishing her face.'

Moments later, Christine Gifford appeared. She was an attractive woman in her late forties, very smartly turned out and obviously freshly made-up. Not a woman to be caught in disarray, Randall thought. He offered her his hand.

'How can I help you, Inspector?' Her handshake was firm. She turned to the boy. 'Mark, go upstairs to your room, please.'

The boy left and she indicated a dining chair. Randall sat down. 'Please excuse the intrusion, Mrs Gifford.'

'It's not Mrs Gifford anymore, Inspector. It's Miss Ellis. I changed back to my maiden name after—anyway, call me Christine.'

'I'll not beat about the bush then, Christine. I retired last week, so I've no real call to be here, but I still had in my possession the item that Graham Hindle took from your daughter. The letter—I'm sure you'll recall its contents.'

'I thought it might be about pressing charges against Ian. I'm not weak, Inspector, but I decided against that some time ago.'

Randall listened intently and nodded. He'd not given much thought to this possibility. He considered it now. The word of a young woman now deceased, concerning events that happened many years before, against her despised step-father. It was hard enough to get a conviction on rape and sexual assault charges when there was somebody to plead the case. The vast majority of rapists walked free from court.

'I think that was probably a wise choice,' he said, 'after everything you'd been through.'

'Nothing to what my daughter went through, Inspector.'

'Of course,' Randall replied. 'There was nothing you could have done, though.'

'It's hard to know that you didn't protect your child. That you exposed her to a—' Christine searched for words. 'A predator,' she said finally. 'But then to be robbed of the opportunity to repair that damage. To know that she would never have been on the street in the middle of the night if it hadn't been for that letter you've got there, Inspector, is a great deal of guilt to bear.'

'I don't think your daughter would want you to blame yourself. Her precious life was taken by the random act of a mad man.' Randall knew his words were futile as he said them, but he said them anyway.

Christine Ellis stared straight ahead. 'I've a young son to think of. That's what keeps me going.' She shook her head briskly and rearranged her face with a hollow smile. 'You have my daughter's letter?' she said holding out her hand.

Randall handed it over.

'Thank you for returning it,' the woman said calmly, standing to show him out.

'I'd like to visit Eleanor's memorial before I go back, if you wouldn't mind?' said Randall on the doorstep.

'Not at all,' Christine said, and then gave him directions to the crematorium. 'You'll find her under Eleanor Knightly. That was her real father's name.'

It was another two weeks before Randall felt the time was right to return Reeva's belt-buckle to her children. The meeting with Christine Ellis had taken the wind out of his sails a bit. She'd seemed damaged, irreparably, and it had left him with a vacancy where feeling should have been. He'd been on autopilot ever since.

It was through his contacts in Social Services that Randall had managed to track Levi and Desiree down. They were in care, still waiting for a foster home to be found. There wasn't a queue of people ready to take on two grieving, emotionally crippled black kids. Randall had made an appointment with the childrens' key worker, someone called Claire Symonds. When he arrived he was shown into the kitchen by a cleaner. It was a big space, with a huge dining-table in the middle to seat the twenty-odd kids who lived there. The walls were covered in children's drawings and Randall walked around admiring the work, standing back from some pieces, as a person would in any art gallery.

'Inspector Randall?'

He turned around to find a young woman, still in her twenties, Randall guessed, looking expectantly at him. Her mousey hair was tied back in a pony-tail, and she wore ripped jeans and an old shirt, borrowed from a boyfriend by the look of it.

'Yes, and you must be Claire.' Randall held out his hand. The woman seemed unused to such formality and her grasp was limp.

'It's about Desi and Levi?' she queried.

'Yes. I take it that you're aware of their background.'

She nodded. 'Yeah, poor kids.'

'How have they been?'

'They're okay. They're inseparable, actually. That makes it a bit hard to know how they are as individuals, if you know what I mean.'

Randall raised his chin in a questioning gesture.

'Desi looks at Levi before she speaks or answers a question, even if it's just what cereal she wants for breakfast. He won't let anybody near her. So it's impossible to gauge what's going on for her—and as for Levi, he's a mystery. Neither of them misbehaves, but they don't engage, either. It's kind of like passive resistance, you know?'

'So they don't mix with the other children?'

'Not at all. They're not nasty or anything like that. I'll give you an example—Desi did a picture of her mum and her and Levi holding hands, and I thought it was a bit of a breakthrough and really praised her, and I put it up over there.' She pointed to a spot on the wall now housing a child's rendition of Leeds United winning the cup. 'Then Levi came in from school, and when she said she'd had her picture put up, he just went over, took the drawing-pins out, folded it up and put it in his pocket. Then he took her hand and they both went upstairs to their rooms. It's like he thinks their grief is nothing to do with anyone else and he doesn't want any help.' Claire gave a resigned shrug. 'They're the only Afro-Caribbean kids here, so that might be an issue too.'

'Do they have any family? Father, grandparents?'

'There is a dad but he's not in a position to have them. I don't think he's had a lot to do with them to be honest, and the grandma's back in Jamaica and ailing, we're told. What did you want to see them for, anyway?'

'I've got their late mother's nurse's belt-buckle.' He held up the padded envelope in his hand. 'It was part of the evidence at the trial and I'm trying to return things to the families. Will the children be back here soon, or should I call again?'

'Oh no, there'll be here any minute.' The carer looked at her watch. 'The school kicks out at three-thirty.'

'Oh well, I'll wait then, if it's all the same to you.'

'No problem,' she said and went off about her business elsewhere in the home.

Randall sat at the big table as kids of all ages came in and emptied their lunch boxes on the counter. Once they'd done that, and cleared away the rubbish, a care assistant issued each of them a carton of orange and a biscuit. The cheapest money could buy, he noted. None of them took any notice of him—they were used to strange people in the kitchen. Levi and Desiree came in a little after the others and, once they had their rations meted out, Randall stood up smiling. 'Levi, Desiree—hello, I'm Inspector Randall.' He looked them over. They were peas in a pod. No mistaking that they were brother and sister at all, both tall and wiry with high cheekbones and beautiful golden-brown skin. Desi looked at her brother for direction. He put his arm in front of her and stared at Randall unsmiling. 'I've come because I have something that belonged to your mother and I thought that you'd like to have it.' They still said nothing. 'It's her belt buckle, solid silver, I think.' He took it from the padded envelope. Levi stepped forward and took the heavy metal clasp from Randall. He examined it closely and handed it to his sister.

'She was a nurse,' Desiree said softly.

'What's happened to him?' Levi asked, staring at Randall unflinching.

Randall met his gaze. 'He's in a special hospital, lad. He'll never be released.'

'Did you catch him?' Levi asked.

'In a way, yes, but I had a lot of help from ordinary people.'

'Would I go to prison if I killed him?'

'Yes, you would.'

Levi just nodded without changing his expression.

'Your mum would want you to be happy, you know? She'd want the very best for you, and that can't come from hatred and revenge. That man's taken away enough of your family's beauty and joy. Don't let him take anymore, son. You should honour your mother's memory by being all that you can be.' Randall knew he was pushing it.

'All I can be?' Levi repeated. 'Black bastard, nigger, wog, coon, sambo. That's my career choices. You be the fool if you think otherwise, mister.'

Randall was at a loss to respond. He'd been witness to enough racism in the Force to know that the arguments forming in his head were misplaced. The boy wasn't wrong and he was 'the fool' for not realising that, without a mother to love and guide them, these black children were at the dubious mercy of a prejudiced and heartless system. Desiree stared wide-eyed at her brother, their mother had forbidden swearing of any kind and he'd have been on the receiving end of a swift clout if she'd been there to hear him. Levi turned and walked out of the kitchen. Desiree watched him go. She stood motionless for a moment, took a quick glance back at Randall and then ran after her brother.

Maggie had been horrified by her husband's report of the meeting with Levi and Desiree. 'Why are you doing this to yourself?' she'd virtually shouted at him when the bleak depression that overwhelmed him following his visit to the home had been like a cloud around him for the best part of a month. And the truth was, he didn't really know. He just felt compelled to see it through to the bitter end. A copper was usually done with a crime after an arrest and conviction. Now that did not seem enough. He needed to witness the continuing fallout to fully comprehend what had happened. He'd needed a bit of a break to recover from his visit to the care home but he was ready now to finish the job.

Randall turned the powder compact over in his hands and carefully opened the clasp. His fingers traced the initials engraved on the inner lid:

MC. It had belonged to Rosie Johns. He'd interviewed the junkie boyfriend, James, back when the souvenir collection had been found and that poor wretch had identified it as Rosie's, and he'd wept when he told Randall that she'd taken it from her beloved teacher's handbag when she was a girl of thirteen. He couldn't take it to him though because James had died earlier that year. His body had been found in the flat he'd shared with Rosie, after neighbours complained of the smell. A batch of unadulterated heroin had come onto the market and killed three addicts on the same day. James was the last to be discovered.

Rosie had grandparents still living in the North West and Randall decided to start there. Maybe they'd want their grandchild's treasured trophy, he reasoned, though from their attitude during the investigation he wasn't certain that any reminder of Rosie would be welcome. They'd behaved as though it was all a bit inconvenient and damned inconsiderate of her to go and get herself murdered.

The journey to Cheshire was hot and unpleasant, and as Randall pulled up on the drive outside the substantial Johns residence he felt his shirt sticking uncomfortably to his back. A maid opened the door.

'I'm Bill Randall, formerly Detective Inspector. Would it be possible to speak with Mr or Mrs Johns?'

'Wait here, please,' the maid said primly and closed the door.

A full five minutes must have gone by before an elderly gentleman in old fashioned corduroy plus-fours appeared from the side of the house.

'I am Gerald Johns. How can I help you, Inspector?' the man said. He didn't extend his hand.

'I have an item that belonged to your granddaughter, Rosie.' Randall took the compact from his shirt pocket and held it in his palm. 'As her nearest relatives, I wondered if you'd like to have it.'

'No thank you. My wife and I have done our best to overcome the unpleasantness of the past concerning Rosemary. Now, if you'll excuse me,' Johns said coolly and turned to walk back around the house.

Randall was speechless for a few seconds. Then he called, 'Do you know who MC is?'

Johns turned around. 'No, Inspector, I do not.'

'What school did Rosie go to when she was thirteen?'

Johns thought for a moment and then said, 'St Margaret's Girls Boarding School, just outside Shrewsbury. I think you'll find that we afforded Rosemary the very best education money could buy. Good day to you, Sir.'

Randall got back into his car and checked the map for a route to Shrewsbury. He thought perhaps he now understood a little better why Rosie might have ended up a drug-addicted prostitute. The journey took just over an hour and gave him time to reflect again on the lives that had been taken. He couldn't properly explain to Maggie what he was doing, but he was on a path and he was learning things, things that he had to know. He was thinking about this learning process as he followed the drive that meandered through the grounds towards Rosie's school. He realised with a dry smile of recognition how his thoughts mirrored his journey's progress and it struck him that he must be doing something right.

The school was a magnificent building set in several acres of prime parkland. He parked his car and followed the signs to the reception area. It was summer recess, he realised, so there were very few signs of life about the place but the big door swung open and admitted him to a large entrance hall complete with a broad, sweeping staircase. The reception area was a modern glass-fronted office adjacent to the main hall. Randall tapped on the window and the two women inside looked up, surprised, from their typewriters. A severe looking woman in her fifties slid open the window and raised an eyebrow.

'Good afternoon, ladies.' Randall bowed his head slightly and tried for charming. 'My name is Randall, Detective Inspector. I wonder if you can help me. I'm looking for a former employee of the school. But I'm afraid all I have to go on are her initials and that I believe she taught art here in the early 1960s.'

'Ooh, what fun—a mystery, Deirdre,' the woman said to her colleague.

Both of them wore twin-sets. Deirdre's was pink, the older woman's beige. Randall wondered if perhaps they consulted each other on their choice of office apparel, to make sure that they coordinated perfectly. He showed them the compact and explained why he wanted to contact the owner. 'The initials are on the inner lid,' he said handing it to the beige one.

'We do keep employee records, Inspector,' the woman explained as she opened the compact and shifted her glasses to see the engraving. 'But, oh my goodness, I don't need to find them—I'm sure I know whose this is. MC stands for Marjorie Clewes. Quite a character. A spinster—devoted to her girls but, how can I put it?' She cocked her head to one side. 'A little eccentric.'

'Do you have any idea what might have happened to her, where I might find her now?

'Well yes, as luck would have it I do know. She's quite a well-known artist, locally at least. She still does the odd talk for the girls here but she went over to the state sector.' She said this as if it was somehow emblematic of the woman's eccentricity. 'Very well- travelled, I believe— she left us to go off on a jaunt, round India I think it was. Very daring.' The woman looked at Deidre and they both chuckled at the thought of such unconventionality.

'So she's still teaching?'

'Yes, I believe so. Part-time, I think. She holds exhibitions too—of her paintings. She had one over in Ironbridge. She's at the comprehensive in Penn.'

'Thank you, ladies. You've been a tremendous help. You wouldn't happen to have an address? I'd like to see her before the start of the new term if possible.' Randall gave them his most appealing smile.

'We sent some flowers when she judged the sixth-form art show last year. I'll jot it down for you, Inspector.' Beige lady scurried away to a box file and came back moments later with a piece of folded paper which she handed to Randall.

It was nearly teatime when he finally found Miss Clewes' cottage tucked away in the maze of streets on the banks of the Severn in Ironbridge. She answered the door in baggy green dungarees over a man's shirt, with untidy wisps of grey hair poking out of some sort of turban. 'Hello,' she said, peering at him through wire-rimmed spectacles.

Randall explained who he was, and the purpose of his visit, for the third time that day. As soon as he mentioned Rosie Johns' name he was ushered into the house. It was tiny, and crammed full of canvases and half-finished artworks.

'Oh, I was devastated when I read all about those awful murders in the papers, and then realised she was one of the victims. Such a talent. Such potential. But she had no-one, absolutely no-one. Did she suffer? No, don't tell me. Of course she suffered—she suffered all her life.'

Randall just nodded. 'Not what you'd call a happy existence—at least that was my impression. She did have a boyfriend who cared for her as much as he could manage. They were both—well, troubled,' he said diplomatically.

'But why come to me Inspector?' The artist's eyes narrowed with sudden suspicion.

Randall took the compact from his pocket. 'Is this yours, Miss Clewes?'

'Oh.' Her hand flew to her mouth.

'The killer stole this from Rosie. It was found among other items when he was finally captured. It struck me as wrong that these personal effects should just moulder in a police store somewhere.' Randall shrugged, 'So here I am.'

'I thought I'd lost this. I suppose Rosie must have taken it?' The thought obviously deeply saddened the woman.

'Yes, Miss Clewes, she did. Her boyfriend told me that it was something to remember you by. You seem to have occupied a very important place in this young woman's life.'

'So it would seem. She was such a promising young artist. I could count on one hand the students I've taught who seem to have some sort of, almost visceral, talent and Rosie was one of them. I do have a couple of her pieces that I kept from my St Margaret's days. I thought them so powerful. Would you like to see them? I dug them out when I read the newspaper reports— it won't take a minute to find on them.'

Randall was left to look around the jumbled living room while Miss Clewes went upstairs. He could hear her crashing and banging about for what seemed like ages before she reappeared carrying two large pieces of yellowed cartridge-paper. She held them up. 'It's hard to credit that she was just twelve when these two pieces were done,' she said, looking admiring from one to the other.

Randall gasped and the small hairs on the back of his head erected. In one of the pictures two elephants stood magnificent with their trunks entwined. In the other, a monstrous, black bird swooped, its claws outstretched above a small, hunched figure shielding its head with arms crowning into praying hands.

'What is it Inspector? Can I get you a drink of some sort? You don't look very well.'

'Rosie painted this bird—it's a Condor, I believe—on a wall just hours before she was murdered, Miss Clewes.' He offered this coincidence without explanation—the complete picture was only just now assembling itself in his brain, and it was too outlandish to detail.

'Good heavens. How strange. Art is a powerful force, Inspector.'

'Could I have a glass of water, please?' Randall asked, still shaken.

As Bill Randall drove home that evening his thoughts were at once a jumble of half-remembered conversations and at the same time crystal clear. In his head he replayed the interviews he'd held with Sandra, recalling all the twaddle she'd talked about that bloody bird. Except now he could no longer comfortably dismiss it as twaddle. Rosie's painting had reinforced Sandra's conviction of foresight and seemed to tap deep into a consciousness that he'd never have given credence until now. He had learned something that day, he'd been dead right on that score. It just wasn't something that fitted into his experience of reality.

By lunchtime the following day Randall was disembarking from the ferry at Dun Laoghaire. He had Colleen Doherty's parents' address on a scrap of paper, and her little gold crucifix in his pocket. He intended to find a Bed and Breakfast and have a few pints of Guinness that evening. It seemed rude not to if you'd bothered to come to Dublin. He took a cab to the address. It was miles, or more likely the cabbie went a long way around—standard practice for fares with an English accent, he suspected. The house was the end of a shabby-looking terrace. Randall asked the cabbie to wait. He didn't fancy being stuck miles from anywhere in a strange city. When the bell seemed to make no sound, he knocked on the door. A sound of shuffling came from inside. Randall waited but no one answered. He knocked again more loudly, and this time the shuffling progressed down the hall and the door opened. A grizzled man in a dirty singlet stood before him.

'Are you the father of the late Colleen Doherty?' Randall asked, putting his foot over the threshold as the man tried to close the door.

'She's no daughter of mine. She was a whore and she bought disgrace to this family.'

The man's breath was pungent with the odour of cheap wine. 'Could I perhaps speak with Colleen's mother?' Randall assumed that leaving the crucifix with this obvious dipso would only finance that evening's binge. Since Colleen had held onto it to the end, in spite of her heroin addiction, he wanted to see it go to someone for whom it had meaning.

'She killed her mother, so she did. That sainted woman died six-month after we heard about Colleen. Who are you anyway? And what do you want?' The man's voice was guttural and his expression repulsive.

'I'm the police officer who was in charge of the case. I have something I think belonged to Colleen and which she seemed to treasure.' Randall held the crucifix up in front of the man, who followed its trajectory blearily like a man being hypnotised. Then he reached out to grab it. Randall snatched it away and put it back in his pocket.

'You give that here. It was given to that slut by my darling wife's mother. So now it belongs to me, man.'

Doherty's sickly, insincere fawning about his dead wife made Randall's flesh crawl. He remembered the mother turning up to formally identify Colleen's body—a downtrodden and timid little woman with alopecia and a black eye.

'Is your wife's mother still living, Mr Doherty?'

'No, she's been passed years since, so she has. Now give me that fockin' necklace.'

'You'll need to put in a formal request to the police headquarters in England, accompanied by evidence in writing that you are, in fact, Miss Doherty's only living relative.' Randall wanted to punch this piece of shit in his fat gut but he thought better of it and took out his wallet. He handed

Colleen's father a fiver. 'Get yourself another bottle, Paddy,' he said with a sneer and walked back to his cab.

Dead end, Randall thought to himself on the drive back to the city centre. 'Know any decent B&Bs, mate?' he asked the driver.

'I'll take you right to the best in Dublin, if you like,' the driver replied, and then kept up a steady stream of information about the whereabouts of the best pubs and the finest pints of Guinness to be had in the city. Randall was glad of the local intelligence and the distraction from the nasty taste that old man Doherty had left in his mouth. He stared out of the window and listened. On every other lamppost a local election poster advertised the skills and commitment of the handsome young Fine Gael candidate. Randall watched the image of his face flash repetitively by. Timothy Monaghan for Dublin Central, the posters read. On three of them in a row someone had drawn a penis and written 'knob' with a red marker. Randall smiled. And he looks like one too, he thought obscurely.

That night, Bill Randall phoned Maggie to explain that he wouldn't be home as early as he'd hoped tomorrow. He was going up to Liverpool to see if he could root out anyone who knew or gave a toss about Colleen. Maggie was patient with him, as she always was. It was getting close to their American trip and she was busy planning their route from San Francisco down to New Orleans. He hadn't given it much thought, besides wanting to please Maggie, but now he realised how much he was looking forward to a proper holiday. He also spoke to Hill and asked him to find the name and address of the friend of Colleen Doherty's who'd been the last to see her alive.

Hill called back five minutes later on the payphone in the hall at the B&B. 'Her name's Angela Kershaw.'

'Right—that was it.' Randall remembered a tragic-looking girl with scabbed needle-tracks and bruises. 'Have we got an address?'

'Yeah. Well, record says it's a knocking shop. Not clear if she actually lived there but it's where her Giros went.' Hill read out the address. 'Why d'you wanna know? You're supposed to be retired from all this shit.'

'Just tidying up a few loose ends, Sergeant. Have a good evening,' Randall said briskly and hung up.

It was raining when Randall knocked on the door of the Faerie house in the early evening and the wind from the Mersey was cutting. It was a big three-storey place, grand in its day but that day was long past. A girl of about twelve answered. She was a bonny lass with a mop of the loveliest red hair that Randall had ever seen. 'Is your mum or dad in, love?' he asked smiling friendly.

'Ma—it's the busies,' the girl shouted over her shoulder.

Rita Faerie came bundling down the hall. 'Go up to your room, Brigid,' she said to the girl. Her fleshy face was a maze of deep lines and she looked much older than her sixty years. Randall wondered how she was even remotely this child's mother. 'I'm Detective Inspector Randall,' he said, deciding that, if he still smelled like the law, he may as well take advantage of the additional clout that gave him. 'Does an Angela Kershaw reside at this address?'

'Off an' on. Why—what's she been an' done?'

'I just wanted to speak to her in connection with Colleen Doherty, the girl who—'

'Ahh, Colleen—she was as dear t'me as me own flesh an' blood. Poor thing, if only she'd have stayed here with us,' Rita Faerie simpered.

Randall knew flannel when he heard it. He wrinkled his nose in distaste. 'So you knew Colleen?'

'I did. She lived here with us just after she come over from Ireland. Oh, it'd be twelve, thirteen years gone, now.'

'But she didn't stay in touch with you after she left?' Randall's detective mind was busy processing and classifying the information, figuring out just what the relationship here had been.

'To be honest, the girl brought a bit of trouble to the house—an' we couldn't have our own children unsettled, if you follow me, Inspector.'

'I can't say that I do follow you, Mrs—?'

Rita Faerie had said all she was going to. Her eyes were hard, something like cruelty in them, as she stared Randall down. She was a woman well-used to dealing with the law. 'Shall I tell Angie you called, if I see her?'

'No, don't bother yourself, I doubt she'd be able to help,' Randall said and turned away. He walked slowly through the back streets to his car, dissatisfied with the encounter. The whole business of Colleen had left him troubled. The cobbled streets were slick with late-summer rain and he trod carefully as he mentally sifted arbitrary glimpses into the young victim's life. Joining Hardman Street, the main road, he noticed a florists shop still open. He crossed and went in, and bought a little pink and white posy wrapped in cellophane. Colleen had been given a paupers funeral—at the expense of a grudging state. Randall recalled that her ashes had been deposited in a cemetery on Smithdown Road. He drove there and parked in a side street. He wasn't even sure she had any sort of memorial to find, but wandering around a graveyard in the encroaching twilight matched his mood somehow.

A gang of kids were sitting smoking weed on a grave and he gave them a wide berth. 'Don't trouble, trouble,' he thought. After he'd tramped around for half an hour reading the stones and the light had almost entirely waned, Randall found himself with the strongest sensation that he was being watched. He continued walking slowly along, and then turned suddenly, hoping to catch whoever was about to jump him in the act. There was no one there. He walked back to check that some little bastard hadn't dived behind a headstone; and then there she was. The small white stone read simply: Colleen Brigid Doherty 1954 - 1980. He kneeled and carefully laid his posy in front of the stone. His hand shook slightly—if it wasn't for his weakness this poor girl would still be alive. Not much of a life, perhaps, but at least she wouldn't have suffered that monstrous death. 'Colleen Brigid.' He felt a need to say it aloud. 'Brigid,' he said again and the pieces fell into place. He ran back to his car as if the devil were at his heels.

The lights were on in the Faerie house as Randall parked outside. He didn't know how he would play this one as he knocked the door, but he felt his luck had changed. The red-haired girl answered again. Yes, his luck had changed. Before she could speak he hushed her. 'Brigid,' he whispered. 'I've something for you—a gift in a way, but I think it really belongs to you.' The girl looked bemused as he dropped the crucifix into her hand. 'Keep it safe, and maybe one day you'll want to know about who owned it. Her name was Colleen Doherty.'

Randall left the girl standing on the step frowning into her hand. As he looked back, she closed her fist and went inside.

It was one of those lovely golden mornings as summer melts into autumn when Randall paid his last call. Even the hallways in the flats were forced to admit a few shafts of sunlight. He was still on a high from his shrewd insight in the Colleen Doherty case. The successful return of the crucifix had helped to assuage his guilt just enough for him to face Sandra Jacques. Anyway, he was going on holiday the next day and he wanted his undertaking complete before he went.

The front door was open and the radio was blaring out Dusty Springfield's 'I Close My Eyes and Count to Ten', and he could hear Sandra singing along. Randall tapped and ventured inside. The living room was stacked with boxes. Smoke from a cigarette burning in an ashtray drifted upward, a plume of blue calligraphy. He could see Sandra in the kitchen wrapping glasses in newspaper, and he recalled the day, nearly two years before, when he'd called after Ginny Hames' body had been found. He didn't believe in God, but he gave thanks anyway that someone had survived. Her hair had grown back and was tied in an untidy chignon at the back of her head. A handwritten letter lay open on a box labelled 'Vince'. He started to read the first page. He didn't want to, but thirty-five years of being a copper had left its mark. Feeling a bit sly, he cast his eye over the big sloppy scrawl.

Dear Sandra and Tracy,

I'm writing this from a beach café in Santa Barbara. Sounds dead glamorous, I know, but I'm really homesick. I can't believe how much I'm missing the rain-swept bleakness of the northern streets. I just wanted to say a massive thanks again for all your help and patience with my PhD dissertation. I will find a way to repay you, one day. I finished editing the final draft on the plane coming out here and I honestly think it's the best piece of work I have ever done. I'm enclosing a copy so that you can give it your final approval before I submit.

When you asked me, Sandra, if I was absolutely sure about this move at the leaving party, I lied. There were a lot of factors pushing me, and I can't exactly complain about the weather out here, but I'm not sure about anything. I was right to break up with Jon. He wanted kids and all that and just a different life to me. It wasn't fair on him to string it out (Thanks, Tracy, for looking after him by the way) but a big part of me will always imagine an alternative life, one that I could have had. I guess we could all say that. Then, when Sylvia was born, the house seemed to change and I felt like I didn't belong. Rach and Jo are great parents but I couldn't relate to all the baby stuff, especially after Izzy moved to London and I was the only single woman – to quote Tracy, I felt like a spare prick in a prostitute's parlour – haha.

I wasn't helping Irina either. She seemed to shrink from the sight of me, and if I'm totally honest, I couldn't look her in the eye without a horrible feeling of repulsion. That wouldn't help her to get better. After my dad died I went through a bit of a cataclysm as you know. What you don't know is—

That was the end of the first page and Randall did not dare turn over. That would really be pushing his luck, and if he was caught out any goodwill he might draw on would be irretrievably lost. 'Hello, anyone home?' he called loudly from the living room door.

'What the fuck?' Sandra span around.

'Sorry, Sandra.' Randall held up his hands. 'I didn't mean to make you jump, but the door was open and I couldn't make you hear.'

'What's happened?' Sandra turned the radio off.

'No, nothing's wrong, honestly. I'm retired from the Force now,' Randall explained amiably.

Sandra looked at him askance. 'I'm not doing business anymore.'

Randall coloured to the thinning roots of his hair. 'Oh no, no, no nothing like that,' he managed to stammer out. 'I've been trying to tidy up a few loose ends since the Hindle case ended and you're the last on my list.'

Sandra stared at him in baffled silence.

'You'll remember that he took things from the victims? Well, I've returned them to the relatives. These things tend to just get left in a police evidence office somewhere and I just felt they should be offered back to the families. Well, in your case of course, things turned out very different I'm glad to say.' Randall blethered on while Sandra nodded suspiciously. 'I suppose I just wanted to see that you're doing well, after all that happened. Is Tracy still about?

'Yeah, she's just taken the first load of stuff to the new house. We're moving.'

'Oh good, these flats aren't up to much are they? Especially now you've got the lad back with you. Have you got a bit of garden where you're going?'

'Yeah, it's up Lennon Drive, near where Sheila Hames lives. There's a decent size garden at the back. The council gave us the move 'cause we're overcrowded since Vince came home. We told 'em Tracy lives here an' they said we needed three bedrooms.' Sandra's laugh was infectious.

'Ah, well there's some advantages to you bein' two girls then,' Randall laughed along with her. 'I saw Sheila Hames a few weeks back and she mentioned that you see a bit of Michael.'

'He's a smashing kid. Poor little sod though—he misses his mum terrible. Tracy's dropping our Vince at Sheila's to play with Mikey today as it happens. Give us a chance to get sorted.'

'Sandra, can I just say how sorry I am about what happened. I'll never be able to put things right but I should have acted on your word and I didn't.'

'Another girl died.'

'I'll have to live with that, though it's nothing to what you or Michael Hames or any of the others will have to live with. It's a dark shadow over everyone's lives.'

Sandra just nodded.

'Are you still in touch with Hindle's sister-in-law—Selene was it? She had a young man,' Randall followed up disingenuous, his copper's instinct prompting him to confirm the existing evidence.

'Oh, she ended it with him soon after. Shame, he was a nice fella. She's gone to work in California. She's a lecturer at a university out there. I think she just wanted a new start, an' this job came up so she took it. She'd got no ties and her dad died, and I don't think she got on very well with her mum. Her sister's is in a loony bin you know? She tried to kill herself.'

'Yes, I did know that. We can only imagine what she has to live with.'

'You've got some fuckin' front coming 'ere.' Tracy had come in behind them and stood staring belligerently.

'It's alright, Trace. Leave it. He's said he's sorry.'

'Well sorry don't bring that poor fuckin' girl from Liverpool back, does it?'

Randall shook his head. 'I made a mistake, Tracy.'

'And what about that psychiatrist bloke hey?' D'you think all the shit he said to Sandra made her feel good when she was already on her fuckin' knees?'

'Don't darlin'. It's water under the bridge.' Sandra moved to Tracy's side and touched her cheek. Tracy put a protective arm around Sandra's shoulders.

Randall hung his head in a turmoil of shame at his own actions and embarrassment at this unexpected tenderness between two women. In a strange way he felt glad Tracy wasn't letting him off the hook. It meant that someone else recognised and understood his sorrow and regret. 'I'll leave you in peace—but I am glad you're doing well, and I wish you all the luck in the world in your new house.' He fingered the lipstick in his pocket as he turned to go. 'I'm guessing you won't want this back,' he took it from his pocket.

'I don't use that shade anymore, Inspector,' Sandra said and smiled.

She was so beautiful Randall could barely look at her. 'By the way, you'll remember the bird that Rosemary Johns painted on the wall the night she died?'

Sandra's hand went automatically to the scar beneath her hair. 'Yeah, the council finally painted it out just last week.'

'She painted that exact same creature when she was a girl of twelve. Her old art teacher showed me it. The only difference was that the original painting had a figure crouched in front of it like this.' Randall bent his head and raised his hands in supplication.

'That's because she stepped out of the painting that night. It came true. Just like Sandra's dream. They all saw that fucker coming but they couldn't stop it.' Tracy spoke with absolute conviction.

'It was certainly a peculiar coincidence. Maybe there was more to this than any of us really grasped.' He shook his head in incomprehension. 'Anyway, look after yourselves, ladies, and thanks for putting up with me—I know you're busy.'

'No, thanks for coming, mate. You didn't have to,' Tracy offered slightly grudging.

Randall smiled and allowed himself one last look at Sandra before making his way downstairs. He found a bin and put the lipstick in it before he went to back to his car. It was parked next to a van with the legend 'Tracy's Transport and Removals' emblazoned on its side.

Sandra packed the last of their boxes and Tracy carried them down to the van. She was concerned that Randall's visit might have set Sandra back, when she'd spent the last eighteen months trying to repair her damaged girlfriend and rebuild that feisty, confident woman she loved so much. 'Stupid bastard,' she mumbled to herself in irritation.

When the last of the boxes had disappeared they stood together for a moment and gazed around the empty rooms. 'We had some good times here though, didn't we?' Tracy said.

'Yeah, we did.

'Glad to be leavin'?'

'Not half.'

They closed the front door behind them and headed down to the van with the last few carrier bags full of clothes and the rubbish. 'I'll take that,' Tracy said. Sandra hadn't been to the bins since the attack and she nodded her assent, and then climbed into the passenger seat of the transit van to wait. Tracy hurled the bags into a bin. The paint was still fresh from where the council had painted over Rosie's last work, and a small piece of black and yellow crime-scene tape had embedded itself into the corner of a fence—the last remaining trace of Ginny. Tracy said a silent prayer for her lost friend at the place where her life had ended, turned her back and walked to the van. 'Sorted,' she said as she climbed up into the driver's seat.

'Weird about that girl's picture, hey?' Sandra ran her finger along the ridge in her skull.

'Don't go back there, babe. We've got to think of the future and Vince and all that. This is a new start for us.'

'I know.' Sandra nodded and closed her eyes.

'Anyway, I've got you something.' Tracy leaned over to the glove compartment.

'You silly bastard—we 'aven't got a pot to piss in.'

'Yeah, we have. I've paid Rachel and Jo all the money back on the van, and I've got that regular run now, so stop worrying.' She took out a small brown envelope and handed it over.

A ring dropped into Sandra's hand. It was a gold band with a faceted red stone embedded into a raised circle of gold.

'Look inside it,' Tracy said.

Tracy loves Sandra—now and forever. Sandra touched the engraving. Then she locked the ring inside her fist and closed her eyes as a fat tear crept down her cheek.

'Well? D'you like it?' Tracy stared, expectant.

Sandra nodded silent. Tracy frowned slightly as she pushed an escaping tendril of Sandra's hair back behind her ear. With her lover's tears wet on her fingertips she looked behind and carefully slid the van into reverse.

The End

Acknowledgements:

The inspiration for this book came from the gruesome tales of true murder told to me in childhood by my mother, Dorothy.

I also owe a debt of gratitude to some wonderful thinkers and writers whose work has influenced my own. First, to Nicole Ward Jouve, whose brilliant feminist analysis of misogyny, patriarchy and serial murder, 'The Streetcleaner', gave me enormous insight into the context of the crimes of Peter Sutcliffe. Pat Barker's exceptionally powerful novel, 'Blow Your House Down', and Gordon Burn's biography of Sutcliffe, 'Somebody's Husband, Somebody's Son' were also both crucial to my understanding of violent crime from the perspectives of both perpetrator and victim.

I am blessed with a gifted array of family and friends who test-read this work, or parts of it, for me. These include Gerry Newman, Gail Ward, Phyllis Inez, Sue Stratton, Carrie-Ann Woodall, Colin Povey, Julia Ferrebe, Jan Stevenson and Kim Ribbans.

My eternal appreciation goes to the many folk who helped me to polish the work: Jude Ramsdale, whose Post-it notes have saved me from many serious crimes of grammar; Alistair Fruish, who read the work aloud, haggled with me about every 'and', and then stole them all to put in his own novel; and Alan Moore, whose constant encouragement and support gave me confidence to write in the first place. Thanks on my part would not be complete without recognition of the kindness and cheerful support of the late Steve Moore, who sadly died just before I sent him the first draft of the manuscript. This work is the poorer for his passing.

I am forever indebted to my dear friend and quite brilliant editor and publisher Jamie Delano (no relation). Thank you for putting up with me these thirty-five years.

Last, thanks to my partner and co-plotter, Martine Bourdeau. Marrying an accountant is the single most important thing an aspiring writer can do.

♀

Deborah Delano lives near Hebden Bridge in West Yorkshire with Martine, her partner.

Also Available from Lepus Books:

"Book Thirteen"
A novel by A. William James (aka Jamie Delano)

"Kiss My ASBO"
A novel by Alistair Fruish

"Leepus | DIZZY"
A novel by Jamie Delano

"The Things You Do"
A memoir by Deborah Delano

And coming in 2015/16:

"The Sentence"
A new novel by Alistair Fruish

"Wilful Misunderstandings"
A collection short stories by Richard Foreman

"Leepus | THE RIVER"
A second 'Leepus' novel by Jamie Delano

Lightning Source UK Ltd.
Milton Keynes UK
UKOW02f1813110716

278122UK00005B/243/P